DOMESTICITY

DOMESTICITY

Joris-Karl Huysmans

TRANSLATED BY GEORGE MACLENNAN

WAKEFIELD PRESS

CAMBRIDGE, MASSACHUSETTS

This translation © 2025 Wakefield Press

Wakefield Press, P.O. Box 425645, Cambridge, MA 02142

Originally published as *En ménage* in 1881.

Cover image: Eugène Atget, *Intérieur de Monsieur T., négociant, rue Montaigne*, 1910.

All rights reserved. No part of this book may be reproduced in any form by any electronic or mechanical means (including photocopying, recording, or information storage and retrieval) without permission in writing from the publisher.

This book was set in Garamond Premier Pro and Helvetica Neue Pro by Wakefield Press. Printed and bound by Versa Press in the United States of America.

ISBN: 978-1-962728-03-4

Available through D.A.P./Distributed Art Publishers
75 Broad Street, Suite 630
New York, New York 10004
Tel: (212) 627-1999
Fax: (212) 627-9484

10 9 8 7 6 5 4 3 2 1

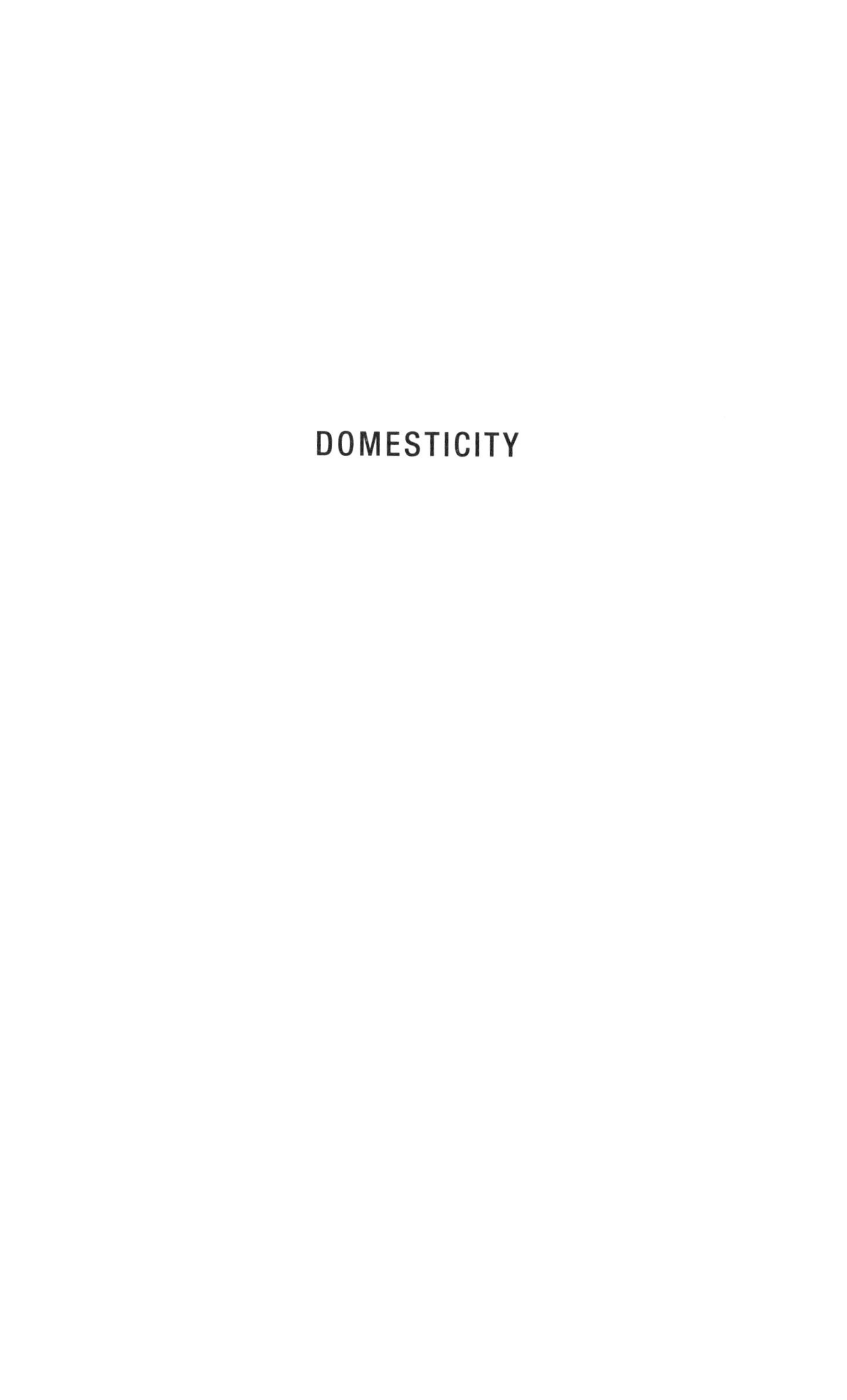

DOMESTICITY

I

Their cigars burned and stank like smoldering bits of charred wood.

As he was buttoning up his breeches which had come undone, Cyprien exclaimed: "Two whole hours spent in a corner watching puppets jump about, soiling gloves and smearing glasses, constantly on your guard, then fleeing when the hostess, whichever room she happens to be in, comes poaching for quarry for the dance, well, if that's what you call pleasure, however used to it you've become since you got married, then you're not hard to please."

André shrugged and, spitting out the tobacco juice that peppered his mouth, merely said: "Ah, you learn to live with it."

There was a moment of silence. They were walking slowly, side by side, when midnight struck. Two clocks blended their chimes; the one that was farther away reverberated softly a second later than the other; the closer one marked its hour clearly, almost gaily.

The two young men were walking down an empty street, and their steps rang sharply on the pavement. Their shadows sometimes broke against closed shops, sometimes preceded or followed them, spread flat on the flagstones, paler at certain moments, darker at others. They often tangled, merged, joined shoulders, formed nothing but a trunk with arms and legs branching out, surmounted by two heads: sometimes they separated, gathered underfoot or stretched out disproportionately, were decapitated in doorway recesses.

The sky was like a landslide of black ramparts. Huge clouds rolled by like factory plumes, sliced open by the roofs of houses, then patches of sky, starry with white fire, glittered through enormous breaches in these immense blocks of cumulus, but were soon extinguished by the opaque veil of the creeping clouds.

Walls, illuminated every now and then by lit-up gas lamps, stamped thick marks in the dark. The sidewalk was dry, streaked in places with rivulets, and the joins of its flagstones were picked out in black. A drainpipe near the road, a gridded cast iron plug with a hole piercing the middle of its circle, gleamed on some ridges that had been sharpened by the rubbing of boots. Kitchen scraps, vegetable peelings, and torn-up posters were moldering in a puddle. A rat snaked into a waterspout.

The half hour was chiming when André and Cyprien reached the end of this street and arrived in another, better lit and still quite lively. A wine merchant was about to shutter his windows. In a room partitioned by frosted glass panes at the back of the shop, a waiter was covering up a billiard table and wiping with a rag the chalk marks on the rim of the felt; another, seen from behind in the first room, was rinsing bottles above a vat, back bent, nape and hips wiggling with the waddle of a bird; a third was hauling away two tubs made from half-barrels and planted with oleanders; two dirty circles marked the place where they'd sat on the sidewalk.

The owner was getting ready to sluice down his doorway. A bucket between his legs, he yawned, stretching, arms in the air, fists clenched, and, behind him, his wife, bottom flattened against a banquette, breast collapsed on the rim of the counter, was berating the waiters, plucking hairs from her nose, balancing the books.

The street was nearly silent; two policemen were strolling mournfully, speaking low, stopping once in a while and then continuing on their way; in the distance, a team of sewage collectors passed by with a muffled rumble, lashing horses harnessed to numbered barrels, to carts that smelled abominably, packed with vats and pumps.

The noise grew feebler and more indistinct. The bouncing rattle of a hackney cab could be heard as it came into view, lights burning, the cabdriver asleep under his hat of boiled white leather resembling a chamber pot, chin on chest, whip at rest, nags exhausted, stumbling, making the rattletrap jolt on the roadway, then the sound faded, and the racket of closing shutters died away; the neighborhood fell asleep, everything went silent.

Cyprien continued to grouse into his beard; he was getting more and more exasperated after the evening he'd endured. He launched into an attack on the drinks, the women, claimed that the punch had been bought readymade from a grocer and cut with water to sanitize it; he repudiated the charm of the young girls tapping out tunes or pecking at ice creams, he mocked the host, standing by the piano, putting on a show of smiling, and he went at it again: "Ah, they're nice, your uncle's parties! A real luggage room scrum! Only those people who've marked the cards have the right to sit down! And there they are, with balding heads, white compresses around the neck, swollen bellies, strapped into tight pants, preventing a tough digestion from settling down! And the salon, with a tapestry of old ladies sleeping along a wall or jabbering with nose in a glass, and conversations raining down, the flood of drivel, the endless shower of polkas and waltzes! And everything, everything, and that flock of imbeciles inviting pink or white dresses to shake out their pleats! And the young ladies! Those adorable vessels of new flesh rejuvenated by the vices siphoned off from their mothers! Oh yes, let's say something about that! You should see them when they shake a leg in their skirts! Handkerchief on knees and pouts on their beaks, there they are, wriggling on their chairs—whispering grubby stupidities that volley back and forth behind a balletto of fans, like a classroom of mischievous schoolgirls, suddenly taking wing with a horrendous cackling of parakeets let loose! Then there's the nosedive of solemn curtsies, the crinkled nostrils and dazzling dentures, the yeses mummy, the noes my dear, the blah blah blah, and so on and so on, the knowing laughs, the discreet effusions . . . The little girls! I've kept an eye on them this evening, oh yes, there they go: physically speaking, a catalogue of unripe bosoms and padded bums; morally speaking, an eternal winter of the intellect, a dung-heap of thoughts in a pink brainbox! Oh yes, those ladies intended for me, hoping that the day will come when, tired of reading in my bed and peacefully smoking my pipe, I'll accept the misery of a bed for two, insomnia or another person's snoring, the nudging elbow and kicking feet, the tedium of compulsory caresses, the boredom of inevitable kisses!"

André was smiling. "Well," he said, "it's really quite simple. Outcome of your theories: all passions confiscated, the prostitute enthroned on high—the three-penny cathouse!—and to top it off, let's glorify the housemaid who helps herself to your candles and sugar! Yes, firing off paradoxes is great fun, but there comes a time when the fireworks get soggy and fizzle out! There's no laughing then—for sure, I got married because the time was right, because I was tired of eating cold meals off a cheap clay plate, dinners rustled up by the housemaid or the concierge. My shirtfronts were gaping open and losing their buttons, cuffs were worn threadbare—like those you've got there, actually—I was always short of clean handkerchiefs and wicks for my lamps. In the summer, when I went out in the morning and didn't come home till evening, my bedroom was a furnace on account of the shutters and the curtains staying closed against the sun; in the winter it would be an icebox, fire unlit since twelve noon. That was when I felt the need to stop eating congealed soup, to have lamplight after dark, to blow my nose in crisp linen, to be cool or warm according to the season. And you'll get there yet, my friend; come on now, tell the truth, is that a life worth living, the one that used to be mine and that's still yours? Is it a life to have your heart perpetually smeared with the muck of whores?[1] Is it a life to desire a mistress when you don't have one, to be bored rigid when you do, to have your soul scraped raw when she drops you, and then find yourself even more sovereignly bored when a new one takes her place? Absolutely not! If you must be an idiot, then better a married one. So, it dilutes the urges and dulls the senses, does it? Well, that's not its only advantage! Just think, my boy, it's a savings bank, where you deposit care for your old age! It's your legitimate right to offload your resentments onto someone else's back, to get sympathy when it's needed, and even love sometimes!

"Ah, if only there was an emetic that could make us puke up all those old sentimental feelings bottled up inside us! Of course, that would be ideal, but it's impossible; the wisest thing is to take a chance, to try and be happy with a woman we think is decent and well brought up. Good lord, I'm starting to speechify like you, and what with all this talk it's now twenty to one. I'm going to wish you goodnight and go back home."

Cyprien seemed disinclined to head for bed.

"You've got plenty of time," he said. "When you go out other nights and your wife isn't dead set on coming with you, you never get back from Désableau's before three. Isn't that so? Admit it, you were damn lucky to come across me in that hothouse. I made you make a run for it. I've given you three hours, give me back one of them and let's go for a stroll."

"Oh!" said André, "I'd gladly give you eight or ten hours, if I wasn't so tired. I'm supposed to go to see what a slaughterhouse is like at the crack of dawn for the sake of my novel, and I told my wife not to expect me before eleven o'clock tomorrow morning, but even so, I have to decline the invite, I'm worn out, I'm cold, and what's more it's about to rain; come on, it's time for bed."

But Cyprien wasn't admitting defeat: he persisted, harping on the laziness of his friend who wouldn't find it easy to get up early another time.

André agreed. For heaven's sake didn't he know it, since he'd deliberately chosen the day when, in not going to bed, he would still be up at dawn! But Cyprien reeled out his arguments to no avail: his friend stood his ground, took the homeward path, and arrived at his house. There, he rang the doorbell and leaned against the wall, waiting for the door to open, listening to the bell's shrill call in the distance, the dull twang of the bell pull, the creaking of the door, ready to open. The handle had been tugged in vain so he rang a whole chime that frisked into the night, and the bolt clacked, releasing the lock. He shook Cyprien's hand and closed the door again.

Avoiding the doormat, the shoe scraper jutting up from the first step, he struck a match and climbed upstairs with the haste of a man burning his fingers and eager for relief.

Hand on banister, he doubled his steps, and, as the lit match brightened in the breeze, or was nearly extinguished, the spiral wall of the staircase gleamed with faux marbling in the dark.

Copper doorknobs glinted on each landing, then a red spot glinted on the varnish of the walls as the flame died and the matchwood consumed itself in embers.

After he had entered the outer room and taken a candlestick from a low stand, he advanced cautiously for fear of waking his wife. Try as he might to walk on tiptoes, his boots creaked.

He came to a sudden halt, surprised, hearing a cushioned bump, like an object falling on something soft, like the impact of naked heels on a carpet. He thought his wife was even more unwell, or that she had risen to fetch a handkerchief or to satisfy another sort of need, but an appalled murmur reached him, whispered phrases choked by anxiety, words spoken nearly aloud, then mumbled in a prayerful tone, others, barely distinct, as though ground between clenched teeth.

He feared a tragedy, crossed the room, rushed into the bedroom, saw a frantic man in shirtsleeves by the unmade bed, whirling round, knocking over the furniture, pulling an armchair toward himself for shelter, hindered by a chair positioned behind. The woman gave a strangled cry, fell back, stupefied, eyes goggling, haggard.

André choked down a "Christ almighty!"

One sensed a dreadful rout in the room, an immense panic. The man didn't move, barely breathed, the woman was shivering, distraught, pressed against the edge of the bed, legs and breasts exposed, her right hand dangling, her left gripping the sheets.

Everyone stayed still, unspeaking. Then in the great silence of the room, André's hand, holding the candle, trembled and the candle ring tinkled softly, tapping against the copper base.

This slight noise seemed to shake off the woman's tremendous stupor; she let out a long sigh, tried to speak, sought for saliva, found none, pulled her nightgown back around herself, covered up her bosom.

André had deposited the candlestick on a table; seeming indecisive, he paced up and down, halted nervously, ashen, staring at his wife. Only the sounds of his footsteps were heard, sharper and duller depending on whether he drew near or moved away, walking on the wooden floor or treading a carpet.

A puff of wind from an unlatched window made the candle flicker and trickle. An azalea in a ceramic potholder was shedding its flowers, blood-spotted petals scattering drop by drop upon the reseda bouquets of a rug; a petticoat, thrown over the back of a chair, slowly slid down, spreading out like a white pond on the parquet. A penetrating *odor di femmina* from bare arms filled the room, commingled with a very subtle breath of frangipane, evoking the discreet gratification of intimate toiletries, luxuries lost since marriage and now rediscovered, of opal-tinted waters bathing the blue reeds imprinted on the bottom of large wash basins.

When André stopped pacing the clear chatter of the clock spelled out its monotonous tick-tock, interrupted by the creak of a wardrobe, the cord of a blind tapping against the panes.

André took a step, stopped in front of his wife. He was trying hard to be calm, but the words came haltingly, in a voice that trembled. "One o'clock in the morning," he said; "if we're to keep up appearances, it's time for Monsieur to get dressed and leave."

The gentleman made a vague gesture. The woman's shoulders drooped still further, her hand opened, allowing the sheets that she had been clutching to gently loosen, like damp linen.

"Come, Monsieur," André continued, "let's wrap this up; I have no interest in contemplating your physique; the situation is ridiculous enough, let's put an end to it.

"When you think," he went on, "true enough, that by virtue of studying women and learning how to hold them in utter contempt, one only reaches the point where the fool begins! But I'm chattering on and time's passing. Ah, for the love of God, that's enough; aren't you ready yet?"

The young man pulled on his pants, and his badly tucked shirt made lumps in his underpants at the rear. He barely buttoned his waistcoat, put on his boots and his frock coat. He regained a little self-assurance when dressed, looked the husband in the face, stammered some incoherent words, and felt inside the pocket of his frock coat.

"You're looking for a visiting card," said André, "of course one never finds it when it's needed. It's like a fait accompli. But it doesn't matter, your family name is of no interest to me; as for your first name, my wife must know it, and if she shouldn't happen to know your address, you'll be able to send it to her tomorrow so that she can meet with you if she sees fit. Now take your hat and let's leave."

Despite everything the young man was suspicious, fearing an ambush. He was worried that the husband might oblige him to go first and wasn't overjoyed at the prospect of groping about in the dark. But André preceded him, candle gripped in hand. They went down slowly, not another word exchanged. At the bottom of the stairs, by the glass knobs of the banister, André turned and, lifting the candlestick, simply said: "Take care, Monsieur, there's a step"; and he added: "I'm warning you so that you don't fall. We don't want a noise."

He knocked at the concierge's windowpane, the door opened, and he shut it behind the young man, who let forth a long sigh of relief and murmured:

"Christ! I was lucky to get off that easily!"

II

Yes, Cyprien wasn't wrong. It was madness to get married, without being wealthy, when a man can, with a little inconvenience, dine at home and be almost well catered for. Those are the kinds of trouble that ought to be left to the poor! Poking logs on those winter nights when, supine in his armchair, he was reluctant to go and lie down in a cold bed, André had often turned things over, taking his own pulse, wrestling with the idea that recurred every time he passed an evening on his own, whether to put bachelor life behind him for good, disturbed as it was by carnal appetites, by the need for caresses and tenderness.

He didn't like children, saw no purpose in procreating; taking it as axiomatic that people who aren't rich are the ones that breed the most, he feared making a wife swell up ten out of twelve months, and yet the miserable ordeals of inadequate housekeeping, drunk caretakers who don't turn the mattress, had, as he admitted to Cyprien, thrown him on the limed twig of a family in quest of a son-in-law.

He had married his wife half-heartedly, without enthusiasm. On meeting, he'd found her as unremarkable as most young girls; she played the piano, copied Bouchers and Greuzes onto porcelain plates, possessed, along with that, an affectedly graceful manner at home, a stiff poise outside; in short, you could take her out without feeling ashamed, or keep her at home without wearying of her. All the same, he'd been foolish! Her eyes were black with a light in their depths, the eyes of a mistress who had once duped him in grand style. He should have been wary! should have known that in deciding to join one's name to another's behind the doors of a city hall, a man ought to be able to measure how profoundly frozen is the sensibility of the one whom he's marrying, or her capacity for utter stupidity! And, standing, fists clenched, he was a man in pain, thinking about his wife, filled with astonishment at not having detected in certain lines of her face, in certain words, the storms brewing under her cold calm.

Now he hesitated over what course to take. "I've avoided a scandal at home, that's the crucial thing," he thought. "If I return to my wife, I'll have to suffer torrents of tears and laments, and, that being the case, I'll no doubt be naive enough to forgive her! Or else I'll have to listen to improbable excuses or insolent comments, and then I won't be able to keep from throttling her. Both roles are equally asinine. On the other hand, to say nothing, to stay, that's hell, that's to light the fuse at any given moment, that's the unavoidable revelation, one day sat at table, in front of the maid, of how much we hate each other, that's the whole neighborhood congregating the next day to noise my misfortunes, that's the events of tonight distorted and exaggerated, spreading from the butcher to the baker." And, in the midst of his temporizing, he was coming back round to the course of action that had first occurred to him when, having got rid of the gentleman, he'd gone back upstairs: resume his former mode of life, cancel out the last two years, try, through his work, to forget the exasperating memories that his wife would bequeath to him.

His resolution grew increasingly firm. He made an abrupt gesture, put his papers in order, tore up some of them, burned others, and remained melancholy, absorbed for a moment in the sparks flying in the fireplace, in the breeze that stirred the ashes and lifted the black and red heap of charred paperwork. Then he sighed, tied up some books, searched through a chest of drawers, placed a pile of clothing on an armchair. He had to find his suitcase, stored in a lumber room by the kitchen, and he pushed the door gently, listening closely, hearing no sound, almost afraid of meeting his wife.

When he entered the kitchen, he halted, stricken, in front of the leftovers of a meal: He was moved by two plates with forks and knives crossed on top; seeing those dishes wiped clean, those two glasses from which they had drunk, he relived the tête-à-tête of their last dinner, his wife's adorable movement in lifting her sleeve and serving the sauce, the unsuspected ending to a whole, comfortable domestic intimacy.

He took down his suitcase and, unsettled, less resolute, returned to his quarters, listening, almost hoping for a cough, a cry, that would force him to heed his wife, run to her side. A great silence pervaded the house. André went back into his study. The room was hopelessly disordered. The half-open drawers overflowed with vests and articles of clothing; shirts were tangled together, holding out their sleeves, opening their collars, hanging upside down, folded as though hinged, lamentable and grotesque with their empty arms and bellies, their chests open and hollow to the spine; cravats lined the yellow flannel of waistcoats with a thin black thread, gloves extended their glazed fingers, color of dust and mauve, over the light brown of the underwear, over the creamy white of silk scarves.

The candle had burned down to its glass collar. The desk drawers, not fully closed, folded the papers in two, and the rubber bands that bound the bundles had fallen to the floor, resuming their round shape.

André parted the curtains. The blinds were closed. The glow of early morning, leaking through the slats, laid down bars of pale blue at equal intervals on the floor, made the reflection of walls in the mirror retreat, kindled the gilding of the frames at certain points, harshened the white of the muslin hanging from the windows, the azure white of the linen. André looked at the shut windows of the houses on the other side, the immobility of the curtains behind them. The uninterrupted silence of the courtyard seemed gloomy to him; he came back into the room, remained ill at ease before the pool of light that was spreading, as sad as a moonrise, becoming no less white and blue. He saw himself in the mirror, sunken cheeks, eyes dark-rimmed. He quickly finished packing his case and, gripping it in one hand, he closed his study with the other, and when he reached the outer room, he turned the handle of the door. There, he felt himself falter. He was seized again by the regret that had taken hold of him in the kitchen, almost bringing a tear to his eyes. Leaving a state of well-being behind him, he was suddenly sad. The door to the stairwell opened onto a horizon of boundless misery; on that landing he invoked the abandonment of a whole future of peace and happiness; past his thirtieth year he must now relive his eighteenth, but now without hope and confidence, and with his currently ruined stomach and need for comfort.

The door opened quietly. He stood unmoving, suitcase at feet, beset by a growing cowardice. Ah, if his wife were to dash in, clad in nightgown, hair tossing in the wind, put her arms round his neck, cover his mouth with her hands, stifle even only a semblance of tears, he would have kicked away the suitcase!

Suddenly, he became clearheaded. He envisaged the reservations that would have haunted him after that ludicrous scene. He pictured to himself all the shame of being a cuckold, the mistrust that would henceforth assail him at the slightest word; he envisioned the exchange of mutual bitterness across the dining table, the reconciliations agreed on, tacitly, in advance, among the pillows, the awkwardness of certain tête-à-têtes, the innocently uttered gaffes, the grudges that would result for both of them.

"Well, I'm starting to turn into an ass," he said. "My choice is either to give my wife a slap or else to clear out." He grabbed his suitcase, descended the stairs, crossed the half-open *porte cochère*, and slowly made his way to Cyprien's lodgings.

The air, the walk, did him good. He took off his hat to cool himself and a light wind drank up the drops of sweat beading his temples. He now only had a vague perception, a confused memory of the night's incidents. He put his suitcase down on the sidewalk, picked it up again, simply in a hurry to get there as it was heavy. He had to pause once more, change hands, rest again.

The streets were deserted. The sky seemed to be smudged with blobs of ink and then smeared with ash to dry them. In the distance, a woman street sweeper, head wrapped in a scarf, clogs stuffed with straw, was leaning on the handle of a shovel; by her side, a dustman, pipe in mouth, nose running, was raking at a heap of trash; a worker passed by, jacket thrown over his overalls, left shoulder higher than the right on account of most working people's habit of always carrying their tools and their bread under the same arm; a milk wagon racing at full tilt struck sparks from the cobblestones. André used his suitcase as a seat, glanced round to see whether a cab might not be happening by, reflected that in Paris it's almost impossible to find a cab at half five in the morning when one doesn't live near a train station, and, finally deciding to get up, girding himself against fatigue, he made a final dash, climbed up to Cyprien's, knocked, knocked again, until the slapping noise of slippers on floor could be heard.

Cyprien half-opened the door, looked stunned, mumbled some words, ran to get back under his blankets, and once there, rubbing his eyes, stammered: "Ah, so, it's you?"

André fell into an armchair. "Can you put me up for a few days until I find a room?"

The other waved a yes, and, pawing his hair, completely taken aback, cried out: "But for god's sake, what's going on!"

At that, André stood up. "What's going on is that I found a man in bed with my wife last night, can you believe it?"

Startled, Cyprien let his arms fall, and, sitting up, swiveled round toward André. "Impossible," he said.

But his friend looked at him, nodding his head. They stared at each other without a word spoken.

"Did you kill the fellow?" Cyprien finally asked.

"No."

"That's good—not your wife either, I hope?"[2]

"Nor her either."

"Well, so much the better. Is the man you caught a friend?"

"No, it's someone I don't know."

"That's less awkward," murmured Cyprien.

They fell silent.

André, who like many a nervous individual suffered horrid pains in his bowels at the slightest vexation, left the room.

"That's a good one!" thought Cyprien, and he gave a slight smile as this incident was by no means contrary to his way of seeing things, but he grew indignant all the same, as he found it absurd that a good, strong man should have been duped by a woman whom he saw as a fool and a conceited cow.

When his friend returned, looking fraught, hand on stomach, he leapt from bed, offered him a glass of rum, and listened to his blow-by-blow account of the scene.

"My poor old friend," he exclaimed, "nothing changes! After our mistresses are done with needling us it's the spouse's turn! Oh, I know, it's more aggravating—but so what? It only goes to prove one thing: love affairs, whether they're in polite society or the gutter, come to the same thing, they all crack up and crumble. Well, my friend, that's something you just have to accept, everything in life is on loan. Our affections live in rented rooms, never the ones we own! Oh yes, I agree it's tough; everyone wants their little freehold of happiness and to be its sole owner! Well, my friend, those are peasant dreams, never to be fulfilled! But let's see, how should we arrange things? Simplest would be to rent a bed, we could put it there, next to the window, you could open up the folding screen and feel at home, eh, what do you think?"

"The first thing to do," André said slowly, "is to look for a little place to rent. I'll take the furniture that belongs to me, my bachelor knickknacks; I'll also need to find Mélanie, my old cleaning lady; I seem to have lost her address, but since she was always at a laundress's on rue des Quatre-Vents, it should be easy to find out where she's staying. I need to ask you one favor; I don't want to set foot in my house again, so I'll draw up a list of things to keep, hire a carriage today, and get you to go to my place on your own, to oversee the packing of my furniture and bits and pieces."

And he went on, feverishly rubbing his hands: "Oh, I can't wait for all this to be over and done with! I'm in luck, though, it's half term so it shouldn't be difficult to rent a room. Okay, that's settled! It's back to the bachelor life for me; enough is enough! When all's said and done, you're right, if I was unhappy then it was my own fault; I'd conjured up a whole bunch of notions: solitude, the want of untainted kisses, silence, evenings in bed, not waking up to funny business, the whole flower-shop dream! No matter, it always ends as a farce when you think about it!"

He fell silent, then thought that it would be proper to take an interest in the work of his host; he looked at a painting set on an easel: "Well, so, that's coming along!" he exclaimed, then he listened to his friend's explanations without hearing them and, once more obsessed by his misfortune, went on: "It's unbelievable, you should have seen her two weeks ago when she gave notice to the maid who'd been staying out all night. She's strict, my wife! I pointed out that the girl was a good cook, always did what was asked of her, that it was absurd to dismiss her for goings-on that didn't really cause us any inconvenience. My wife gave me such a look! To her I was clearly a man without morals, I kept quiet, the maid received her notice." He added in a lower voice, "It was for the best that we weren't able to hire another, so that at least tonight . . ."

Cyprien cut him short. His old grievances against women were reviving. "Oh, they're not good-natured," he said vehemently. "And yet that's all we ask of them! Yes, but to be good-natured, you need to have been taken advantage of, like you and me really. When our longings are satisfied with remaining unsatisfied we think that we're happy! We're the kind of people who settle for what's just about good enough. We're full of joy when tiles aren't falling on our heads, and with such a modest ideal it's even more of a miracle that bloody great wallops don't land on our nut!"

Disconsolately, André gestured his agreement. "How about I empty my trunk," he finally said, "then we could get some breakfast and I'll get started on my chores."

Cyprien nodded a yes and went out to fetch some provisions.

André started unpacking his clothes. He was experiencing the devastating vagueness, the brain fog of an individual regaining consciousness after having been almost knocked out. He arranged his shirts on a table, gathered his books and smoothed out their covers with his hand, straightening their dog ears, flattening pages creased by the journey.

"And here's one that my wife found utterly boring," he thought. "As for this one, what a masterpiece it is, I didn't even lend it to her!" And he promised himself he would read it, reproaching himself for having neglected his art for so long. Ah well, she pouted so much in the evenings, when he would have liked to work! And he shivered, dreaming of the pout that wrinkled the corners of her lips so prettily. He tossed the rest of his volumes in a pile, no longer wanting to see their titles, trying to escape the memories that kept coming back to him evoked by each item. His wife had touched them all, mending some, purchasing others, leafing through this book, perusing that one, on those days when she would calmly say to him, "Give me something to read," take a volume, open it, and, returning it to him, say: "Pooh! this isn't much fun!"

He tried to shut out his marriage, tried to bury the present, made himself call to mind a thousand details from his bachelor life that might now be of use. He thought about domestic arrangements, sought to avoid in advance the discomforts that descend on wifeless dwellings; he rummaged in the lumber of his memories, and, as these evocations of things past smiled on him, his life as a married man, by an almost unthinking mental process, leapt before his eyes and settled in for the duration. Once again he felt possessed by irritating resentments, a furious rage that was perhaps further aggravated by this obsession that could only be expelled by the very cause that triggered it.

Then, like those children's toys in which a sentry returns to its starting point after having gone round in a circle on a track, his thought, after completing a thousand circuits, stopped dead at the exact same point: the manner in which his wife had duped him. His anger escalated, his wounded pride bled, for the space of a minute he was astonished that he hadn't strangled his wife's lover.

Cyprien returned loaded with parcels; they laid the table. The painter attacked the assorted dishes with gusto, stuffed himself with brawn and bread and slurped at his drink. André nibbled, picking at his food, swallowing big mouthfuls of watered wine to help the meat slip down, but the pieces stuck in his throat; he pushed the dish away, feeling sick.

"I can't swallow," he said.

The mazagran brought up by a barkeep comforted him a little.[3]

Cyprien had guzzled and gulped for four; he leaned back in his chair and enjoyed the contentment of a satisfied appetite. At that moment he was seeing things through rose-tinted spectacles and, crumpling his napkin, looking at his comrade, he repeated at intervals "Just look at the poor chap!" and regretted that they wouldn't be able to dine together; he was, this evening, quite exceptionally, on family-dinner duty, one of those once-a-year family dinners where everyone gathers, to toast each other and let loose with lame vulgarities.

André made no comment; in a way he preferred being on his own. Cyprien was getting on his nerves; beginning to forget about his friend's bitter predicament, he didn't understand that André, in the grip of an idée fixe, couldn't allow that Cyprien wasn't equally full of regret. With the egoism of persons who suffer, André in fact thought that the painter had far too little sympathy for the misfortunes of others. The writer was exasperated by the words of encouragement that Cyprien had tossed to him like a lump of sugar to keep him from straying: "Chin up old boy, it'll all turn out fine, you'll work better now that you're free, what's the point of torturing yourself since there's nothing you can do about it!" He would have preferred that Cyprien walk on tiptoe, as they do in those sickrooms where the patient is buoyed up with a mere look and a squeeze of the hand. Unfortunately, Cyprien was incapable of soothing a grief such as this. Moreover, like most bachelors, he didn't see that other men's conjugal agonies warranted any great sympathy. He could more readily commiserate with the despair of a man abandoned by a mistress than with a husband cuckolded by his wife. The latter should have expected no less, why on earth did he get married in the first place? Moreover, Cyprien detested the bourgeois female whose low morals dressed up in Sunday-best made his blood boil; he declared that he only felt well disposed toward tarts, who were more honest in their vice, less pretentiously stupid.

So, André was hardly upset about being left alone, but, on the other hand, solitude frightened him; he knew beforehand that he was obsessed with his calamity; what's more, he was feeling anxious, on edge, wretched.

They finally decided to leave. André took his hat and slowly made his way through the streets linking rue Royale to rue Cambacérès, urged on by the superstitious notion that he would only be able to properly smother his bitter memories, really recover his former life, by going back to live in his old stamping ground.

So began for him a long trek in search of unfurnished premises. He walked with his head tilted up, scrutinizing notices. For hours on end he turned the doorknobs of lodgings, received full in the face the pungent odor of boiled beef, the smell of leather being worked, the scorched whiff of sheets being ironed.

In some houses where the concierge's lodge was closed he knocked at a windowpane, went into the courtyard in search of the concierge, didn't find him, asked an old woman who, returning to the hallway from which she had come, cried out from the foot of the stairs: "Monsieur Baptiste, you're wanted!" A voice came from on high: "Be right down!" And the distant swish of a feather duster approached, descending in time with the loud thud of boots.

He found no acceptable lodgings at an affordable price, only sumptuous and expensive apartments with doormen who looked at him disdainfully, or noxious basements hung with dreadful wallpaper, paved with red tiles, embellished with painted plaster fireplaces. He listened to the sales pitch of the viewing agent who tried to bluff the client, swearing that whole families had lived healthy lives in these hovels, had only left them reluctantly and were still missing them.

André was aching, wrung out. He lingered in the rooms where chairs could still be found, sat down, hands on knees, his gaze vacant, listening to the concierge standing and jiggling keys in the pockets of his blue apron, trotting out his little spiel, raising the matter of the short-term deposit.

"Oh! This is a quiet house you know, everybody minds their own business, no gossips, no troublemakers," and he talked about the people from downstairs, tried, given the opportunity, to air their dirty linen, mentioned others, reeled off their important professions, seemed overcome with modesty when he couldn't proclaim a high-flown title, passed hastily over the names of some tenants without any further comment, then he pushed the apartment's window wide open, invited André to lean out, praised the view into the courtyard, transformed into the garden of a nightclub.

And André got up, leaned over the balustrade, looked down into the depth of a cesspool, to a slowly dying geranium. He contemplated the four whitewashed walls, the square of overcast sky, the foul bottom of the hole. "Nice, isn't it?" the doorkeeper said, pointing out colored balls dangling in the ivy, flower beds with box borders and planted with black stakes representing rosebushes that had lost their sap.

And André went back into the room, received a further verbal drenching, ended by taking flight, promising that he would be back with a definite answer. He had already made his way along several streets, climbed flights of five floors, investigated ground floors, probed thousands of closets, lifted every single chimney damper, admired the inconveniences of a number of lavatories and kitchens, when he visited a house on rue Cambacérès that looked decent, a little apartment composed of two tiny rooms, a medium-sized dining room, a bathroom no bigger than a dishrag, a passable kitchen and toilet. There was also a balcony, and all told it cost a thousand francs. That wasn't expensive for the neighborhood, and the place was vacant and could be occupied right away. André took it.

He enjoyed a certain peace of mind now that he had secured a roof over his head. He went to a branch of the Bailly movers situated on the same street and arranged for a house removal for the day after next.

He was hungry. Fatigue and walking had somewhat dulled the sting of his woes. He was almost happy, when he caught sight of a small café with a swollen melon floating in alcohol behind the window.

Rows of bottles, each with lead caps on their tops and stars shining in the middle of their bellies, formed the half-circle surrounding two tiers of little, round, blue cheeses, vinaigrettes veined with cold beef, dubious ragouts of turnip congealed in fat, sponge cakes with burnt black splotches puckering their yellow sludge.

A remaining portion of rice pudding was collapsed in a pewter dish; eggs the color of wine filled a floral salad bowl; a rabbit, spread open on a platter, four paws in the air, spilled the viscous violet of its liver onto a carcass washed in very pale vermilion. A mural of bowls fitted into each other, blue-rimmed saucers raised up in a tower, were preceded, in front of the glass of the shopfront, by an old plum brandy jar full of water, where the stems of wilting gladioli were soaking.

André sat down at an empty table. While waiting for the soup to be served to him, he looked around the room. It was fairly large, with a décor of gas lamps and green lampshades, a cast iron stove, a counter surfaced in faux mahogany with shaded fillets, embellished with a blue glass vase full of flowers, tin measuring rods posed as panpipes, a nickel collection box, a yawning cat, and an inkwell. Stacked shelves behind this item of furniture supported unsealed liter bottles, a porcelain teapot, three-legged white cups with scarlet handles and gilt initials in the center, tarnished with dirt. A mirror fixed in the middle of the shelves reflected the top of the bouquet of flowers marinating in the blue vase, the pipe zigzagging from the stove, three unoccupied pegs fixed to the wall, the frayed lining of a topcoat, the greasy shine of a hat. On a little corner table a Burgundy cheese with a notched belly was collapsing under attack from a thousand flies; close to the racks where napkins fitted with napkin rings were piled, a bread-bin contained meager and limp loaves that nearly reached up to a birdcage hooked to the ceiling. A death had left it vacant, occupied by a lonely cuttlebone, dangling from the end of a thread.

This establishment was part country inn, part slum Parisian café. The owner, in shirtsleeves, with a turned-up nose and stomach pushed out like a hump, was lurking with a serviette on his arm, trailing slippers patterned with dominoes and playing cards through a mire of spit and sawdust.

From out of the perpetually swinging kitchen door spilled noises of pots, pans, and crockery, the music of frying food and a moaning of roux sauce. An angry sizzling of meat sautéed in the pan arrived now and then, and beefsteaks oozing juices on the grill, fetid blue fumes, sudden red steam. At any moment muffled quarrels could be heard, the terse voices of managers throwing their underlings into confusion.

A pale, skinny serving girl, her expression vacant and dejected, tottered unsteadily, worn down by constant vaginal discharges.[4] Another one, with the air of a sleepwalker, lugged piles of plates from kitchen to pantry and from pantry to kitchen, seemingly unaware of the important task assigned to her.

André was starting to lose patience; his soup still hadn't been brought to him. He was tired of looking at the people around him; they all knew each other; he had fallen into a sort of guesthouse, into a manger where a strange bunch of people were stuffing their faces. There were distinct groups, chatting in low voices, smothering their laughter behind their napkins; then there were men singing their own praises, shouting gargantuan jokes at the top of their voices, monopolizing attention with their antics.

The owner, on familiar terms with his clientele, laughed along, with a cry of "Ha! that's a good one!" Suddenly calm, he shouted: "One veal filet with sauce, one filet in tomato sauce, one!"

André swallowed the noodle soup that, at long last, they had decided to serve him. Two gossips on his left dipped into a plate of tripe, dabbled in a snuffbox, and emptied tumblers. Elbows on table, they exchanged exaggerated civilities over a spoonful of sauce, chattered like a pair of mothers-in-law, badmouthed a neighbor, pitied their concierge whose stomach had swollen up while eating mussels.

André began to perk up, but the racket made by a clique situated near the stove drowned out the brouhaha of the other groups.

A hairdresser was holding court, venting truths like, "When you've got money, people take their hats off to you, otherwise, when, like me, you've invested all your kit in stocks that don't yield, you'll hear '*Marie, trempe ton pain, Marie, trempe ton pain.*'[5] Besides, every time I bought shares, they sank like a stone the next day; but I just couldn't help myself, I need a bit of a thrill!"

His friends were delighted, poured him drinks and, looking gloriously cretinous, with hooded eyes, he continued: "Me, I love sex; I'd have to be like the blackbird whistling after its chicks to go without it"; and, making a punning allusion to his trade, he added: "I wouldn't always be a fast bird, I'd be a slow bird."[6]

This salvo of nonsense was met with bursts of joy, incomprehensible mirth.

André hastened to grab his hat, to flee, but the service was in no great hurry. He'd managed to finish off half of some very tough roast beef and, having abandoned the rest, he now ordered a sorrel salad, which failed to arrive.

He asked the owner, who was stupidly elated, if he had a newspaper. *Le Siècle* was already taken. A copy of the *Petites Affiches* was brought to him. He tried to lose himself in it, to isolate himself from the unrestrained delight of those other tables, to block out the strident jabbering of those imbeciles. But he still heard them. He forced himself to read three pages of that rag, pausing at an ad that offered a magnificent opportunity, in the wake of a liquidation of family assets, a dowry of eighteen thousand francs and an orphaned girl. It left him thoughtful. The word "urgent" which figured in parenthesis, at the bottom of this notice, unrolled before him a prospect of infinite vileness. He saw there the impending due dates of childbirths, of bulging bellies after a month of marriage. He mused upon the difficulties that would be experienced in the company of this orphan by the honest fool who'd let himself get caught. He was likely to marry a virgin with a long history of turpitude dating back to a young age! And he thought: It's already difficult enough to avoid being duped when you know the family and have lived for months with your fiancée. Who would ever be able to believe that his own wife would have cheated on him? Once more his thoughts had returned to their starting point, to the wretchedness of his domestic affairs. More than anything he wanted to shake off those memories. He now made himself look at his neighbors, to listen to them.

A shrill falsetto drilled into his ear. The hairdresser had departed without his even having noticed. A gentleman who possessed a nose crossed by golden spectacles above a red beard had taken his place and was explaining the mystery of teeth to a much younger man.

The latter stared, wide-eyed, listening devoutly, no doubt wishing to establish himself in the trade.

"The greater part of your income," the gentleman was saying, "is the fitting of false teeth. They're manufactured in England and sold in the passage Choiseul. Now, there's some serious profit to be had there, just think, you can charge ten francs per tooth and it only costs ten sous without rubber gum-tip and one franc with gum."

"They come in pink and in brown, don't they?" the young man timidly interrupted. "Me, I'd rather the pink."

"Well! You aren't a slowcoach!" the other responded. "The brown gums are for poor people! They're less expensive, but you sell a lot more of them!"

His young devotee gawped in astonishment. "And the dentures of hippopotamus ivory?" he ventured.[7]

The man in the golden spectacles raised his arms to the heavens.

"They're proper sculpture, those! Think about it, the tooth has to be chiseled from solid ivory, mounted in a gold frame, all that costs a mint!" and he went on to explain the backroom of his trade, admitted performing useless operations on the stumps of his patients and taking advantage of their state of stupefied agony to sell them his toothpaste concoctions at a premium.

These appalling revelations were too much for André. His sorrel salad had been eaten. Infuriated, he insisted on receiving his bill, refused to order a dessert, paid the sum of one franc and forty centimes and was opening the door when, from the back of the room where some people were lingering for an eternity before their tiny glasses, a voice full of conviction said, quite simply: "Women, they're no big deal!"

André closed the door, thinking, not without a certain melancholy, that, of all the banal chatter he'd overheard, this thought was maybe the only profound one, the only one that was true.

III

It was nearly nine in the morning when Cyprien stretched and noticed that his mouth was stale. That was unsurprising; last night he'd enthusiastically toasted the health of his family.

He groaned, coughed, and, shaken by the chronic phlegm of smokers, retched and spat in his chamber pot.

The noise awakened André, who yawned loudly.

"Are you okay?" Cyprien called between two burps.

"Not too bad. And you?" André sat up and folded back several sections of the screen.

"As you can see, I'm hawking it up," Cyprien replied, showing his face, skin sallow, eyes swollen, the prominent clavicles of the skinny man revealed under the unbuttoned collar of his shirt. He rolled a cigarette, asked his friend whether he'd found lodgings the day before.

André reported on his day's doings and added: "I'm off to look for my old housemaid."

"Good, I'll come with you," the painter cried. "I need some fresh air. I'm not feeling my best this morning, my heart's all in a flutter. Say what you will, but families are damned inconsiderate. They pass on to you all the bad health they've inherited, and on top of that they throw you out into the world without a penny to your name. Two generations on down, I really don't know what can be left of a failing stomach that gets more and more dyspeptic as it gets handed on to the next in line. It ends up as a bit of fiber. Reduces a man to drinking this here juice." And, leaping from his bed, Cyprien drank tumbler after tumbler of water.

"Shall I get up?" André inquired unenthusiastically.

"That wouldn't hurt," the painter replied.

Once on his feet and done with his ablutions, André brushed himself down and proceeded to the landing ahead of Cyprien, who shut the door.

André remained silent as they walked. He wanted beforehand to avoid indiscreet questions from the housemaid he'd dismissed on the eve of his marriage. Obviously, she would ask for news of Madame, want to know the reasons for the breakup, feel the need to commiserate with the fate of her old employer. André had decided to simply tell her that his wife had traveled to a warm climate for the sake of her health.

"What I've cooked up isn't very convincing," he told himself, "but it'll do, seeing that Mélanie isn't the sharpest knife in the drawer."

This was as far as his reflections had reached when they reached rue des Quatre Vents. The premises they were looking for were tucked into a corner, daubed in black from top to bottom, decorated with stripes and canary yellow letters. It was a model laundry that had seen better days, a murky shack decked out with three knitted caps adorned with chou ribbons[8] hanging in a showcase. Near a door with glass panels on which fingers had drawn figures of eight in the dust, a senile and paralytic old man was sitting in an armchair with a hole in the seat, breathing in mouthfuls of air. When he saw the young men coming he lowered his head and, before they could even start talking, he salivated copiously on his linen and muttered in a low voice that combined despair with confession: "Me, I don't know . . . don't know . . ."

The old man was dismal, and he stank.

André and Cyprien went inside. At the rear of the shop, an imbecilic-looking girl was amusing herself by singeing a lock of her hair on the top of the stove, and when it shriveled up she lifted it to her nose and seemed to enjoy sniffing the smell.

André declared the reason for their visit. She giggled and seemed even more half-witted. Luckily the proprietor emerged.

"If you want to talk to Mélanie," she said, "you need to go to number 46 rue Duvivier at the Gros-Caillou,[9] that's where she lives, but if you want to wait, she'll be here in not more than an hour; she does housework in the neighborhood and she always comes here for a chat before heading back home."

They decided to show up at the stated time, and, as they were at a loose end, they strolled under the Odéon.[10] The new books were quickly browsed.

"How about a walk in the Luxembourg?" Cyprien suggested.

They entered by the gate on rue de Vaugirard.

"Hah!" said the painter, "would you believe the memories we've planted in this park! All the same, what a pain in the neck that they've all been switched around, along with the paths![11] Look, let's head up to the terrace, they've forgotten to patch its gown and tart it up with hair lotion."

And he walked tranquilly, hands behind back, needlessly spitting to the left and right. "All the same, that spot there, that's where, after being slapped around as a kid, I was robbed of my tender years by women!" he resumed. "There's where I first met Héloïse, the big fat blonde mamma—ah! no, it's true, you never met her. Well, my friend, she took pity on my sixteen years; she swiped all the coins in my pocket, and as I didn't have the look of a man who's satisfied she said to me, straight out, calm as you please, 'It's not me who's got you all worked up, is it?' She hoodwinked me beautifully, really mothered me, and she was dignified too. I often missed her when I'd had others."

They'd arrived on the terrace and strolled up and down.

Time and again they passed by two statues. Cyprien hardly bothered to conceal his contempt for them. He stopped in front of one and, with exaggerated gestures, contemplated an Anne of Austria, carrying a scroll of paper in one hand, a little girl's music case and a scepter in the other, like those back-scratchers found in fancy goods stores and perfumeries. She was puffed up, bags under her eyes, looking grumpy, without any cleavage or backside to speak of, in short, a wash-house queen who wasn't yet completely drunk.

The other one stood in an attitude that was perhaps less imposing and looked, if possible, even more unsavory. Labeled "Anne of Brittany, Queen of France, 1476–1514," she held a cord between two big fingers as pudgy and soft as oatmeal puddings; no more of a cleavage or backside than the previous. With her louche looks, upturned beak, lips like the rim of a vase, and beefy belly, she might have been taken for a sailor woman about to tow a boat.

"It's not necessarily country girls like those who'll debauch the young folks who lurk around these parts. These here princesses are old girls from dens of iniquity." He looked for the names of the sculptors on the plinths, was astonished that they didn't bear the signature of Maindron, deeming these works worthy of the sculptor of *Velleda*, a surprising statue.

André had settled himself down on a bench. The park was almost deserted. It wasn't yet that time of day when seated women compete in boasting about the excellence of their boys, who, on a more distant path, were nipping each other and throwing sand in each other's eyes. The little girls weren't yet strutting about, displaying embroidered bloomers, white petticoats, acting snobbishly, looking down their noses at the children of the same age who invite them to play, turning away from them if their dresses were washed out and their coats had seen better days.

Ten o'clock sounded. Here and there, between the trees, gangs of plebeian brats started making a racket.

André and Cyprien traced circles in the sand with their canes. They had fallen silent, were listening, in the silence of the garden, to the shrill cries of the kids, the crunching of gravel under passing feet, the sound of a siren in the distance.

All around them they felt a silence that was enveloped in sound; the muted and distant noise of the neighboring streets spread itself out and died away in the paths near the gate. Here and there some sparrows chirruped; elsewhere pigeons hopped on bowls of flowers; hobnailed shoeprints were everywhere visible in the sand.

Cyprien, elbows on knees, head in hands, whistled, contemplating the grimy block of apartments behind the trees, the Pantheon's dome arching its gray skullcap against a flaxen blue sky intersected lower down by a line of water, a line formed by light glinting off zinc rooftops.

No one strolling on the terrace. About a hundred feet away little girls from poor families were skipping rope, bonnets fallen back and tied to the neck by an elastic string. They shouted out, "Salt, pepper, mustard vinegar!" and little white calves and very long feet could be seen under their lifted skirts.

"So," André murmured, eyes fixed on the pebbles; "That was the time when the family gave us ten sous every week to buy lollipops or chocolate from the concierge's cupboard; on Thursdays when we were free to roam about,[12] when this terrace was a meeting place, we stopped playing card games so we could talk about women. That takes us a pretty long way back, doesn't it?"

"Nearly twenty-five years," Cyprien replied. "We've known each other for more than just a few days, eh? I can still see you when you arrived at the boarding school. You were crying fit to burst—but you had nothing to moan about, not you, you had a family that laid siege to the visitor's room; you got out of the joint nearly every Sunday. Me, I was almost always stuck there. I'm damned if I don't get a chill down my spine when I think of the schoolyard's sheer misery on that day, deserted, the endless gloom of schoolwork, with the monitor sprawled in his pulpit, sullen, bad-tempered, dreaming of bingeing on booze and billiards, taking his boredom out on us, refusing permission to leave the room when we raised our hand for the loo."

"Ah well," André resumed, "if you think that the free days were happier on the outside, think again! My whole day was spoiled in worrying about having to go back in the evening. My family would check the time. My mother would say, 'We need to get a move on, it's getting late.' I left the table after the second course, carrying dessert in my pocket, and then, after the hugs and kisses and being told to be a good boy, Irma, the housemaid took me back. The streets full of people made my heart sink, I would see children hanging round in front of shops dotted with lights. I was jealous of the penniless urchins who romped on the sidewalks. They were free! As for me, I had to get a move on so as to arrive on time. Oh, the streets on that particular evening, the noise of cafés full of people, the theater posters that seemed to me an invitation to untold delights, all that was salt in the wound! I tried to walk more slowly, but the maid was in a hurry to get rid of me, no doubt to go and meet a lover. She went twice as fast, at last we were in front of that sad lodge where Piffard was keeping watch behind his glass partition. As soon as I set foot in that room I felt an icy cold on my shoulders, as though I'd entered a cellar; the back of the maid as she went away made me want to burst into tears and run for my life. You remember, when we reached the dormitory; the monitor threatened us with detention on the following Sunday because the noise we made with our heels was too loud. We took off our shoes and, without any slippers, in that dormitory that was lit as though for a mortuary wake and looking sinister with its row of white beds, we slid between the sheets as fast as possible, and heard all the others coming back, going to the pots lined up along the windows, pissing as much as they were able, whispering under the threats that the monitor yelled from between his blankets.

"To think that there are people who claim that later in life we feel regret for our schooldays. Ah, no! No way! However down in the mouth I might feel I'd sooner die than relive that barrack-room life, be bullied by bigger fists than mine, by the vicious spite of the monitors.

"Monitors! So, let's talk about them! Let's feel a little bit sorry for their fate. They have a hard life? Yes. Is there anything worse than supervising and incubating the vices of a heap of brats, and then it's lights out and waking up with them at stupid times? And after that? Aside from one or two waiting for better days in that dump, I've only known absinthe addicts, people racked by those diseases that get special treatment in the law courts! Apropos, do you remember Bourdat whom we called 'I gotta go'—he spoke just like that—do you remember him? With his shabby suit, dragged through all the dives and booze shops, his mangy and threadbare hat, his muddy mustache, his chin spotted with pimples, filthy lecheries oozing from his eyes? He kissed the boys that still didn't have hairs on their chins, swiped our pennies, confiscated our tobacco so he could smoke it, sold the books he borrowed from us, drank like a fish and made us pay two francs for a release from detention. He was really one of a kind . . ."

"He was the best of them all!" Cyprien exclaimed. "When we didn't have money to buy our way out of detention he gave us two days credit. I don't deny that deep down he was a thug, but a decent thug. I swear he's only one I've still got any respect for."

And as memories resurfaced they each took turn. Now it was the food, always the same on any given day: leg of lamb on Monday, with suet and beans in warm water; veal and chalky cheese on Tuesday; carrots in red sauce on Thursday, nauseating sorrel, macaroni without parmesan or gruyere, badly creamed peas, potatoes sautéed in black fat; then they remembered the dreadful hardships of study evenings in winter, when you dozed off, stupefied by the oppressive heat from the stove and the gas fumes, startled awake by the monitor, by a friend who poked your elbow; they recalled the anxious wait for the moment when the dictionaries were closed, when, at the sound of the bell, they were lined up in the snow, when at last they were able to stretch out in an ice-cold bed in a dormitory left open from morning till night on account of hygiene, and both of them remembered how they shivered when stripping off, keeping their socks on to alleviate the cold, coat and smock spread out on the bunk. They slept, and at half past five the next day a cleaner jerked you from your warm bed with the horrible din of a brush that he rattled between the shelves of the shoe rack.

If possible, summer was even worse. Every Saturday fortnight they washed their feet in the refectory; but come the evening some were still fetid, and a stale odor, a nauseating sickly sweetness, rose up from certain bunks, permeating the entire room.

And it went on like that for months on end, for years; you left one class to go to another; you studied new books, had to admire Horace's weighty gibberish, Homer's stupefying mishmash, recite from Virgil, Cicero, and Boileau, review all the solemn boredom of the classical epochs, copy out hundreds and thousands of lines, learn nothing useful into the bargain, and so the weeks followed on, one after another, bringing the same tasteless food, the same water, either tinted with red wine or untinted; the days flowed by, equally sad, between the desolation of Monday morning when you woke up, dismayed at the prospect of another week to get through, then on Thursday you were seized by the hope that you would make it through to Sunday.

The only light shining in that unending night of aggravation showed itself toward July, with the approach of the summer holidays, when, with the discipline relaxing somewhat, the faces of the monitors, cut out from pieces of paper and colored card, were stuck to the ceiling with wads of chewed-up paper.

And the very image of their boarding school appeared before them: the two sheltered playgrounds, that of the younger pupils and that of the older ones, separated by a wooden fence, the four latrines with a clock on top, the fountain where they gave themselves attacks of colic thanks to swallowing so much of its water. The three acacias whose flowers they ate, the shed in the big playground with a chapel above it and a pigsty below, the classrooms surrounding the little playground, the dormitories reaching up as far as the roofs, with their big windows veiled with white curtains, the kitchen in the basement areas with two barred basement windows at ground level, the parlor where piano and violin lessons were held, and, opposite, two more floors of classrooms with a hanging staircase for access.

André felt queasy thinking about the old study room with its tiers of desks of low-quality black wood, incised with pen-knifed initials, pierced with ringbolts for the chains, and he could clearly see the room before him, the shelves running all round to accommodate the Alexandres and the Quicherats,[13] the two gas lamps whose glass shades cracked when spat on; he remembered the interminable arguments, the ferocious rivalry to capture a place near the top of the room, near the stove and far from the monitor, the petty acts of meanness perpetrated in order to secure a less damaged desk, one that closed more easily; but one figure dominated over the schoolyard, the classroom, the teachers, like an apotheosis of disgust, the figure of the soup seller, bawling with a stentorian voice, slapping faces with all his might, leaving behind the red imprint of the bezel of his ring. André saw him again with his massive belly, his calf's head, his Herculean arms, he remembered his vile tricks, his blatant lies, his display of a book containing portraits of men grotesquely ravaged by syphilis. "Look, my young friend," he said, "see, you'll end up like that if you carry on playing around with your little buddies." And the foul image was lodged in your head by his repeated slaps round the ear.

And Cyprien and André helped each other to remember. They recalled the sissy boys for whose caresses they competed, the cigarettes smoked in the loo, the religion instilled by dint of punishment drills, the painful envy felt by the orphans who were visited by neither friends nor guardians, the tortures suffered by the disabled pupils, mocked by the whole classroom, shoved, beaten up without being able to defend themselves, the miseries of the bastard children whose mothers were insulted, the baseness of the monitor who looked the other way when the assailants were his favorites and his pets.

And other memories arose, yet more; the terrible panics, taking flight at the repeated yell of "look out, look out, there's the monitor!"—the hullabaloo in the streets when old mother "That Stinks" headed toward the school, a street seller near Saint-Sulpice who shot up with a howl when they spat on her cooked pears or poultry, "Pichi," a dealer in curios on rue de Grenelle who was infuriated with that nickname, and the wicked jokes: the hard, rolled-up pieces of paper folded in two and catapulted at the bellies of horses that reared up, threatening to wreck their cabs, crush passersby, and everything, everything, the terrible worries when you started for school without having prepared your lessons, the hellish storm of detentions and confinements, the family's reproaches, the soup-seller's rages!

"What shitholes, all those boarding schools!" André ended up saying, and Cyprien, in full agreement, spat his contempt on the sand.

"And yet," he resumed after a silence, "you've got to admit we had some good times in this here park. The days when we were kept as reserves in competitions, we ate the traditional slice of paté on this bench and emptied a pipe of wine wrapped in netting. We smoked damp cigarettes behind those trees"—and he pointed to distant embankments tinted red and yellow by flowers, thickets blown open by a gust of wind, letting stars of blue sky be seen through the gaps in their leaves—and he added in conclusion, "the Luxembourg is the only stretch of raked ground that still interests me."

André mournfully poked at pebbles with his cane. "It's all of my younger days here, a boyhood full of humiliation and failure," he said. "With a widowed and penniless mother, a scholarship to support me at school and reduced fees, I couldn't protest when the meat was rotten and hordes of cockroaches danced about in it. Ah, I knew what was going on, when the kitchen lad brought the plates to the cook and whispered to him the names of the pupils he was going to serve, the plate came back to me with scraps and blobs of fat, bones or fishbones! I ate badly and not enough, and I was regularly picked on to recite the prayer. Added to that, no end of punishments—others got a hundred lines, me five hundred. No congratulations when I came top of the class, looked down on when I came third—anger and contempt when I came eleventh. My boots were always patched and repaired. Waistcoats tailored from old ones that an uncle passed down to my mother for me, a Sunday uniform that was always faded from want of reconditioning. Well-to-do friends abandoned me at the school gate on free days because I didn't have straight collars and blue cravats like them. I didn't drool over manilla cigars, no, not me, I sucked on penny butt ends. That's what I see when I go back, a deplorable procession of miseries and insults, cartloads of refuse, jailhouse vices and abject galley slavery.

"And yet I wasn't a cretin, or a troublemaker either—no—I wasn't anything—I was just mediocre. I wasn't exactly lazy; in all conscience there was nothing that could be held against me except reading prohibited books behind my desk, the tales of La Fontaine, who at that time I saw as a great poet. Things carried on like that indefinitely. Years butting into yet more years, monitors wore out and were replaced by different ones, the housemaster got old and hit you less hard, the study walls got stickier and more stained, the tiers of benches caved in more and more, and life carried on in the same way, sad and stultifying.

"It's true that once I'd passed my baccalaureate things were hardly more appetizing. I had to give Latin lessons to a family on rue d'Anjou. It involved stretching the hopelessly limited intelligence of a clotheshorse. My uncle's inheritance finally turned up when my mother was dead of sorrow. My God, what a heap of muck we stir up when we look back."

"Oh!" Cyprien replied, "We don't even need to think about our school years for buckets of dirty dishwater water to splash down on our heads. As for me, I don't need to go as far as that. All I need to do is conjure up memories of my old mistresses, Céline Vatard among others,[14] and that's me done for!—And when you think that I had an income of three hundred francs a month for eating and that I ate up the capital with loose women with the excuse of doing a better job of painting them! My canvases should have compensated for what I paid for the flesh of the model—a lousy investment—I learned nothing. My paintings have been turned down in all the galleries and haven't sold. I've still got them at home, and it's been a long time since the originals were bought and I no longer have them!—Still, it's some consolation that if people like us aren't worth envying, our old school friends don't seem to have done any better—at least from what I gather." And he mentioned a name: "Letousey, for example, remember, when the monitor wanted to thrash him, he lashed out with that never-to-be-forgotten yell, 'If you come near me I'll knock your stinking teeth down your throat!' Well, I'm told that he works for a salary of 1,800 francs in a ministry."

"Flat broke!" André replied. "A wife no doubt—children, lodgings on the fifth floor—a petrol lamp for lighting the house—imitation oak sideboard—mahogany piano—the wife nursed the babies herself to save money—breasts gone all saggy. On Sundays, the latest brat wheeled around in a little pram stowed away underneath the stairs come evening. Nights spent watching the milk teeth coming through. Dogged needlework on top of that, material from the top of the pants taken to sew on a piece needed at the bottom. Flat broke! Or else the bride is painting the town red!

"And Degagnac, you remember him?" he resumed. "That maniac who was shortsighted because his nurse was myopic—anyway, that's what he said. Degagnac, the man who sucked the milk of blindness, what the hell has become of him?"

"I don't know," Cyprien replied. "That customer must have seduced his mother's maid and they're living as man and wife. In the evening, when the old unmarried couples come from the alleys, you're bound to see him alongside a fat critter in a run-down neighborhood, sucking a five-cent cigar, chattering to the porters, sitting astride the chairs in front of the doors."

And such and such? And a procession of names paraded past, one by one—faces that were sometimes specific, sometimes vague, barely sketched. André remembered this one but Cyprien didn't. Cyprien still clearly recalled that one whom André struggled to put a face to. Out of all those whose image they summoned up, none appeared bathed in an aura of wealth and well-being. There was one single exception, the stupidest of them all, the son of a dealer in pigments. He'd made his fortune with white lead, and his income was spent on draining mugs of beer and betting on the races.

"Hey, there isn't much consolation in any of that," Cyprien muttered—"and no panoramic views either, no wide open spaces! Nothing anywhere but a long wall of need. The old friends, the comrades we meet, the acquaintances we greet, all of them condemned to berths in beaneries, rationed love affairs, proposals to other men's women, troubles with the landlords, agonies when the bills fall due! Everywhere you look, an eternal and incorrigible deficit! Here, look, see that young man going past; his overcoat is almost new, but his ankle boots have had it, the elastic's gone, the heels are lopsided, the bootstraps burst. His tie is worn long to hide his shirt. Oh, the sickly shirtfronts! I know them well, the shirtfronts we examine every morning, gaping open, buttons you fasten under the starched front with a bit of thread so as not to lose them. And to cap it all, just imagine seeing the underwear of that there gentleman! . . . Underpants with filth supplied free of charge! The seat of his pants as thin as onion skin, just as weathered and rust-colored, socks that are worn for a fortnight, with black creases at the heels, sepia streaks on the instep, toes the color of terracotta!" After a moment's silence he pointed a finger at the children who had gradually collected and were prowling about the terrace. "There are plenty more," he continued. "They'll simmer away miserably on the cooker. That'll be a real stew!"

Then, without another word said, they looked at the brats, shirts hanging loose from pants, sloping shoulders, the appearance of rickets, necks with dry, scrofulous holes, they almost felt pity for the bundles of red flesh, packed in swaddling, carried by ragged girls, fidgeting bundles from whence came cries, piss, tears. Further along, a big, pale, emaciated lad at the age when the voice breaks, with overgrown legs and a bizarre voice, was bullying a smaller boy whose smock was decorated with a lead medal, and, just opposite them, three little girls were making mud pies in red-painted metal buckets. They were squatting, their backs turned, and they lifted and lowered themselves in time, revealing little white backsides with a cleft down the middle.

Eleven o'clock chimed. André gave a start. "Let's go and find Mélanie," he said, and then, "I've had more than enough of

Luxembourg; this park is a sink of misery! The hell with you and your childhood memories! Come on, let's be off." And they made their way down from the terrace to the paths that border the parterres, hugged by railings in front of the Senate.

They walked quickly, overtook a priest grunting over a book bound in black cloth, a man off to work, nose buried in a newspaper; they skirted lines of workers stretched out on the benches, smoking cigarettes, hands raking out fleas from under their shirts, edged past an old man knocking the dottle of his pipe out on the green tub of an orange tree, their eyes followed the swaying hips of the young worker girls, no doubt more or less honest ones, for they were in a hurry, carrying their lunch in a leather satchel. André went faster, pushed aside a kid heading toward the pond, a model boat in his arms, swore at a scamp of a girl who threw her hoop at his legs.

"Let's get a move on," he repeated, "I mustn't miss Mélanie."

At last they arrived at the laundry.

"Sit down for a minute," the laundrywoman said to the two young men. "Mélanie is next door with the neighbor; I'll go and find her."

They grabbed chairs. The old man, put to bed in the back room, could be heard moaning. They saw that his backside had been smeared with bacon lard to prevent the skin from rubbing raw. An old woman emerged from the shop's backroom and threw away the scraps of the bacon near the mechanism, at the bottom of a heap of dirty linen.

Three laundry women were handling shirts. The apprentice was seated on a chair, her feet on the rungs, knees raised. She muttered in a low voice, eye unfocused. Unconsciously, almost aloud, she said, "I can't hear my sheep!"

The laundry women stopped working and chorused, "There goes a dirty rookie! You're getting on our nerves with your sheep—should've stayed with them!" The old man shifted restlessly on his bunk. His cramped arms, which he was still able to move, knocked against the partition. He swore in a dull voice. A laundry woman went over to comfort him. "Come on, uncle, that's enough now! If you don't pipe down your wine won't get sugared!" And the grizzling of a scolded child made itself heard: "What do I know? . . . I don't know . . ."

"Is he your uncle?" Cyprien asked the woman.

She shook her head. He was nobody's uncle. He'd been taken in simply because he had a disposable income.

"It's only a shame that the old pig there had a bit of a life annuity," one of the women who were ironing said judiciously.

Cyprien thought it best not to reply to that comment. Besides the new girl astonished him; he'd never seen so many red marks on a face, arms even redder and hands blacker. He was yanked from his contemplation by the arrival of Mélanie who stopped in front of her employer, dumbfounded.

"Hello Monsieur André," she said. "Is Monsieur still keeping well?" And she looked to see if he had a crape band on his hat. Not seeing any, she no doubt concluded that the wife of the house wasn't deceased, as she'd thought.

André took her aside, told her that his wife was very ill, that she couldn't come back to Paris for a long time yet. He cut short the loud lamenting whines that Mélanie thought proper and simply proposed thirty-five francs and board to her for preparing his meals and cleaning his rooms.

She hesitated. "The thing is, I've got a lot of houses to clean," she finally said. Nevertheless, she accepted the offer, declared that she couldn't come to work for him before the beginning of the next month. André wanted her to come in three days' time, when he was due to move in. She refused: she couldn't abandon clients whose praises she sang. André stopped her, accepted her conditions, gave her his address, remembered that she was married, asked after the health of her husband, the police officer, once more cut short the lengthy details that she proceeded to itemize and, on exiting, in the street, suddenly forgetting the unhappiness of which he'd made a song and dance, took Cyprien's arm and, cheerfully, said, "Oof! At last I can breathe! I can see the coast clear. In a week or so I'll be pretty much settled. This time I've got all the trump cards. Someone to light the fire and the lamp too, my clothes brushed and mended, supper ready on time, feet in slippers, I'm going to have all that, and treated with respect too for my thirty-five francs a month; I'm saved!"

"The dream, eh?" Cyprien concluded. "All the comforts of marriage minus the wife! On top of that one evening lost every week to carnal horseplay; peace, quiet, and well-being on all the other days, trouble-free love and your work done at a stroke. Watch out, eh? I'm not joking, old girl. There you are on the train, don't get off at any stops, you'll find there are whores waiting on the platform."

"Oh, no need to worry about me on that score, thanks. I've paid my bill . . ."

"You never know," the painter murmured. "This Paris of ours stirs a man up, with its growing juveniles and their obscene innocence, the forty-year-old women and their sympathetic hysterias, the older bourgeois wives with their complicated vices! Ah! it's a ginger that a man really likes to taste! Then, you see, for all that they might be muzzled, all the old passions that we weren't able to tranquilize still get up on their hind legs and howl when a petticoat passes by! Watch out, my poor friend, watch out, let's stick together, let's keep a tight hold of each other."

"And let's go eat," said André who was affected by Cyprien's melancholic fears. "So, after the breakfast that buried my boyhood, I now offer you the dinner of my divorce. We'll order burgundy wine and try to soak and soften all our old grudges in it . . ."

"Agreed!" Cyprien said, and, arm in arm, they passed through the door of a restaurant where they were greeted by a flunkey bowing almost to the ground, the bow squashing his florid dewlaps against the starched breast of his shirt.

They sat down across from each other, studying the menu, straying off into the wine list.

In hushed tones André named the grand crus; Cyprien listened, lingering dreamily over each name.

Romanée and Chambertin, Clos-Vougeot and Corton paraded royal feasts before him, abbatial ceremonials, opulent, gold-embroidered vestments ablaze with light! He was dazzled above all by the Clos-Vougeot. This wine seemed to him the nectar of great dignitaries. The label glowed before his eyes, like those crowns of light set behind the Virgin's occiput in churches.

"No, not those," he said; "Let's order a more modest wine. Let's see, going down the pecking order we arrive at the unfussy bottles that don't put on any airs. No high and mighty dames, they've had their day; let's look for modest and saucy little ladies, bottles with a touch of elegance but relaxed about letting us caress them!"

"Volnay, Nuits, Beaune, Pomard?" André continued.

"Pomard, eh?" Cyprien said, his eyes greedy; "How about that one?" And he made imaginary brushstrokes, saw an already completed canvas; a comfortable dining room, devoid of women, happy partners at table, swollen bellies, shiny red mugs, the air of gorged gluttons, the laughter of guzzlers sozzled with wine! He saw artists making merry at leisure in a warm room, carpet underfoot, cushioned seats, a well-organized waiting service, random outbursts of good cheer, paradoxes waltzing on tightropes, falling onto trampolines, bouncing back and spouting phrases in sparkling verbal pirouettes like the sequined costumes of somersaulting clowns!

"So, are you going to decide," André groaned, losing patience with Cyprien's dreamy manner.

"Well then, the Pomard," he replied.

They ordered a bottle from the sommelier and filled their glasses.

"I can't see anything anymore," the painter said to himself. The delightful vision of the disordered table littered with wine glasses had vanished. He drank wine that wasn't disagreeable but that was about all.

Disillusioned, he gazed at the restaurant that was now abuzz and, swallowing two mouthfuls, exclaimed: "No, it's not the vintage that makes for good wine, it's the décor, the atmosphere you drink it in! This here wine, well, it would only be Pomard if we were to sample it at home, in a deep armchair and in a pretty glass. Here, it's Château-Velisy, it's no more than three-year-old Saint-Clamart! Look, order an intimate wine like this in a restaurant, take a deeper dive if you want; choose the Maçons and the Beaujolais, drink Thorins and Moulin-à-Vent, that's really stupid! We should have asked for table wine, wine that's drunk out in the open with a breeze blowing between the legs and plates clattering in the ears, champagne in fact! Yes, in classy eating joints our tongues should be slurping drinks that make you want to quit the table before the coffee arrives, not enjoy the false feeling of well-being that sends your legs to sleep and glues you to your chair. Without that it's just a nonsense.

"Enough said!" he resumed, examining his friend who wasn't listening, seeming to have relapsed into his black mood; "We simply made a mistake." And he added to himself while swallowing a mouthful of fish that tasted of the napkin, "All the same, there are people who are really happy. They get a little bit of illusion on top of what's due them by way of mealtime eats and pleasure in bed! Us, nothing at all. We're the unlucky ones forever going somewhere else to look for a bare allowance of stew in a bowl! What I'm saying isn't very uplifting, all things considered. But André too, why is he looking so sorry for himself? The truth is, he makes me feel bad."

* * *

Like those who suddenly see the calamitous notice of a closure on the doors of the theater where they'd gone to purchase a few laughs and then stare in despair at the doors, Cyprien and André, after having expected the joyful enchantments of wine, now gazed, disheartened, at their glasses.

IV

The room was oblong, hung with wood-colored wallpaper, embellished with a craquelured white ceramic stove with copper doors, a mahogany sideboard, six rush-seated chairs, an extendable table on castors.

A felt carpet was on the floor and round green esparto mats in front of each chair. A mirror, unwelcome in the other rooms, stood isolated from other furniture on clawed feet alongside walls paneled to waist height. Its gilt sides, through which the red base was showing, were flanked by a cigarette holder with a worn emery paper surround showing blue scrape-marks, and an almanac illustrated with colored lithographs, given away by a store. Facing the mirror were a siphon barometer, a colored map of Paris in uniform tints dating from 1860. The room's decor was completed by a mezzotint depicting the crossing of the Alps, with a Napoleon parading on a rearing horse like a circus rider, and two cameo plates in lilac and bister, a portrait of Mme Vigée-Lebrun and Girodet's Atala, fastened to wall by hooks.

The faded, urine-yellow damask that, as in the majority of bourgeois dining rooms, formerly served the living room as curtains, now decorated the connecting room where meals were eaten, while the drawing room had been refurbished and renovated. Since that room possessed only a single window, the material that had previously draped the living room's second window had been attached, in the form of a hanging, above the door joining the two rooms.

Residing on the sideboard shelves: a britannium teapot, a Minton dinner service, a teak liquor cabinet on which two Gien vases were permanently placed, decorated with horns of plenty and surmounted by a bouquet of dried reeds; on the stove's marble, a cup of water, a snot-colored porcelain lamp wearing a miniature fez with a blue tassel on top of its glass, both of them leaning against the pipe looped by copper bracelets, crowned at its summit by some kind of diadem in white ceramic.

To save money, the Désableau family lit the stove an hour before supper and spent the evening there.

The maid had swept up the remains of the meal from the table and wiped down the oilcloth cover with a rag when Madame Désableau brought in her workbasket. She took out a box of needles in the form of an ivory bean, the stub of a wax candle for her thread, scissors, a thimble, the yellow ribbon of a tape measure. Finally, she took from a chair the pattern of a dress cut out from an old journal.

She spread this out on the table, rummaged in an old pastille box for pins scattered among buttons, cut out the paper, attached the segments to it and, looking thoughtful, having planned skillful, strategic cuts, made a determined start on the material.

Her husband laid out his cards for a game of patience. A little girl, playing with non-toxic pigments arranged on a pad, laboriously colored in a penny image, sucked her paintbrush, turned it between her lips to give it a point, then stuck it in the hole chafed through the middle of the paints.

A young woman with a matte complexion and brown hair, brilliant teeth, a droll overbite, gazed in boredom at her uncle dealing out his cards. After a moment she got up, went over to the stove, opened the little hatch of its door, toasted her feet, appeared to lose herself in a newspaper.

Throwing light on the table, an overhead copper lamp left the young woman's face in the shadows, cast its full light on the fingers that were sewing, or dealing cards, a bobbin of white thread, a cardboard star round which black thread was wound. The face of the little girl leaning over her picture entered the circle of light that cut off, at the midpoint of her arms, the sleeves of Madame Désableau, who was now sitting back a little and leaning on the backrest of her chair.

"And the coffee," the man said. "Is it coming?"

"Eugénie, what's gotten into you," the woman cried out. "Can't you see, girl, that Monsieur is waiting for his coffee!"

The maid carried in a bowl of sugar, a cup, a spoon, poured the coffee from a little pot. Madame Désableau soaked a lump of sugar, let the child take a bite, blissfully melted the rest of the piece in her mouth.

In the eight months since he'd been promoted to second in command at the city hall, M. Désableau had at last fulfilled a long-cherished desire to take a coffee every day after his meals. Until then, his wife had forbidden it as an extravagance. "It's not so much that coffee is expensive," she'd said, "it's the sugar that's added to it."

Obliged to live the obnoxious and reduced life of slim purses, the Désableaus, to make ends meet, had had, every weekday except Sundays, to deprive themselves of the paltry luxury of the demitasse that concierges and laborers don't deny themselves.

For twenty years M. Désableau had written up reports in both italic and copperplate, filed away in boxes of useless paperwork, maintained a voluminous register bound in green leather. After this length of time, he had acquired the mannerisms requisite for ordering others about; no doubt the powers that be, before promoting him and awarding him a decoration, were waiting until he had succumbed to the infirmities of people who spend too much time sitting in a chair.

Solemn with respect to everything, he looked the part of a busy and earnest man, wore stiffly starched collars, black cravats wound twice around the neck, riding high at the nape, tied under the chin in a very short knot. He liked to hold forth like a lawyer, hands in pockets, legs spread. Under pince-nez with lenses encircled by black buffalo leather, he opened, when relaxing, two astonished eyes that belied the typically thoughtful gesture of his fingers combing through sandstone-colored whiskers.

His wife was plump, with big, vacant eyes and the complexion of scalded white meat. She had a huge chin falling over a smaller one, and along her lips a sprinkling of gray hairs that defied depilation.

She sweated blood and tears by day to safeguard her household; in the evening she curled up on a chair, lowered her chest and lifted her stomach, said to her daughter every ten minutes, "Justine, straighten up," turned toward her niece, asked for a summary of the news reported by the *Petit Journal*, listened to her husband who grew heated as soon as talk turned to the Chamber of Deputies.

M. Désableau's opinions were simple; he believed in the honesty of politicians, the valor of warriors, the independence of the magistracy, the conspiracies of the Jesuits, and the crimes of the agitators.

Having chanced to read eulogistic platitudes about America retailed by doctrinaire thinkers, he exalted that odious country's mode of life,[15] wished that ours resembled it more closely, advocated utilitarian ideas, the benefits of learning, progress, the limited freedoms of republics.

He further aggravated these exorbitant naiveties by the sententious way in which he pronounced them; his wife remained mute, blissfully ecstatic as soon as he opened his mouth.

By nature she was both weak and grasping; greedy for gain, with a weakness for pleasure, she would have trimmed ten centimes from the daily groceries to spend her savings on giving a ball.

A daughter was born belatedly from her union with M. Désableau, the girl presently busy spoiling a penny image. They had always wanted a son, would have liked to found a dynasty of employees, imitating those families whose offspring endlessly succeeded each other to the same chair, living and dying in dire poverty, without even having tried to strike out for the horizon.

M. Désableau said it was an honorable situation if poorly remunerated, and one that offered security too. And he promptly added, "In our capacity as civil servants we represent the flower of the bourgeoisie."

Their prayers remained unanswered. No son was born to them. On the other hand, they were able to complete the education of a new girl. Their niece, Berthe Vigeois, lost her father suddenly and went to live with them. What's more she came at no extra cost, the sixty thousand francs that came with her even helping the household's halting progress. For her benefit they annexed a bathroom adjoining a bedroom, stored there as best they could all the furniture held back from the sale of the estate. The tranquility of the family, unsettled by these developments, was gradually reestablished; they made the soup go further, were able to buy real meat more often, able to invite a few people to gatherings.

At that time Berthe was nearly twenty years old; her mother had died when she was twelve. She grew up near the armchair where her restless and sickly father emerged from his traveling blankets at nine in the evening. Then the maid was summoned to prepare the beds, to warm Monsieur's, and Berthe crushed the embers in the warming pan with a shovel, put the fire guard in place, offered her forehead to her father, lit her candlestick and, in spite of the cold, postponed the moment of going to bed, delaying the maid who had come to pull back the sheets, listened to her recital of the household woes, all the malicious gossip of her neighborhood.

Henry Vigeois, her father, a retired dealer in Rouen printed cotton, was a man who had, notwithstanding his honesty in business dealings, succeeded in amassing a small fortune.

Puny and meek, he had, throughout his life, given way to his wife's slightest whim. A commanding woman! Now that she was dead, he was in denial about his subjugation to her, squawked like a magpie as soon as his daughter and his maid didn't obey his slightest order. Relations were difficult at first, but Berthe manipulated him with matchless ease; she turned him inside out like an old glove, broke off when he frowned, waited till his temper had improved, overturned his resolution at a stroke, in a sudden sortie. Sometimes, however, when he was twisted with rheumatism, her attacks failed, but she patiently restated the matters that he had refused to consider, presenting them to him in a different light, led him to agree, listened to him repeating once more that he never went back on his word.

These daily battles soon quickened her maturity. She was ready for marriage at an early age. In bed too early, she meditated for a long time before going to sleep and in this way prepared terrible trials for the husband who would want to marry her. Never having been in a boarding school or convent, she might have been less cunning, but the ennui of gloomy evenings beside her father had prodigiously whetted her appetite for pleasure and luxury. In marriage she saw her chance for revenging her monotonous and dull life, she saw the future as a mad whirl through theaters and balls, a whole horizon of visits and dinner parties.

Evoking the prospect of future joys consoled her for her present circumstances; she sat in dreamy absorption in her chair, read on page four of the newspaper the program of performances, thought about *Fra Diavolo*[16] which she had admired on a previous occasion, felt a vague desire for the tenor who filled his white breeches so proudly and emitted cooing sounds in statuesque poses.

Like almost all women she'd conjured up an ideal of a grease-painted thespian, then, gradually, had come to realize that these seductive individuals were in fact no more than vulgar buffoons, grubby machines spitting out notes.

Her ideal then grew more nebulous and confused. He was hardly embodied in the amiable freebooters described by Fenimore Cooper, in the heroes contrived by George Sand or the elder Dumas. She quenched her raptures and fevers by pouring them out on her piano which, for months, resounded with lachrymose reveries and Turkish marches.

She came to her senses in good time, recognizing how fatuous her dreams were; her thoughts now dwelt on something solid, on the comfort of an affluent situation. She sighed less often and understood that the stultifying life she was leading wasn't without its advantages. In the absence of parties and divertissements she at least enjoyed a certain measure of freedom; her father allowed her to go out with her maid and she had the run of the department stores, smiled gladly at the compliments of the drapery salesmen, yearned, in her idleness, for intrigues. Her uppermost concern was to be elegantly attired, and she trimmed money from the household budget to pay for more elegant lady's boots and more expensive stockings. She'd even purchased a box of talcum powder and, as her father wouldn't have tolerated her flouring her cheeks, she dusted them lightly[17] in the evening in front of her mirror, in this way tasted intimate and forbidden coquetries, quietly descended to more banal maneuvers in order to satisfy more costly ones, encouraged by her maid who was rewarded with Mademoiselle's slightly soiled gowns as the price of her complicity, permission to enjoy greater liberties, the right to shamelessly engage in substantial pilfering. Sometimes M. Vigeois ventured a remark, claimed that female trappings had been less costly in the days of his deceased wife. Berthe calmly replied that the cost of living had tripled since that time. "You spent less on food," she said, "and yet our meals haven't changed."

Her father agreed, and a few days later, she carefully waylaid him, persuading him step by step of the need for new cosmetics, and he finished by giving way, flattered that, all things considered, his daughter was pretty and dressed in the latest fashion.

Furthermore, like most young women who lose their mother at an early age, she was badly brought up. She saw in her father a banker whose reserves of cash were earmarked for all her needs and whims. And in this we see the eternal female; here was the whole woman, honest or not, who thinks it only right to squeeze as much money as she can from the man on whom she relies, whether father or protector. The battle, incessantly renewed, was between the man's rooted willpower and the woman's obstinate blandishments; and right from the start the man and father had, of course, already been defeated by the woman and daughter.

What's more, the expensive boots and the gala of gowns emboldened Berthe's ambitions. With the aim of hooking a husband for herself she persuaded her father to entrust her to relatives who introduced her to society.

She achieved some victories. Almost unhoped-for opportunities came her way. None of them pleased her. This one looked like an apprentice upholsterer, hair like drumsticks; that one had an awkward and clumsy manner, the flesh round his eyes was inflamed. She wanted a man who would look the part, provide her with pleasures, guarantee a life of sweet luxury. For the space of two years, she judged all those suitors by the shape of a nose and the cut of a suit and rejected them. Practical though she was, all these blunders resulted from her shallow female brain.

Her ideal had already suffered plenty of knocks and bruises, when her father collapsed on the carpet, felled by a stroke; her life changed overnight. Life with the Désableaus bored her to death. The freedom she'd enjoyed with her maid came to an end; her aunt accompanied her wherever she went. Her prolonged shopping trips were no longer possible; the strings that she had pulled so easily with her father stood no chance of working with a thrifty woman like her aunt. She had to satisfy herself with the modest allowance granted by her uncle for the cost of her toiletries.

This state of subjection, without any compensating advantages, weighed on her. She'd rarely gone out when she was with her father because he was almost paralyzed; she hardly went out much more when she was with her uncle, and she had to suffer the sad disappointments of these two petit bourgeoisie, infuriated in spite of everything with their inferior status, nevertheless making an effort to put on a show, eating meat and drinking rape wine,[18] hosting a soirée and improving their wardrobe. Accustomed to a tolerably comfortable way of life, she lived in a state of monotonous and niggling chagrin.

She pitied the wine bought by the quart in a grocer's shop and decanted into carafes for the table; she was disgusted by the second-rate meat, pretentiously dished up, the fish that was past its best and yet served on a napkin; she smiled contemptuously when the Désableaus, taking advantage of a bonus payment, supplied their front door with a bell. The imperious door chime seemed aristocratic to them, suitable for earning the esteem of the people who rang it. However, as the kitchen and the dining room were separated from the hallway by a long corridor, and not being able to hear the ring of the chime, they had kept the old bell that, as before, ding-donged nearer to them and alerted them to a visitor waiting on the landing.

It was at this juncture, after those evenings when Berthe regretted not being married, staring at the family at table and engrossed in tedious pastimes, that André was introduced to the household. He neither pleased nor displeased her. It seemed to her that he possessed distinction. The Désableaus did not approve of this marriage. The profession of man of letters frightened the husband. He foresaw all kinds of unconventionality, a tempestuous marriage, a slovenly life, carelessly tailored, bursting at the seams; his wife too viewed André with an uneasy eye; for her a man who must have dined with actresses boded nothing good. Berthe merely remarked to her uncle that all the reports were favorable and that although an artistic type the young man possessed an income. Moreover, she declared in no uncertain terms that André suited her.

The marriage was celebrated. She remained dismayed. All her girlish dreams fell away, one by one; all the joys divulged by her girlfriends, whispered in the corner of the window, all the expectations of paradise suddenly unveiled behind the curtains, came to grief. Sensually cold, she found nothing in the transports sanctioned by the Church but a revolting convention, a distressing dirtiness.

And then the character of her husband seemed to her prematurely old. After her father's grumbling affection, her uncle's upright rigidity, she would have liked a freer rein, the benefit of childish intimacies. André had adopted a paternal and benevolent manner. He was always on the defensive and, behind a display of affection, sought to take the measure of his wife. Not to shock her directly, not to fly red rags in her face, to keep hold of her so that she wasn't too aware of the leash, wrap the harshness of a refusal in a delicate tenderness, such was his method. Moreover, when she sought to impose her will on him through a hidden war, as formerly on her father, he promptly took into account the force of her calculated inertia, her tireless cunning. He resisted at first, then finally, with the melancholy experience of those men who have often frequented young women, admitting once more that he lacked willpower, gave way for the sake of peace; except that, in saying "yes" to Berthe, the word laid bare before her eyes the workings of the apparatus she was employing. One day, when he was in a good mood, he even said to her, at the very moment she commenced her maneuvers; "So that's what you want. In a week you'll bring your artillery out into the open; so go on, do it straightaway."

She blushed, sulked, mortified at having for adversary a man who stopped short in front of her traps and laughed, pointing them out with a finger before stepping into them.

In the early days they remained, generally speaking, in an alert and uneasy intimacy. Both spied on each other, suspecting under all these skirmishes, all this front-line combat, a stubborn and inexhaustible struggle. Disarmed, like all unfortunate creatures who have lived alone for a long time, by the slightest token of affection and small signs of caring, André sometimes told himself that while his wife was willful and obstinate, she was at heart a decent, honest girl who truly loved him. Then there followed a truce that lasted several months; he believed that Berthe had abandoned her schemes, was tired of wrangling; he didn't understand that, in a new initiative, she had time and again beaten him right across the board. In fact, she now employed a sure tactic. She made a show of wanting something that meant nothing to her and that she knew her husband would disapprove of; then, to please him, she readily renounced it. It only remained for André to give way to her on those things that seemed less important. Although he was still distrustful, he got caught in that trap, proving once more the indisputable fact that, stupid and dim though she might be, a woman will always get the better of the most cultivated and intelligent man.

In spite of everything, their ailing marriage hadn't yet reached a crisis point. Hostilities didn't emerge into the open until André had the unwise idea of inviting to supper his oldest and best friend, Cyprien Tibaille, who came unenthusiastically and donned gloves for the occasion.

The welcome couldn't have been colder. Berthe's insolent silence at table, her hurried serving of the dishes, her acid tone of... "no one wants any more leg of lamb?" accompanied by a ring of the bell to summon the maid, left André in torments.

He made every effort to find witty things to say, to enliven the meal, winked at his wife who, following her usual habit, rolled a bit of bread crust between her fingers and even avoided replying to her guest's polite remarks.

All the platitudes had been trotted out. The conversation died out on a Delft plate hanging on the wall. This meal, gulped down at full gallop as though in a railway station buffet, nevertheless seemed interminable. When it came to an end, however, Cyprien, more and more offended by Berthe's persistent refusal to pay him any heed, managed to regain the upper hand; he poured out the wine she failed to offer him and, elbows planted on the table, he turned toward André and, sweeping aside with one accord the heap of banalities they'd piled up since the soup course, both chatted to each other like in the good old days. They remembered amusing stories, laughed openly, no longer paying attention to the woman. Berthe decided it was time to intervene. She said in a voice that was half grating and half amiable: "Come now, Monsieur, I hope you aren't going to make my husband remember his bachelor days?"

She cut their conversation short. Silence reigned for several minutes. André kept himself under control, determined not to aggravate through quarreling the icy embarrassment provoked by his wife. He wanted to react, tried to light a firework; it sputtered out, the atmosphere was too saturated with malaise. Cyprien, for his part, wanting to shake off the lethargy that was getting the better of him, did everything in his power and talked uninspiredly about the silver-plated portable stoves placed on the table. Seizing the opportunity, André launched into a pointless discussion of the value of britannium and nickel silvers; his words dropped without echo into a miserable silence. Then he made an effort at joviality.

"Well now, old chap," he said, "Make sure you don't take them away with you!" And, addressing his wife, he joked complaisantly, "Berthe, you'd do well to keep an eye on Cyprien when he leaves."

She replied with studied coolness: "Why? You know what to expect. Monsieur is your friend since you brought him here."

After that display of rudeness the conversation shuddered to a halt. Dessert was rapidly dispatched. Cyprien stretched his hand toward a plate of nectarines, Berthe pretended not to see the gesture, rang to have the dishes removed and coffee served. Both men hoped she would leave them alone. She didn't budge; when her husband took out a cigarette she merely declared that tobacco smoke didn't bother her at all, and she leaned back, eyes on the ceiling, seeming to ignore André's search for matches, the painter's arm straining to reach a bottle of rum.

"Wait a bit, I've got to give you a taste of this kirsch," André said. "Berthe, fetch us a bottle, will you, it must be there at the bottom of the sideboard, on the second shelf."

She got up with bad grace. "I can't see it."

"For God's sake!" André broke out impatiently, "I'm telling you, there, behind the cognac."

Finally, she grasped a liter bottle of white liquor. They uncorked it, it was marc brandy.

This time she got up with such a dour and peevish look that Cyprien felt compelled to cry out, "Madame, I beg you, don't go to so much trouble."

Exasperated, André had gotten brusquely to his feet, and seized a flask of kirsch from where he'd pointed. They drank a little glass, then Cyprien apologized for not being able to stay longer. Berthe maintained her glacial attitude, didn't even have the grace to ask if he really must go, and he quit the premises, irritated and on an empty stomach.

As soon as the door was closed, the storm burst, horribly. André gave his wife a harsh shaking. She resorted to tears and hysterics. He ended up feeling sheepish, afraid of having gone a bit too far, lifted up his wife, kissed her, almost made excuses to her.

From that evening, the conflict intensified.

Berthe never forgave her husband for treating her like a child who was unfortunately now too big to be spanked; nevertheless she had achieved the goal so ardently pursued by all young wives—slammed the door of her house shut on the friends of the man they've married; she might, as a result, have shown greater indulgence; but the uncommonly high-handed way in which André had rebuked her left her outraged, then he was stupid enough to let her see that, like all weak people, he felt sorry once the reprimand was served. All of a sudden, she understood how insecure his firmness really was, how his clear-sightedness, so hazardous at first, was blurring; until now she had neither loved nor hated, now she came to detest him.

The more she thought about it, the more she became convinced that marrying him had been a stupid mistake. After letting more advantageous matches slip through her fingers, she should have waited longer. Among the people eagerly surrounding her in the rare salons where her uncle agreed to introduce her, she could have found a richer, more fashionable suitor. On returning home still damp from the sweat of waltzes, she dreamed of the dancers who had embraced her, imagined that she would have been happier with one of them. In every case, those individuals had worthwhile positions, might, through hard work, increase their assets, allow the life of their wife more scope. André was absorbed by literature, a circumstance disdained by all the families she knew, an occupation that consisted of twiddling his thumbs and writing at a rate of two words a day. Besides, he couldn't have much talent, as the few books he'd written sold hardly any copies.

Thanks to him, her life remained humble and low status; thanks to him she was the unhappiest of women, and, with smothered rage, she felt sorry for herself, during long evenings stared at her husband working hard on phrases. She shrugged her shoulders at his hesitations, the furious way he chewed his pen, his scoring out of entire lines, his overwriting of words already crossed out, his inky cancellation of repetitions; she finished by losing patience with his obstinate silence, his annoyed grunts, and she interrupted him with remarks like, "You're going to stain the table with your pen."

It seemed to her that if she'd learned a craft she would have performed it without so much floundering. She didn't believe that putting words one after another was more difficult than filling the canvas of a tapestry with woolen stitches. She was irritated by her husband who, on evenings when she would have liked to go out, protested that he was in the mood for work, harnessed himself ferociously to a chapter, stopped, no longer so certain, sat in a brown study for hours, rubbing his glowing hands.

One day she said to him, "For the tiny amount of work you've managed to do this evening, you might just as well have taken me out to town."

Her intolerable buzzing and pestering would have done a fly proud, and her husband could neither brush her aside nor complain, for she was never in the wrong. She asked him in an impassive voice if his book was progressing, looked at him doubtfully if he said yes, disconsolately if he said no. The books she read were an opportunity for damning reflections, saying on the evenings when André was struggling over his sheet of paper, "It's really enjoyable, this novel I've just finished reading, it's written with great facility!" And she added some minutes later, "Do we need to turn up the lamp? If you have to stay up late I'll top up the oil."

André swallowed his anger, sometimes replying like a man losing patience. She then adopted a tone of entreaty: "Please, don't speak to me like that. It isn't my fault if you aren't able to do it."

At other times she affectedly sang the praises of the work of major writers whom André adored. "They well deserve all the money they earn. They've got real talent!"

She managed to make her approval of the artists he best loved disagreeable to her husband!

She successfully sharpened the sting of her pricks; moreover, like the majority of women, she viewed her husband as a beast of burden and was indignant that, in spite of her jabbing him with spurs, he didn't work flat out so she could multiply her extravagances. If previously she'd taken her father for a banker, she at least accepted that he doled out to her a sum of money that was adequate to his means; now she would have taken it for granted that her husband should work his fingers to the bone, should slave like a laborer with no aim other than to provide her with the means of increasing her spending.

Her father had gotten off lightly and received the woman's affectionate gratitude as reward for his largesse. Not André. Besides, she would have considered his capitulation to the most exacting of sacrifices as no more than her due; he wouldn't even have been compensated for his efforts by as much as a speck of gratitude.

In her view, he deserved neither encouragement nor pity. He was stupid and clumsy! To think that he wasn't even resourceful enough to enjoy what all writers profit from: securing complimentary tickets to theaters and concerts. In marrying him, she'd promised herself those pleasures that had long been denied her, to occupy a comfortable seat in the balcony without having paid for it! When she plagued him to see a play, he bought tickets with his own money like an ordinary member of the bourgeoisie.

In the end, she no longer wanted to go to the theater under such conditions. The pleasure she derived from it was spoiled by the thought that she could have enjoyed that without opening her purse.

But the time came when she grew weary of remaining constantly at odds; then she fell into state of miserable lethargy, led a numbed existence without hope or any chance of novelty. She lay long and late in bed, lingered at length in an armchair. Her maids grew bold, stole from her as they pleased. André ventured some reproaches that she received with the air of a victim who expects the worst. Then he kept quiet, tried to bury himself in work, watched the disarray of his household gather pace; then, alarmed one day by his wife's air of wretchedness, he decided to cheer her up; he even endured the torture he'd always avoided until then and dragged Berthe to social salons, even got used to it without enduring too much tedium. It was a wasted effort; in spite of everything she got bored in his presence, saw him as a killjoy.

In that disordered life, the gossip of her maids became an enticing distraction, just like when she was a young girl, but she only really felt pleasure in the company of some friends, young married women like herself. Then, during the day, with menfolk absent, they installed themselves near the fireplace and the chitchat bubbled up, intimate secrets danced in their smiles, confidences that were begun ended in a fluttering of fans. Each one complained about her husband, but their eyes all sparkled when, insensibly, the conversation halted before the breathless intimacies of the night. There was a pause, little silences interrupted by whispers behind fingers, invitations to speak out more loudly, prudish and envious exclamations, bursts of tremulous laughter. Berthe kept quiet, wondering just what kind of flesh she was made of, why her nerves could remain so slack, how her transports amounted to nothing.

"The blame lies with Monsieur, your husband," one of them said. "Good God darling!" another chimed in, "If it were me in your situation I'd die." They all tried to extract from her the precise details of the inept lovemaking she'd had to suffer. Berthe defended herself, supplied only vague particulars on which they pounced with alacrity, slashing away at her husband, portraying him as a coarse creature and a fool.

Berthe managed to persuade herself that if she'd married another man, things would certainly have been different; the few doubts that she still entertained suddenly melted away. A dancer at a ball, inviting her to waltz, squeezed her hand ardently and she felt a delicious sensation throughout her whole body, a kind of vertigo that threw her into a swoon, locked tightly between his arms.

The man who moved her in this way was a tall lounge lizard with hair that was sparse on top, slimed to his temples with brilliantine, spread out in a fan on his brow. He was dolled up in the very latest fashion, collar flared like a soup tureen, a fob watch with a double chain, a bulging dickey, trousers with narrow bottoms and wide feet. He rattled off the monstrous idiocies of the salons in an indolent voice. Little by little he pushed his luck, was supported in his schemes by all of Berthe's lady friends.

They disparaged her husband who, fearing their influence, had forbidden his wife to see them; they disparaged him because he didn't mix with their husbands, retailers busy with commerce or the pleasures of baccarat and the races. The wives who themselves didn't yield to temptation urged the undoing of their friend in order to heighten their own self-esteem; they urged her undoing through the cowardice of children who, lacking the courage to behave badly, persuade the stupidest among them that she must do it, even at the cost of rejecting or condemning her after the event.

Berthe rebelled, deciding it undignified to cheat on a husband, even an unloved one. She wrestled with herself while, alone, she let her thoughts go astray, ended up rehearsing the agreed-on arguments, the rationale prepared and served up by whole generations of women, the excuses for every base act, every fault.

The young man became more and more pressing, persistently begged for rendezvous. She was besieged from all sides; he pursued her, his eyes made her blood seethe in her veins, and her friends endlessly extolled this boulevardier, praising his rare qualities, his charms. She gave him two or three rendezvous, didn't keep them, received him at home one day when André was away, surrendered herself in a corner, out of the way; she was left as though shattered. The promised land that she'd glimpsed remained out of reach. The palpitating carnalities of adultery did nothing to uplift her. With the lover, as with the husband, sensual feeling was stillborn, the tempest so eagerly anticipated didn't arrive. She thought she was going mad but still determinedly pursued those passions that failed to come to fruition; she took refuge in this liaison, making herself think about her lover during her idle hours, willing herself to want to love him.

Then she stopped grumbling about her husband, who congratulated himself on seeing her finally mild and obliging, but she put the blame on her family, her luck, the heavens, the tough stuff she was made of, the benumbed nature of her passion, the trivial reality that took the place of her dreams just when she thought herself on the point of realizing them.

Buried in his books, over which he sweated strenuously without ever being satisfied, confident of his wife's virtue, André never doubted her. It took his precipitate return one evening for the disgrace of his menage to be fully exposed to him.

When her husband abruptly showed up that night and surprised a man in shirttails beside his wife, the shock Berthe received was terrible; she remained on her feet, already no longer knowing where she was. When the two men went downstairs together, she collapsed on the floor. She regained consciousness long afterward, lacked the strength to get up, only instinctively comprehended, amidst the lethargy that was crushing her, that everything had crumbled around her, that she was buried forever under the rubble.

In the morning, she hauled herself vacantly onto her bed; the memory of her misfortune hit her; she sobbed desperately, no longer knowing what was to become of her. One single thought floated in that sea of misery; that of not being confronted by her husband.

Rather than suffer the bitterness of his rebukes, stand shamed in his eyes, she would sooner he killed her. She had only one aim, to flee, and, in haste, as though delirious, she got dressed, ran away from that house as from a threat of destruction.

She walked down the street, repeating to herself that after such a catastrophe all that was left was to plead with her accomplice. She stopped suddenly, remembering that he lived with his family, that he couldn't receive female visitors; then she continued on her way, telling herself that in such a fiasco, the proprieties mattered little.

He was still abed when she knocked on the door. She was panting, winded by climbing five flights; he remained dumbstruck before her, then cleared his discarded clothes from the armchair where they were piled.

"What's the matter?" he asked, in a tremulous voice. Then she lost what little composure still remained to her. She clung to his neck and babbled words mingled with tears; "You're all that's left to me now, save me, tell me, you still love me, don't you?"

The young man's expression became more and more worried. He stammered, "You know very well that I love you," and, while buttoning up the collar of his nightshirt, he doled out some scraps of affection, then awkwardly trotted out the predictable stories; she wasn't thinking; she was making herself a fugitive from the law, risked being forcibly returned to her husband's home, dragged before the courts. She and her family would be shamed, her escapade would be retailed in every newspaper along with her and her father's name. He himself would never recover from such a scandal; his parents would throw him out. Oh, they must think hard before taking such a drastic step! And then, what kind of life would they lead! He couldn't leave his own people, had no money of his own, they were letting themselves in for black poverty. Oh! There was no doubt about it, his father would be inflexible and curtail his allowance. He might come in now, see a woman in his son's room, and certainly wouldn't let them leave the room alive.

He held her hand, pathetically explained his situation, repeated the same arguments over and over, sought to see from her face the impression he was making, choosing to emphasize the actions of the law, how their families would be shamed.

She listened white-faced, didn't breathe a word.

"You see," he resumed tearfully, terrified that she might stay with him, afraid that she would finally understand that his only goal in seducing her was to keep a bit of cost-free love on his plate;

"... you see, everything I'm telling you is for your own good; it doesn't matter to me that my own life is ruined, I love you enough for that! But, when all's said and done, things could be a lot worse. Your husband could have reacted much worse than he did; he'll maybe forgive you if that's what you really want. Look, he doesn't seem like the nasty type, you'll get off with a good scolding. As for me, I'm ready to make the sacrifice, I won't see you again, I'll try to forget you if that will make you a happier woman! Ah, it hurts me to talk to you like this, to argue against my own heart, but I owe it you after the harm I've done you without intending to, for love isn't reasonable, I want to stop you from crowning your calamity with a scandal. My God! My God! How sad it all is my poor darling; oh, we aren't lucky! Heaven's my witness that if it were up to me, but I don't know, what can I do, tell me, what?"

He looked so hangdog and disconsolate that she almost felt sorry for him.

There was a discreet knock on the door, then a woman's voice could be heard: "Monsieur Alexis, breakfast is ready. They're waiting for you."

Berthe remained dumb. She gazed at that man putting on his coat and brushing his hair before going downstairs.

Then she reflected that while everything had collapsed around her, while her life was forever blemished, he, her lover, was calmly going to join his family, taking breakfast as usual. The immense catastrophe that had engulfed her hadn't even touched him. And yet he was as guilty she was! That twist of fate made her indignant. For this popinjay she had cheated on a husband who was certainly worth more than him; for this coward who was only concerned with getting rid of her she'd fallen into more mud than she'd ever be able to wash off.

She dried her eyes with her hands, rearranged her skewed hat and, unconsciously, instinctively, retied the hatstrings with trembling hands, tucked her hair behind her ears.

His eyes lit up joyfully. "You're leaving," he said feebly, and he brought her the umbrella that she wasn't looking for. She didn't even hold out her hand. He felt obliged to murmur, "I'll see you again? Where?"

She gave him a level stare, opened the door, went out without even turning to look back.

"Bon voyage," the young man said. "Ah, damn it to hell! But I can't afford to get tangled up with a woman."

Berthe strode down the road. All other thoughts were overridden by the shame of having been rejected like that. Her contempt for that man knew no bounds. Oh! She'd had enough! She would return to her husband; he'd do with her whatever he thought best! She returned, saw that André had taken his trunk, understood that he wasn't going to come back. She collapsed, exhausted, in an armchair; even her misery subsided. She no longer felt her tribulations. In the buzzing that filled her head, she seemed to hear only a furious knell sounding horrible disasters, irremediable grief! A kind of light suddenly penetrated the fog of her ideas; the filth seemed to pile higher around her; she got up, overcome with fear, then she fell back on her seat, her teeth dry, her gaze distracted, a frenzied look on her face.

Worried at not having seen her the previous evening at the soirée, and, in spite of the husband's reassurances, afraid that she was seriously unwell, Madame Désableau arrived just then and shook her, terrified by that broken stiffness, by those shudders, by those groans; she begged her to speak, asked her where André was, rushed through the rooms in search of a phial of Melissa oil,[19] realized from the prevailing disorder, the front door left open, that the house had been battered by a storm of misfortune that had left it upended top to bottom. She returned to her niece, hugged her, understood from the broken phrases that she managed to extract that André had fled, wrapped her in a blanket, and transported her back home in a cab.

There, Berthe calmed down and consented to tell everything. Stunned, Désableau cried out "Wretched woman!" Then his anger went into reverse and lashed out at André. He was a good-for-nothing who must be keeping company with whores; after all he'd only gotten what he deserved. But as Berthe suffered nervous spasms at the slightest allusion to her marriage, crises that threw her hectically against the furniture, her uncle was obliged to hold his tongue; but he swore to himself that he would vent his spleen on the day she was fully recovered.

Little by little, the soothing atmosphere of the family calmed her. She sat back, huddling on a chair, cooling down for hours on end; gradually, she weakened, desired one thing only, that she not be roused from her languor, that like a hurt animal she be allowed lick her wound in the corner where she'd taken refuge.

Several days flowed past in this way. Languid and as though diminished, she had a convalescent's softness, the good nature of a little girl; she now happily accepted the monotony of family evenings, the unvarying conversations ebbing and flowing around her, saying nothing.

One evening when they were all gathered together, seated in the dining room around the table, the mother trimming fabric, the little girl smearing paint on a picture, the father sipping his coffee and playing hands of patience, Berthe daydreaming about a news item, feet in front of the fire, Madame Désableau, who had completed tacking the bodice frame, spoke to her daughter. "Come here Justine so I can try out your dress," and she slipped over her a sleeveless and rough-sewn blouse stitched to a gray lining.

"Stand up straight now." She lifted the child's arm and, taking her time, put darts in the surplus material under the armpits. Then, taking her by both shoulders, she spun the girl round like a teetotum, giving her little taps on the fingers with her thimble to make her remain in place. She wasn't satisfied with the collar; she joined the two flaps of the lining, fixed them with a pin, with the flat of her hand tucked in the material that dropped straight down, forcing it to follow the contours of the bust as far as the swell of the hips and, busily, she yet again roughly adjusted her pattern, considered the spots destined for the buttonholes.

"There, that'll do," she said, cautiously removed her assemblage and spread it out again on the table, took out the pins she'd fastened as guidelines and silently started to put her alterations into effect.

Nine o' clock struck.

Monsieur Désableau spoke in turn; "Justine, darling, it's time for bed."

The child protested but her parents were inflexible. Madame Désableau lit a candle, took the palette, the glass of dirty water, and carried them to her bedroom. To delay her bedtime Justine gave her father and Berthe long hugs, asked them questions, took her time in looking for a ribbon mislaid beneath the table. Her mother grabbed her and pushing her forward regardless of the stamping of her feet, closed the door behind her.

Then Désableau raised his head slightly, adjusted his pince-nez and, riffling the pack of cards between his fingers, turned to his niece: "Now that Justine had gone to bed, let's talk. I received a letter from Maître Saparois inviting me to attend his office. I'll sum up our conversation for you.

"Your husband who, in this instance, seems to have every right on his side, will be happy to avoid the scandal of court hearings and notices in the press. Also, he won't formulate a demand for a formal separation;[20] he simply proposes an amicable arrangement. You'll each of you live apart, he'll provide no alimony, but he'll return your dowry in its entirety.

"Those are the proposals that Maître Saparois has put to me in his name. I told this solicitor flat out what the situation was and what I thought of the conduct of your husband. It seemed incredible to me, I added, after mature reflection, that Monsieur André Jayant might be in a position to return the whole of the dowry with which we endowed him. I didn't hide from Maître Saparois that I'd always had a poor opinion of the projected union between your husband and you. At the same time, I drew his attention to the scandalous ideas that André had advocated in his books, and that I'd been bound to conclude that he must have squandered in orgies the money that an honorable family had agreed to provide him with."

Monsieur Désableau took a deep breath and paused for a moment. He recited a screed he'd rehearsed for three whole days in his office. He carried on in an even more emphatic tone of voice. "While agreeing with me that such literature was odious, and after he too, as any honest man would, had deplored the excesses of those villains who have no scruples about insulting all that's respectable with their scribbles, Maitre Saparois, however, didn't acknowledge the justice of my conclusions. He claimed that because André took pleasure, artistically speaking, in wallowing in unspeakable filth, it didn't necessarily follow that he'd gobbled up your dowry.

"After all," Désableau resumed, seemingly more thoughtful, "perhaps the solicitor was in the right. It could be that your husband hasn't frittered away the money, no doubt he's a man who lacks the audacity for vice! It's a fact that there are scoundrels who through the sheer intensity of their wrongdoing achieve a kind of grandeur. Of course, from the point of view of your financial interests I'm pleased that your husband doesn't belong in that company; but, my girl, let's admit that the vices to which André lays claim are so banal that he leaves you full of disgust."

Berthe defended her husband vehemently: "You shouldn't accuse people like that," she said. "My husband is neither dishonest nor a scoundrel, and what's more, as you well know, I'm the one who's to blame for this wretched separation."

"No, not at all," Désableau cried. "While admitting that you're to blame, the fact is that you aren't. A wife becomes what her husband wants her to become. Look at my wife, your aunt; ah! I can swear that never, never once has there been the slightest divergence of ideas between us, not the slightest cloud! And more than that, under my guidance she's contributed to the prudent well-being of a hearth and home that everyone rightly holds in high regard. No, I say again that if you'd married a respectable man instead of a dubious artistic character, you'd be a happy woman, like my wife."

Berthe lost her temper. All of a sudden she shook off the apathy in which had smothered her since her fall. "I forbid you to speak like that about my husband in front of me!"

Désableau choked, thrown off balance. His pince-nez leaped into the air. "That's enough," he stammered. "I accepted the solicitor's proposals, but I reserve the right to express my opinion of André, and I'm expressing it!"

Happily, Madame Désableau came to put an end to the turmoil. She ordered Berthe to her bedroom.

"We can talk about all that again when our heads are cool," she said, and added, "this is stupid, you're shouting so loud that little Justine can hear everything in the other room."

Then her husband lowered his voice. "You're right, my angel," he murmured. "We must protect our little girl's childhood from these revelations, they're humiliating and dangerous. All the same, though, I told your niece, told her good and proper, that her marriage was a foolish one, that she was marrying a man with the eye of a mountebank. She didn't want to listen to me—she's well on her way now. But enough, let's drop it. These kinds of upsets just put my head in a whirl!"

He took his watch out, satisfied himself that there was time to play two or three hands of patience before bedtime, sat down again, shuffled the cards, held them out to his wife so she could bring him luck by cutting the pack, and laid out equidistant rows of cards.

Worried by her husband's red-mottled face, Madame Désableau silently prepared a glass of water sweetened with orange blossom and placed it on a plate, on the table, before him.

Désableau smiled sweetly. "You're the best of wives," he said.

And they felt a mutual tenderness, thinking that in this deluge of sordid baseness they were sheltered in their little household as though on the ark. Their niece's misfortune had cheered them up without their being aware of it. The placid life they had enjoyed for so many years, and which had been made to seem the natural state of affairs by force of habit, suddenly looked to them like a special favor. They went through to their bedroom almost cheerfully to surrender themselves to sleep, that symbol of death as Monsieur Désableau called it, and, after having wound up his watch, the husband divested himself of his suit and his waistcoat and revealed a back that was quartered into a St. Andrew's cross by two pink suspenders.

Then he removed his trousers and socks, slipped between the sheets and there, looking at his wife, who had removed her false chignon and tied her hair into a topknot, he pointed at the bunk where his daughter was sleeping, moved into their own room since Berthe's return.

"Let's hope that one day our Justine will marry an employee, a worthwhile man and not, like our poor niece, an acrobat and artist."

Madame Désableau's mouth was full of the grips that secured her mop of hair. She confined herself to raising her eyes to the heavens as though she too was imploring this favor, climbed into bed in her turn and turned down the lamp, but the charcoaled wick broke on the rim of the nozzle and sputtered, spurting oil against the glass, spreading an acrid stench. Madame Désableau hastened out of bed, carried the lamp into the other room, blew it out, promptly returned to press herself, shivering, against her husband.

Then everything returned to normal. The jeremiads against shopworn wicks, the threatening diatribes against art came to an end. The movements of the two lumps beneath the blankets stilled, the pillow corners bent. Nothing more was heard save the regular tick-tock of the clock, the imperceptible gallop of a watch, then the soft "put, put" of a snore rose up, light as a breeze, its sustained note trembled for some time in the silence of the room, gradually weakened, and expired in an elusive sigh on the lips of the couple.

V

André took a childlike delight in his new place of residence. After a frenzied chase round the four corners of Paris to purchase the utensils he needed, after the agonies of moving in, managed as usual by half-drunk workmen, the difficulties in arranging the furniture without compromising access to the windows and doors, the battles fought with brick walls that resisted and bent nails, the tiresome searches on all fours among the piles of volumes unloaded en bloc on the parquet floor, André, with Cyprien's help, had at last succeeded in organizing his apartment. With all his good spirits revived he strolled the streets for entire days, rubbed the cracks in his ceramics with bleach to clean them, used the leaves left at the bottom of his teapot to refresh the colors of his rugs, dreamed of improvements in comfort, new acquisitions of books and bric-a-brac.

A week passed; everything was ranged in definitive order, papers stacked on the table ready for work. He had resumed his little daily routine with Mélanie.

He found her much as he had left her, thin, not much to look at, hooked nose, round eyes, a hairy patch on her upper lip, a ruddy complexion under blonde hair, tanned by open air and face cream. She wore the same frilled caps, the same peach and gooseberry ribbons, the same sleeveless bodices decorated with braiding, the same brooch whose glass enclosed a photograph of her husband in his police uniform, his hair combed in pigeon wings, mustache waxed, eyes fixed and smug.

She was neither older nor fatter, still with the same Auvergnat obstinacy, quasi-honesty in cheating, delight in cooking and mending other people's socks.

Just like before, she was incapable of laying a fire, put two little logs at the back and a gigantic log on top, heaped up the ashes under the andirons so that they hindered the draught, or else she emptied it all out and so gave the hearth the sorry look of a new fireplace! She went on usurping his newspapers to cover the table and the office sideboard, cut his writing paper with pinking shears to make a valance for the kitchen mantelpiece, broke the cup handles, stuck them together after a fashion, so that her employer, in picking them up, might think he'd broken them himself, broke the pencils that she'd pinched under the pretext of writing a list of expenses, persisted in compulsively putting matchboxes in the ash-trays, waxing the polished tip of his ballroom pumps.

Just like before, she poured boiling water over glasses and knives to wash them and was stupefied when the former cracked and the latter lost their cutting edge; she regularly forgot to remove bundles of laurel and thyme from her sauces, left her feather duster on the furniture when sweeping the front room, forced her employer to daily clear away the pile of newspapers and books that she collected from the rooms and heaped up on the desk just where he wanted to write.

These rediscovered faults didn't displease André. He expected to find them the same as ever, greeted them as old acquaintances, was surprised, nevertheless, to find them no better or worse than before. He was satisfied that his maid's stupidity had remained unchanged. Then those failings he'd forgotten about reasserted themselves, one by one as the occasion arose. He had to repeat, for the thousandth time and without the slightest chance of success, the same comments he'd made before his marriage. He begged her not to fill the chamber pot with soapy water, not to leave the waste basin unplugged,[21] not to wipe the inside of his tea pot, finally not to add to the freshly ground coffee the old grounds that she persistently retained in the filter. In the same way, he insisted on having large loaves and not the high-fiber bread or the baguettes she preferred, protested the objectionable use of mushrooms in sauces, her obsession with sugaring the spinach and cooking the meat until it shredded into long, soft strands under the knife.

All things considered, he had no cause for complaint. Along with her clumsiness and blunders, Mélanie brought qualities unknown to latter-day housemaids; a marvelous cleanliness, a rare care for the household, a certain affection for the interiors that she swept. She refurbished, scoured, polished from morning till night, mended clothes, provided shirts with new collars and cuffs, managed the house in such a way that he neither had to worry about the laundry nor all the headaches and trifling annoyances that plague even the most incorrigible and resolute bachelors.

For the moment, André sank comfortably into his happiness, got up late, lingered in shirtsleeves, smoked cigarettes until his housemaid arrived, bringing the newspapers and brushing down his outfits; then he went out for a walk, came back for breakfast, filed his notes while waiting to resume work on his book, halted since the overthrow of his domestic arrangements.

He was at first disturbed and somewhat affronted by the new arrangement of his furniture, finding it particularly constricted in this little cubbyhole by comparison with the vast room he'd previously possessed, but as the memory of his conjugal living room faded, he gradually came to feel that the room was bright and cheerful.

Soon it seemed to him to be already imbued with that indefinable charm acquired by dwellings one inhabits for days on end and not merely used as a place to sleep, dwellings where, in the evening, following the silence of working hours, the laughter of friends meets and mingles, enlivening the contemplative air of the walls.

Finally, he came to view as sufficiently spacious and convenient that tiny room so stuffed with knickknacks and so crowded with furniture that it could scarcely accommodate more than three people at a time.

From floor to ceiling, the walls disappeared under a jumble of china, pictures, brasses, Japanese porcelain, in the middle of which two impressionist watercolors sparkled in their gold frames on the bister background of the wallpaper: an image of stage wings with dancers in pink gauze relaxing before props daubed with shrubbery, exquisite little minxes teasing big ninnies stiff in their ball gowns; an image of a salon with bored and affable gentlemen, exciting and frivolous women tightly laced into pale silk armor, arms and shoulders bare, the corsage wide open, propping up with their concealed stays the white mounds of their breasts.[22]

Then, with the little available space shrunk still further by their ledges and edges, a table, chairs, an old oak stand, and a divan upholstered in gray-brown fabric embroidered with amaranth flowers made their entry, flanked on the right by a large bookcase where an army of bradel bindings[23] in canary yellow and oxblood lined up in battle formation and blazed away, their firework suns overshadowing all the quieter items, the sad and discreet La Vallière,[24] the stern Jansenists renouncing gilt lace or frills, the ordinary, easygoing, and somewhat rascally jackets, stiff in their blue or gray cloth boards, the shagreen bindings looking bourgeois and priggish; on the left, another bookcase, a smaller one full of sewn softcover volumes, and there, again, two large swathes stood out, two rows of volumes marching tumultuously, beating the drum, wearing the yellow uniforms of the publisher Charpentier,[25] the red tunics of Hachette's foreign legion.

André frequently rearranged his books and pictures. After trials and test runs, he'd finally organized the whole collection with the shapes and colors complementing each other so that the flaming punch lit up the beveled mirrors, so that the lights falling on the gold lines of the frames and in the iridescent hollows of the plates helped brighten a room that remained somber when the grave and dark tone of the walls showed between the trinkets and the furniture.

A number of weeks went by. The tranquility of that new mode of life put a spring in Andre's step. His convalescence reached full term; after the debility that followed the crisis, he was en route to complete recovery, thought less often about his wife, simply retaining a slow and sad memory of her. At times he seemed to have always been a bachelor; the past looked distant and confused, like those vague memories left behind, even after recovery, by the hallucinations glimpsed in the course of a fever. He believed that the wished-for deliverance had been achieved; he no longer doubted this cherished dream; canceling two years of his life was finally possible.

He succumbed to the all-embracing cosseting of his housemaid. Mélanie, an excellent cook, sought to reassert her influence in the house, prepared mouthwatering meals for him; astonishingly tasty fried dishes, authoritative remoulade dressings, exuberant shallot sauces, even several fine traditional dishes such as braised veal, stew browned with mustard, rabbit and apples sautéed in incomparable wine sauces.

Then there was Cyprien who often came to take potluck in dining; and there were delightful meals where, elbows on table, they discussed art, sipping drams, waving away the cigarette smoke that wafted up in whorls under the lamplight.

On these occasions Mélanie was in superb form; caught unawares, she served up an adequate and acceptable meal in a matter of minutes, supplemented insufficient dishes with marvelous cheese omelets, was ready for anything, fetched coffee, then, basket on her arm, rolling the strings of her apron between her fingers, recited her regular evening formula: "Does Monsieur need anything else?" "No, Mélanie." "Then good night, Monsieur." And she left to rustle up the policeman's meal in turn.

The distraction of lengthy discussions, the laughter of a friend chattering uninhibitedly, indulging in the racy language generally in use among artists and men of letters, the medley of slang and jargon that provide a lively seasoning, the give and take of questions and retorts, infused André with a fresh zeal; after the chilling boredom, the drenching cloudbursts of married life, a spell of sunshine seemed ready to break through. The return of his old brother in arms refreshed him, he was hungry for work and, excited by all these discussions around the table that made the pulse quicken, he wanted to demonstrate that he wasn't burned out, that his talent had escaped unscathed from the skirmish.

But, in the early days, his good intentions, his upswings, came to nothing. As obsessive as the majority of artists, he could only work in an environment that was thoroughly well known to him.

So that his eye wouldn't wander off in spite of himself to the decorations hung on the wall, he needed to be well acquainted with the angle and colors of these objects in order not to become aware of them at any given moment. His obsession was overwhelming. He couldn't even work on a table unless it was in its customary position. So he devoted long hours to examining, one after another, his curios, his books; then he surveyed the ensemble until his eyes were so glutted that they lost their appetite for distraction. That was an affair of at least two weeks. That time had already long since elapsed, and yet however much he tried to get into harness, his efforts failed. He would seat himself in front of his desk, visualize the scene he wanted to describe, seize his pen and remain there, listless, like those people who, after having waited a long time for supper, can only swallow a mouthful when finally seated at table.

He ripped up his paper in a fit of anger. He would, at a pinch, have considered himself an imbecile. He feared that his wits had suddenly deserted him. He mourned, thinking that he would perhaps remain stricken with impotence, then he bounced back, remembered, so as to shore up his courage, the several fine pages he had formerly written, followed the advice of Cyprien, who urged him not to overtax himself, to leave the mechanism in peace to resettle itself. He busied himself with revision, improved ungainly terms, filled in gaps, pruned the foliage of his prose, waited like the engineer who takes his beast out on the rails to start it up, ensure that it's sufficiently warmed up to set out. And it was a matter of long internal debates, battles fought with Cyprien who, seeing him indecisive, his ideas less firm and comprehensive, tried to convert him to his own theories, corrupt and morbid theories that André usually rejected while at the same time acknowledging the interest and justness of some of them.

Cyprien renewed the attack and, misled by his friend's silence, thinking him irresolute, reiterated his arguments one after another, explained at great length the novelty of his insights, quoted examples to validate them.

The accent of a landscape derived, in his view, from the factory chimneys that rose above the trees and spat flakes of soot to the clouds.

He laid claim to a euphoric delight when, sitting on the ridge of embankments, peering into the distance, he saw gasometers lift up their contemporary and sky-filled carcasses like circuses built with blue walls and supported by black columns. Then the site disquietingly came to signify suffering and distress for him.

In that countryside whose scarred epidermis is as though pockmarked with hideous scabs, in those flayed roads where trails of plaster resemble the flour shed by a diseased skin, he saw a plaintive rapport with the sufferings of the wretched man coming back home from his factory, exhausted, ground down, sweating, stumbling over the rubble, losing his footing in the ruts, choking on coughing fits, bent under the pelting rain, under the wind's scourge, puffing resignedly on his clay pipe.

He saw nature's leper house in the banlieues that stretch out around impoverished Paris, the Saint-Louis hospital,[26] landscapes and sites and melancholic delights came to him, a charitable sympathy for that sickly nature which, with its deadly exhalations, hastened the incurable diseases engendered by alcohol and famine.

"Ah!" he cried on the evening of an expansive argument, one of those evenings when, under the stimulus of a few drops of liquor, his conversation flowed freely. "Ah, Pantin! Aubervilliers, Charonne, those are the charming districts, the consumptive ones! And, by God, you needn't look at me like that! I already know what you're going to say; that it's not just those districts! But I like the others too. Not so much, it's true, but I love them just the same. Yes, I love the big boulevards with their noisy crowds, their packed cafés, the hubbub of their dandies and stock jobbers, and above all I adore the nighttime, at about two in the morning, when the street girls are so miserably on the hunt. Well then, with my reputation for being very exclusive in my opinions, I hope you won't mind my saying so, but I think that I'm a lot more eclectic and broad-minded than you because, when all's said and done, for me the street, however it might be, rich or poor, opulent or miserly, is always beautiful! I feel a tremendous delight, in the evening for example, when the gold letters on the fascias or the glass doors of shops sparkle in the gaslight. I read them, I learn the name of the shopkeeper, I see that he's the son-in-law or the successor of so-and-so, and through the window panes I look at the whole family seated around a table in the back of the room: the mama dozing, snoring, hands on her belly, the father, the daughter, the son-in-law, and successor playing *trente-et-un* and chattering with their eyes glued to their cards. That makes me want to go in, to offer enormous discounts on the price of their wares, and so give an unexpected bit of real meat to the rot that these fine folk will talk until closing time.

"Yes, my old friend, there you have it. And these delicious joys of the street, I enjoy them in the morning too when I go for a stroll along the sidewalks. Then I study the little ladies who've been awake all night and who dart along, giving their skirts a bit of a shake, lowering bruised eyes, scampering along the asphalt with their scuffed little boots. There's something languid and pale about them that reveals the hard-working insomnia of their night, a certain something about their linen which is still clean but a little rumpled, about their slow pace, their way of wearing their veils and lifting their dress that speaks to their putting on their clothes in a hurry, the difficulties of a toilette that couldn't be done at home.

"Some of them are delightfully embarrassed and a little nettled by my fatherly smile. Those ones make off more quickly, and in gazing after them, I indulge in private satisfactions, I sense erotic or monetary disappointments behind the mutinously graceful way they walk, the disorder of pillows in warm bedrooms and the secret satisfaction of the Monsieur who, after the long kiss customary in such cases, sees the woman finally heading out of the door.

"Seen in this light, the street is always splendid, always new. However jaded it might be, it's brimful of countless delights understood by very few, for the Holy Scriptures are right; the world is full of eyes but cannot see, and alas we all belong more or less among them. So there's nothing else to say, my friend, we're soaked and saturated in a whole basinful of platitudes and truisms! The picturesque is what we need, striking architecture, bizarre streets with moonlight, mountains and forests, we need subjects that lend themselves to description! Ah! They really drive me up the wall, all those people who go into ecstasies over the apse of Notre Dame and the rood screen of Saint-Étienne-du-Mont! That's all very well, and as for the Gare du Nord and the new Hippodrome, they don't exist. Ah, for sure they're nothing but a heap of old buffoons who foist their enthusiasms on you to order when they prattle on about ancient basilicas or castles of dressed stone that they call marvels of Greek art! They're full of it! Eh, they can go to hell with their Parthenon. If they love that kind of building let them plant themselves in the middle of the Place de la Concorde, then they'll have two Parthenons, one in front and one behind; let them strike camp in front of the Bourse,[27] they'll see yet another one, cheerier though, because a clock has been very sensibly placed on its facade and chimney stacks stuck on its roof. At least that interrupts the harmony of its big, stupid lines.

"And just think, that's going to carry on like that for years yet, just think, whole generations of artists are going to buy their scaled-down copies of the Venus de Medici, a prude who has a pin head on the torso of a fairground wrestler! A good thing that that fatso can take advantage of arms to hide her belly! The Venus that I admire, the Venus that I'd kneel down to worship as the archetype of modern beauty is the girl who larks about in the street, the worker girl in her coat and dress, the milliner with a drab complexion, rascally eyes with pearl glints in them, the dressmaker's girl with a pale little face, an impish nose, whose breasts jiggle on hips that sway!

"Oh, the chlorosis of the little worker girls and the warpaint of the tarts on the prowl! That makes my pulse race and I dream about them! When you think that in all Paris there are maybe no more than three of us painters who think like that! And that's the way the world is, and the Messiah hasn't arrived! Ah, if only we all, such as we are, weren't afflicted with the gangrene of romanticism. If instead of curing our infection we merely stopped at whitening it, if an iodide was invented that could purify the brains of artists, we'd for sure see lots of other beauties of modernity that pass unnoticed."

And Cyprien swallowed tumblers of water, walked up and down, continuing to voice his laments, lectured the four corners of the room on his hopes.

André let him have his say. The painter's exasperated tirades interested him. They reminded him of the time when they would argue for whole days. Right now, Cyprien was a voice crying in the wilderness. André contradicted him as little as possible, having long since understood that his friend was one of those people who, once possessed by a subject, don't even listen to contrary points of view, and, regardless of rebuttals or replies, continue to resolutely outline their doctrines and systems.

André, though, didn't accept all his friend's ideas. Starting from a shared point of view, both smitten with naturalism and modernity, they'd linked arms so much that they shared a similar outlook, a melancholy vision of life, innate with Cyprien, less instinctive and more synthetic with André, colored by friendship with the painter, and gradually increased by difficulties and setbacks, and yet they didn't see things in the same light. At the first fork on the road they traveled together they each went their own way. They were temperamentally different.

Big and blond, thin and pale, with long, slender, and tapering fingers, Cyprien had a pale beard, restless hands, a sharp gray eye, a head bristling with white hairs.[28] He was knock-kneed, wore out the bottom of his trousers, usually too short and also too wide for his spindly leg bones. With his slight stoop and his lopsided left shoulder, he looked unhealthy and poorly. His manner of roaming the streets was odd to say the least. He progressed by fits and starts, stamped his feet on the spot, suddenly shot forward like a big grasshopper, made off at top speed, holding his umbrella under his arm like a schoolmaster, rubbing his hands together for no reason.

Cyprien was indeed the man of his painting, an anemic rebel with thin blood, a victim of his nerves which were always on edge, an inquisitive and sickly spirit, with the dull, obsessive melancholy of neurotics, spurred on by his feverish nature, with little self-awareness in spite of his theories, led on by his maladies.

Ill-balanced, tilting to the left and right, he was incapable of producing a major work, but from time to time he possessed an intensity, a boldness in creating distinctive paintings, an often successful exploration of daring effects, above all a scornful and cruel treatment of the whore, showing her as she is, with her disgracefully derelict underwear and her opulently corrupt outerwear.

Andre, not so lethargic or nervous, less of a rebel and less bitter, was also in the vanguard, but though less excitable and less given to preaching, he was more thoughtful. He was a well-built lad, neither fat nor thin, with a touch of yellow in his complexion as though bilious, with a short and bushy brow, his little black moustache tousled like a cat's, a dimpled, blue-shaven chin, broad and hairy fingers, mild eyes with long lashes, pale lips and bad teeth. His clothing was conventionally bourgeois, worn without either carelessness or ostentation, and he was a member of that race of people whose suits never get muddied and always seem new even when threadbare. Under the guise of a man of decision he concealed the timidity of a young girl, a terrible fear of what people might think, and of being ridiculed. He hesitated before the simplest of life's circumstances, he dithered before choosing a side, saw difficulties in every direction, sometimes resolved them with the courage of a coward, and felt regret, two minutes after his show of firmness.

He knew enough of life to reveal to you the inner workings of his neighbor's virtues and vices. He explained clearly the character of other men's wives, spelled out the measures to take in order to avoid their treacheries and deceptions, but little by little lost his analytical lucidity where his own domestic menage was concerned, or else, when clear-sightedness prevailed, he parried the blow that threatened him, then, tired, exposed himself and let his adversary, whom he'd first annoyed by resisting him, strike him all the harder.

And this common sense and finesse that were so quickly dulled, so quickly betrayed, trailed after him in his books. There, as in his life, he was both stubborn and feeble beyond measure. Stubborn in advancing an idea that he'd decided to communicate, feeble before the difficulties that arose when he had to flesh it out and present it. He persisted in his purpose but didn't even try to overcome the obstacle, limited himself to keeping a weather eye on it, waiting for an auspicious moment, an opportunity. In essence, he blockaded a work so as not to mount an assault, and once camped in front of it, he relaxed and subsided into inaction. Although he avoided starting on a chapter other than the one he was struggling with, he wasn't able to take action against his characteristic failing, against his ennui. Once begun, the thing tired him. He reread the chapter in progress, then walked about, seeking the continuation, ended up leafing through a book while buried in an armchair some distance from his desk, giving no more thought to his work, absorbed in the work of others.

He lacked Cyprien's ferocious instinct for attack, his unexpected frontal thrust, but on the other hand, were it not for his inconsistent working method, his apathetic approach to life, his puny mode of attack, the oeuvre he created might be less brilliant, less fitful, less haphazardly accomplished, but was more discerningly conceived and solidly achieved.

With the requirements of his impressionable temperament, with his need for tranquility and well-being, his disdain for things taken for granted, his lack of resilience when facing opposition, his fickle and unsteady character, he had, unavoidably, ended up in his books with one or two slowly quarried and laboriously constructed novels, and, in his life, with the wished-for placidity of marriage, with an easygoing love in a bourgeois sphere.

After having wandered the streets, Cyprien, with his anemia and his unhealthy dawdling, had to work in a whirlwind on his days of effervescence; after having dreamed at length, he had, in life, to necessarily seek the satisfaction of his carnal ferments in casual beddings. With both men badly singed by women, André no longer dwelt on them save with a certain sad mildness while Cyprien saw them in a fervent and disquieting light. That difference of character marked their works. United by a shared hatred of the dominant prejudices of the bourgeoisie, they spurred each other on, scorning public opinion, defying it, accepting lack of success, set apart from the world of arts and letters, regularly pilloried by all the journals, by all their confreres who faulted them for their isolation and disdain. Their childhood friendship was reaffirmed by the struggle they withstood; they'd always lived together and, aside from a few squabbles resulting from female tittle-tattle that had understandably set them at odds, no fight, no quarrel had ever come between them.

It had taken André's marriage to suddenly shatter the intimacy of their relationship; disunited, they missed each other. The episode of the supper left Berthe's spitefulness in no doubt. Soon, André only saw his friend in the Désableau house, where he was invited in the hope that he would restore a family portrait for free. Thus were Cyprien's prophecies fulfilled; a stupid and peevish woman, friends shown the door, and, at last, like the final rocket burst, the crowning point of these annoyances, cuckolded by an insipid lounge lizard.

Moreover, it was a pleasure for André to find himself once again close to the painter, for the latter's feverishness inspired others with the urge to work. He now prodded André, sword in the back, no longer accepting the excuse of disrupted routines and freshly acquired lodgings. He hounded him so that André reattached himself to his book.

The wheels of the machine seemed to have been repaired, but it ran slowly. He brooded for whole days over a page, but on the whole he was well satisfied. The warming up stage of his work was over, he was no longer worried, had no doubt that he could get the job done soon enough, just like in the good times, and delightful days were spent working and wandering the streets, pegging away with little strokes, rubbing his hands together exuberantly, sunning himself on his balcony, smoking cigarettes, staring in curiosity through the windows of the Ministry situated opposite his window at the interiors of offices, the rows of green boxes with copper handles, black wooden tables, filing cabinets, rush-seated chairs, baskets, bowls and carafes, cabriolet armchairs[29] full of files, enormous piles of dossiers. Opposite him two employees were shut in the same room, one whose puffy profile could be seen, the other one bending a back whose spine jutted out. Then a white patch glimpsed at the back of the office, behind the windowpanes, disappeared, opening one day on another room and people came in, papers in hand, chatting to each other, sat on the corners of the tables then, on leaving, they moved the white patch out of the way and put it back in place.

All this carry-on interested André. He started to know the routines of his two neighbors. One of them, a man of about fifty, with a shabby and benign look, arrived early, changed out of his suit and boots, took his time in settling in, arranged his pens and pencils neatly, read the *Petit Journal* through to the classified ads, ate a two-penny croissant at 3:00 p.m., dealt with a good deal of yellow paper. He no doubt lived far away, for example Vaugirard or Vanves, was married but uncomfortable at home. He snuck out furtively during the day, came back from time to time with a little packet that seemed to contain children's shoes, and he received letters in his office.

The other man, younger, arrived late, a shagreen satchel under his arm, morose and out of humor, barricaded himself behind high piles of paperwork, hid the papers on which he scribbled as soon as the door was opened, and made an early escape. This one must be doing outside work, and no doubt a bachelor, judging by how hastily he made off, by the toothpicks from cheap chophouses that he chewed on while writing.[30]

Above and below him, from the top to the bottom of the Ministry, through the high windows of the first floor, through the lower lattice windows of the other floors, through the constricted dormer windows on the roof, André saw men of a similar type, smoking, writing, reading newspapers, swerving and turning, paired together in similar rooms.

Then he got tired of contemplating the boredom of these hapless individuals and, leaning on the balustrade of his balcony, he swooped further down, his glance taking in the entire street which, with its roundabout, as sad as the small plaza of a low-grade subprefecture, had the look of a distant town; here and there, near a depot where a lame old man kept an eye on carriages, hotel cooks yawned in their white chefs' aprons, swapping small talk with coachmen dishing out oats, with kitchen boys lurking behind mesh-covered windows, with the commissionaire prominently positioned at the doorway of the wine merchant.

Mournful in the morning and deserted in the evening, rue Cambacérès only started to come alive toward 11:00 a.m. Then hordes of office workers poured out from the bar, going to the Ministry, carrying mazagrans and small carafes of cognac, plates of eggs, sealed bottles, covered or steaming dishes, and there they assembled in groups, laughing, hands full, with a policeman on duty near a coalman's barrel, with workers in blue overalls, with the roadman whose job was to sprinkle the street with water.

Then visitors, at first infrequent, now flocked in droves. Cabs rushed in from all points of the compass and, stopping in front of the entry decorated with a tricolor flag, near an official's unoccupied gatehouse, emptied onto the sidewalk busy people with newspapers, books, papers under their arms, who vanished under the vault of the carriage entrance, reappeared long afterward, consulted their watches, most of them seeming annoyed.

Others, like scene shifters and bit-part players who know where the backstairs are in the wings or the stage, disappeared through a neighboring door, through the little door of no. 9, similar to the artiste's entry to this theater, and old ladies with hair in ringlets under their bonnet strings, like typecast actresses,[31] coming there to beg for pensions, or for support, arranged their contrite looks and prepared to shed tears on making their entry.

But it was particularly toward 3:00 p.m. that the bustle in the street increased. A procession of important persons marched through, Deputies, Senators, Prefects, and other gentlemen decorated with red cockades emerged from the offices, shook hands respectfully, and went away, stopped in their turn by people who spoke to them deferentially, hat in hand.

In the silent street, in spite of its uninterrupted shuttling of crowds, in that road where the subdued rolling of cab wheels on the asphalt could be heard, a man walked by on certain days of the week, wearing a black leather bowler hat adorned with white-painted scissors, a little box strapped on his shoulder, chanting lugubriously, "Animal-barber here, dogs shaved, cats neutered, and whatever you got!" At other times, a cry of "Ho, glazier" arose and sustained its shrill note, or else a knife grinder rolled his little grinding wheel in front of him, ringing a little bell with each step, accompanied, from a distance, by the sour solo that a fountain seller played on a horn.

At about 4:00 p.m. on Tuesdays a new noise drowned out the others. Private vehicles containing a flotilla of light, bright dresses stopped in front of a little one-story hotel contiguous with the building where André lived, and the vivacious peal of a doorbell rang out, announcing the visitors, followed by the heavy slam of the door closing again.

André started to classify the various noises that rose up from under his balcony. The particular life of rue Cambacérès became less and less confusing to him, little by little he saw emanating from these buildings that were discolored or distempered with yellowed ocher the melancholia of places left empty for months, blinds and doors closed, the banal opulence of a family boarding house, the sadness of a ground floor unenlivened by any trade or business.

Some kind of ennui prevailed, the ennui of a place one passed through without stopping, the ennui of people visiting this district solely out of obligation and necessity, not dwelling there, and in spite of the fugitive and artificial life that the offices of the Ministry breathed into the street, it had the gloomy tone of a dead province.

All things considered, André congratulated himself on residing in such a reticent and tranquil neighborhood, but Mélanie, unconcerned with the particular atmosphere of these streets, merely considered this corner of Paris to be dishonest. Life here was twice as expensive as elsewhere, she said, and you had to walk for hours before finding a grocer or fruiterer. She bombarded her employer with complaints, declared that she didn't want to go to the market because all the peasant women were hagglers and cheats; from now on, she concluded, she would buy her provisions in the morning when crossing the Gros-Caillou; according to her, the avenues behind the Invalides were a land of plenty where the traders sold at a loss. André merely replied that she was perfectly free to heft a full basket for miles if that was what she wanted; he had little faith in the savings she claimed to make through this method as every second day she continued to produce an interminable list of expenses.

Free to shop however she wished, Mélanie kept her word, and so earned the reputation of a tough customer in the Anjou-Saint-Honoré district. The shallow flatteries initially trotted out by the greedy retailers were succeeded by active hostility, then muffled quarrels broke out, and, spilling onto the sidewalk, flooded the porter's lodge like a stream of greasy water. Furious at not being entrusted with André's housework, excited by the angry resentments of the shops that his wife patronized, the concierge brandished a regulation that forbade the fetching of water and wood and the shaking out of carpets after ten in the morning. There was daily conflict between the lodge and the kitchen, relentless warfare over a drop of water, a twig from a fagot dropped on the stairs.

André was worried, afraid that these clashes might affect him. He ordered Mélanie to keep her temper, greased the palm of the porter with handouts and small tasks in order to arrive at a kind of truce. To compensate his housemaid for having to put her aggravations on hold he went as far as listening to the tall stories that she thought it worth her while to tell him. Office boys and even employees from the Ministry leered at her as soon as she appeared on the balcony. She pretended to be angry about this but actually wasn't, being in fact flattered by these attentions, about which she told André in unnecessary detail, saying she resented them.

André shrugged his shoulder; Mélanie's virtue was of little interest to him; what he wanted above all was that she not bring the nosiness of the street down on her head.

He had paid a price for his knowledge of what to expect from the prattling race of shopkeepers! The gossip and slander reported by Cyprien on the day when he'd come to oversee his friend's house removal had surpassed all known floods of nonsense.

From the coal merchant to the fruiterer, from the fruiterer to the baker, from the baker to the pharmacist, it had been a hailstorm of abuse and insults. All these people's opinions coincided with that of M. Désableau. André kept a seamstress, everyone had seen her, they even described her, a tired blonde with a toothless mouth. All the household money was gobbled up by her upkeep; he let his wife languish in a corner, a poor little woman who looked so sweet and decent. "Me, I'd have sent her packing instead of his respectable wife," one woman said. "Ah! you'd no more have sent her packing than anyone else," retorted a neighbor who got knocked about by her husband, and the woman who kept shop, while taking advantage of their quarrel to give them short weight, restored harmony by asserting that all men were cut from the same lousy cloth! And every day it was a case of absurd new revelations, remote connections were made between André's departure and newspaper reports of abandonment, there were opinions asserted by inveterate gossipmongers, allusions to other menages in the street, tired old smears on both the one and the other were suddenly resuscitated. "The mistress of that lad there is a circus horse rider," the baker declared summarily, knowing that André was a writer, and, as a proof of his declaration, he cited nebulous chatter and arguments that proved nothing. Where they all agreed was in claiming that André looked the part. The wretch would have attracted less odium and enmity had he fled to avoid paying his debts.

Then, one fine evening, amidst this concerto of curses, the concierge, inflamed by cassis, contributed her two pennies' worth. She revealed unexpected details about André's wife; then tongues that were flagging wagged more than ever. She had a lover, he had been seen in the night while André, holding a light, was showing him out. They were accomplices, no doubt about it, the lover was the son of a tycoon, he supported the husband and wife. André was a shoddy good-for-nothing, a jobless idler, a journalist, a flaneur who trafficked women. Then Berthe acquired the reputation of a Jezebel and a hypocrite. Her pale complexion which at first was that of a poor woman abandoned by her husband and eating her heart out, became the disgraceful pallor of a woman exhausted by debauchery, then there was a renewed shift of opinion in her favor, it was that swine of a man who had corrupted her! She came from a good family; M. Désableau, her uncle, looked like a respectable gentleman and the abuse he had heaped on André in the presence of a number of people showed the contempt he felt for his niece's husband.

Cyprien was left stunned. In a state of resignation, he watched this cartload of slander tipped out over his friend. The calumnies now oozed out of all the shops, lingered on all the pavements, and from there accumulated in all the concierge lodges, spread through the courtyards, filtered like fine smoke under the doors of the landings, filled the kitchens, accompanied the maids to their employers' dining rooms, penetrating as far as the sleeping closets.

This was the shopkeepers' revenge for the sudden winter; shut up in their cages, doors closed, not even able to take advantage of bright spells, in rubbing with their fingers the misted glass that veiled the street they moped behind the silver ferns of ice on the panes of their windows; housemaids' tittle-tattle couldn't satisfy their hunger; on the lookout behind their counters they tried in vain to keep the passersby under observation and spit on the backs of the persons from whom they made a living.

The curb imposed on them by the cold made them fierce. All the ways that André was able to think of for subduing the glare of his misfortune went for nothing. For the space of a fortnight his departure was the only topic of conversation, and Cyprien, who kept him informed, in toning down the clumsy idiocies that were said about him, might have added still more if he'd known that he himself hadn't been spared. He was the husband's bosom friend, cast in the same mold, no doubt living on the earnings of whores. The baker gave a somewhat different view of matters. He readily allowed that the painter was a scoundrel, but he thought that it was he who had seduced André's wife. What's more, he supported his view with a profound thesis based on the friendship uniting the two men. A man is only ever betrayed by friends, he said; but, then, in that event, André was no more than a dupe, a husband one could pity and not attack. That assumption was inadmissible; nevertheless, one part of the neighborhood was given pause, but the day was carried by the concierge, who declared that Cyprien, viewed from behind, bore no resemblance to the lover who, as much as she was able to make out in the night, had broader shoulders. People were more than happy to denounce André, Cyprien, and Berthe in equal measure; suddenly the reason for such a rapid turnover of housemaids was clear, and why they were finally left without any at all. Any self-respecting girl left the house after a week. As little disgusted as the last one might have been, who, although looking like a proper trollop, had gagged and thrown down her apron in horror! A real brothel, the district chorused in conclusion; really, what were the police dreaming of, in tolerating such filth.

André was immediately tempted to go and break a stick on the noses of the baker and concierge, then he reflected that this would be stupid and he'd get all the blame. He fumed and kept himself under control. He had, after some time had passed, arrived at a quiet and thorough contempt for these swine, when the disputes between Mélanie and the concierge reawakened his rage and made him fear for a similar explosion of filth in his new street; he held his breath and was only able to feel himself again after the quarrels seemed to have finally reached a conclusion.

One, two, three more weeks flowed by. A period of complete quiet arrived, he worked flat-out, sheltered from the demands of Berthe and the Désableaus who accepted the conditions offered by the solicitor, protected from annoying contacts and the onerous duties of the world, household troubles alleviated, savoring the peace of a man continually unbuttoned and in slippers, he little by little recalled his bachelor enthusiasms, luxuriated in a blissful state of ease and good food; in a word, he found perfect contentment.

VI

Then came the petticoat crisis.

Hard-won peace and calm gave way to an undefined malaise that worsened, peaking in a kind of spleen that he attributed to the languor of springtime with its accompaniment of strained nerves.

An aversion to his domestic interior, so much to his liking, showed itself. He was now irritable, unsettled by the slightest noise, and, bored stiff at home, went out, and, even more bored outside, came back and fell, harassed, into an armchair. He remained there, unmoving, lacking the willpower to shake off the enervation that overwhelmed him, waiting till the soles of his feet were tingling before getting up, until his hand, propping up his head, prickled almost painfully, becoming inert and numb, as though paralyzed.

He remonstrated with himself, was willfully blind, going off on a tangent, fearing, through probing, to put his finger on the wound that he felt reopening and so inflame it. So, wasn't he happy? From the moment that he had the means to allow himself a housemaid he led the same blissful existence as before his marriage, well coddled and well fed, master of his actions. Tired of these evasions, he acknowledged to himself that this mode of life wasn't the same as before, that, under an appearance of sameness, it had somehow changed, more or less completely.

His marriage finally loomed up before him. It intervened between his present and past lives. Like those mirrors that distort the objects they reflect, it fogged and spoiled the egotistical image of well-being he had once enjoyed and that he hoped to enjoy once more. The admission slipped out; he wanted a woman.

Ah, Cyprien was right to say a man couldn't live all by himself like that! The petticoat crisis that exploded after André was freed from his initial bewilderment, and was no longer troubled by concerns for the functioning of his reorganized and renewed existence, was ripened and accelerated by Mélanie's condolences. She felt the need to ask after his wife every time he received a letter. In fact, her fear was that Madame was restored to health and would return to take over the running of the household. In that event she would, in all likelihood, cut back on the expenses and dismiss the policeman to whom, during his free time, Mélanie had delegated the waxing of the apartment's parquet flooring, the cleaning of the tiles, and the smoking of André's tobacco; but as her employer's nose got out of joint every time she spoke about his wife, Mélanie concluded that Madame's health was no better, and, remembering the name of the illness that André had mentioned to her, she took the precaution of consulting the Gros-Caillou chemist, who took the view that the patient would expire sooner or later.

Reassured, Mélanie nevertheless believed that it was her duty to persist with her laments and, having helped hasten the crisis, she was responsible for aggravating it. Meanwhile, André now languished in a state of idleness lit up by sudden alarms and rages when he was at home, but at suppertime his anger was succeeded by a great despondency. He ate quickly and without appetite, like a man in a hurry to finish a troublesome duty. The bell summoning

Mélanie rang again so promptly that she was left openmouthed, craw filled with soup while he demanded cheese and dessert. Nose plunged in a book that he wasn't reading, his thoughts wandered and no sooner did he finish his meal than he took his volume with him and sprawled out in an armchair in his workroom.

He despaired at the increasing springtime daylight. It was above all in the evening that the acute stage of the crisis declared itself, like the fever that overtakes the invalid tired out by daylight hours. He wasn't so much haunted by lascivious scenarios as by a vague, nervous longing, a confused reverie. He wanted a woman not for the carnal embrace of her body, but for her skirt whisking against him, her tinkling laugh, her purring voice, for her company, not least for the atmosphere she radiated. Without her, his apartment seemed joyless.

Incapable of doing any work, wearied by whatever he read, oppressed by an inveterate dejection, tortured by a sullenly mutinous nature in revolt against this cloistered life, he watched the gradual decline of the day and, in the sorrow dispensed by nightfall, he felt a sad and consoling pity that furnished him with a kind of mild support.

Boyish dreams bloomed in this sadness, the light-minded solace of an urchin. Like many another, he'd known ideals to die under him, and memories of juvenile amours suddenly awoke in the breast of this skeptic.

He was obsessed by a girl, a girl he hadn't loved in the way that, by common consent, one loves in novels, but who had pleased him, who had been the first to charm him after he'd left school. He remembered days in the country with an astonishing vividness of impression, intimate conversations at a little distance from suspicious parents, smothered laughter, the foolishness of picked flowers, a whole passionate courtship that made him shrug his shoulders subsequently at the time of her marriage.

He remembered still more clearly a certain scene one evening. They went for a walk in the park under the chestnut trees while the family was playing a card game in the front room. She'd sat down on a bench in the shadows and said to him in a changed voice, "Sit here"—and there they remained, holding their breath, she prodding the dry chestnut husks with the tip of her foot, he, hands trembling and heart pounding, not knowing whether to hold back or take the risk. They had been fetched back and the young girl had been soundly scolded. The family had certainly believed there was an intention to misbehave, of which for his part he wasn't guilty.

That scene was so clearly and exactly evoked that André felt the same shiver, the same embarrassment as when it had happened. Following that stream of memories, he suppressed all at once the breach created by the marriage of that young lady and he imagined that, having married her, a sweet and peaceful life unfolded between them, then, returning to reality, he cursed himself for being a puerile imbecile, lit the lamp whose brightness dispelled all these floating reveries that were suddenly filled with emotion after slumbering, seemingly dead, for almost fifteen years.

But the cheerful light didn't stop his mind from continuing to dream. If the darkness helped him to recover the most distant memories, the light rejuvenated them, bringing them closer, making them more precise. Jumping abruptly from one epoch to another, André bridged the intervening years, the casual love affairs, and, an association of ideas being necessarily established between the only two respectable women he had courted, his thoughts once more alighted on Berthe.

She now arose before him and from the moment of her approach swept away with a gesture all the slowly drifting, foundering memories. She and she alone held sway. He brought her into focus, saw her as she was and, by dint of focusing on her, ended up not even seeing her very distinctly. There was a moment when he positively sought to picture her face. A new rage against her and her lover galvanized him, then, when the feeling dulled on account of its very violence, he was seized with cowardly regrets. Ah! Without a doubt it would have been better to remain with her. After all, he wasn't the first victim of an event like that. So what if it was a ridiculous role to play! The opinion of the world concerns itself neither with the character nor the needs of individuals and measures all species by the same yardstick. If it could be relived, he would be reasonable, would accept the partnership of mutual indulgence so frequently found in Parisian marriages. They would remain good friends, pardoning their mutual indiscretions, each making allowance for the other in order to lead a tranquil life; he wouldn't be reduced to living alone like this, and he drifted into incoherent reveries where a woman passed before him, cajoling him and seeking his pardon, and a respectable nursemaid cared for him, smiling and gossamer reveries that were rudely interrupted by footsteps mounting the stairs, footsteps striking at his heart and that, half awake, he took for female footsteps, Berthe's footsteps. Ah! If she'd had the idea of coming to knock on his door; inventing a pretext for a visit was so easy! He would pardon her; once inside his apartment, it would all fall into place so naturally; they'd be able to get along and agree with each other.

Then he gave a start and, sobered, cursed himself, and relapsing into his thoughts which, now freed from the image around which they had gravitated, gradually diverged, veered away from

Berthe and, turning in the same circle in spite of everything, returned to their point of departure—to women—he went on to think of a period of his life remaining till then in the shadows, he conjured up his old liaisons and, irresistibly, he alighted on Jeanne, a mistress he'd possessed for a few years before his marriage.[32]

It was the first time in an age that he'd been assailed by this memory. She alone had remained in a corner of his brain as a fine, curious young woman, a little worker girl, somewhat unfathomable, either very corrupt or very naïve, but in any case, tender and making do with what little she had. They had quarreled angrily over a trifle and, proud and touchy as she was, he'd never seen her again.

He could hardly remember her face. As much as that power of vision acquired by memories of one's extreme youth made the face of the girl with whom he'd conducted a chaste love affair appear very clearly before his eyes, so, for all that he tried to throw light on the features of the woman who slept beside him for months, they shrouded themselves from him. He saw certain of her traits, but the ensemble danced to and fro. In recollecting her, he perceived, vaguely at best, bright and inquisitive eyes, a trim and supple waist, an elegant figure in a little dress, a retroussé nose under blonde hair, adorable arms, slender feet, pretty hands, a pert and provocative plainness, but however faint and incomplete the image that presented itself to him, he felt that he would recognize her among a thousand in the street.

Suddenly, as soon as his mind dwelt on Jeanne it went no further. Tired of dreaming about his wife whose charms, enhanced by her absence, seemed to him more attractive than they really were, the evocation of which left him, in spite of everything, with dull fits of anger, he inevitably ended up clinging to the memory of the only mistress who had attracted him, and the same phenomenon repeated itself. He remembered nothing but Jeanne's good qualities, finally finding them superior to those of Berthe, whose more recent absence left her less idealized, and also toppled her from her pedestal when the scene of their rupture came mind, a fixed point amidst the fluctuations of his dreams.

What had become of the girl? Frail and delicate, she possessed at that time a perfumer's disquieting pallor; no doubt she had died, and he was suddenly seized with a childish compassion for this woman whom, in truth, he had never loved; he was astonished not to have thought about her sooner, and he went on to reflect that life was really bizarre, that one unites one's life with someone else, tells her everything, each tells the other all there is to tell—the man at least—and then, several years later, everything is gone from memory and nothing further is shared in common.

There were almost tears in his eyes when he repeated to himself that Jeanne must be dead, and, recalling their white nights together sharing a bed, he admitted that he'd have done better to cohabit with her, which was what she herself had one day wanted. He would have been no unhappier and no more of a cuckold, and he told himself sadly, "I've long since reached that time in life when a show of affection is enough to satisfy me; even allowing that she was never in love with me, it would have been enough if she'd learned to play her role well enough."

And he retired early on those evenings when he was cast down by despondent moods, lingering in front of his bookshelves searching for a book that would make sense of the thoughts that agitated him. He would have liked to find one that provided consolation while at the same time reinforcing his feelings of bitterness, one that told of even greater troubles and yet were the same as his, one that would solace him by way of comparison. Of course he found nothing; so he took out a volume at random, stretched out on his bed and, unable to follow what he was reading, he carried on dreaming, brooded and pored over his troubles, was eager for sleep to blanket them, and even when sleeping remained harried by an indefinite ennui that made him suddenly start up with the terrifying anxiety of someone who falls down a staircase in dreams.

Such petticoat crises occurred with increasing frequency. Previously they hounded him for a day or two then disappeared for weeks altogether; now they were protracted, and when they appeared to have finally quit the scene they resurfaced in thought at the flimsiest pretext.

André wondered if his late arriving sexual chastity didn't play a part in precipitating these sad and dispirited phases.

Just like those invalids who, hearing the news of an infallible remedy, persuade themselves, even before having tried it and in spite of the costs they've already incurred from similar claims, that this latest one is more effective and that it alone will have the virtue of putting them back on their feet, André, thinking that he was saved, experienced a moment of joy. He wanted to sample therapeutic debauches, heightened his senses by means of lascivious memories, and on various occasions gave himself over, on that account, to downright bouts of intoxication.

As a result he procured a species of relief; he returned home shattered and fell immediately asleep. The following day his head felt heavy, but skirts were no longer a torment to him. His desire for affection remained unsatisfied, but they clamored less loudly in his sated flesh. André was delighted with his experiment and repeated it to the point of exhaustion. Then the briefly conquered yearnings reappeared, reasserting themselves even more keenly. He had overdosed on this sedative that now exasperated him, like those potions containing excessive amounts of opiate that produce an effect opposite to what would have been obtained by a correct dosage. Far from distracting him, these episodes of love on the fly distressed him; his depressions became even more pronounced and peremptory, with the mental lethargy that follows carnal excess. A comparison made itself unavoidably felt between these women who facilitated ecstasy by the prompt removal of skirt and blouse, losing no time in sending him on his way in order to go down to the street or the salon to swallow glasses of wine or beer, and Berthe and Jeanne. In the former he found no semblance of either sympathy or consideration, even less of any kind of pleasure.

Schoolboy memories came back to him, memories stupid enough to make him weep. He left boulevard Bonne-Nouvelle one evening and stole through one of the foul streets where, in every kind of weather, the waste basins protruding from the walls emit the nauseating smell of old cauliflower. With one of his friends he ventured with timid steps into those black alleyways where two gas lamps flicker at second-floor level, their dirty light illuminating the sills of windows cluttered with sick plants, veronicas and wallflowers, mustard pots full of parsley and water, faded blouses drying on clotheslines; there, three or four women, with big bellies under ill-fitting clothes, too short in the front, showing heads with barbarically rouged cheeks, gossiped among themselves, in a circle around a streetlight.

With faltering hearts they listened to the invitation of these Jezebels. They hesitated, hostage to horrible fears, sudden shame, doubts about this unknown world into which they were venturing, then they both revolted against their better selves and, as though approaching ladies, politely offered their arms to these fat drabs who were amazed by such good manners. So the couples had crossed the street, showing the grotesque retreating backs of the scrawny youngsters and the enormous shoulders of the hussies who waddled along like ducks.

No sooner than sequestered in a shabby room badly lit by a candle stub, before an unmade bed and a basin in permanent residence on the floor tiles, André felt an urgent desire to flee. His schoolboy desires no longer heated his blood. The brutal act was there. The fear of looking childish and naive added further anxieties.

Luckily he'd fallen on a good-hearted woman who took an interest in this avid and troubled youth. She had a certain tender care for him, an almost maternal welcome; she emptied his little purse, stole, by appealing to his kind heart, a bottle of eau de Cologne that he'd brought as a hygienic safety measure, and with soft words and big kisses, with loud sighs and pretended joys, she made him giddy and at ease.

He exited this hovel along with his friend, thinking in the street, "so that's all it was!" and making an effort, in spite of everything, to get worked up, imagining that they'd drained potent intoxicants. Out of bravado, each, in telling the tale of his pleasure, exaggerated it. They now looked more proudly at passersby. They were men! They put on brash airs, would have like to shout the story of their adventures to all and sundry, meet a friend, an acquaintance and tell them all about their feats! At times, though, they were tormented by a terrible fear, that of having contracted an incurable disease, a disease that would wreak havoc on the scalp and eat away the nose, but they were still full of the enthusiasm that they both maintained, keeping it warm for as long as it threatened to go cold. Disillusion only really materialized when, going their separate ways, each had returned home to stretch out on his bunk.

André's thought was that, at the ripe age of thirty, he'd regressed to the amorous escapades of an eighteen-year-old! After gallivanting all over he'd returned to his beginnings in love! He paid more money, went to respectable cafés instead of sitting down in pothouses, but what he consumed was no different; it all left a sour aftertaste, a new thirst for delicacies that were unsoiled.

His haste to possess something feminine that simulated grace, pleasure, was further quickened by the revulsion he felt. These female clowns didn't perform their act at all well. They no longer put a smile on his face now that, being older and less high-spirited, he found it more difficult to lose his head at the critical moment.

His wife, cold though she was, seemed passionate alongside these female fraudsters, but here he was haunted, and still more keenly, by the memory of his former mistress, her trembling, her swoons when he rocked her in his arms. Ah, that one, the blood really danced in her veins and the course of her raptures wasn't calculated in advance.

Not knowing whether she was living or dead, he longed for a similar demoiselle, for a new mistress, then admitted to himself that he was no longer of an age to seduce a woman.

What stopped him was the thought of going to exchange discreet signals through the windows of milliner's or cobbler's premises, letting himself be snubbed at the door, wasting his time with such carryings-on, the fear of being ridiculous. Besides, he harbored few illusions about his attractions. He knew he didn't have the special something that enables even an ugly and physically impaired man to charm a woman. He knew enough about life not to be unaware that intelligence, distinction, are only meager assets when it comes to young women, who fall for the most appalling louts because they have a roguish or ferocious eye, who fall madly in love for reasons that they themselves aren't able to fathom.

Besides, the more he thought of the difficulties of the undertaking the more his timidity increased. Having had enough of paid streetwalkers, he now wanted to address his attentions to girls who earned their bread in another way, to the lower-class girls who choose a lover and are only unfaithful to him by fits and starts, depending on when their rent falls due or meetings arranged on leaving their shops.

Then, toward eight in the evening, finding himself by chance or as a result of an errand, on place du Carrousel, seeing the midinettes escaping their workplaces, returning in pairs to the left bank, laughing, tripping along, he followed them with a sorrowful eye. The blonde girl, the one on the right who scampered along, would have done nicely for him; she had a sweet look and seemed as though she would laugh easily. It's true that those sweet-looking cheats are worse than others and that they're the ones who mock men and give them a proper dose of pepper.[33]

Sometimes he sat down on the stone benches of the Turgot Pavilion,[34] unconcerned with his neighbors, workers busy reading their newspapers and sleeping, business representatives resting and wiping their brow near their offices, people removing boots to ease their swollen feet, or else old couples breathing in the serene evening air, the husband's hands leaning on a cane, the woman holding a basket on her knees; he watched the flow of the crowd, the private coaches and hackney cabs speeding by, the hired carts swaying, full of furniture, pulled in front by harness straps and pushed from behind by men's arms, and once more he told himself that among all these swarms of people crossing each other's paths at that time of day, many of them were no doubt going back to a woman. Alert to the froufrou of skirts, he also thought that all these women, however unprepossessing and ungainly they might be, have a man whom they satisfy and pamper while deceiving him; his dreams were even bolstered by the little girls in aprons running in front of their mothers, blonde hair swept up in front by a comb and falling in bunches on the neck, with powdered hands and cheeks smeared with recent tears. He saw in these brats, whom age would refine, the future suffering of little kids who would become increasingly stupid as they grew up.

Utterly disconsolate, hands placed flat on his crossed thighs, he contemplated the marvelous and terrible sunset that stretched beyond the black foliage of the Tuileries; he contemplated the raw stains of the new buildings, the little Arc de Triomphe cut out and prettied up like a puppet theater, and, devoid this evening of both perspective and surrounding air, was stuck almost flat against the ruins whose purple masses, breached with holes, raised themselves on the crimson flames of the clouds.

Then his gaze descended, and, looking all around, fastened on the unfortunate soldier on guard duty. He followed his measured steps along the length of the Louvre. Was it possible that this infantryman didn't have a sweetheart from his native province, a girl of any description who hugged his body in her arms on a folding bedstead or in a kitchen corner, regaled him with a torrent of big kisses on his neck, or fondly trimmed his moustache? He must be really happy, him over there. At least someone was waiting for him when he was off duty! Then André shrugged his shoulders, acknowledged his own stupidity, for, all things considered, better to give up the ghost than lead the miserable life of that poor devil.

Those evenings ended with him dragging himself back home, in the kind of stupor felt by people who, after having wept for hours, are numbed with an almost agreeable lethargy.

Once in bed his wound still ached. More than ever, he dove down into his sorry dreams. Ultimately, he envied those men who, satiated with a woman, don't how to extract themselves from her caresses. He'd never been pursued by a woman, he was yet to experience the torment of those who are vulgarly said to cling like leeches. He'd never known how to keep hold of a mistress, was always the one who was dropped first.

After having congratulated himself on never having known such entanglements, after even having made fun of friends who'd been besieged by their lovers, now he was jealous of them.

In his lucid moments he sought for a remedy that would suppress the illness from which he was suffering. The only one he was able to imagine, seducing a girl who was almost chaste, seemed impossible. Inevitably, he would be obliged, as before, to target a girl on the game who would share him in common with others. He would have his day and he would be well received by her, knowing him for a regular client and that he received the pleasures for which he'd just paid in gentlemanly fashion. Finally, he decided to adopt that scheme, persuaded that in Paris it was impracticable to possess a woman who was his alone, trying to convince himself, with the help of supporting arguments, that if he'd been averse to street girls, it was simply because he'd visited a different one every time instead of always resorting to the same one.

But here it all depended on chance. He could roam through powder rooms and sleeping closets for months before finding an agreeable woman, one who would satisfactorily feign the effusions of the nice girl.

He searched and only found sad comediennes in thrall to pimps whom they hurried to rejoin as soon as his back was turned.

In this debacle, the memory of Berthe once more took root, but the accompanying cortege of rancor and rage had disappeared. André had lost all firmness of purpose, all resilience. He desperately wanted to see his wife again; he wandered the streets neighboring the Désableau house, meeting none of them; he finally learned second hand that they'd all left for the country.

From time to time Cyprien cheered him up. He understood his friend's silence, lips kept sealed about his failings. Sometimes they spent an evening together, and there, while they smoked their pipes, without chatting, the painter strove to shake André loose from his leaden inertia.

"You're wrong," he said to him one day, "to let yourself carry on like this. Watch out, you're hoping for women down on their luck so that you can console them, you're going to dream about your own incredible sensitivity and no less incredible gratitude from her whom you'll oblige by sleeping with afterward! Come on, we'll see about that, but that kind of absurdity should be rejected out of hand. What then? You know very well that if you manage to really tie a woman to you, she'll flay your soul, she'll skin you alive while seeming to bandage your wounds! That's how Providence has ordained the relations between men and women. I'm not saying that's a good thing, it's just how it is!" And on these evenings Cyprien invited his friend out for a stroll, dragging him on epic excursions, trying his best to tire him out so he would sleep.

VII

One evening, André almost perked up.

Tired of banging his head against unobtainable desires, he quit the blind alley where he'd been getting nowhere and, without even being aware of it, quietly retraced his steps. The petticoat crisis had little by little exhausted itself; a volte-face took place in this soul that, unable to settle securely, jumping from one extreme to another, now wanted laughter and boisterous pleasures.

Come the evening he needed the illuminated gaiety of Paris. He wanted to mingle with noisy crowds, intoxicate his eyes, like them, with tinsel and gaslight; he wanted purely animal distractions that would absorb his curious gaze but bypass his state of mind which, tired of digesting painful thoughts, demanded rest, the absolute diet.

André went out and, not knowing how to pass the time, headed toward Cyprien's apartment.

When he went in, the painter was seated in front of a table, near a plate bearing the remains of a veal stew, and was finishing a drawing stretched on a board by four drawing pins.

André examined the drawing and was taken aback. A plaster bust of Hippocrates on a pedestal under which two turtle doves struggling in the coils of a boa were bordered by two medallions, much as the stem of a nautical telescope is by its two lenses, one medallion representing an opera ballet, the other a clearing in a wood where two lovers were kissing. To the left and right of these, two other figures were standing, a young woman in a white skirt, crying, and a young man in a dressing gown, desolate. Behind and in front of them, under their feet and over their heads, snakes coiled round palm trees or, on the ground, rearing on their tails, hissed and twisted while their tongues flicked out.

"A pediment there overhead," Cyprien murmured, "a few beakers, some phials, and, set over the whole, a caduceus in the clouds and two syringes put crosswise and this symbolic effort will be finished."

Then he leaned over to André and said, "This here isn't, as you might think, a sketch for a big canvas, no, quite simply it's a pharmacist's leaflet that will be cut in wood, printed, and rolled around a bottle, adorned with a sacramental red paper label, 'for external medicinal use only.' You get it, don't you? Shall I now explain to you the philosophical significance of this work? Listen.

"First of all, this proves that if you manage to pick up persons from dancing schools, or any other school for that matter; that if you go on exorbitant binges with them, you get sick. And that's the righteous punishment visited by heaven on profligacy.

"Then again, that proves that if, instead of being lecherous and rich, you're poor and your soul is ethereal; if instead of getting blind drunk with flighty women, you love a young person whom you take to be chaste, ah well, you get sick just the same. And that too is the righteous punishment visited by heaven on the naive.

"As you can see, then, this brochure is above all modern and humanitarian. It's morality at work. The young lady and gentleman beating their breasts are destined to serve as examples to youth and show that no matter what it does, it'll cop it. All in all, this elevates the soul and offers no consolation! There you have it, but," he continued, looking at his drawing in a mirror to better judge its overall balance, "enough for today. Hey, if you've got nothing better in mind, how would you like to come with me and breathe in the delicious stink of the streets?"

"Where to?" André enquired.

"It doesn't matter where, so long as it's noisy and there's gaslight on painted faces, for instance at the Palais-Royal, in the boulevard, in the passageways. Do you fancy that?"

Instinctively, for no reason, through one of those primary impulses that decide a man, André hid the pleasure that this offer gave him and replied as indifferently as he was able that going to one place rather another made no difference to him. Cyprien made so much of an effort to entice him through singing the praises of these convivial locations that André, annoyed, wanted to contradict him through finding fault with the routes, one after another, over which he rhapsodized. He felt that strange need to condemn and belittle what has just been praised to the skies.

Once outside they got underway, dawdling through the streets with little steps, noses in the air. They now spoke at random about anything and everything. A pharmacy that grease-painted Cyprien's face green and pink as he passed by a shelf of light-reflecting jars led André's thoughts back to the painter's leaflet.

"So, you must be really hard up to take on that kind of work."

Cyprien heaved a sigh. "You don't say," he murmured. "Flat broke, utterly, catastrophically. As the croupiers say in the casinos, *rien ne va plus*. My work might just as well be sold going door to door, with six kitchen knives laid out in a case, the little silver-plated spoons, the discounted candlesticks and toy playsets specially produced by street sellers or else stolen—that's how it is now." And switching topic like a man who talks about anything else in order to avoid an unpleasant conversation, he pointed to a fire station where some gleaming helmets could be made out, lit up on high shelves, and he ventured this question: "Why the devil is it that whenever you see the firemen in their barracks they're always writing? It's true," he continued, without waiting for a reply from André, who was playing hide-and-seek with other gentlemen in the metal shell of a urinal, "that it would be just as difficult to explain why it smells of cloves in the Louvre on Sundays, and why, on a different track, bookbinders are always the least punctual of tradesmen and pharmacists the biggest thieves."

Not finding his comrade at his side he looked around for him, finally saw him exiting the pissoir which at that time resembled those Nuremberg cuckoo clocks where, as soon as one figurine emerges from a niche, on the hour, it's automatically replaced by another stationed behind.

The two young men walked on silently with nothing to say to each other, each thinking of personal concerns, letters to be written the next day or the unstamped ones left on their tables, troubles, possibly still more serious matters.

"Very nice, the poppet," Cyprien suddenly cried, brushing past a little minx who fluttered her big eyelids suggestively. And he lapsed back into wordlessness, no doubt mentally undressing the little nymph.

He suddenly spoke again. "I'm thirsty, what do you say we stop for a quick one."

They went into a café and sat at the back of the room, under a mirror that, behind them and over their heads, put a reflected image of the lady at the bar busily piling up little sugar cubes with fingers loaded with rings. Cyprien, legs outstretched, neck buried in the leatherette, wondered what might be going on in the mind of that young woman, probably the offspring of a whole generation of barkeepers, raised amidst pipe smoke, the rolling of billiard balls, and shouts for bocks.

Then he watched a bewildered head emerging from a staircase that corkscrewed up to the floor, followed by bare arms, laden with trays and mugs, finally, slowly ascending, a complete body enveloped in an apron of blue cloth spattered with big black stains where it had been splashed by water.

Sliding on sorry old slippers, the dishwasher plunged into a furious coming and going of waiters charging full speed ahead, shouting "Boum,"[35] juggling carafes and saucers, dazzling the eyes with the white trajectory of their aprons, and he stopped, winded, putting his burden down near a counter where the proprietor was using a wooden spatula to clear the head of some beer mugs, emptying the slops and the froth into fresh glasses that he filled with newer beer.

Cyprien soon got tired of contemplating this little kitchen, drank his bock, benumbed by the heavy fumes that were still perfumed by a faint smell of absinthe, glanced at the newspaper André was reading, received without turning a hair the smile of two tarts whose noses disappeared into the make-up of harshly lit faces. Two pink stains, two black circles, and two streaks of blood-red rouge were all that, at the front, accentuated cheeks, eyes, and lips, relegating to the background all that part of the face encrusted with bismuth powder and white grease.

"Ugh!" he said to himself, "those two aren't the ones who'll light my fire!" and without paying any further attention to their giggling and ogling, he contemplated the joy of people absorbed in shuffling games of piquet and écarté, and, leaning over to André, who was yawning, he murmured, "So you see old friend, Monsieur Gringoneur, who invented cards, had no idea how important his discovery would become.[36] He believed, poor man, that he was merely relieving the boredom of a doddering old fool and a madman and without knowing it he created a grander and more devout work; he helped to suppress the free trade of human folly! Because, well, I'm making an exception for these here players. Idiots or not, well or badly bred, the great majority of these here are either men cohabiting with women or husbands who hang around taprooms because they detest their wives, or are bored with them, and Lord knows I forgive them! But in the drawing rooms, in the world at large, cards only serve to mask the poverty of idle chatter, weakness of intellect, hollow men with nothing to say when gathered together; all the same it's amazing how the futility of the bourgeoisie comes into its own in a game of whist."

But André motioned him to keep quiet. A fat, bald gentleman was coming toward them, steering between tables, his overcoat snagging on the corners. The three of them exchanged unenthusiastic banalities and the usual handshakes, expressing surprise at the chance that united them in a café none of them usually frequented.

"I won't ask for news of madam your wife," the newcomer said to André, who turned pale, "because I had the pleasure of spending yesterday evening with her."

"Bah!" Cyprien growled.

"Yes, I was back from a trip and, well, I went to pay my respects to that fine fellow Désableau at Viroflay. By the way, did you know that they've managed to find a very nice little house that isn't too expensive. The garden isn't so big . . ."

"Yes, but the woods are only a few feet away," Cyprien interrupted.

"So, you've been there then? And yet Désableau declared that he hadn't seen you for months."

"I've never set foot in the place," the painter replied, "but since every time a country cottage is said to only have a little garden, it's the done thing to immediately compensate by adding that a wood isn't far away; I thought, and I was right, that the same applied to the shack rented by Désableau."

"Well," the man continued, somewhat disconcerted by that opinion, "it remains the case that our friend has reached the goal he was aiming for, since his daughter can run around and play in the fresh air as much as she wants; but, good heavens, you rascal," he continued, addressing André in a friendly voice, "when I asked after you, I was told that you don't go there very often. Ah, you devils of artists, you're all the same, you need the pandemonium of Paris, the cafés, the balls, life as grand opera. All the same, just between us, you're lucky to have a little woman who's so accommodating. As for mine, let me tell you if I don't come back home on time every evening, well, there's hell to pay! 'Where have you been, what have you been up to, you stink of cigars and beer, those women are cheating you, they're laughing at you, you're too old for that kind of fooling about!'"

Cyprien thought it was time to apply the brakes and steer this unfortunate conversation away from André's wife.

"Hey, look at that," he said, "the man who's smoking his pipe over there, hasn't his head got a really funny shape?"

This ploy failed.

"Always observant, our Monsieur Cyprien," the fat man said to no one in particular. "But to come back to the point, tell me my lad," he went on, fixing his calf eyes on André's beard, "are you still at odds with old Désableau? Bah, you know you mustn't hold it against him, it's understandable, he isn't in our line of work; your books annoy him, he doesn't see that business is business; I've told him straight out that the wares in each of our shops are specific to what our customers want, we only stock items that we have a chance of selling. Look, in my premises for example you'll find specialty underwear that you won't find in Maison Buquet because they wouldn't easily be able to shift it, and yet it's a major outlet. But, all the same, as my wife maintained the other day, and you can rely on her judgment for that because she's a woman with her head screwed on who always likes to have her nose in a book, 'Why can't Monsieur André write something nice, something sensitive, you know a story that would feature a love interest, something that would soothe and touch the soul?' The public adores novels of that type, and it would please your family so much!"

"Hey, André," Cyprien flung out, beside himself with rage, "What's his name hasn't shown up, we've waited long enough, what say you we lift the siege?"

André immediately agreed.

"Ah, so, what with all that, what time is it?" the man asked.

Cyprien didn't think that checking his watch was the best idea; he preferred to consult the café clock, which was always fast. "Twenty past ten," he said.

"Damn," the fat man cried, "I've got to run." And he added in a complaisant voice, "are you coming with me?"

"No, not yet. Since we've already waited so long for the friend who arranged to meet us here, we'll hang around a little longer."

Then all three got up, shook hands, and the man said to André, squeezing the tips of his fingers, "delighted to have met you my good friend, I'm sorry I can't stay longer, but you know, however good the company, we have to leave at some point; my best wishes, if you please, to madam your wife when you next see her."

"Oof," the painter groaned and, arms crossed, shaking his head furiously, he gazed at André, who didn't reply.

Cyprien's attempts to divert the conversation had in fact been in vain. A single word was enough to make André's numb misery well up. From when their acquaintance had mentioned his visit to the Désableaus, André had only half listened to his gossip and his advice. He'd been transported to the Viroflay house and could have described it, he saw it so clearly, white and bright with green shutters preceded by a lawn dotted with rose bushes and China asters, a lead tank in a corner, in the middle the few stone steps of an entrance stairway adorned with cast iron pots planted with ivy leaf geranium, and his wife sitting on a folding stool under a tree spreading a bit of shade, her workbasket at her feet, knitting near her little cousin, sitting on smaller stool, learning her lessons, putting down her book from time to time so she could be made to recite, faltering, repeating the same word four times, fumbling for the next.

André felt a great tenderness enfold him. The crisis resurfaced once more, like those diseases that flare up more briefly and feebly each time before dying out completely. The rage against his wife and her lover, the pain, mixed at first with hatred then dominating it and absorbing it completely, the regret for a lost domestic life, the mad desire to see Berthe again, all these symptoms of the acute stage of the disease had reached an end. André was suffering secondary symptoms.[37] He now felt the slow and sad emotion inspired by the memory of the beloved gone far away forever. Then that languid and melancholy fatigue, born from a hope recognized as utterly impossible and unrealizable, also melted away and next, in the soul that was at a standstill, remaining for a minute immobile and inert, a frightful jabber buzzed like a confused noise, suddenly penetrated by a furiously repeated whine, piercing like the note of a harmonica, the name Désableau. André's thoughts went on the warpath again, inspiring him with renewed anger against that man who now occupied the foreground. The cold contempt for him that André had felt for years suddenly caught fire and exploded with rage. He remembered his typically tiresome twaddle, his eternal grievances; he saw him again, grumbling about his office work, voicing the responsibilities that burdened him, the shortcomings of his unfortunate underlings, saw him proclaiming handshakes with his superiors, reading certain promises in their smiles, or returning home worried, shattered when their greeting had seemed to him colder or less cordial.

And, suddenly coming back to the countryside, the tedious evenings he had been subjected to in the little family dining room after his marriage, with a bed folded in the corner, André thought of Désableau saying solemnly after supper, after the removal of the tablecloth, "No, no games of patience this evening, work calls before all else my children," and from a voluminous shagreen brief case stamped with his insignia, he pulled out the minutes of employees that he crossed out from top to bottom and started to rewrite in a stiffer and more dignified language. André had a new vision of the family invariably occupied in this way; Madame Désableau looking at hovering houseflies from between two knitting needles and silently advising her daughter, with winks, not to disturb her father's work by moving about; Berthe sewing, her nose in her work, exchanging every fifteen minutes some banality or other with her aunt in a quiet voice, or getting up on tiptoe, cautiously opening the door to go and look for something forgotten in her bedroom; at long last, in the silence disturbed only by the distant sound of dishes being washed, the scratching of pen on paper, Désableau, paused before a phrase, hesitating for hours between one word and another, cradling his chin, chewing the whisker on his right side, grumbling, complaining about the racket made by the housemaid in the kitchen, the noise of the little one pushing her chair back.

André felt a profound disgust for this bourgeois full of prejudices, for this official puffed up with self-importance, with no sympathy for a flight of the imagination or a whim, for this narrow-minded old man entrenched in his manic habits, offended by any new idea, whose habitual talk, when it didn't address politics or morality, condemned with unappeasable rage the hostility of his subordinates, the machinations of his office boy who dared to bring him the low-grade lamp of ordinary employees rather than the better-quality lamp to which he was entitled, appropriate to his rank.

André now felt astonished that, back then, he had so good-naturedly accepted the admonitions of that imbecile. He excused his wife who had been raised in that depressing environment, and he pitied her for having fallen back into it. How bored she must be at Viroflay! Ah, but she really must be a fundamentally decent person, he thought, because most women would have gone off with their lover or would have entered into a new liaison rather than consenting to a life like that! "Wait," he suddenly said, without even being aware that that he spoke out loud, thinking now of the chatterbox who had just left them, "I should have asked him when they'll come back from the country."

"I'll find out from the concierge if you want," Cyprien suggested in a low voice.

André blushed and shut his mouth.

Moved, the painter looked at him, following the trail of these griefs. His thoughts followed his friend's train of thought, step by step, and if they briefly lost sight of it, they invariably caught up with it again at a turning in the route. He sought for ways of distracting his friend and planned an energetic application of moxibustions,[38] of getting him drunk. Seeing a woman seated in front of their table, the idea of launching her on his friend suggested itself. "If he can go with her this evening," he reckoned, "he'll be saved. Of course it'll be a sour awakening, but at least he'll have avoided something worse, going back home alone this evening." And, preparing to make an overture, Cyprien let his cigarette papers fall under the table and apologized to the woman, who graciously moved her feet aside under the bench so he could retrieve his leaves.

He picked them up wet with the saliva that soaked the floor. The woman gave a moue of disgust, to which Cyprien responded with a friendly smile, carefully separating out the leaves that were still dry. A conversation got under way. Cyprien included André who was busy examining the face of the woman, her veil lifted to take a sip of beer.

She was a fine-looking female of about thirty. Her flesh seemed firm and her slightly tired face, white as a turnip with cheekbones tinged with purple, was as though febrile, with two big, pale blue eyes, refracting to sea-green in places, the eyes of a bold jade thought the painter, who had known women like that. She vaguely possessed the voice of a well-bred woman, talked with a certain glib turn of phrase, her dress was simple, but came from a first-class dressmaker, her fine jewelry gave the painter food for thought in guessing what price she might be worth.

André found her charming. On emerging from his reflections and unhappiness, he saw in her a caring womanliness eased by a semblance of education and decorum. Cyprien excused himself, pretending to go for a newspaper and, on returning, refused to resume his place, pushing André closer to the woman. He gave a fresh impetus to the conversation, which was slowing to a halt, and prompted André to let loose with the mediocre banter that never fails to amuse women.

She laughed, replied to him with little taps of her fan on his fingers, showing her arm, which was white and a little plump, chattering about some or other things like a good housewife, not set on taking the initiative, with the air of a woman who had come into the café by chance rather than from need or to pursue her profession.

André sustained a seamless stream of gallantries. His tongue acted of its own accord, his mind acted in another sphere. A wish to possess that woman, a need to escape his solitude, to break at all costs with the dazed monotony of his life, the hope of having a mistress who would lull his greed for tenderness, not least the thirst of his lips for female flesh. His abstinence melted away, a murmur grew in him, then distrust, good sense gained the upper hand, he was suspicious of the usual strings attached, the predictable languor. He remained sunk in his reveries, without even realizing that his tongue had ground to a halt, that he was no longer talking.

Cyprien then assumed the role of those fellow weavers who, picking up the thread dropped by their friend, knot it off. He carried on André's interrupted phrases, rounding them out.

The woman was astonished by the young man's silence.

"Have you got something on your mind, then?" she asked him, smiling.

He woke up, and, somewhat at a loss, looked at the sea-blue silk stockings shining under her raised dress. He complimented the woman on her small foot, repeated the vulgarities that this topic usually inspire; she laughed like a woman used to showing her ivories as soon as the favors of her person were praised. A flower seller approached them just then, but the woman refused the rose that

André offered her; she also refused any further drinks. On the insistence of the two young men, however, she accepted cherries soaked in brandy, and she swallowed them gracefully, twisting the stalk between her fingers, fooling about with her tongue which wriggled between the white rows of teeth, nibbling the cherry, spitting the stone into her hand, whose rings flashed.

André asked her name and the street where she lived; she said she was called Blanche and lived on rue de la Bruyère.

"That's some distance," he said, for the sake of saying something.

"So you don't live in this neighborhood?" she replied.

He pointed out his street.

"Ah yes, rue Cambacérès." She knew it. "Near the Madeleine, isn't it?" One of her friends once upon a time … and she spun a story in which, little by little, the friend in question figured as a woman who had taken advantage of her to cover her with filth.

Cyprien yawned. André listened, greatly seduced by tricks played by a cute mole, the color of cork, on her upper lip.

At length they exited the café.

"Well then, I'll leave you now," Cyprien said after André had hesitantly offered his arm to the woman.

"Won't you keep us company as far as the end of the road," André protested.

"No, no." And the painter said good night to the woman and ran for an omnibus. He got on it and climbed to the upper deck. The coach banged his spine against the bar of the backrest in time with its jolting, rolling along the cobblestones with a terrible din of metal and a hail of shaken windowpanes, diminishing, almost dying out as soon as the carriage met with asphalt.

He dozed, a cigar stub clenched in his mouth. The conductor who, leaning on the upper rail, cried "Fares please," jerked him abruptly from his nap. He handed over his three sous and, uncomfortable, chilled by the wind, turning up the collar of his overcoat, gazed in fright at the streets in flight behind him. Midnight chimed; the windows of the houses, where a sudden tilt scraped the wheels against the sidewalk, were almost all black.

In the upper areas, however, near roofs where feeble lights glanced off gutters, big squares of light blazed in somber facades. Sometimes the two lattice windows of the same room, unequally lit, flashed past, followed by closed shutters, sketching alternating rows of light and shadow.[39] And still others, large or narrow, higher or lower, flew past at a gallop, the latter all a-shimmer, lending the color of their light to the closed curtains, these almost black, pricked only by a candle almost level with the railings, by a yellow star, its meager rays dissipating in the dark of the room.

Melancholically, Cyprien surrendered to contemplation, arranging peaceful lives wallowing cozily under quilts in gaily lamplit rooms with closed doors, bourgeois couples sleeping, bottom to bottom, little puffs of air snorting from their lips, wheezing through their noses under the blankets, then, before the room's shadows, he imagined the disarray of people not yet returned home, lingering in taverns, prolonging the evening only to delay for as long as possible their solitude in impoverished rooms.

"Enough of that," he suddenly declared, returned to the thought of his friend going with a woman by the sight of an open first-floor window furnished with a stitched muslin curtain behind which the globe of a lamp could be seen, and a bit of an old, fat face soliciting from the window;[40] "Now's the time when André enters a completely unfamiliar room. The woman takes off her coat and says, 'Make yourself at home, darling.' I can see the scene from here—Blanche kissing her cat or dog to show she has a heart. André half undressed, leaning on the console table between two windows, contemplating the unwrapping of skirts and corset and seeing that he's been taken for a ride. Blanche coming over to him in her chemise, taking him in her arms, head slightly tilted back, eyes half-closed, lips pouting, murmuring in a fluty voice 'You're going to make me rich, aren't you, my little man?'—and I can see Andre's nose just as clearly from here, and hear his wary reply, 'Well, that depends!'"

Cyprien's monologue continued while he got off the omnibus: "And yet I shouldn't be making fun of him. If I'd received the money for my flyer maybe I'd have bought a few sedative hours for myself. No matter," he thought after a moment of mental silence. "What luck! I'm going to go to bed alone to sleep in peace," and without conviction he heaped praise on his hearth and home, the pleasures of a bed in which one can stretch out comfortably, and yet, troubled, he felt threatened by the onset of the fever that he'd thought he'd finally vanquished in all the years that, disdainfully, he'd lived in unconditional solitude.

VIII

In the morning, André, legs weak, head empty, eyes tired, made his way down to the street. He strode down rue de La Bruyère, in a hurry to put that woman's apartment behind him but not knowing why. He slowed down as soon as he'd turned the street corner. There, in a shop mirror, he saw himself, pale and drawn. He brushed his hat with his jacket sleeve, retied the knot of his cravat, and blushed at the idea that anyone might guess the bleariness of a night without sleep from his unpolished shoes, his creased shirt, his pallor.

The idle neighborhoods through which he passed were hardly awake. On his way, he met only policemen, deliverymen with bundles of newspapers, dairywomen. Here and there, tired people like him were going back home, bruised eyelids blinking in gaunt faces. They looked at each other as they passed, no doubt brooding over identical thoughts. Sometimes, more dignified individuals paraded in their costumes, black suits, white cravats visible above overcoats with collar turned up, the worldly excuse for their tiredness.

André's dry mouth tasted sour. It seemed to him that he'd been sucking copper; he tried smoking a cigarette to combat that horrible taste, but it left his tongue still thicker and tore his lips where the paper adhered.

Just then he exited rue Blanche, which was sad-looking at any time of day. He hurried to reach the entrance to the gare

Saint-Lazare to find an open café and get served something warm, and as he made his way there the alcoholic grogginess, the exhausted prostitutes from the Bréda district, yielded to an increasing activity, a feverish coming and going, an uninterrupted bustle of commercial interests on the lookout for the arrival and departure of trains, always on the move, speculating on the throng of passengers, in expectation of trolleys full of luggage and engines whistling.

He went into a café under the railway arcades. At that hour the waiters were dusting down the seating, sweeping under tables with a broom, while others, already neatly uniformed, tore the wraparound bands from newspapers and arranged glasses. André ordered a mazagran, took a magazine sleeved in black cloth boards, but the printed letters fluttered before his eyes and scattered in disarray. An extreme lassitude overtook him on his bench. He tried to shake off the lethargy that was engulfing him now that he was no longer walking, forced himself to stare at a pair of travelers busy buckling a belt round a plaid cloth with black and green squares that served as wrapping for a bundle of coats and shawls, umbrellas, canes with handles and ferrules protruding. Exhausted though he was, he smiled, noticing that the waiter, as usual, brought the change back to whichever of the two travelers hadn't paid him.

Nevertheless, he was starting to see more clearly. Shafts of sunlight that shone through the display window cheered him, lighting up the red underside of the copper letters embossed in reverse on the window glass in the café interior. He amused himself by deciphering "breakfast *à la fourchette*,"[41] composed in a curve on the pane, then, stimulated by a mouthful of black brew, he congratulated himself on the previous night's godsend. He'd really struck it lucky. Instead of the intolerable parasite that he'd feared from his experience of Parisian amours, he'd chanced upon a nice girl, friendly, not given to quibbling, trusting in the good faith of her clientele. He'd been no less charmed from yet another point of view. Instead of the shopkeeper wanting to avoid damage to her wares, allowing the slightest of her playthings to be handled only with an ill grace at best, he'd found a retailer offering herself for trial, happy to grant buyers the same pleasure that she took in selling.

The tedium of going to bed in a room that wasn't his own, the difficulty of not feeling regret for what, it can be argued, is the only complete happiness to be found in this world, namely to feel warm in one's own bed, free to smoke, read a book, with no kind of inconvenience, without being required to listen and reply—there had been none of that.

In short, there had been no deceit. Just naughty enough and not prudish, no visible bad faith in her effusions, with a restorative good humor in her caresses, the woman had delighted André.

They had awoken in the morning, and the embarrassment of two people who, scarcely knowing each other, find themselves with swollen eyes, stale breath, legs entangled, had been dispelled by Blanche who gently wound her arms round André's body. They had kissed, and then the young man had leaped out of bed, begging her to not to inconvenience herself, as she proposed, by getting up to show him where the bathroom paraphernalia could be found.

Once in the small room where a marble-plated washbasin took pride of place under a shelf full of petite ladies' boots, amidst a jumble of camisoles and skirts, André, face in the basin, making like a dolphin with his nose, had continued to exchange endearments with Blanche, who shouted from the bed, "You know the facecloth, it's the first on the left, on the dryer."

"Near the chamber pot, yes?"

"Yes darling. Have you got the soap?"

"Yes, yes, don't worry," and in a trickling of water, a sound of washing, affectionate messages were passed back and forth without pause from one room to the other.

Once dressed and back in the bedroom, they had parted as very good friends. She hadn't asked for any money and he had delicately left a twenty-franc coin not too conspicuously on the mantelpiece. Blanche's eyes opened and her ears pricked up at that moment, but she promptly turned over, plunging her nose under the blankets.

André smiled jubilantly, telling himself that he'd finally found the remedy for future petticoat crises, the poultice for his heart that he'd sought in vain for months. All very well for Cyprien to say that all women are modeled on the same pattern, that differences of caste are determined by more or less luxurious lingerie and stockings, and by words and deeds that are more or less hypocritical, all so much hogwash! Then again, while it might be amusing to mock women, one can't do without them . . .

Only one thing puzzled him: knowing to which class of coquette Blanche belonged.

She didn't ask for payment in advance so she clearly didn't belong to the class of sidewalk stalkers who ensnare passersby at random with their eyes. The same consideration banished the idea of a man behind the curtains waiting to pounce, or in a kitchen, waiting for the money exacted so he could go on a spree, and then too her lodgings were good, comfortable, with imitation Boule furniture,[42] a big bed taking up the length of the bedroom, high at the bedhead and low at its foot, without a metal or wooden headboard, upholstered in cretonne similar to what was on the walls, with vast lace pillows and embroidered monograms. The living room boasted a pedestal table and a rosewood piano, and in the dining room, an entire service of Baccarat glassware[43] and English china with blue flowers baked in the white porcelain, under glass in a substantial walnut sideboard with black trim.

From another angle, it was unlikely that she was kept by one man only and, simply from womanly sentiment, had a lover who from to time offered her a jewel or a gown; otherwise André probably wouldn't have been able to take her on the first night without meeting resistance. Besides, her lodgings didn't indicate the presence of a gentleman lover who, paying the rent, thought himself almost at home, owning a pair of pumps or slippers in the nightstand, on the shelf below the pot.

André finally settled on the supposition that Blanche belonged to a particular brigade, probably a member of the regiment of women whose task, both moral and lucrative, consisted of gladdening the hearts of married men and sending them back to their families feeling more soothed and less stressed. By certain signs he thought he'd recognized the distinctive character of this genre of women; a good-natured, gracious voluptuary, destined to stand apart from the sour and tedious home-loving hausfrau, and, with that, a certain attitude, a simulacrum of decorum, useful for not creating an overly abrupt transition between the legal wife and the loose woman, the dream of married men without their perhaps being aware of it, no less immoral than the mistresses they'd known in their youth, before marriage, but with better taste.

That must be it, he murmured, calling the waiter; feeling delighted, he paid for his mazagran, and, lighting a cigarette, made his way homeward.

The closer he came, the more his fear of what people would say grew. Since taking up residence he'd never once stayed out all night. This escapade would be all too evident to the concierge, would renew the malicious gossip of the lodge, and then there was Mélanie who at this moment would no doubt be looking worriedly at the bed—wasn't she going to imagine an accident? She was capable, in her anxiety, of conferring with the doorman and both of them drowning their old rows in inexhaustible tittle-tattle on his account.

He stopped on the sidewalk, hesitant, almost ashamed, feeling himself not young enough for these goings-on.

He finally decided not to return immediately. That would be better, he thought, "I'll be able to better give the appearance of a man who has risen very early and gone to the public baths."

Then he was ashamed of his cowardice, sought for excuses that would justify himself in his own eyes, the need for a walk. He thought of going to see Cyprien, but told himself that would delay him too much, that Mélanie, maybe still uncertain, would be bound to make a scene in the house, and he sauntered on, nose held high, hands in pockets, trying to take an interest in not much at all.

Then a remarkable phenomenon occurred, as though to justify his feeble reasoning. Little by little, his brain fog disappeared, thoughts about Blanche and his housemaid were abandoned, and suddenly his organism felt curiously clarified. His nerves vibrated at a higher pitch, and he was struck by a thousand details never previously noticed although he saw them daily. At a stroke he discovered his neighborhood.

Looking at the streets from top to bottom, correlating thoughts that had perhaps already come to him at random, he suddenly became aware that his neighborhood was, for the most part, inhabited by old solicitors, by what was left of the old Orleanist nobility,[44] by old dignitaries of the Second Empire,[45] by lawyers from the appellate court, by auditors from the Council of State, claims advisers at the Revenue Court. That explains, he thought, the unhappy and fretful air of people perched on stilts meditating on solemn bunkum, passing by with the pinched look of old judges, sober and stiff; the very stones seemed bored, impregnated as they were with all the pedantry emitted by those people!

"There it is then, the general coloration, the milieu,"[46] he continued, trawling through rue de Roquépine, rue d'Aguesseau, rue de la Vieille Éveque, rue des Sussaies, and rue d'Astorg. "Let's see, let's put our ideas into some kind of order; this district is a complicated one, but I'll untangle it. It derives its individual stamp from two distinctly different elements, and yet one dependent on the other. All the cheerful unscrupulousness of the servant class is thrown into relief against the backdrop of sad and banal affluence.

"Ah, that's the true note," he murmured, enchanted by his observations, "the exact note, with its garish embellishments of boozing and funny business overlaying the gray and starchy theme. The life of these sidewalks, hardly trodden by rich folk, is appropriated in its entirety by their menials; they alone fill the pavement, breathe life into the bars that have been opened specially for them, English shops with Stilton cheese, celery, bottles of pale ale and stout. Besides these bars, the only enterprises that can thrive in this district are those of saddlers and coachbuilders. Let's check them off from memory," he continued, counting on his fingers: "As adding to the note of dryness and boredom, to the predominant perfume of the stable and horse dung, check, a riding school, a seed merchant, a farrier, a veterinary surgeon, a shop for farm animal feed, two or three dealers in secondhand clothes and trinkets for chambermaids, a tack shop, a grocery store selling preserves and sauces from London, and finally, completing this forced and ill-assorted hotchpotch, perfecting the ensemble, further darkening the sad color but without being able smother its lowlife geniality, there are Protestant bookshops, societies for Lutheran propaganda, Bible agencies, and finally, three churches for reformed religions, including a Methodist chapel and an English church, flooding the scene with gloom, further supplemented by puritan rigidity, English frigidity.

"That's it exactly," he continued, "that's what it is—there's nothing like continually living in a street for knowing it; in the end it makes you farsighted, for," he continued, pushing his analysis of the neighborhood to its conclusion, "there's no denying the absolutely original, absolutely unique character of this district, inasmuch as it differs from the one that it most resembles, the faubourg Saint-Germain. Just like this one, it too boasts evangelical chapels, and it has its lords and its lackeys, yes, but the noble faubourg doesn't smell of clergymen and coachmen the way this one does. The grooms aren't the same, that's all. Those of rue de Grenelle and rue de Varenne perfume their soil, they fill Belleville and the Grand Duchy of Luxembourg with fragrance; those of the Anjou-Saint-Honoré district exude the smell of the Thames. That explains the principal difference between types, shops, streets. No pubs hung with pleated plaid but good wine merchants with red grilles, no old gin and whisky, but spicy wine and *trois-six*.[47]

"A small volume could be written about each of Paris's arrondissements from this point of view, a guide for artists and the cultivated;[48] I must talk to Cyprien about it, but, good lord, it's nine o'clock," he soliloquized listening to a clock chiming the hour. "Time to go back home," and without further loitering in front of shops that he didn't even bother to inspect, absorbed as he was by his meditations, he made his way to his lodgings.

He adopted a casual expression, making his boots ring as he crossed the yard, braved the astonished look of the concierge leaning on his broom, climbed the stairs, found Mélanie busy shaking out the carpet on the balcony. She turned round at the sound of the key in the lock, gave her employer an eloquent stare, then, little by little her owl eyes shifted and her lips opened.

"A package hasn't been delivered for me, has it?" André rapped out, wanting to stifle any questions she was about to ask.

"No," she replied, her wide-open eyes fixed on him, then her Auvergnat tenacity overcame her fear of displeasing and, folding the worn overcoat on the back of a chair, she said: "Monsieur is looking tired, should I pull back the covers?"

She was disconcerted by a sharp "No" flung from the bathroom where André was brushing his teeth. She pocketed her curiosity, reserving its satisfaction for a more opportune moment.

When she served breakfast, André buried his nose in a book. She brought the dishes silently, furious at being kept at a distance, considering her employer's muteness a personal affront. She wanted, however, to unlock his tongue and when she brought the coffee she enquired if Monsieur had time for the accounts.

He would readily have sent her to the devil. Nevertheless, he raised his eyes from his volume, saw her standing straight before him, her hand holding a classroom exercise book with a purple and black marbled cover, bulged out in the middle by a white pencil placed at an angle, one of those penny pencils sharpened with a table knife whose lead breaks under the least pressure and makes no mark even when licked.

He held out his hand, took the notebook, and, grumbling, laboriously totted up the numbers.

"I don't think this bill is included," the housemaid interrupted, shoving a receipt for meat under his nose.

He muttered, losing the thread of his count. He had to abandon it, leaf through the pages, check back through the items already entered, search among bizarrely spelled words that zigzagged one under another to see if the beef figured in the expenditure; it was there.

"Of course it's included!" he cried, annoyed.

"Oh well," Mélanie replied very calmly, brushing away a sprig of vegetable stuck to her bodice, "I thought that my husband had forgotten it."

He didn't reply, resumed his calculations, worked out the sum spent against the sum received. "You should still have three francs and fifteen centimes," he said.

"Monsieur is absolutely right," Mélanie proclaimed. "See, I took the money from my home," and pulling a long, greasy purse, she touched each of the coins and each of the sous it contained and gazed vacantly at the furniture. "I'm short of three sous," she murmured. "Is Monsieur really sure of not being mistaken?"

Harassed, he recommenced the addition for the third time, swallowing occasional mouthfuls of rapidly cooling coffee. He didn't arrive at the same result, lost his temper, rechecked the figures, this time taking them from the foot of each page. "You should have three francs twenty centimes left over," he said.

Mélanie uttered the cries of a fishwife.[49] Then she would be short of four sous! That wasn't possible.

"What the hell," André growled striking the exercise book angrily with the pencil, pitting the paper with blows from its point. "The accounts are there. Take it, there's your book, your husband will confirm it if he sees fit. As for me, I've had enough for today," and he flung his napkin on the table and disappeared into his little drawing room, slamming the door.

It was a bad day. André realized that his bad temper was stupid, then the moment of digestion arrived and a terrible heaviness, weighing on the wrecked machine of fatigue, made him doze off in his armchair. He felt shivers down his back while his temples and the palms of his hand felt hot. The coppery taste in his mouth was succeeded by a still fouler taste, that of a burned match, that of sulfate and soda; to get rid of it he drank a big glass of water that froze him, and, ill at ease, shivering, he walked up and down, looking at his bed, not lying down out of shame at vindicating his housemaid.

The other times when he came back from Blanche he managed things better. He hardened himself against the alarmed or mocking looks of the building and let Mélanie talk as much as she wanted.

"Ah well, since Monsieur's wife is still ill, Monsieur might as well see someone else!" And, very titillated by the idea that her employer, whom she imagined was demanding, would seek out only chic women, she tried to get information from him, and at home, joining her husband in bed at night, she recounted at length the scraps of information she'd manage to collect while he smiled and twisted his goatee, thinking of the more or less pretty whores he'd had the good fortune to arrest in his capacity as policeman.

André was frugal with information when Cyprien quizzed him on the events of his nights.

To the painter's malicious insinuations, describing the inconsistent lures of the woman as though he had tasted them himself, he merely replied that he was wrong, that Blanche was hardly mutton dressed as lamb.

"Ah, well then, you've been cheated," Cyprien riposted, "because you thought the goods you bought were past their sell-by date and you've gotten stuff that wasn't! In your shoes I'd ask for a refund!"

André decided to break off the conversation every time that Cyprien brought it round to Blanche. He was afraid of seeing the painter demolish the woman's surface attractions. He now visited her at fixed times, to be sure of meeting her alone, and he exulted when, knocking on her door, he heard the tip-tap of her slipper heels and saw her, dressed in clean lingerie, smiling in the shadow of the hallway.

The welcome was always the same, feminine and juvenile, a kiss on the mustache, his head taken between her two hands and gently cradled, then, holding each other by the waist, they both retired to the bedroom, and there, she quickly removed his hat and overcoat, offered refreshments, and, as soon as he was sitting down, jumped on his knees, asking him if he'd been a good boy, affectionately calling him a rogue, repeating, "Are you sure you aren't thirsty? You know you mustn't stand on ceremony, there's brandy and wine here."

More than once he asked about what kind of life she was leading; she told him about trivial doings and lied ineptly; finally one day she talked about a very gentlemanly individual whom she praised at length.

André inwardly reproached her for this tactlessness for which, however, he was responsible. He decided to stop questioning her, but in spite of himself broached the topic several times. Then Blanche cut her replies short and confirmed him in his idea that every afternoon she received men who had to be at home in the evening, and he was annoyed that she might be entertaining a series of men! He felt some resentment, thinking it natural for her to have one serious lover, but not two, three, four: she seemed to him too much of a whore.

He questioned his own motives and felt chastened, wondering sadly what had become of the hard lessons learned from his old amours. He was just as stupid as before! He had, with exceptional luck, found the woman he had long desired, and instead of remaining in intelligent uncertainty, and influenced by a silly feeling of amour propre, of jealousy, of God know what, he was about to pry into her business, to expose himself to uncomfortable truths or flagrant lies.

And yet he wasn't in love with Blanche! And he was afraid of examining his emotional malaise too closely, of ending up with a pathetic diagnosis; the fear of not being her preferred suitor. Given two lovers, that was something he could still believe, being the one who didn't support her financially. Given three or four, that childish illusion disappeared.

He remained worried, analyzing how stupid his thoughts were where she was concerned; and sometimes Blanche questioned him, uneasily, thinking that he was possibly in trouble, and to soothe his worries she sat at the piano and banged out waltzes, badly. "I'm making progress, aren't I?" she said.

He replied "yes" out of politeness.

"See, I'm taking three lessons a week. Really, it would be too bad if I applied myself and didn't get any further forward!"

André nodded his head.

"What's more I have a very capable tutor. One can learn from her lessons, it's not like with my French teacher; one day, would you believe, she looked up a word in the dictionary? Hey, I could do the same thing for heaven's sake! Of course, you know, I thanked her."

Evenings with Blanche followed on, each gloomier than the last. André started to see her as somewhat lacking in character, notwithstanding her brutal enthusiasms and her combativeness in bed, then the overnight trysts worsened for him. Two out of three times he came back feeling ill, head on fire, heart in a stir, and he had to stretch out on his bed, rub opium onto his temples to deaden his pains, try to sleep.

Then the inconvenience of nights spent away from home made themselves felt; the ennui of awakening in an airless room, muggy and reeking of musk, the impossibility of performing his morning wash in a toilet full of clothes that got splashed, the necessity of going to fill the jug almost emptied by demands of the night, the lack of hairbrushes, toothbrushes, and slippers. The disgust of picking up a brush bristling with hair, and digging out the facecloth, smeared with cold cream, from where it was buried in a pile of underwear near old hair tonics, was repugnant to him. He swore to stop spending nights away and adopted a different system. He ate supper with Blanche and came back home toward 11:00 p.m. This procedure seemed satisfactory to him at first, then he decided it was costly because he left ten francs over and above a gold louis to pay for the meal. His means being insufficient to support such expenditure, he visited less frequently.

A cooling of relations resulted. The slender threads tying him to Blanche steadily loosened. He saw that she lived some distance away and neglected her more often. On her side she counted him among her unreliable clients, no longer made an effort and wasn't at home on number of occasions when he visited.

These absences dealt the finishing blow. On those evenings he had dismissed his housemaid and came back down from the woman's lodgings feeling at a loss; he roamed the street, needing to kill an hour by walking around before going to throw himself down in the corner of a restaurant. The melancholy of those meals disgusted him still more than the capacity for surprise that wasn't to be found chez Blanche.

As ever, Mélanie made matters worse, expressing astonishment that Monsieur didn't spend nights away or dine in town. "Well now," she said amiably, "I see that Monsieur likes change." And by way of boasting, by wanting to demonstrate a strength of character he'd never possessed, he replied casually: "Well, it's been going on for too long, I'm finished with her."

Mélanie who feared the arrival of a mistress no less than the return of the legal spouse to a household that she managed in her own best interests, went on at length on the vices of those "creechers" as she called them, irritated her employer so much with the tall tales she told about the fancy women of the officers who lived in her street in the Gros-Caillou, that André, annoyed, begged her to go to the kitchen and keep an eye on the stew.

Incapable of realizing that she was able to try the patience of a saint, Mélanie concluded that the unpleasantness of the breakup was responsible for her employer's fits of temper. She also guessed, with the instinct of a woman accustomed to giving orders to her husband, that André wasn't able to keep a woman under his thumb. So she adopted an air of concern and discretion, sure in her own mind that, in the end, it was André who had been dropped.

All this fuss and bother, all this monkey business to which other people would hardly have paid much attention, made André want to weep. Naturally thin-skinned, he had been hypersensitive ever since the misfortune that had overtaken his menage. Little by little, however, a spell of greater calm arrived. What had seemed to him a sovereign remedy for short-circuiting the petticoat crisis, the once-a-week woman who isn't a mistress and who is already more than a casual pickup, acted efficaciously, but with results different from those he had foreseen.

The cure took effect not through the action of the remedy itself, but through the revulsion caused by taking it. Tired of feminine stupidity, André was cured of the female. He slipped into serene apathy, a growing need to remain unmoving in one place, a kind of Flemish bliss, comfortably seated, happy with just a well-filled belly and toes kept warm. No more rambling abroad, mourning over the images of mistresses, dissatisfaction with work and solitude. He had returned to that state of mind he'd enjoyed after taking up residence in his new lodgings. Once more, he found himself perfectly content.

IX

Two months later, over breakfast, André finished spreading his bread with redcurrant jam bought from a grocer; the jelly trickled over the crust in sticky red teardrops. André rang the bell and when the housemaid brought his coffee, he begged that from now on, when she planned to buy jams, she should choose cherry, plum, apricot, pear, whatever she wanted, with the exception of redcurrant and candied fruit that he suspected were old leftovers of New Year's Day sieves disguised as jams of the Midi, in sugared syrup.

Mélanie got ready to fire off some judicious views on swindling grocers when the doorbell rang. She scuttled to the door, opening it to a delivery boy with a letter.

The maid went back to her kitchen. André unsealed the envelope and, suddenly turning very pale, he read these lines from a friend he hadn't seen since his marriage.

"Émilie, my ex-mistress, has written to me to obtain your address for Jeanne, your former lady friend, who would like to see you again. May I give it to her? Please reply immediately to the bearer of this letter."

André hesitated, stunned. A whole flock of amorous memories flew up from the paper. The only mistress he had ever cared about wanted to see him again! In a momentary flash he saw her throwing herself into his arms, clinging to him, kissing his eyelids and neck. He was filled with a mad desire to renew ties with her.

He was ready to reply yes, but stopped, troubled. How stupid was he? What! Here he was, cozy in his nest, and he was going to lose the benefits of his hard-won tranquility! He was going to yield to the expectations of women, to pose! Ah, no, really! That game was all very well at twenty! No need to hesitate, he made up his mind to answer no, but all the happiness he'd previously tasted with Jeanne, all his youth, happy for a moment, came alive, invaded all his thoughts, submerging his instinctive caution and fear. He dashed down a yes on the paper. The delivery boy made his departure and André was left quivering on his chair, immediately deploring his soft-heartedness and cowardice. He was about to write to tell his friend to treat his letter as not having arrived, then he was afraid of looking like an idiot. Little by little, by dint of thinking things through, he decided not to get back together with Jeanne. He jotted down a letter to this effect and had no sooner dropped it in the post than he regretted it. His friend informed him by return mail that it was too late, that his address had been sent. Then André felt a measure of relief. For better or worse the thing was done, now out of his hands. And then, after all, what did the return of Jeanne commit him to? Would a renewal of carnal relations necessarily result? "Ah yes," he exclaimed, "yes, no point in deluding myself, I'm done for if I see her again."

He forgot to drink the coffee brought to his room by Mélanie, astonished by her employer's state of agitation. "Ah, I was so calm," he muttered from time to time, "Good God, what a curse, being so spineless." Now he thought of nothing but Jeanne; she forced herself on him, never leaving him, when eating, in the street, in bed.

Nevertheless, he fought a final battle the following morning. Cooler, calmer, he had heroically decided against muddling up his life with a woman when the concierge showed him a letter.

That was the crowning blow; his courage deserted him. The writing, that he particularly recognized, unclear, scribbled, dancing madly, every letter hooked and tailed, demolished him. Badly shaken, he read:

Dear André

You must have heard my news from Monsieur Jules who received a letter from Émilie asking for your address. What am I thinking, you'll say, after a silence of five years, but better late than never and I'll prove it to you.

Do you remember a *Manon Lescaut* illustrated with plates. I've come across it again, in very poor condition; in spite of that, a doctor who collects books wanted me to give it to him. Seeing how keen on it he was, I felt guilty about giving it away, knowing that it's as important to you as to him, and above all it belongs to you.

I don't know if you'll think well of me, but as Monsieur Jules in writing to Émilie told her that you would be happy to see me again, *I dare to*; if it weren't for that you wouldn't have heard my news, but is it for me or for your book? Well, you can act as you see fit after such a long time; in spite of everything it would give me the greatest pleasure to see you again, but how? Here's how it is, I'm still working on rue du Quatre-Septembre, at the Maison Larmange which you're familiar with, and most days I leave work at 8 o'clock. If you can come one day or another this week, Thursday for example, I'll leave at 8 on the dot; or else write me if you aren't free;

come anyway, one day or another, we'll share our old memories.

While waiting let me kiss you like in the old days.

With all best wishes

Jeanne

If you can't come, write me care of Madame widow Laveau, 18, rue Sauval.

He immediately replied that he would go to rue du Quatre-Septembre, Thursday, at the specified time.

He was elated, altogether changed; the struggle had reached its conclusion, his indecision at an end. It was only on rereading the letter that he thought further about it: "Jeanne must have been sent packing by her lover, so she's short of money," was his first thought, "because the story of the book is nothing but an excuse, one that's all too transparent. But how the devil could Jules, whom I haven't seen for years, know that I'm living on rue Cambacérès? And then, who is this doctor, lover of old books, and this Widow Laveau who takes delivery of letters?"

Finally, he searched on his map of Paris for the location of rue Sauval of which even the name was unknown to him. He found that it was a kind of alley near the Grain Exchange. This gave him an excuse for a walk. He went for a stroll along this street, saw the correct address, an old building with windows veiled by poor quality curtains and a courtyard befouling the air with piss and chlorine. The look of the place gave him no idea of what the occupations of its inhabitants might be. It was sad and stinking, nothing more.

He went back home where Cyprien was waiting for him, seated in an armchair. Not without hesitation, he told him about his adventure. The painter listened, his cigarette glowing as he puffed on it, blowing the smoke from his nostrils, merely nodding his head.

His guesses were the same as André's. It was a return motivated by an urgent need for money. "Two things," he said. "One, either Jeanne is staying with the widow Laveau, and for want of being able to pay the rent for a room the widow has let her know, as a friend, that she'd be happy to see her pack her bags and clear out. Or else this widow is set on hanging onto her friend so she can tempt and exploit her clients. It's my honest opinion that they're crafty and poisonous harpies, both of them. Whatever the case, whether Jeanne fools around with Tom, Dick, or Harry, or whether her status is a nearly respectable one of dignified poverty, it'll add up to the same thing, you'll be royally fleeced."

"But," said André, annoyed by these assumptions that, coming from someone else's mouth, soiled the memory of his mistress, "you're building a case without a shred of evidence! You don't know any more about her than I do; besides, this Laveau woman to whom you're assigning a leading role that no doubt she doesn't play, there's nothing to prove that she isn't quite simply a workmate who, for a reason neither of us knows about, does nothing more than receive and pass on letters."

The tone of André's voice, piqued, almost aggressive, wounded Cyprien, who retorted in a dry voice, "When it comes to women, I always reach for the least favorable hypotheses; that way I'm sure of not getting fooled."

"Come on now," André responded, sounding increasingly resentful, "don't play the hard man, it doesn't suit you."

"The hard man," the painter cried, "God, but you're an idiot! When there's any risk of being within reach of women, all my boldness consists in avoiding them and fleeing the scene; something you well know. And on that note, good night; my advice is to haggle over the affection that's being sold back to you and check the scales to see where the weight lies!" And with that he made an exit, leaving André irritated with this fierce skepticism, seeing it as ridiculous because his friend applied it to matters that were intimately personal to him.

Thursday was a long day for André. It seemed to him that the time would never pass. Fearing that Cyprien might come, he ordered Mélanie to serve dinner earlier than usual and he got dressed in advance, thoroughly sprucing himself up, putting on his smartest clothes. He ate without appetite, went out and, as he still had several hours to kill, he strolled along, imagining the meeting of two lovers who hadn't seen each other in five years. He was afraid of finding Jeanne fleshy and gone to seed. What had become of her after this length of time? What tribulations, what highs and lows of destitution had she endured before coming back to him? Perhaps she was now ugly, skinny or disabled? In that case, he told himself, she certainly wouldn't have wanted to see him again. Ah, who knows. Maybe it was an act of desperation, a howl of dreadful impoverishment! And he already felt softhearted, prepared to make sacrifices because, at the moment, a resurgence of affection propelled him toward her.

He checked his watch, held it against his ear, thinking it had stopped working, but it was ticking steadily. The minutes seemed to him a slow drip, like hours; then he tried to imagine their tête-à-tête. "It's going to be hellishly embarrassing," he thought, and tried to find phrases that would rescue the situation but didn't find any.

Bored and exhilarated at the same time, he saw his reflection in shop windows and made sure that his collar and cravat were in order.

He was now patrolling the Palais-Royal; he lingered in the arcade where Chevet's was located,[50] a short arcade near the Théâtre-Français, which invariably combines the sweet perfumes of a flower market with the pestilential bouquet of a cesspit and, smiling, forgetting for a moment the length of his wait, he entertained this thought: that through the open basement window under the shop of a manufacturer of meerschaum pipes located opposite Chevet, in the same gallery, there arose, each time he passed through, a smell of shallots and onions roasting in hot vinegar in a frying pan. He dawdled, retracing his steps, inspecting the alluring window of a grocery shop with turtles sleeping under a flow of water in a basin, big smoked fish the color of strong gum, oranges wrapped in tissue paper like the orbs of breasts in a bodice, knuckles of ham, mortadella sausages, fattened chickens, and fruit of such size and excellence that they seemed handmade.

And, having reached the colonnaded square that serves as forecourt to the galérie d'Orléans, he took out his watch once more and stopped, enraptured, in front of that shop where the extraordinary muskets of the old guard, the improbable schapskas, the exorbitant kolbachs[51] of the soldiers of the First Empire lie at leisure, and his mocking thought was that it all stank of Laurent de l'Ardèche and Marco Saint-Hilaire, history written for Les Invalides that we forgot to put out of its misery![52]

Then, turning on his heels, entering the glass-windowed arcade, he wondered if he would be able to recognize Jeanne. The woman's image persistently misted over before him. Perhaps they had both changed to such an extent that they'd pass each other by without noticing; but that fear only held him for a moment, it wasn't possible that they wouldn't suddenly remember their features on seeing each other—and, sunk in thought, he didn't even inspect the long windows in front of which he stood, the windows of bookshops lit up like cafés where books with gaudy and meretricious covers were displayed, books that whored themselves in colored peignoirs for three francs and fifty centimes.[53]

The harsh lighting of this shop and the whole passageway irritated him. He ventured into the corridors that bounded the inner courtyard, but there too he found the glittering of jewelry under the gaslight wearying. People were transfixed in front of the jewelers' gold and the bureaux de change. He turned away from that crowd, left behind the manufacturers of mess tins and military insignia, all the retailers of honorific brassware, and going into the deserted, almost pitch-black garden, disgusted by the horror of the Parisian shop-ware he had seen brazenly glittering under the archways, he remembered that phrase coined by Cyprien one day when, fleeing from rain, they both wandered through the Palais-Royal: "It's a place with shops full of food that's never eaten and books that are never read, shops where gems for women and crosses for men, everything that provokes human nastiness, are displayed on velvet!"

And that bleak declaration returning his thoughts to Cyprien, André told himself that the painter would certainly laugh if he could see him wandering like this, counting the minutes to a tryst, in this place teeming with foreigners and prostitutes. He still bore a certain grudge against his friend; "he's an anemic hypochondriac," he said to himself, "I'm wrong to be annoyed with him." But this reasoning didn't pacify him. His disgruntlement flared up at the very memory of the unintended wound he'd received.

He took out his watch again. The time for the rendezvous was approaching. He exited the garden and headed into rue Vivienne.

"All the same, I'm lucky that it isn't raining," he muttered, looking up; it was only drizzling; the pavement was damp and greasy. He quickly reached the Bourse; he was only two steps away from rue du Quatre Septembre. He sat down on a bench, looking as though from an embankment at that ocean of Parisian thoroughfares where high-class carriages, business vehicles, and cabs for hire are incessantly churning. He remained there, contemplating the flow of passersby, walking, running, crossing each other's paths, exchanging a few words and going on their way again. People escaped from doorways onto the sidewalk, others went into shops to a tinkle of bells, still others spoke to concierges, or, with time on their hands, sat in cafés and quarreled with waiters, newspapers, and cards.

It was the time of day when the marketplace goes quiet and the pleasures of the evening are about to make an entry. The tremendous activity that moved around him, the ferocity of commercial power, embracing the whole of this district and spreading through the entire city, gradually died away; the pursuit of a living wage, the battles fought by retail stationed behind its shop fronts, these came to an end, and the Bourse, devoid of noise and clamor, slept silently in its bed of dark streets.

André realized with childish joy that his watch was five minutes slow; he adjusted it from the Bourse's illuminated clock dial. Hardly forty minutes now separated him from his rendezvous. He planned to be at his post sooner, knowing the habit of women, that they never show up at the agreed time, but either earlier or later.

He arrived at the door of the Larmange building, an open *porte cochère* showing the end of a peristyle and the steps of a flight of stairs, and he bought a newspaper from a neighboring kiosk so as to appear occupied, but the gas lamp against which he leaned gave off a dim light. His feet were cold and he walked slowly in front of the establishment, occasionally stopping in front of shop windows, surprised, contrary to expectations, not to see men loitering, biding their time.

Idly, he tried to interest himself in a dealer in hairpieces, a shop full of women's model heads, cheeks pink, eyes blue, lips red, adorned with every shade of hair, cinnamon, orange, salt and pepper, chestnut, studded with taffeta flowers, birds of paradise, ears of corn in silver or gold, and all those figurines were truncated at the bottom of busts emerging from a mirror as from groundwater, and to indicate the price of their head of hair, they bore cardboard labels stuck on the wax of the skull.

Behind the display window a shop assistant was smiling as she stared at him. He fled in embarrassment and continued walking back and forth, forfeiting his male status, acquiring that of a prostitute pounding her patch, observed from behind a clock-seller's merchandise by young women who whispered in each other's ears, with a burst of laughter, "Another no-hoper hanging about." He distanced himself, going as far as a shop specializing in Japonaiserie where he resumed his melancholy toing and froing on the sidewalk, soon driven away by a pair of eyes that laughed behind grotesque oriental figurines and cabinets of faux lacquer. Then he recrossed the street and stationed himself once more beside the gas lamp, standing near the door of the building where Jeanne worked.

A clock sounded a quarter to eight. Good lord but the time dragged itself out! Disappointed, he looked up, saw, stretching out as far as the eye could see, enormous gold letters, cyclopean inscriptions piercing the mist: "coats and gowns"; "ready-to-wear garments for ladies"; "bustles and petticoats"; "dresses and mantles." Everywhere nothing but adverts for women's clothing, running and winding the length of the facades, creeping above doors, clinging to balconies, terrace balusters, climbing up to the sixth floor, as far as the tops of roofs, and he remained there, eyeing the sky, contemplating that street that oozed wealth and bankruptcy. A street that survived from day to day, subject to the fads and fancies of a whole clientele of actresses and whores!

The cold that once more froze his legs roused him from his reverie and he checked his watch yet again. It was almost eight o'clock. He shivered and, his face somewhat concealed by his newspaper, he waited, wanting to be recognized first, eyes fixed impatiently on the door.

Soon two young women appeared, making off to the right at top speed, then two others who made off to the left at top speed, then a whole whirlwind blew onto the sidewalk, squealing, kissing each other on cheeks, and scattering in couples in all directions.

André edged forward, fearing that Jeanne had run away without his noticing. Perhaps she had already fled. At that thought, a terrible anxiety seized him. But worker girls were coming down, still spreading out. Suddenly Jeanne emerged, arm in arm with another woman. He took a step forward, she stopped, and, blushing, they took each other's hands, not daring to kiss in front of everyone, asking after each other, with tremors in their voices.

"How are you? Still well I hope."

"Yes, thank you, and you?"

"Yes, as you can see."

He offered her his arm. "Where will we go?" he asked.

"We'll go for a meal, it's just over there, not far."

They went into a side street on the right and climbed the stairs to a restaurant located on the second floor.

The room was empty. André hastened to relieve the women of their coats and sat down opposite them.

"Everybody's eaten already," Jeanne said, smiling, and told him that she came every day with the widow Laveau, here with them now, to eat in this same room.

André inspected her; she was the same as before, fresher, even more fleshed out. The little tip of the nose the same as ever, smiling under ringlets of light-colored hair in a pale complexion; those mobile eyes the same as ever, sparkling at the slightest word, that pretty figure, those delicate hands, the piquant allure of a Parisian woman, slightly "flash" as she used to say, talking about herself.

She was better turned out than formerly, clothed all in black, with a cameo medallion that he knew from back then, turquoise and pearl rings that he remembered, and earrings and good luck charms that he didn't remember seeing her wearing in the old days.

"You think I've changed," she said, unfolding her napkin.

"No, not at all; you're still the same!"

"Just like you. But you're even better; your short hair really suits you—you used to look poor with your long hair covering your ears."

They both started to laugh, and the widow Laveau politely imitated them.

The waiter reappeared.

While they scanned the menu, André cast a quick glance at the widow, whom he'd have liked to send home to bed. She bothered him, with her solemn face, her silent reserve, the thin thread of her laugh. He didn't like her but doubted that she was depraved. "Cyprien is absurd," he thought, and he contemplated the big woman with her broad, solid back but simple and meek air, imagining that her love affairs must be humble and robust ones that cost her dear.

"No soup then," the waiter said, bored by the two women's dithering.

"No, we'll have thrushes right away."

The waiter was surprised.

André thought that Jeanne wanted to show him that she ate well; in his turn, he ordered a mazagran.

The conversation resumed. André gazed tenderly at the little lady and, elbows on table, he said to her, "Ah! my poor Jeanne, it's been long enough since we last saw each other! I'm really pleased to see you again."

She smiled in return and declared herself happy to meet once more.

They remained silent for a minute, with more effusive, more urgent questions on the tips of their tongues, but the presence of a third party inhibited them.

The waiter brought the thrushes.

Their knives dealt carnage on the ripe carcasses of the birds. André retreated a little, for the aroma turned his stomach. The two women didn't have the courage to swallow the disgusting mess and they called for the waiter, who sang the praises of the very ripe game without being able to convince anyone and advised a thin cut of veal to the two women.[54] They accepted his advice; he disappeared like a puff of wind and returned almost immediately with a slice of soft, white meat. The widow exclaimed at the single piece lying on the plate, but Jeanne, slightly red in the face, said, "Bah! Let's eat, we'll see afterward."

The waiter smiled, still taken aback; André no longer doubted that the two friends were accustomed to sharing a single portion and he remained embarrassed by seeing them consuming such substantial and choice fare in his honor.

With that, he ardently longed for the end of the meal, hoping that the widow Laveau would leave so he could be alone with Jeanne. She must have had the same idea, because she hustled her friend to finish the meal more quickly.

The service unfortunately took its time and the heat of the room with its very low roof, with its half-moon windows, was overwhelming. André was stifling in his overcoat.

Jeanne suggested that he take it off.

"It isn't worth the effort," he replied, "since you're about to finish."

The conversation still dragged while they pecked at raisins and, disdaining nutcrackers like the majority of women, broke almonds and hazelnuts between their teeth; Jeanne explained to André while looking for philippines in their shells,[55] that it was a restaurant where all the shop girls dined, the ones who didn't eat at their workplace. She also mentioned certain dishes that were always reliably good and could be ordered with full confidence, for example rabbit sauté, calf brain au vin, and the widow Laveau, still silent, nodded in approval.

The *mendiants* were definitively consumed.[56] André took out his wallet and asked for the bill, but the two women were having none of it. He insisted, again unsuccessfully, and paid for his mazagran, feeling embarrassed by letting the women pay, in the presence of the waiter who, this time, looked at them with no trace of surprise.

They went back down; Jeanne took André's arm. At the street corner Madame Laveau declared that she had to go back home and, after having pecked Jeanne on the lips, she said goodbye to André and disappeared.

Now they were alone! Then both glanced at each other, and André squeezed the arm with linked with his.

"My little puppy," he murmured very softly, "the name I used to call you in the old days, eh? I'm really pleased to see you again—really pleased."

Fearing to fall back into the repetitions of the restaurant, he stopped, but Jeanne interrupted the banalities with a mad laugh.

"Guess what," she said, "I've forgotten your book."

He waved this away, indicating how unimportant the book was to him.

She spoke again: "Oh! I've got it at home. I'll bring it next time . . . if I see you again . . ." she added hesitantly.

"How do you mean, if you see me again?"

At last they touched on the goal around which they'd been circling for hours. Then Jeanne, chivied by André's questions, said that she was happy, that there was nothing she needed, and as for the rest, she'd been busy at work ever since their breakup.

"But have you got a boyfriend?" André asked, rather anxiously.

She admitted to having a boyfriend, but he wasn't in Paris, he was doing his voluntary service in a city in the East. "You know, he still sends me my money," she said.

André guessed that this gentleman was rather young, but he kept that thought to himself. He now called Cyprien's nonsense to mind. How wrong he was! She wasn't in need of money! He forgot that he himself had believed that Jeanne's reappearance was not unmotivated and imagined that his first suppositions were the same as those he now entertained; a reappearance prompted only by the desire to have a lover who would satisfy your carnal needs and then take you out and about.

While he muttered, looking down, Jeanne skipped along on his arm, showing a glint of teeth under her spotted veil, fluttering eyelids, sparkling eyes. She asked in turn what he had been doing for the last five years. "I was afraid of writing to you. Well, you see, you might be married, I wouldn't have wanted to cause you problems on my account. It's for that reason I got Émilie to write to M. Jules."

He then inquired about Émilie. What had become of her?

Nothing. She was living with one of the friends of Jeanne's lover.

"And M. Jules?" the little woman asked.

"Nothing either. I don't see much of him," André replied, embarrassed.

"Ah, I see, but wait a bit, where are you taking me?" she cried suddenly after a silence, stopping.

"Really, I've no idea . . ."

In fact they'd been wandering at random, venturing unheedingly into dark streets. The mist now fell more thickly, the pavement was slimy. Jeanne, who was teetering on high heels, now had to lean her whole weight on André's arm.

"I'm tiring you, aren't I?"

"You? Not a bit of it," and he tenderly pinched her arm.

André spoke again: "Hey, look, here we are on rue du Rivoli." Indeed they emerged from a black alleyway opposite rue de la Tacherie.

He suggested they go into a café so she could rest and drink something warm, and he looked around him, hoping to find a brasserie with not too many customers, without a racket of billiards and backgammon, and while still on the lookout, he took the street that ran alongside the Hôtel de Ville building site.[57] A sad-looking café was there, epitomizing all by itself the mortal tedium of provincial life. André slid a glance between two badly drawn curtains, but the fogged windows were streaming; he couldn't see anything; he listened and heard no noises; he thought that the café was empty, turned the handle of a small door and went inside.

Four individuals were drinking mazagrans around a table; the waiter drank another in a corner; and at the center of the bar a woman dozed in front of a cup. André was delighted with this peaceful locale and ordered two grogs.

"Let's see," he said to himself, "after all this, I still don't know what to make of Jeanne's intentions." He tried to open up a path for her, hoping she would take the initiative, but she talked about this and that, deciding to remain on the defensive, to let him make his move.

"Little vixen," he said to her while she crushed her slice of lemon with a spoon and fished out the pips that danced in the disturbed water, "do you remember the wonderful evenings we used to spend in my room?"

She nodded her head exuberantly and looked at him with slow, liquid eyes.

"Well," he asked, hesitantly and leaning toward her.

Jeanne, somewhat agitated, said nothing.

He took her hand under the table and murmured in a low voice, "Come now, what do you say . . ."

"It all depends," she said, "you know, you can't visit me in my rooms."

These words were a cold shower for André.

The idea of taking Jeanne home knocked him back. He saw an uproar in the bourgeois house where he lived, the concierge looking to pick a fight with the little lady, yelling at her to wipe her feet, asking her every time where she was going; Mélanie indignant, railing against Jeanne, grumbling, growling, refusing to acknowledge or serve her; in a flash he saw the tranquility of his domestic interior sailing away, replaced by a thorough hell of gossip and conflict.

"But it's the same for me; you can't me visit me either."

"Oh well then," Jeanne replied very firmly, "what's to be done? We'll stay as good friends. That's all it'll be."

He was stricken by the thought that he would now see Jeanne for the last time; losing his head, he proposed to rent a hotel room.

"Oh no, really!" the little lady cried, "I know you; you need your home comforts, you'd only come to a rendezvous very reluctantly, and me too! We'd get on each other's nerves; no, it's much better if we leave things as they are!" And she added, after a silence, "You aren't married, you live in your own place, and you can't take me there. Have you got another woman then?"

He swore by all the gods that he didn't.

"So, will I be compromising you?"

Once more he swore not.

"Well then, what's stopping you?"

He reeled off vague reasons; his apartment block was prudish, his concierge was unpleasant, it would be a whole song and dance if a woman came home with him. Sorry to say it wasn't like it used to be!

"Oh you, you haven't changed," she burst out, "you're always afraid of everything, you make monsters out of nothing at all; ah, if only I was a man!"

More and more embarrassed, he went red. "What's to be done?" he stammered, then had the clever notion of turning Jeanne's arguments back against her.

"But you," he resumed, "why can't I visit you since your boyfriend isn't in Paris?"

"Why? Because Émilie and her boyfriend are at my house all the time, because they keep an eye on me, and our doorwoman does too; because I have to watch my step with a crowd of people in our area!"

André was beaten. He held his tongue so as not to admit his defeat straightaway.

They left the café. The mist had lifted a little, but it was bitingly cold. Separated from them by a wall of palings smothered with posters, a monstrous network of planks and beams rose up all along the high carcass of the Hôtel de Ville under construction, climbing up the mist, rising like an open-air palace in the sky, more imposing, more superb, grander than the stone building previously destroyed. In his mind's eye André vaguely saw those terrible etchings by Piranesi wherein enormous monuments arose in a frightful chaos of scaffolding—then he smiled, seeing the moon moving there inside, as though imprisoned in an enormous cage, barred by formidable girders.

He showed the moon to Jeanne who looked up at it, then lowered her gaze without saying anything, and they walked on, silent and unhappy, him annoyed at being thwarted, she irritated by these arguments and constraints.

"Let's take that one," she said. "It's late and I have to get back."

"Don't you live on rue Sauval," he asked.

"No, it's Eugénie who lives there."

"Madame Laveau?"

She nodded a yes; and they remained silent for a long time.

Ashamed of renewing the proposal that he had first rejected, André bit his lips. "But I must make up my mind," he thought to himself; then he set aside his amour propre and declared that, after all, and taking into account certain precautions, he would be able to welcome her to his home, that if she wanted he would come and find her after tomorrow, on Saturday, at her workplace, that until then he would think about how best to introduce her to his lodgings without scandal and without causing a fuss.

Jeanne's face lit up: "You'll see how quickly I eat on Saturday, so I can finish sooner," she said, laughing.

They had reached rue Bonaparte where she lived. Jeanne thought that André was going to kiss her and furtively wiped her mouth, moist with her misted breath condensing under her veil; under the pretense of blowing his nose, he wiped his mustache too for the same reason. And then they kissed, but not well. Suddenly timid, André only kissed her on the cheek and forehead. "Kisses from nana and papa," he said apologetically, but she offered her lips boldly, to which he promptly glued his own, murmuring, "So, it's agreed, I'll wait for you in front of the door. Saturday at eight, yes?"

X

On Saturday morning André awoke with a start; in his still drifting consciousness the idea that he was going to see Jeanne immediately sprang to mind. Having gone to sleep thinking of her the previous evening, he awoke without his train of thought having been altered during the night. Sitting up, he pulled on a knitted, long-sleeved cardigan which he wore mornings and evenings for smoking and reading, rolled a cigarette and, arms upraised, hands clasped above his head, asked himself, "Should I warn Mélanie that the little lady will come this evening, or would it be better to say nothing?"

He was in no doubt that in either event his housemaid would pull a long face and pinch her nose, but his foresight went no further. How would she take the news? He was worried, afraid that she would play her trump card and dogmatically declare her firm resolve to wait on no one but her employer.

"In fact," his soliloquy continued, "I pay her for taking care of my bachelor quarters, and not for ministering to women. Logically speaking, she'd be well within her rights to refuse. For thirty-five francs I can't oblige her to divide her attentions and her scrubbing brushes between both Jeanne and me.

"After that, whether I give her advance warning or not, the situation remains the same; breakfast for two is on the cards, and boots polished into the bargain. Ah," he suddenly told himself, "but I'm being an idiot. Show me the bachelor who doesn't bring his mistress home without their housemaids having any say in the matter. Mélanie will do the same as they do. The thing to decide is whether it would be best to bowl her over her by letting her see a woman under the blankets and so prevent her from preparing her resistance while she's dumbfounded, which always lasts quite a long time with her, or whether it would be wiser to carefully sound her out and so give me time to plan defensive maneuvers for tomorrow, if, that is, she's really determined go on the warpath.

"That's certainly the best course," he thought. "Okay, I'll test the waters fairly soon, or rather, no, I'll announce the news to Mélanie straight off; the positive side of my first option, the hammerblow, will still make itself felt and at the same time, I'll get the advantage of the second option, the possibility of parrying the reply.

"Hang it! It's now or never," he muttered, already not quite so set on his plan, hearing the distant scrabble of the key in the lock.

He wreathed himself in smoke, puffing hastily on his cigarette. Mélanie bustled about in the kitchen, opened and closed doors, then came in holding a newspaper and letters, complaining about the chilly wind, tossing out stock phrases, stored for years in her brain and mechanically churned out with the advent of cold weather at the end of each autumn.

André tore off the newspaper wrap and, while the housemaid quit the room, he reflected again, wondering how he was going to tackle the issue.

Still far from decided, he pulled on his trousers, moved into the bathroom, pushed the communicating door and asked Mélanie to pour a little warm water into his tooth mug.

While she tilted her kettle whose lid, badly attached to its hinges, rattled above the thin stream of water singing in the spout, he said to her, “Oh, by the way, Mélanie, I believe that it’s market day today. See if you can buy something nice and not too expensive. I’ll have a guest for breakfast tomorrow.”

“Very good Monsieur. Would Monsieur like a piece of sirloin, or roast beef?”

“No, I’d like something lighter and more select, it’s for a woman.” And he added, looking her in the eye, “who’ll sleep here this evening.”

Mélanie didn’t even utter a cry; she remained frozen, arms quivering, mouth agape.

“That’s taken care of,” André said to himself, promptly exiting the kitchen.

The day slipped by peacefully. The housemaid prepared and served supper; André glanced at her on the sly and saw her beaten, almost defeated.

“What if I simply make kidneys in white wine,” she said with an effort.

“That’s fine,” André replied.

She twisted her wedding ring on her finger and added, “So Monsieur’s wife has recovered and she’s going to live with us?”

“No, not at all. It’s another woman who’s coming.”

“Ah!”

Mélanie’s astonishment increased, but she smiled nevertheless and went away relieved, preferring the arrival of whichever mistress to the return of the legitimate spouse.

Then André covered his log fire with cinders so that it would burn slowly until he returned, placed a full kettle between the andirons, closed the big curtains and headed out.

The position he took up before the door of Jeanne’s workplace was hardly different from the one that he had already endured.

Except that, ashamed, he stood in front of different shops, not those of the coiffeur and the dealer in Japonaiserie; lastly, to vary his sources of pleasure, he paced up and down the middle of the road then, chased off by vehicles, returned to the sidewalk, saw Jeanne, who came down ahead of the appointed time, preceded by her widow friend, and once more he escorted them to the restaurant. As on the previous evening, he drank a glass of coffee and, stifling under his overcoat, started to sketch a vague and basic map of the place where he lived on the white tablecloth marked with blue, using the burned end of a matchstick.

"So you can see," he said to Jeanne, "there's my house; here's the carriage entrance and an alley leading in a straight line to a big wall; buildings on each side of the alley; well, the start of my staircase is in the building on the right, just at this point where I'm pressing down the black; you only have to climb to the top floor. So, here's the plan of action; I'll go in first, you'll follow two minutes later, and I'll wait for you at the top of the stairs; have you got that?"

"Yes, I've got it, I take the one on the right and climb up to the very top."

"That's right."

"So, what if the concierge asks where I'm going?"

"Well," André replied, somewhat hesitantly, "well, you'll tell him that you have an urgent letter for me; wait, I'll make one up," and he procured a pen, sealed an empty envelope, wrote his name and address on it.

"And anyway," he concluded, cracking his finger joints, "I don't give a damn about the concierge!"

That belated assurance amused the little lady who had known for a long time just what to make of André's valor.

They exited the restaurant, said goodbye to the widow Laveau, and then, for the first time, André talked about Mélanie, saying that she was as silly as a goose and as mad as a hatter, but a fine woman all the same, emphasized that Jeanne mustn't worry about her sour looks if that was how she showed herself, finally declared, unconfidently, that he was absolutely sure that the two women would get on perfectly well with each other.

Very worried, Jeanne didn't breathe a word. She was more than a little afraid of this housemaid installed in the apartment; she dreaded snubs and freezing contempt.

Her anxiety grew when she learned that Mélanie was married.

Her irregular situation, in a domestic set-up that had taken shape months ago and had been running regularly ever since, scared her. It was clear to her that she could be no more than a late-coming outsider; that in this domestic machinery she would only be a spare wheel, added by chance or a whim, and which could shatter without in any way impairing the regular running of the machine. The impossibility of having her lover again and keeping him exclusively for herself dawned on her; she almost regretted the liaison that she'd wanted to renew.

"What's wrong?" André asked, surprised by her silence.

"Nothing really . . ." she said in a low voice.

Her fears continued to grow. The concierge, who had been of little concern to her until now, rose up before her, assuming formidable dimensions; she saw him alongside Mélanie in the courtyard, two angry mastiffs ready to snap at her legs.

She felt lost; however, the jarring perspective of her fears didn't persist. André caressed her hand and she leaned on him in hopes of support and affection, but although sure that she was exaggerating her dread, she couldn't dismiss the image of this Mélanie whom she saw as a great dragon, old and stiff, looking at her disdainfully in her capacity as married woman and retainer, mistress of a house, ruling over André's unreliable character.

She pressed herself still more closely against her lover, almost leaning her cheek on his shoulder, feeling the need to make herself small, promising herself to slip through the half-open door and offer humble greetings all round.

"Ah, it isn't like before," she sighed with a heavy heart.

"Yes it is, kitten, nothing is different," he said, feigning a confidence he didn't feel, for Jeanne's unhappy worries revived his own; "you'll see, it'll be fine; come now Madame, let Monsieur see a nice smile," he said, trying to distract her from her sad thoughts.

She gave a wan smile under her veil. André started to feel ill at ease. Fortunately, they had arrived at his street. He gave the envelope to Jeanne, went in quickly, climbed the five floors and, leaning on the banister, waited there.

A small sharp tap of footsteps soon sounded far away in the depths of the basement, on the lobby paving, then the noise, dulling almost immediately, mounted from the stairwell, coming closer, accompanied by a slight vibration of the banisters moving on their struts and a rustle of starched petticoats sweeping the stairs. André couldn't see anything; the gas lamps positioned below him, separated from each other by two floors, blinded him without illuminating the scene.

At length Jeanne emerged onto the landing of the fifth floor, stepped forward into the light, a little out of breath from having climbed the stairs so quickly. He gave a faint cough; she raised her eyes and they smiled without speaking; finally, she came right up to him; he took her by the waist and thrust her through his door, closing it immediately behind them. Then all his anxiety fell away; he was home and free.

"The concierge didn't bother you?" he asked, lighting a candle.

"He didn't see me, I sneaked past his lodge very quietly. He was reading a newspaper and didn't even turn his head."

"Good, everything's okay; take off your things," and he embraced her tenderly then poked the embers, which glowed red in the fireplace under the cinders; he piled on fresh logs, lowered the chimney damper, helped Jeanne out of her coat, went over to the armchair, but Jeanne refused to sit down, wanting to see the apartment first.

She looked around the little living room where they now were, recognized old curios, a print by Daullé after Teniers, an old engraving after Breughel the Elder, china plates, copper dishes.

"Why, you had that back in my day," she said. "You know, I often thought of you when I saw plates hung up in junk shops," and she added, her eyes dwelling on the Impressionist watercolors that she'd never seen before; "Well, here's something new, it's pretty, but why hasn't it been finished?—Oh!" she exclaimed suddenly, turning round, and, lifting the lamp, enveloped the chimney place in the circle of light cast down from the lampshade. "What's that?" And she gazed with a little horrified pout at an outlandish Japanese chimera armored with red and green scales, paw on a ball, tongue rolled up, plume-like tail, protruding eyes, projected as though on stalks.

"Good heavens, it's really ugly!" she exclaimed.

Then, still holding the lamp, she went, André following behind, into the bedroom separated from the little living room by a door; she looked all around; "Ah, now, that's nice!" she said and admired a Louis XVI rosewood bedside chiffonier table, going into raptures over the new marble, the newly attached gilt locks.

But what most astonished her was the bed; the old iron garret bed that she knew of old was no longer in evidence. André briefly explained to her, while pulling her close, that this was a lacquered whitewood bed in the style of Louis XV.

"Hey now, be a good boy," she said, tapping him on the fingers. He abandoned the game he'd been playing and stated that she would be the first to enjoy this fine bed.

She smiled, scolding him for telling lies so unblushingly.

He repeated that it was true, that he had never received a woman in his apartment and that this bed had been purchased quite recently, since he had taken up lodgings here.

She didn't believe him and he had the good sense not to try to convince her.

Looking at the furniture, Jeanne spoke again. "It's really nice, all this, you know," adding, "and so clean too."

He felt duty-bound to state that, in this regard, Mélanie was a really remarkable woman.

The name clouded Jeanne's mood once more, worrying her; but going into the bathroom, she resumed her prattle. "Ah," she exclaimed in delight, "now this is really very nice; with a room like this it won't be like the old times . . ."

She paused, blushing slightly, and they both laughed, remembering: she certain intimate difficulties, he certain farcical visions that filled his one and only room; feeling a little stirred he tugged at his mustache, then he embraced the little lady again and, in front of the water jug, looked at himself with her in his arms in the mirror hanging above the basin, but Jeanne disengaged herself and started to fiddle with the toiletries. She opened the box of face powder, stuck her nose inside, half removed the puff pressed against the boxwood sides and powdered the washstand with a fine pink cloud, then she ran her fingers over his razors and brushes and moistened the material of her gown with a few drops of oil of frangipane shaken from a vial, at the spot where the tip of the breast nestles.

"Oh, where does that door lead?" She pointed to a glass door between two cupboards, covered with a serge curtain.

"Into the kitchen," André replied, lifting the latch. He invited her inside, but she didn't want to, seemingly afraid of stepping into the lair, even in the absence of the wild beast. She ventured only the tip of her nose, saw the glittering battalion of saucepans and dishes, was even more frightened by a black tulle cap adorned with chou ribbons, with apple green strings that hung down against the ocher wall.

"It's very clean," she murmured and, taking the lamp, refused to cross through the kitchen to reach the dining room, vaguely afraid that Mélanie would know that a woman had entered her kitchen, and she went back into the bedroom.

"You can see how handy my apartment is," André said. "No one room dwarfs the others."

She too appreciated how much of an advantage this was, then went back to sit down in the drawing room. The fire rumbled angrily, spitting embers under the trap. She lifted it with tongs and, noting that André still possessed handsome books, asked if he still had the works of Alfred de Musset and Henri Murger.

He declared that he had sold them because they were cumbersome and worthless.

She was sorry, as she would have been glad to reread them. He offered to buy her copies of those books. She thanked him and gave a little smile as he brewed her tea. She noticed that, after five years, he was preparing the infusion in the same way, warming the britannium metal with water that he poured back into the kettle, opening the lid of the teapot, letting the black rain of tea leaves flow inside, finally drowning them in a deluge of hot water.

She laughed, leaning back into the armchair, saying once more, "Ah, you haven't changed!" The she got up and, entwining her arms round André's neck, showered him with little wet kisses.

"Watch out my kitty cat," he said, "You're going to make me spill the kettle."

"Oh, you haven't changed at all!" And she continued, a little plaintively, "You're still not very keen on being stroked?"

"But I am, I am," André exclaimed, kissing her tenderly, lingering on her lips; then wanting to start a less predictable conversation, he asked her, "Now, darling, what's happened to you in the five years since our separation?"

"Really, nothing at all, I told you already when you asked me." And somewhat warily, she took refuge in vague phrases.

"So, you don't want me to think that since we lost sight of each other, you haven't had ups and downs, and good times and bad ones."

"No, of course I've my bad days like everyone else, for example . . ." And she told the story of how, being unable to get work during a period of unemployment, she'd poisoned herself.

"Gosh!"

"Oh yes, I poisoned myself." And Jeanne told how, having gone to bed, she'd put on a white shift and swallowed a glass of laudanum after having first poured in some drops of mint spirits to make it taste better.

"And so," André asked, "what happened?"

"Nothing, only that I was sick for a fortnight. I vomited it up on the pillow."

"Ah!—Do you want sugar?" And he handed her a full cup of tea.

"No thanks, I only put in one lump."

He said nothing for a few moments, tormented by the fear that Jeanne's flesh had gone spongy. He tried gently to reassure himself, but she begged him to remain calmly in his chair.

Then he spoke about Madame Laveau; he hadn't known her during their time together.

"No, almost exactly next month it'll be two years since we met. It's an odd story all the same," Jeanne said looking thoughtful. "I got to know Eugénie a long time after she became a widow, for she was really married you know; she lived in a hotel on rue Contrescarpe, in the room below mine. One morning, while bringing up my shoes, the porter let me know that the woman and her child in the room below hadn't eaten for two days. I prepared some chocolate and went to see them. Eugénie was in bed sleeping, and her little girl, a tot of six months wearing a gown with a train, cut from an old plaid raincoat, was pulling on the chairs and pushing herself at every turn, on her nose, on the floor, squalling, her legs tangled up in her great big gown.

"So there you have it. Then they ate the chocolate and after that I stayed friends with the mother, but the little one died of the croup a year later."

André was left thoughtful, telling himself this truth: lower-class women help each other and almost all of them look after neighbors they don't know who are hungry or unwell, while, where the wives of the bourgeoisie are concerned, women who give them no pleasure and in whom they take no interest are, as a rule, left to die like dogs.

"Ah, not to say," Jeanne resumed after a moment of silence, "but I can tell you that Eugénie has known some really hard times, and she needs to have a stomach for it, because there were times she could only afford to eat potatoes and drink pure soda water."

André was bound to admire Madame Laveau's really remarkable stomach.

"Had she been ditched by a lover when you found her in that terrible state?" he asked.

"Yes. Oh, her lover was nothing but trash; anyway, you know, men."

"Hey there, come on now, hey!"

She smiled. "You aren't the kind of man who would behave like that with me," she said cajolingly, kissing him on the eyes.

By way of reply he wound his arms round her.

"Listen," he whispered in her ear, "it's half past eleven, what do you say we go beddy-byes?"

She blushed slightly. He went into the neighboring room, pulled back the bedspread, placed the pillows next to each other, then he came back to ask Jeanne if she was sleeping at the edge of the bed.

Certainly, she wasn't able to sleep beside the wall.

Then he went back into his bedroom and buried his handkerchief under the bottom pillow. He arranged the quilt, putting it right, smoothing it out with the flat of his hands, then he went into the bathroom where he lingered for some moments, disrobed quickly, donned his nightshirt, still bothered by a persistent fear that Jeanne had gone flabby.

Everything was ready for going to bed—he'd left out warm water, pulled out the bucket, prepared the towels; he went back to the little lady and held out his hands to help her out of the armchair. All a-quiver, eyes bright, hair spilling over her forehead, she quit the drawing room and disappeared into the powder room where she tried to make as little noise as possible, stopping in confusion when the water jug banged against the basin.

André was stretched out at the far end of the bed.

"My little darling, I beg you, turn your face to the wall," she said when she came back.

He replied, laughing, "Don't be silly, my little puss. Heavens, aren't we old friends!"

But she insisted, almost imploring; then, to satisfy her, he turned himself over. Jeanne undressed as quickly as she could. Did she murmur "Hey"?

He turned his head.

"No, don't move," and, laughing, she slipped nimbly between the sheets. Amused by her childish behavior, he seized her bodily and promptly felt a joyful frenzy; Jeanne was as solid as marble, well rounded and molded just right.

Very late, at daybreak, they closed their eyes; they slept badly anyway, with an impatient and feverish sleep.

At nine o'clock, Jeanne, awakened, was overcome with alarm; the terrible Mélanie, almost forgotten, was remembered again and sent chills down her spine. At all costs, she didn't want to be seen between the covers, and jumped out of bed.

But it isn't late," André protested, "it's Sunday, you don't need to go to work."

She refused to listen. A clinking of keys accompanied by a sound of footsteps entering the apartment terrified her; she would have liked to slither under a piece of furniture, to hide behind an armchair, disappear, whatever the cost.

While gently calling her a coward, André told himself that now was the time to show some mettle and vanquish Mélanie if she looked like she was going to make a fuss.

Jeanne didn't now dare to go into the bathroom; she was afraid of the housemaid opening the communicating door; the slippers she heard shuffling in the kitchen made her head spin and her heart thump; she almost regretted getting up, thinking that if she'd stayed in bed, she would be buried with her nose in the pillow when the housemaid entered.

However, understanding the need for a good wash in the other room, she took the risk, tiptoeing, hid her breast under a scarf, cleansed herself on the fly, returned as quickly as she could, bringing face powder and comb with her to the bedroom, thinking herself more sheltered near the young man.

The latter thought yet again that that he should get up and undertake a reconnaissance of the kitchen, using whatever excuse. For the moment he felt a virile firmness of purpose; wanting to take advantage of this frame of mind, he put on his slippers with a belligerent air, determined to do battle.

He prowled in the dining room, pretending to look for his newspaper and, through the wide-open door, he saw Mélanie's back, her elbows flapping over the stove, quickening the embers with bellows.

She turned and greeted him.

"What time would Monsieur like to have breakfast?" she asked in a gracious voice. And she showed André, with a triumphant cry of "Aren't they splendid, eh?"; kidneys, violet and glazed, hard and elastic, pushed back against her finger as she pressed them.

"Well, let's see, in a quick fifteen minutes," André replied, a little peeved, in spite of everything, at not being able to deploy the provisional courage that inspired him.

He returned to find Jeanne busy heating up tweezers to curl her hair. She was now almost dressed and seeing herself clean and covered up, she regained a degree of self-confidence.

"Are you hungry?" André asked.

"So-so."

"Ah," he suddenly said, "Where are your boots so I can get them polished." But she showed them to him clean and shining like mirrors.

He was amazed.

She confessed laughingly that she had made use of the shoe brushes the evening before when she was alone in the bathroom.

He scolded her, but all the same was grateful for her discretion.

"So then, since you're ready, we can go for breakfast if you want."

She didn't say either yes or no in reply, confined to the bedroom where she persisted in thinking, without knowing why, that she ran less of a risk there. At this moment Mélanie showed up. The two women gazed at each other, Jeanne apprehensively, Mélanie unconfidently.

"Monsieur is served," the housemaid said.

Still confounded, Jeanne remained unmoving; however, she was beginning to recover from her anxieties. The serving woman didn't seem to resemble the fearsome old dragon that her fears had conjured up.

"She's quite young, your housemaid," she said to André; and like a child who, taken to the classroom for the first time, is astonished that the school mistress doesn't look more forbidding and arrogant, she added, "Oh, she doesn't look so very fierce."

The eggs lay under a napkin on the table. André and Jeanne sat down. The dining room was hardly very warm; the damp cold of the end of autumn chilled this north-facing room.

They soaked their bread fingers and drank a mouthful of wine without a word said. The eggshells were emptied, André rang the bell; Jeanne felt extraordinarily uncomfortable. She looked at the young man in astonishment, almost fretfully, and clenched her fingers on his hand as though to prevent him from ringing the bell.

André was at a loss to understand her. Jeanne seemed more intimidated than ever.

The sharp peal summoning Mélanie wounded her. It seemed to her, dining with André, that she was complicit in that curt summons. The thoughts that perturbed her the night before returned and she was dominated by a feeling of decency and embarrassment; it almost hurt her to see herself, a woman of the people, having taken lovers, served like a lady by an honest woman of the people, and she was as unhappy and almost as revolted as though she'd seen an injustice being committed, or inflicted a humiliation on someone before her because Mélanie, not being a poor old woman or ugly, was worth as much as she was.

She lowered her head, eyes on her plate, fearing that the housemaid would see her as a whore and an interloper.

"Madame maybe has cold feet," Mélanie said in an obliging voice and, without waiting for a reply, she fetched a heater and slid it under the feet of Jeanne, who thanked her, almost on the point of crying, but that courtesy hardly cheered her up; she made herself smaller than ever, ashamed of these attentions.

"Are they good, the kidneys?" André asked.

"Oh yes, very good."

"Well then, hold out your plate," and he plunged his spoon into the dish.

But Jeanne refused.

"I've had enough, no, really; you know, I'm not a big eater."

He rang the bell once more.

The little lady plunged her nose into her plate.

Mélanie brought cauliflower au gratin and, wanting nothing more than to be friendly, asked Jeanne, whose shyness astonished her, if the heater was warm enough.

“Oh yes, Madame, you’re very kind,” she said, looking up a little.

Once launched on this trail, Mélanie took pains to find new obliging attentions; not finding any, she went away.

Jeanne was now tormented by a cruel dilemma. She detested cauliflower, which didn’t agree with her as she admitted to André later, and yet she didn’t want to refuse to take any. She begged the young man to give her as little as possible and forced herself to eat them, drinking after each mouthful a glass of water tinged with wine, not daring to leave anything on the plate for fear of hurting the feelings of the housemaid.

Her torture neared its end; the dessert once served she nibbled some marzipan and André, who was sorry to see her so ill at ease, suggested that they quit the solemnity of the dining room and, like before, take their coffee by the fireside in his bedroom.

She accepted with a grateful look and, once seated, comforted by a glass of green chartreuse, she prattled on, saying that Mélanie was a fine person, that she’d been very obliging and polite, and while she reeled off friendly words about her the other woman, in her kitchen, forgot her panic, thinking that this little lady was too humble to order her about. “She’s just as she ought to be, not insolent and not scheming,” and she gave a sigh of relief at how lucky she was not to have to deal with a high-handed and determined woman who would have made both of them spin like tops.

André begged Jeanne to stay for supper, but she expressly refused, not wanting to add to the housemaid’s labors, her woman’s instinct making her aware that her person and behavior had produced an effect that was not at all bad, and intent on not seeming to want to force herself on the menage, wanting, not least, for Mélanie to maintain the good opinion she’d formed of her.

XI

On the following day, a flood of comments came from Mélanie, on Jeanne's nose, her good qualities, her black dress. "Ah Monsieur was really very lucky to light on such an unassuming and sweet little lady!" Mélanie, having only known the women of officers residing in her district of Gros-Caillou, was astonished by that demure little girl, not proud and not louche like most of the females whom she encountered crossing her street bareheaded, accompanied by an orderly in the role of servant, tasked with brushing their clothes and, in the absence of superiors detained by professional duties, to keep them out of mischief in cafés in front of glasses of absinthe.

It was almost with delight that André accepted the full buckets that the housemaid poured over his head. All his trepidations vanished; not even the obstacles were matters of concern; Jeanne found a place in the household without as much as a single outcry or quarrel. It only remained to avoid the trouble that might be caused by the concierge. Mélanie, to whom André let slip some of his fears, screeched in response, feeling a resurgence of her old hatred of the man who forbade her from beating her carpets and shaking out her cleaning cloths after ten in the morning. "Ah well it'd take more than that, for a blabbermouth of a caretaker to lay down the law to Monsieur!"[58] she said; and, without André having asked her, she undertook to protect the little lady, to keep her mouth shut if anyone tried to worm information out of her, not least she offered to snub the lodgers and the doorman at the slightest insinuation.

André cooled down this fine display of zeal, fearing irremediable upsets.

Meanwhile, touching ties of friendship grew between the two women. On the second day that she slept with André, Jeanne, while waking up in bed, was surprised by Mélanie who came in discreetly on the tip of long toes, greeted her, and smiled politely.

"Good morning, Madame, you're well I hope?"

"Yes, thank you very much."

"I didn't know what to buy for breakfast this morning. I've ordered lamb chops in sauce from the butcher. Does Madame like them?"

"Yes, of course Madame, I like all sauces with vinegar and gherkins." And, grateful for the heater brought on the previous occasion, Jeanne asked after the policeman.

Greatly flattered, Mélanie became garrulous. She harped on at length about her husband's rheumatism, talked about his future promotion, the children they'd wanted to have, volunteered, without anyone having raised the issue, that either she or her husband were infertile, maybe both; then she took Jeanne's shoes in spite of her protests, declaring that she would never allow Madame to soil her pretty fingers, and she put such a gleam on the laced boots that André's ankle boots, properly polished as usual, looked like dull and soiled old shoes in comparison. She even pushed consideration as far as warming the laced boots near the fire, heels upturned.

Somewhat surprised, in spite of everything, by this sudden fondness, André wondered what Mélanie's motive might be; he found out when, on coming back home one day, he found the two women sitting in the dining room in front of a table, Jeanne showing the housemaid the best way of tailoring a dress, attaching her sewing pattern to it, like posters, along the back.

He didn't say anything, thinking all the same that Jeanne was going to be thoroughly exploited; he only started to distrust the intimacy between the two women one Saturday when Jeanne declared a wish to dine in a restaurant the next day.

That whim surprised him, knowing that she usually didn't like going out with him for fear of meeting friends of her other lover; he questioned her and she eventually confessed that Mélanie wanted time off. "I'll take care of the cooking if you don't want to go to the bother," she said in a low voice, "you know, Mélanie asked me as a favor."

He didn't want to displease Jeanne and annoy the housemaid; he obligingly conceded the leave and the next day, Jeanne, saying she was a little under the weather, suggested that it would be nicer to eat by the fireside and proposed to send Mélanie to buy provisions. André consented to this; he even agreed to not eating in the dining room because it was much pleasanter to sit in the bedroom like in the old days, and a delighted Jeanne rewarded his amenability; stomach covered by a towel, looking bold and healthy, she laid the table, kissed her little man on the cheeks, whispered in his ear, "Isn't this fun, eh?," remembered the portions of food that, back in the old days when he had no maid, he'd had sent up from a cheap chophouse in the neighborhood, declaring, in spite of André's disparagement of congealed dishes carted through the streets in a napkin, that she preferred to eat like that, informally, without ceremony, rather than changing plates all the time and dining in pomp to the sound of a dinner bell.

André smiled. "Admit it, pussykins," he said, "Mélanie still scares you, doesn't she?"

Turning bright red, she denied it. "Look here, I'm no longer a little girl to be scared of a housemaid. No, I prefer to eat casually because it's a nuisance always having somebody breathing down your neck. Mélanie always shows up like that when we'd like to kiss and cuddle each other; we aren't free and easy, we can't say what we want; you know we might as well say that we aren't really at home."

André wisely decided to keep his thoughts to himself. Jeanne also brought the dishes, cleared the table, pushed it into a corner, and got ready to grind the coffee beans. André offered to take over this easy task and, while she brought the cups and spoons, he awkwardly cranked the handle, between his knees, surprised after all that the device didn't crush the beans more quickly.

Jeanne shrugged her shoulders, took the grinder back from him, and soon finished the job. Sitting side by side, feet on the fender, they talked haphazardly; the conversation languished, only touching on fruitless topics, skimming over indefinite subjects. Like those bits of fluff that drift randomly until they find a place to stick, their words, after having at first grazed the topic of clothes, led there by Jeanne's skirt which was spotted with grease from having served the meal, alighted on the shop where she worked.

Then she explained the disdain that she and the other working girls felt for the models who paraded on the gleaming parquet floor in borrowed clothing. They were tarts picked up daily from fitting rooms by rich buyers for foreign markets; in a word, good-for-nothings.

As for the three classes of women workers—makers of skirts, bodices, and coats—there were very few decent girls among them, and, launched on the subject of the garment industry, she said that the handful of virgins scattered through the workshops were nags, hoity-toities, clever clogs, counting for their future on already fading charms and rancid underclothes; she confessed to spiteful comments exchanged from morning till night, the disgusted and brattish airs of the kept women, wearing the names of their lovers, wanting to be treated as Ladies all the way down the road, and yet she asserted that in spite of exchanges of taunts and curses, they were very polite toward each other, because when a worker came in without a good morning greeting, the whole shop cried out: "Hey there, you've left something behind the door!" And Jeanne laughed, claiming there were plenty silly gooses who went out on the landing to look for whatever they'd lost.

Then, touching on the workshops located in the attics on the sixth floor, suites of garrets, covered with cheap wallpaper, pink flowers climbing gray trellises, lit by skylights, connected by doors with missing panels, Jeanne, urged on by André, spoke about the head outfitter, a hoity-toity who clocks the workers' arrival times, keeps every shade of silk in big boxes, and when you go to ask for supplies shouts, "What, you've used it up already? Show me your reel!" A sexless snitch and old maid, saying to those who spent a night on the tiles, "We know your sort, look there, your collar's dirty and it's Thursday; so you didn't go back home yesterday. That isn't the worst of it, you should see yourself, the state of your eyes!" Or else casting slurs like this at women with swollen bellies, "Ah! The wee girl who's stretched herself out on a pointed stone!" Or else, "So tell me, my little beauty, I see you've been eating uncooked beans, is that what's made you swell up?"

"You find that funny," Jeanne said a touch sadly, looking at André who was smiling with delight in his armchair. "Ah well, if you were shut up in winter in rooms like that, full of drafts, warmed with coke, lit from two in the afternoon by gas lamps hung so low they burn you and make your hair fall out, if it was you stifling in the summer in the middle of a whole crowd stripping off to feel more comfortable, pulling their boobs out of their blouses and weighing them to see who has the biggest and firmest, if you too had to put up with three or four months of off-season, you'd see there was nothing to laugh about. No there's nothing to laugh about," she said after a brief silence.

André apologized for his glee and justified it by the spectacle she'd revealed to him. "All the same, I'd like to see that," he said, cheered by the prospect of blouses allowing the passage, one after another, of a row of white pears with stalks the color of rust, chocolate, raspberry, or mauve, all framed by rumpled underlinen.

"Sometimes there's snuff on top," Jeanne retorted, smiling in turn, "because, you know, we all we all have a little penny sachet that we dry under the flatirons."

"Ah well! There's a fine thing!" André cried.

"It's okay for you! We need to do that to keep us awake, to help us hold out till eight in the evening. Oh! Nobody is sleeping then, believe me; in every workshop you can hear the shout, "It's time!" and the preening and primping begins; we all smooth our hair with a bit of spittle, pull off the bits of thread stuck to our clothes, freshen our cheeks with the powder puff, touch up our eyelids with a hairpin, and then you should see, it's the most stringy ones who do the most to show themselves off, who put on the most innocent and ladylike airs for leaving the workplace."

"Ye gods," André exclaimed, "it's just the same in the rag trade as in the arts. You can be sure that it's those people who live the most degraded lives who write the most sentimental and prudish works! Really, that's how it is!" He sighed, then he asked for some information on what the girls usually ate, learned without surprise that these young folk fed on crudités, artichokes with pepper, cottage cheese with spring onions, green apples, and, when it came to more substantial food, clams, mussels, chops, all of it brought in from outside, in big baskets and warmed up in a special room shared by all the classes of workers, on the seventh floor, on gas stoves, on which however the burners, bagged in advance by the apprentices in every workshop, were fought over.

"Ah well, you must all talk a lot about men!" André suggested.

Jeanne agreed that men were undoubtedly talked about, but the conversations dwelled above all on their dreams. So, every morning on arriving, the dressmakers cried to their friends, "Good morning darling, have you slept well?" "Oh yes, darling, I dreamed all kinds of things that I'll tell you about upstairs, during breakfast; oh, you'll see, darling." And while munching on radishes that they clubbed together to buy, they told their dreams that were interpreted for them by big Amélie, a hefty woman up there who knew the key to dreams better than anyone else.

So, when you kissed a woman or saw her backside, an affront was in store for you during the day; when you dreamed of birds, it meant malicious gossip; fire meant something really joyful providing you didn't see the flames; then again there was the cat, which meant a betrayal; a child meant agony, and a heap of other riddles that Jeanne said she no longer knew.

"And you believe all that?" André asked.

"Of course, why not?" Jeanne's smile was so ambiguous, however, that André was unable to decide whether she was seriously in good faith. "We're all superstitious," she concluded with a smile. "So when we leave the table, we always have wet hair because we pour wine on the table and soak our finger and wipe it on our head to bring luck."

"And does Eugénie believe in all that too?"

"Of course. Besides, she's done well out of believing in it, because her dreams always come true. So, before getting married, she saw a man holding a plane and her husband turned out to be a packer. And the same thing happened with her sister; when she was a young girl, she saw a man in a frock coat and her first lover was a man of letters. So, you know, you mustn't say in front of Eugénie that dreams are nonsense! She'll give you what for!"

"I respect all beliefs, even when they're sincere," André declared. Then, leaning over Jeanne, he whispered a question in her ear.

"Oh, you're filthy!" she exclaimed. "What a question! I wonder what's your interest in knowing if they're on the seventh floor, near where they eat, if there are cigarette butts, blood on the ground, and then if its full of bits and pieces of muslin."

"So then! It's with muslin," André said, laughing. "Apropos of the garment workshops, that's a good point to make a note of."

"What do you mean, make a note of! Ah yes, you're writing all this down. Oh, but don't go putting what I'm telling you into your books, because, you know . . . But I'm being stupid, you wouldn't dare to write things like that!"

"You'll see," was all André said.

Jeanne shrugged her shoulders and resumed the conversation: "So you're working as a journalist?"

"No. It's more than three years since I gave up journalism," and he went on, speaking more to himself than to the little lady. "I've had enough of editors, a parcel of eunuchs who want to command and control the virility of other men. Before handing in my notice, I really should have written a heartfelt article demonstrating the utter uselessness of criticism; but then again that would have committed a financial heresy in the eyes of my colleagues; those cretins wouldn't even have understood how human my idea was; talk down the métier that supported my livelihood! What both of us are doing right now," he went on, turning to Jeanne.

He fell silent, overcome with melancholy and disgust. He'd hardly done any work for months on end. He was living through a period of discouragement and abandonment, chewing over the terrible arguments of the man of letters tired of work and glutted with art. What's the use? What need is there? Best to read the work of others and not write oneself. Then, in this letting go, in this rout, the novel he had begun work on appeared to him in a distant and magnificent perspective. He said, "All the same!" then, realizing that the work written with great effort would necessarily be inferior to the one he had dreamed of, he collapsed back into his initial melancholy, repeating to himself as an excuse, "Today I'm not in the mood; we'll see later."

And that today was tomorrow, was the following days, weeks, and months; by dint of waiting he'd lost the advantage of the motivating force he'd felt on moving into his apartment.

And then . . . And then . . . he was married. Already he saw only a few people. The marriage had made him break off relations with all the people who might have been able to give him a nudge in the right direction and lend a helping hand. He was still held back by the fear that his cuckoldry was known to everyone, the shame of explaining the separation between his wife and himself by means of a lie, which would lead to smiles on the lips of others. The benefit of those labors completed during the time he toiled in the brothels of the press had now been abandoned. He was forgotten, condemned to a hole; through absenting himself he had closed all the doors, he was ignorant of the current open sesames and passwords. The difficulty of putting his finger on an editor was the same as in the beginning, a difficulty that, although his first books had sold badly, was at one time almost a long way away, if only he had persisted on staying on the job. His instinctive laziness was now allied to the pointlessness of new research, the tedium of making fresh efforts.

"It's a funny thing," Jeanne resumed, changing the topic of conversation on seeing André's gloomy expression, "in the old days you had lots of friends who came to see you, and Mélanie has told me that now you don't see anyone. Is it because you're angry with a little man, uh, I don't remember his name, you know who I mean, a little man who always wore pince-nez and polka-dot La Vallière cravats?"

"Ah, Eugène; no, he's married and, well, you see, lots of relationships are broken off as a result of marriage."

"Yes, and what about you? Have you never wanted to get married?"

"No."

"It's a funny thing that you don't end up like the others when you love your home so much."

André, who had become very unsettled, took a deep breath. Jeanne certainly didn't know that he was married; Mélanie hadn't said a word, taking an exceptional degree of notice of the orders she'd received.

"So you didn't think I was a bachelor then?" he asked Jeanne.

"No, it was rather that I thought you were dead."

He made no reply, thinking that he too had thought that Jeanne was deceased.

"But let's see," she carried on, trying to remember, "you used to be friends with a big skinny chap with a beard."

"Cyprien?"

"Yes, him. And so, don't you see him anymore?"

"Of course, we're still friends," and, though he added "we even see a lot of each other," he reflected that the painter had refrained from visiting or writing letters since Jeanne had been once more back with him. "I must go and see him," he thought to himself.

"There you go, staring into space," the little lady said, somewhat put out by seeing André woolgathering, far away from her, "what's got into you? You're out of sorts this evening!"

The fact was that tonight André was poking about in a heap of cinders; he found some still live bits of coal sleeping underneath, memories that glittered all over, and, his head now leaning on Jeanne's shoulder, so as to at least make a show of being concerned with her, he dreamed, eyes unseeing.

"It's a pity you're no longer a journalist," she sighed, "you could have got me theater tickets."

Those words set him off on a new track. Ah! How many times had Berthe, his wife, said she would like that! A slew of reminders of persistent demands came back to him; he embraced Jeanne, happy to hold her close. A detailed parallel between the two women now formed in his mind. Berthe, prettier, with her regular features under chestnut hair, her deep black eyes, the droll overbite in a rosy mouth; Jeanne, her features less certain, her brash nose quivering and retroussé, her voluble eyes ardent and mild, her hair scattered in a fine blonde rain over her forehead; she was unfussy, funnier, possessed a more provocative figure, and above all had a sweeter character, a fear of causing problems, a discretion that was delicious for a man who had put up with the harsh despotism of a wife, sitting in judgment over everything, deciding everything, imposing her ideas, her preferences, a decided member of the bourgeois class who, on the day she took possession of her married quarters, unleashed the dictum that still weighed on André's heart; "You absolutely must remove those prints; prints are never hung in a drawing room." And he had to accept the vile pictures chosen by her and relegate his fine engravings to the hallway.

These memories made him lift his eyes to the same prints that now covered the walls of his little front room.

"Get away, you wicked fanatic," Jeanne said, spying the direction of his gaze, "there you go, still looking at your old knick-knacks. Wait," she went on, laughing, "that frame is lopsided," knowing André's habit of repositioning pictures that Mélanie, skew-eyed like no one else, relentlessly left tilted.

He got up, straightened the frame, happy to amuse Jeanne, then sat down again and plunged back into his reverie.

He told himself yet again that, with her high spirits and affectionate nature, she was also kindhearted and charitable, which was proved for him one evening when he was unwell, hammered by a migraine, and she had gently applied compresses to his forehead, hugging him like a child one consoles, saying with a kiss, "And so, darling, is your wee head any better?"

That evening she'd had a delightful way of calming his ailment. André, who was usually consigned to the cares of a maid, found in her a properly devoted servant right up to the time of her departure, but he suffered appallingly when unable to tolerate light and noise. Mélanie brusquely brought in a lamp, banged a cup on the floor, and besieged him with useless offers of help, misguidedly plying him with infusions, harassing him until he swallowed indigestible soups.

As for Berthe, in such cases, she fulfilled her duty as dictated by decency; she sent in the housemaid from time to time to inquire if Monsieur needed anything, rang for her so that she could prepare a glass of water sweetened with orange blossom and take it to André, then she undressed on tiptoes at the usual time, taking precautions in lieu of caresses, murmuring, once in bed, things like "You're really hot, you must have a fever," turning her back and turning down the lamp.

That matter of the bed led André to still more intimate comparisons between Berthe and Jeanne. The latter won out with her pretty pantomimes, her shivers and bodily commotions, her head promptly whirling, and her words all hashed up. The former was cold, unyielding, accepting with an ill grace, rejecting his hands, turning her lips away, never passionate.

"Really, you're still the best of them all," he suddenly said.

But Jeanne sulked, reproaching him for thinking of his old mistresses.

Astonished himself by the phrase he had uttered aloud, he cajoled her, and in order to appease her submitted to an operation he had deferred for months. Jeanne insistently begged him to let her remove the two worms that had, it seemed, taken root under his forehead.

Then she squeezed them between her sharp fingernails, so that he started to cry out, but she threatened to use the point of a needle if he didn't keep quiet, then gave him a tender kiss.

"You're much better-looking now. Really, take a look at yourself."

And he had to get up to stare at himself in a mirror. He deemed himself neither better nor worse; he declared, however, that his head was improved by having undergone the extraction of the sebaceous matter.

And there were further evenings like that one, gradually releasing all the childishness contained in the man and woman.

After supper, they drank a drop of Benedictine or sloe gin; sometimes André even went in search of chestnuts and sweet white wine and, both of them nibbling and drinking, they swapped those banal effusions, those comfortable endearments that are the prerequisite of continued affection and relaxation of the intelligence.

On other occasions, when Jeanne had arrived early in the morning, André proposed that they go out for some fresh air after supper, and, in the sharp cold, at those times when the limpid moon shone in a hard blue sky, they sped along rue St. Honoré, Jeanne wrapped up in her tightly buttoned fur overcoat, and, arm in arm, they entered the arcades of the Palais-Royal, stopped for a minute in front of the watches in the jewelry shops and, harried by the wind, numb with cold, they took refuge in a German brasserie located in the vicinity.

There, huddled in a divan, in front of a table, they gluttonously ordered sauerkraut, Westphalian cured ham, sausages with horseradish, and black bread; and their appetites were roused by the tart smells emanating from the plate, and their thirst, whetted by the salted bread and the sour sugar of the juniper berries that they munched in the sauerkraut, caused them to gulp down mugs of Munich Salvator: a magnificent, mahogany-colored beer, oily and sweet.

Then Jeanne stopped eating to laugh, seeing André's mustache white with creamlike froth. Dazed by the warm atmosphere, blinded by the continual serving of bocks, they had the inebriated fancy of sampling all those bottles, ranged on a shelf in battle array, shimmering with gleams from the gas lamps.

"It's wonderful here," Jeanne said, breathing hard and holding out her plate. André replied with a yes; and no further words were spoken, their eyes engaged in contemplating a buffet full of fat, golden smoked joints of ham, some of which oozed drops of pale jelly on a plate, others showing bloody cuts letting the bone be seen under sliced-open flesh.

Although they had eaten a full supper, they felt something approaching contempt for Mélanie's fine and ephemeral fare; their mouths watered, captured by a raging hunger before this buffet laden with big, substantial cuts of meat, flanked and further pressed in by kegs of herring rollmops, baskets of fennel-flavored bread, crackers and bream, salad bowls where brawn was marinating in vinaigrette, bell glasses under which high Munster and Limburger cheeses were liquefying.

And both of them, with stuffed and flagging stomachs, lingered on their banquette until closing time, Jeanne, somewhat dizzy from tobacco smoke and fumes from the beer, André dreaming with eyes open of the potent drinking bouts of Alsace, seeing in his mind's eye red waistcoats and tricorns filing past in front of him with blooming noses and round bellies, a whole procession of comical drunkards boozing and circling around the enormous paunch of a terracotta Gambrinus that stood on a counter of the brasserie, glutted and triumphant, astride a bolt of lightning and raising a glass in the air.[59]

XII

André and Jeanne now called each other gourmets and surprised each other with this newborn gluttony. Each accused the other of being responsible for their respective failings and vices, and here something odd occurred: the unexpected advent of a new predilection in Jeanne who usually had no qualms about eating in cheap cafés and couldn't be reasonably considered a gourmand or glutton; disdain for a whole history of culinary indifference on the part of André, who took his mistress to brasseries he would never have frequented on his own, and now purchased early-season fruit and vegetables from market sellers encountered on his walks, saying, "There, we'll have a taste of that at supper this evening with Jeanne."

This vice affected Mélanie, even rebounded into her household. By dint of devising artful cuisines her palate became discerning and her husband, who, not unreasonably, took an interest in what André was eating, encouraged his wife to devote even more attention to preparing their dishes, above all to refine the ones he preferred.

"Hey, Monsieur Denis!" Jeanne cried one evening when, stretched out on the bed, they had run out of talk, weren't even thinking about kissing and cuddling.

André, who was snoozing, lifted his nose above the blanket. "What is it?" he asked.

"Well," she replied, "you know, we might as well begin to sing the chorus of the song, 'Do you remember . . . , do you remember . . .' because, don't you see, when we enjoy stuffing our bellies like this then it's goodbye to those happy nights when we don't sleep."[60]

She wasn't wrong; eating in style had established itself as a new source of interest for them, brought about by a diminishing interest in sensuality, like the passions of priests who, deprived of the joys of the flesh, bray over refined dishes and old wines. Their revived love life having run out of steam, André and Jeanne were soon reduced to exchanges of blissful tenderness, the maternal satisfactions of sometimes going to bed together, simply stretching out side by side, to make small talk before turning back to back to sleep. So they tasted the monotonous happiness of long-lasting marriages interrupted by the inevitable and feeble disputes arising from prolonged snoring or bodies jostling clumsily during the night.

In that tranquil existence, in that cozy domesticity enjoyed in the heart of Paris as though in the provinces, André soaked himself as though in a soothing and sedative bath; Jeanne's caresses healed the wounds inflicted by Berthe's betrayals, which had hardly been bandaged by Blanche's easygoing nature. For possibly the first time since he had parted from with his wife he could think of her without distress, without regrets.

"It's too good to last," he told himself, surprised at how easily all his wishes were fulfilled, for the much-feared concierge maintained a peaceful truce and Mélanie was unfailingly obliging; "it's bound to off the rails." And in fact, little by little, an issue emerged that he and Jeanne, by mutual consent, had always avoided—the question of the maintenance money paid by another gentleman, from one end of France to the other.

At first, it wasn't this callow lad they talked about, but rather his older brother, M. Auguste Vidouvé, a retired furniture dealer, a man of forty, a rich bachelor who, thanks to some bottles of champagne, had become one evening the lover of widow Laveau. The widow's tippling was a disaster for André's household, for this gentleman felt it necessary to spy on the morals of his faux sister-in-law.

Then, on certain days, there were mad chases across Paris. Dogged by the retired dealer, Jeanne climbed into tramcars, exited in a street in Montmartre where her mother lived, climbed two floors, waited an eternity on the landing, surveying the street through a window, and when she no longer saw the imbecile, she flew downstairs in a whirlwind, leaped into another tram, fled along branch lines, arrived at André's apartment by way of a connecting omnibus, dying of cold and hunger, breathless, laughing, crying out, "Well now, I've had a really hard time of it!"

Jeanne's filial affection was the excuse for some of her late morning homecomings, but the man didn't trust her, and, as he was little acquainted with women, gave himself the job of visiting her very early every day, declaring that on principle he didn't accept the usual excuse for going out, namely the public baths.

Then, while calling on new resources, Jeanne didn't dare to spend a night away. Tracked to her place of work by the spy who thought himself unseen, she managed to lose him in heavy traffic and crowds, ran to André's apartment and, retaliating furiously against these obstacles, their senses violently heightened, they flung themselves on each other, tumbled in a heap on carpets and on chairs. Then Jeanne went away again quickly and returned home, listened to the man saying to her with conviction, "You know, my girl, there's no point in you running, see, you can't fool an old dog like me."

He did so well that, while he kept a check on his brother's woman, his own woman, Eugénie, though not given to excess, and who, by a lucky exception, he completely trusted, took time out in the home of every tenant in his building so as to get revenge for Jeanne.

"One more," she said when he returned home.

"One more what?" he asked.

"You know very well," and she mockingly lifted two fingers in the air.

He shrugged, thinking that if she were telling the truth she wouldn't dare admit it to his face.

These goings-on didn't delight André, left despondent by all the obstacles that this liaison entailed. Soon he feared more serious troubles. Jeanne seemed to lose all her cheerfulness. He plied her with questions. She replied vaguely, only complaining about Eugénie's lover, saying that he was a horrible man, a hypochondriac who lived a loose life, poorly educated and yet demanding correct and careful language from his mistress who was obstinate, replying to his furious exhortations, "Really, since we say 'carriage,' then why can't we say 'omnibus!'"

"Do you know, he gives her a slap when she speaks back to him?" Jeanne added. "Ah, well, you can be sure I wouldn't live with him even if he were to give me more money than he gives Eugénie!"

Eugénie's faulty language and the blows she received weren't, it seemed to him, sufficient reasons for Jeanne's dejection. He accused her of no longer being in love with him, but that invite, usually followed by protestations and heart-to-hearts, was unsuccessful. Jeanne's only reply was to kiss him tenderly and remain tightlipped about her own situation, returning instead to the subject of her friend, telling him that Eugénie's faulty pronunciation was in her blood, that he was really someone to be afraid of, finally that the man would stop providing for her when he got tired of insulting her.

These details of widow Laveau's unfortunate fate started to irritate André. He felt that the gentleman didn't knock her about nearly enough, and, as he now started humming when Jeanne recounted the man's wrongdoings, the girl stopped talking. Tired of brooding all alone over her troubles, however, she finally talked about herself one evening. "If you want to know," she said, "well, my lover's spell of voluntary military service is almost finished and he's coming back; there you have it!"

André didn't flinch.

She entered into more detail. Her lover was a sharp dresser, proud as punch of his high collars, a dandy, lighthearted, not as malicious and uncouth as his brother, but oafish, incapable of understanding a woman and entertaining her, in bed or out. "Just a boy," she said, putting it in a nutshell, and she continued, "Yes, he's coming back, but what's not so funny is that as soon as he arrives back in Paris he's going into business with a banker and he's getting married." She added in a lower voice, "I really don't know now what I'll do to get by."

André, aghast, looked down and said nothing, for, with the best will in the world, he couldn't provide for Jeanne. He didn't earn a penny with his pen and Mélanie swallowed up his meager income in cooking for him and exploiting him. Several times already he'd been left penniless near the time when the rent was due. The few cash advances he'd possessed at the time of his breakup with Berthe had been eaten up by furniture and linen, the costs of moving house. In fact, his household was in a real mess, a scene of plunder; everyone helped themselves and the bitterest pill was the housemaid's husband, who carried off waistcoats and socks, gobbled up mad amounts of money in buying wax and nitric acid cleanser, helped to empty bottles of wine, and made sure that the brandy didn't grow old in the cupboards.

Every morning Mélanie required twenty francs from him.[61] André balked at this, declared that he couldn't carry on at that rate, that she must curb the expenses of his household, no matter how, and she, for her part, replied that that was impossible, that the cost of living was sky high, that her management of the house was as thrifty as possible. His only options were to hold his tongue or else dismiss his housemaid. He felt he had no alternative but to keep her on, dreading the collapse of his way of life.

All these reasons, spelled out to Jeanne to excuse his real inability to help her, left her unimpressed.

"Get rid of Mélanie, who's robbing you blind," she said, and little by little she delicately insinuated that, just like before, they could live more cheaply in setting up house together.

That suggestion dismayed André. He tried to gain time, countering these attacks with his powers of inertia, having made up his mind in any event not to cohabit with Jeanne and not to dismiss his housemaid.

Once or twice on certain evenings Jeanne risked further discreet approaches; then, although she had once solemnly announced that, since her lover's marriage had been celebrated, she might return to spend the night with him as before, she avoided reopening the topic of a shared life and discarded her air of gloom.

André welcomed this change and regained confidence; he prudently arranged his business affairs, sold off some bonds, passed small amounts of money over to Jeanne at intervals calculated in advance.

One or two months flowed by; February was reaching an end. Completely recovered from his fears, André breathed easily, thinking himself in the clear, when, one day, looking somewhat drawn, Jeanne declared that her situation was about to change.

André was alarmed by these words, which rang in his ears like a threat; he bent his head, expecting the worst.

She sought for words. "Yes, so you see, in the end I've got no choice. I've had to accept. So, next Monday I'm leaving for England."

He was flabbergasted, and, after a silence, while she went over to him, he recovered a little, looked her sadly in the eyes, and said in a tremulous voice, "So, you're deserting me?"

"Oh, it's mean of you to say things like that!" she exclaimed. "No, you'll always be my little man, how can you think that I don't love you anymore? But you have to understand that a woman can't live on thin air! My God, I know that you've done everything possible, and I don't hold anything against you, but now that the workshops are idle and I can't even earn enough to keep myself in food, I'd be leading a life of poverty in Paris. Look, would you prefer me to misbehave with whoever comes along?"

He shook his head, sighing, admitting to himself that he would perhaps have preferred Jeanne to be promiscuous without telling him, rather than brutally abandoning him like that.

She took his sigh for a sign of the desperation he felt at the thought that his little Jeanne might give herself in public to the first comer. She sighed in turn, then deprecated the perils of the crossing, the miseries of seasickness, the cheerlessness of a country whose language one didn't know, then she kissed André on the eyes, murmuring, "Don't be sad, my little baby, you'll see, I'll come back, it won't be long."

He didn't reply.

Then she spoke again: "Look, don't be like that, say something to me, you can see that I'm not happy about it either, say you aren't angry with me?"

He gestured vaguely, she kissed him on the mouth and smiled a little. "Really, it's been a month since I signed my contract, I knew that it would make you unhappy, so I couldn't make up my mind to tell you; I went to rue Richelieu to Madame Tricot's agency, a big woman, very funny looking, with round glasses on her nose and Queen Amelia style ringlets on her cheeks. She checked with the shops where I worked and made me sign up for three months.[62] She's a decent woman who specializes in sending workers abroad and who's a swimming instructor for ladies in the summer when the market is on hold."

And Jeanne started to laugh, hoping that André would cheer up too, but the portrait of Madame Tricot hardly touched him and, on the contrary, ill-disposed to that tradeswoman who sent his mistress so far away, he inveighed against her agency, declaring that it was a nest of vipers, a meeting place for bawds, swearing without any proof that Jeanne had been robbed.

But the little lady shook her head, maintaining that she was running no risks, explaining how these matters were arranged: "These are the conditions; I'm employed for one hundred and forty francs a month plus food and lodging (for example a bed for two of us girls); as for the agent's commission, it's paid by the London firm, which also pays the travel costs."[63]

André remained unconvinced and launched into a fierce attack on the quality of the food that would be served up to Jeanne, spoke of the disgust she would feel in sharing a bed with someone else.

"Anyway," Jeanne went on, "even if you're right, I can't back out now. The contract is signed and I'd have a big penalty to pay if I didn't go."

André didn't continue to insist.

For all that Mélanie went out of her way to rustle up treats and tasty dishes, it was wasted effort from thereon out. Gone was the gourmandizing of the good times; born all of a sudden, it died just as quickly. André and Jeanne were now cloaked in an air of sadness. The thought that "we've only a few more days left together" continually weighed them down. André's distress was so devastating that he hoped for Jeanne's departure as a deliverance. Although he kept turning over the same thoughts for hours on end, he possibly suffered less when he was alone. The sight of Jeanne heightened his bitterness and regret; the sadness of each of them augmented that of the other, becoming intolerable for both of them.

Fortunately, their meetings soon grew less frequent, for Jeanne only visited him occasionally, busy, so she said, with preparations for her journey.

Finally, he received a letter stamped from Boulogne-sur-Mer. Jeanne had lacked the courage to kiss him before leaving.

"What's the point of us being miserable?" she wrote. "It'll be less painful this way." And she added. "When you get this letter I'll be at sea on the passenger ship."

André collapsed into an armchair.

So, it was over. Jeanne too had left him! His life was now complete, it could be summed up thus: he'd been fooled by his mistresses, cuckolded by his wife, and abandoned by Jeanne! And he raged against the little lady's lover boy; "What a simpleton! I ask you, twenty-two years old and gets married! He must have been in a hurry to get taken for a ride, or, still worse no doubt, not to be, thanks only to the disasters of pregnancies and all those infirmities that were specific to the little ladies of the bourgeoisie! As though he wouldn't have done better to keep Jeanne and carry on enjoying an obliging mistress, as though it wouldn't be in his own best interest to not disrupt the course of three lives happily proceeding in parallel.

"The truth is," he told himself, "I'm wrong to blame that gentleman, it's down to me, it's the money that I don't have! Jeanne wouldn't be in London if I'd helped her," and he almost understood the ignominious behavior of the crowd, the degradation of society at large, lying flat on its belly, nose in the muck, drinking in foulness, sacrificing friendship, beliefs, everything, for money, which renders all things faultless and sublime, ruling over the despised law courts, the prisons, providing everyone, according to preference, with the respected joys of the family or the coveted orgies of the wealthy.

Besides, why did he earn nothing? Why had he always worked at unproductive jobs, professions of no value, like tutoring and authoring? Why hadn't he accepted the dirty work of his métier, become a serious journalist? And yet he had known people who had cooked up complete poppycock rightly valued at a king's ransom because every night the smart set inanely repeated it when dining with their fancy women! Yes, but then he would have needed to be stupid enough to dream it up and audacious enough to write it down; what's more he would have needed a heart stout enough not to keel over every day at the miserable labors required by current events, fashion, and there rose up before him a sudden vision of the hours wasted in the newspaper office. He saw himself leaning his elbows on a green tabletop, looking for his proofs, while toward three in the morning, like love's handmaidens shut up in salons furnished with divans and gas lamps, his colleagues dozed, stretched, yawning, asking what time it was, smoking and drinking, awaiting the longed-for moment of release from work and going home to sleep.

Ah! That life of girls on the game, resigned to obeying Monsieur's demands and satisfying the whims of regulars and passersby, had filled him with revulsion, and then he had higher ambitions, he wanted to be an artist, but was he? Had his work shown talent? Was he recognized in the world of letters? Had he elbowed his way through the crowd? Was he, at last, seated on the rostrum, in front of the public, subduing it with his audacity, or bringing it to heel with sentimental or solemn farces? No, he had attempted nothing, run no risks, accomplished nothing. He had taken the wrong direction, should have kept to the main road, become just like any other worker or shopkeeper. "Ah no," he cried, "I've learned nothing and I know nothing!" And indeed, he'd obtained the baccalaureate!

Manual employment? But he would have needed years of apprenticeship! Some kind of trade? But he knew nothing of either bookkeeping or business! He'd learned neither English nor German, learned nothing of practical matters, nothing. Was he able to measure cloth, tie up a parcel, seal a bottle or hammer a nail? Could he, like an old official, write pages in slanting and round hand, or, like an ex-corporal, groom and curry horses? Formerly he had known a little Latin and a little Greek; now he knew a little French, and that was all! And he reproached his family for his empty education, the wasted expense of school, the sacrifices to which it had readily submitted in order to make him unfit for ever earning a living!

Then again, it wasn't his family's fault; the comment that habitually marked his classroom exercise books, "adequate," had stalked him all his life! After having labeled him in the eyes of the monitors, it now labeled him in the eyes of the world. He had been unfailingly adequate—adequate in his school exercises, adequate in his tutoring, adequate in his books. And that wasn't all; in his private life, in his household, in the company of his wife, of Jeanne, he had been revealed as neither a cold nor a heated lover, neither bold nor cowardly. No, he had been Mr. Anyone, an insignificant personality, one of those poor folk who don't even have the supreme consolation of lamenting the injustice of their fate, since an injustice presupposes at least an unrecognized merit, a strength.

So, like a man waking up, he looked around him and the drift of his thoughts paused, then quickened again in a tidal surge of troubles. It might, all the same, be said that he had been unlucky because before his marriage he had made an effort, had shown promise in some people's eyes. Only after the separation from Berthe had he become seriously sterile. She it was who had always undermined his energies and his hopes. Now Jeanne's departure was the finishing stroke. And in his mind's eye he saw cohabitation disappearing in the distance, arm in arm, warm in the sunshine, united against the slings and arrows of fate, against the ills of aging. The irregular liaison that he had summarily rejected appeared to him as a safe harbor, like a Saint Périne caring for the infirm and the unwell.[64] "I should have made a commitment to Jeanne," he told himself. "Ah, if she comes back!" And he smiled sadly, knowing very well that she would create a life for herself over there, that without a doubt he wouldn't see her again.

"Poor darling," he murmured, "she's far away now," and he forgot himself in her, identifying himself for a moment with her sex, sewing in London, in the middle of a workshop lit by murky windows, in a dim day among a charivari of foreign words, and, called seamlessly back to himself by his slipper bumping against the floor, he found himself once more on rue Cambacérès in a state of bewilderment as noisy laments arose once more in his soul, leading the funeral music of a life riddled with misunderstood loves, stubborn sorrows, and fleeting joys.

Then, as when in a funeral mass a soft sad voice arises in the silence of the church when the organ falls silent, a voice sounded plaintively, in the annihilation of his soul, imploring vague mercies, uncertain pities, soon drowned out by the return of the great organ notes, by the vehemence of the petticoat crisis that broke out again, tearing at the wounds, opening them wide, ripping off the bandages applied by Jeanne.

It was the end. The tertiary disorders emerged.

After the resentment of the offense he'd received, the wrathful protestations and the bitter regret for absent caresses, after the reawakened memories of times now long gone and dead love affairs no sooner resurrected than reburied, after the aching hunger for a climate of femininity and violent revolts against a cloistered existence, deprived of daylight, of interest, of women, the first bout of the crisis had terminated.

Then, no more piercing torments, burning fevers, obsessions, no more frantic failures and dreadful fits, but some kind of beguiling languor, like a convalescence, a slow calming of his thoughts, complete resignation, a limpid tranquility, melancholic and smiling reveries, tender and consoling feelings such as are sometimes felt on All Soul's Day, before the tomb of a long-dead friend.

Then these symptoms of the second period also passed and the malady seemed to have spent itself when, suddenly, on receipt of Jeanne's letter, it reemerged in a brutal outbreak; then, overwhelmed by an incurable distress, an unrelieved chagrin, an abdication of the self, he gave way under the collapse of a life that, scarcely rebuilt, crumbled once more, burying his last hopes under a noisy heap of ruin and destruction.

XIII

"This staircase is abominable," Désableau thought. "I really don't know how anyone dares live in such a wretched-looking building—I beg your pardon Madame," he said suddenly and flattened himself against the wall, making room for a woman coming down escorted by a litter of grumbling snot-nosed kids, swinging milk cans and clanging them like cymbals.

"Here we are at last," Désableau sighed.

He had arrived in front of a yellow-painted door, adorned halfway down by a black iron doorknob. He looked in vain for the doorbell, then knocked with the handle of his umbrella; the door yawned open and in the half-light he saw a fat woman and a red cat.[65]

"M. Cyprien Tibaille?" he asked by way of greeting.

"He's here, Monsieur."

Désableau deposited his umbrella in a corner by the door, passed through a dark anteroom, opened another door and paused, eyes wide, dazzled by the bright sunlight, seeing Cyprien stretched out, his arms around his head on the pillow, the stub of a smoking pipe in his lips.

He shook the other man's hand and, sitting down on a chair at the foot of the bed, said he hoped his friend was in good health.

Cyprien thanked him for his good wishes, saying that alas they fell short of the mark as he was suffering from an inflammation of the stomach lining.

M. Désableau was one of those people who promptly propose the most wide-ranging remedies to sick people; he therefore advised pills and capsules concocted by such and such a doctor, electuaries,[66] tisanes, and the boluses regularly promoted among the adverts on newspaper back pages.

"Nothing too serious besides that?" he added in a confiding voice.

"No, nothing serious, I'm even allowed to get up tomorrow . . . Alexandre!" he suddenly cried, addressing the cat that had gone inside Désableau's hat after having sniffed it for some time. But this cry had no effect on the beast, whose hindquarters alone were visible, its red-striped tail swaying erect.

Désableau got up, put his hat somewhere safe, and, affably, wanted to stroke the cat, which came forward crabwise, stalking, its ears flattened, its whiskers bristling, and its tail low.

"He's going to scratch you," Cyprien said calmly.

Désableau retreated and sat back down, wishing he'd kept his umbrella as a defensive weapon.

There was a moment of silence. Cyprien, greatly surprised by this visit, looked inquisitively at Désableau, who was crossing and uncrossing his legs with an air of absorption.

"You've moved house," said the latter, finally letting his legs rest, and, raising his head a little, looked around the room, murmuring, "It's very nice, very bright," and, after a pause, "You're still doing lots of work?"

"Yes, lots," and the painter gestured at the watercolors scattered on a table.

Désableau got up, put on his pince-nez, and asked if, without being indiscreet, he could look at them.

"Of course, my dear sir, look as much as you like."

Désableau retreated, feeling nauseated before these watercolors that depicted a whole spectrum of skin diseases, a whole scale of sores and pustules.

He pushed the plates away indignantly and, with poorly concealed disgust, "So that's the kind of subject you enjoy painting?"

"Excuse me, but it's not at all for my own pleasure that I paint these watercolors. I'm simply carrying out a commission for chromolithographs from a doctor. I have to go to the Saint-Louis hospital, install myself in the wards in front of the subjects pointed out to me, enforce a dietary regime for the ones who refuse to let themselves be painted, and all that to earn ten francs for each plate! There's really not much there to enjoy, contrary to what you might think."

That statement was followed by a pause. Deep in thought, Désableau rolled his handkerchief and for no obvious reason flourished it under his nose.

"He obviously hasn't come to buy one of my paintings," the painter thought.

At this juncture the fat woman who had opened the door came in and sprawled herself out in an armchair. Désableau felt even more uncomfortable; he stole a look at the woman, squinting politely from under his pince-nez, not daring to stare at her face.

She looked too obese to him, and well past her prime; tied up like a parcel, her cheeks refurbished with blusher, her hair reduced to dandruff at a parting, her eyes as watery as a dog's, he saw in her something of the doorkeeper, the nurse, and the whore.

"She's really unspeakable," he thought.

Cyprien lost patience with this scrutiny; he stared at Désableau and said, "My dear sir, if you have something to communicate you mustn't worry that Mélie is here. She's a little on the curious side and you can bet that if I asked her to leave the room then I'd have to repeat our conversation word for word after you left; so perhaps it would be better to forget she's there and we can talk quietly together."

This explanation did nothing to lessen the embarrassment of the visitor who, to save face, breathed on the lenses of his pince-nez and polished them carefully with his handkerchief.

The painter was busy speculating about the reason for this visit. Wanting at any rate to break a silence that threatened to prolong itself, he politely asked for news of Madame and Mademoiselle.

Désableau visibly brightened. He relinquished his pince-nez and replied eagerly, "Thank God, all the family is in good health . . . My wife, you know her, she's a workhorse, a rare soul sharing her affections between her daughter and me . . ."

He stopped short.

The cat suddenly leaped from Mélie's lap, took to bolting madly about the room, darting under chairs, rolling on its back and wiggling, its four paws in the air, righting itself with a flip of the back, and, looking alarmed, jumping on all the furniture.

"It's his fleas," Mélie said sententiously.

Désableau looked at her sideways and, picking up the thread of his ideas once more, he carried on speaking: "Yes, my wife is keeping well, and as for our little darling, she has a delicate constitution as you know, but really her health is as good as we could wish. Besides, the child is a source of great satisfaction for us. Her character is as straightforward as her mother's; she's never disciplined in the classroom, and always comes top of the class; the schoolmistress cites her as setting a good example, and Monsignor was good enough to compliment us on that last month when he came to the school to confirm the young pupils.

"What have you got in mind for your young lady when she grows up?" Mélie asked in a friendly voice.

"Shut up Mélie," Cyprien barked, "and stop Alexandre from jumping about like that."

Mélie grabbed Alexandre and, while she clutched it to her, a silent battle was fought, marked by the cat's tail whipping dully against the woman's belly.

"Well," Désableau resumed, somewhat hesitantly, "everything is for the best, and yet, you know, one's happiness is never complete. Yes, when a man is satisfied in one direction, he isn't in another. So, I can tell you, the health of our poor Berthe is a worry to us. You see, her morale has been affected by all the misfortunes that have befallen her, the separation from André, all that, and as a consequence, her physical well-being too; in short, while there's no immediate danger in our house, our niece's condition isn't without giving us some serious cause for concern."

Cyprien, paying close attention, stared unwaveringly at his visitor, who spoke again.

"Yes, lots of care and attention are needed, and fresh air ... The doctors we've consulted are unanimous in prescribing a stay in the country, walks in the woods, peace and calm, no emotions and no worries."

And after a pause he continued in a lower voice. "It's really regrettable that André hasn't agreed to the request concerning this that I submitted to him through the office of M. Saparois, our solicitor."

"Ah!" went Cyprien.

Désableau continued more animatedly: "This refusal is all the more inexplicable as it's a rare opportunity for Berthe. Just think, a house at Viroflay, which is to say a few leagues from Paris, a good-sized garden with a vegetable patch, only ten minutes from a station, a train every half hour, and all that for twelve thousand francs! And then again, even more than the material advantages that would accrue from that purchase, there are reasons that surpass all others, humanitarian considerations that no one with a heart could reject . . ."

The painter interrupted him. "Excuse me, but I haven't fully grasped the story you're telling me; let's see, you want Madame Berthe, your niece, to buy a house at Viroflay, no doubt the same one you rented last summer?"

Désableau nodded an affirmative.

"Good, and, since her status as married woman means she can't buy anything without her husband's approval, you've sent a solicitor to André to obtain his authorization."

Désableau nodded again.

"And André has refused?"

Désableau gave a silent nod.

"Good, I've got it now. If you'd like to continue, I'm all ears."

But Désableau declared that there was no need to continue. He even apologized for having bored his friend with this lengthy story, but he couldn't help himself; he'd been too unsettled by André's response! He'd been suffering from a bad stomach since learning the news. He loved Berthe like his own daughter. In raising her he'd made no distinction between her and his little Justine, and here was the poor child, after all her misfortunes, suffering a new setback just as her hardships were beginning to subside in the serene company of her family.

"Oh! I'm not forgetting," he cried, "that André's religion should come as no surprise and it would be a really good thing if a friend were to open his eyes, were to make him understand how lacking in humanity his behavior is."

"In other words," the painter murmured, "you're asking me to talk to André about this business. But really Monsieur, why not talk to him yourself?"

"Because . . ." Désableau replied, blushing slightly, "I'm afraid that M. André is prejudiced against me, and then again, I have to confess, I'm afraid of getting carried away in the argument and making things worse."

"Okay, but your reasons for thinking that André isn't well disposed don't apply to Madame Désableau. Why doesn't she go to see him?"

Désableau didn't immediately reply to that question. Well, he reflected, just think, a decent woman visiting a gross type like that! and he shuddered at the thought of Madame Désableau coming into contact with this fat drab who was lazing in an armchair with her cat if she instead of him had visited Cyprien.

"Discretion," he said at length, "prevents my wife from going to visit a young man who might not always be alone when at home."

"Good lord!" Cyprien replied. "I'm not saying that I'll refuse the service you're requesting, although, given a choice, I'd rather not get my fingers caught in the doorjamb, however . . ."

Désableau didn't let him finish. He got up and seized him by the hands. "I expected nothing less from your friendship," he cried. "I said to Madame Désableau yesterday, I'm sure that M. Cyprien will acknowledge the justice of our aims. And my wife was of the same opinion, insisting that I scold you a thousand times, because you've become a rare visitor—you've absolutely forgotten the path to our door. Let's see, you must come to see us and share our supper, as informally as you like. Dammit! Just because André is angry with us, that's no reason to join in his quarrels with us! Besides, you know that my wife likes you."

"I've never doubted it," Cyprien replied.

"Well then, it's agreed. But what an idiot I am!" he suddenly blurted. "What with all this, I forgot the reason for my visit. We still need to have the portrait of my father restored. Before we left for the country you were good enough to promise to take care of it yourself . . ."

"Yes, yes," Cyprien replied very coldly. "I'll come by to pick it up one of these days."

"Yes indeed," Désableau cried. "Come whenever you want. We dine at six in the evening. There, it's agreed. Look here, your cat is shedding its hair," he said after a moment's silence, looking at the animal that was arching its back and slowly rubbing against the bottom of his trousers.

"It's nothing to worry about, Monsieur," Mélie exclaimed, bringing over a scrubbing brush.

But Désableau protected himself. He never would have accepted a lady taking that trouble. However, pushed by the fat woman, he consented to put his foot on a chair and let her brush his trousers energetically.

"Cyprien," Mélie cried, kneeling in front of the chair, "it's time for your rub down."

"Oh," the painter groaned, spreading camphor balm on a length of flannel.

Another moment of silence ensued, during which time a smell of camphor arose faintly from Cyprien's stomach, gradually thickening in the room while the sharp sound of cloth raked by the brush was the only one to be heard.

"A thousand thanks, madam," said Désableau to Mélie, then, on both feet once more, he pulled out his watch. "Damn! I'm going to be late to the office. So, here's wishing you good health," and he shook Cyprien's hand. But, becoming very undecided, he didn't leave, wondering if he should remind the painter of the intervention he had requested between André and Berthe, but then felt that it showed more dignity to refer again to the painting to be restored, and let it be vaguely understood that he would pay the costs involved. "So, goodbye once more, and take care"; and, shaking the painter's hand yet again, he added, "I can tell my wife that she can count on you?" thinking in this way to make a discreet allusion to the main reason for his visit.

Cyprien gave a vague nod of the head and, preceded by Mélie and the cat, Désableau, with a last look round, exited the place, and, as soon as he was down in the street, he grimaced, thinking that, all the same, a decent man would be really out of luck if he had to live like that with a whore. "Everybody's leavings, a beast, a piece of filth, and this Cyprien, a sewage worker and a gipsy," he mumbled. "Yes, like attracts like, he's well paired with André. All the same I must say what a lousy job it is, having to go and ask for help from people like that, and if you have to play the diplomat with them then make sure to wear mittens, gloves. Oh, that poor devil Vigeois can boast of putting us to the test in bequeathing his daughter to us!"

And he strode on, angrier than ever, fulminating against shady menages. "Annihilation of the moral sense, that's the only way to explain these aberrant lives," he thought, and consoled by these reflections, he went into his office and furiously berated two unmarried employees who had arrived late, declaring that they couldn't claim domestic responsibilities as an excuse since they were both bachelors, and that the administration couldn't accept reasons that no doubt it was unable to decently acknowledge for late-coming prejudicial to its best interests.

And while the employees patiently endured their boss's dressing-down, Cyprien, who was in no doubt about the deplorable impression Mélie had made on Désableau, laughed to himself, stroking the cat, curled into a ball on the bed.

"Alexandre, you Rustbar," he said, "the monsieur with whiskers you've just seen is a serious man, a man with connections. Married, the father of a daughter, and recently promoted to the coveted grade of second in command, he looks like an impressive figure in the eyes of small-time shopkeepers and rentiers. Well then, this civil servant must have left with a poor opinion of you, because you're dishonest, you poked your nose into his hat and covered his left leg with hair; but you mustn't let that bother you my poor pussy, because, you see, you can be sure that M. Désableau has an equally bad opinion of your father, Cyprien, who right now is holding you by the paws so you don't run away.

"Yes, this gentleman despises us, me and our good friend Mélie. Why? Well, that's not so easy to explain to you, because your mother Mélie took pity on you and had the Pont-Neuf gelder tear from you in advance the seed of certain ideas that would otherwise have taken root in your soul. We've sliced off all your instinct for amorous prowling, all your future desire to utter heartrending howls among the rooftops. We did you wrong, because you're a monstrous and superhuman creature, a beast that has been robbed of the most holy laws of nature by the removal from you, right from the start, of moral grief. But that isn't the point at issue. Forgive the digression, don't bite me or else I'll spank you, and listen now.

"You see, puss, society has decided, on a day of delusion, God knows when, so much has that been lost in the dark night of time, that every man who wants to live with a woman, in the same room, in the same bed, must first step in front of another man who, after having put a cotton sash round his waist, will ask them some questions.

"That procedure, my dear pussycat, is called marriage; it's the honest thing to do, it's respect from the whole nation, the whole world, it's protection wherever one happens to be as guaranteed by the legal establishment and the gendarmes.

"So! Your daddy Cyprien and your mommy Mélie haven't paraded in front of the well-known sash I told you about, they just live together as you might have done with a lady cat, without having first obtained a license from another cat. This is to inform you that, whatever they do, they'll always be reviled, always held in contempt.

"And there's nothing to be done about that," Cyprien added with a touch of melancholy. "No clever tricks to dream up. If I were to buy a wedding ring for your mom, if I were to throw silk over her back and a feathered hat on her head, that wouldn't stop us from having the particular look of unmarried people. If you want to be sure of that you only have to look at us through the window when we walk out together; that, it has to be admitted, is a fine sight! Mélie walks with a lurch, and she can't keep up with me; she whines and blows her nose, wipes her face, shouts after me, calls my name out loud in the street, while my long legs plow through the air twenty steps ahead of her. Now, is that what can endow us with the honorable look of a married couple? No, right?

"Oh, if we were laborers, if Mélie wore old camisoles and soft bonnets, and if I was wearing overalls with a cap on my head, I'm not saying we might not be able to fool people, since everyone among the common folk gives the impression of cohabiting."

Alexandre stirred restlessly and meowed desperately.

"Well then, I'll cut it short," Cyprien said, "because I'm beginning to think that you aren't very interested in these explanations. In fact, the two cents of liver that you eat every day are neither better nor worse, whether it's Mélie-daughter-of-Aulanier or Mélie-wife-of Cyprien-Tibaille who cuts them up for you and kneads them with bread dough, but all these details were necessary for you to understand the depths of disgust M. Désableau felt at the sight of us three."

Impatient with this speech, the cat rolled its black eyes, barely circled with yellow at the rim, and writhed still more angrily between the painter's hands.

"Let him go," Mélie protested, "do you think that animal can understand all the stories you're telling?"

"Your mother is right," Cyprien declared, "So off you go, my boy, you must be fully enlightened by now"; and he released Alexandre who leaped down from the bed and briskly shook a shower of red hairs onto the parquet.

"Good heavens, Cyprien my old friend, what an idiot you are!" Mélie sighed.

"You sometimes hit the nail on the head," Cyprien replied.

Their conversations often ended this way.

The two of them together were model cohabitees, on the basis of a reciprocal forbearance, a union in which sexual attraction had little place, the alliance of two worn-out people, managed by a woman who was no longer young and who, through debaucheries undergone as one submits to the exhaustion of a dangerous job, had only one idea, one goal: to find a man who would consent to pull her out of the water and land her on the shore, safe and dry. Her nose smelled a rescuer in Cyprien; she saw that he no longer shared a young man's concern with finding an appealingly pretty mistress to show off to others; her fat waist, her coarse form, her penchant for boozing and sipping little glasses of vermouth between meals, made it impossible for her to find a situation with men enamored of distinction and possessed by the ideal of a delicate woman, with no natural disabilities, who feel the need to probe their mistress's past, force her to tell jokes so as to allow themselves to deliver the punchline, and who drop them in the end because they've met another woman more elegantly dressed and with a better complexion.

She saw Cyprien as a street urchin worn out before his time, like an invalid who only wants to be tucked into bed, and she attached herself to him, dreaming of merely becoming his housemaid, but a maid with whom one can talk familiarly and to whom one can, from time to time, give little pats on the bottom.

Then this mild, good-natured whore who had been constantly tricked by men without, for all that, harboring any resentments, embraced a simple idea. Vigorously broad-backed and overweight, Mélie felt a certain pity for the painter's delicate gauntness. "He needs to be fattened up," she often said to herself, and she worried about him like a youngster whose forehead one wipes after he's been running. She checked his clothing when he got ready to go out, stuffing scarves into his pockets, making him strip down from head to foot when he came back soaked on rainy days, going to bed before him in the winter so he could stretch out in warm sheets.

They had crossed paths one evening when she stood on a bridge idly staring at nothing in particular; accosted under the most fatuous of pretexts, she invited the painter to get lost. Cyprien had then spoken of the fraternity of souls, took the woman's arm in his and, in spite of her attempts at refusal, had taken her with him, dazzling her with impenetrable phrases, impressing her with the certainty that she was being taken in tow by a gentleman who had received an education. For the rest, she was enchanted by the painter's hospitality. This was the courteousness of draper's assistants and hairdressers, always sure to produce an effect. To that, Cyprien added a gracious, easygoing quality that Mélie found comforting, already pleased as she was with his good manners.

Cheered by strongly spiced grogs, she felt a maternal pity for the gaping seams in the painter's clothes, and she supplied some stitches here and there, a bit of darning. Then, satisfied with Cyprien's low expectations and generosity, she came back of her own accord, several times, coming in with the humble air of a dog that expects to be chased away, but the painter, thinking of the future of his wardrobe, good-naturedly let her prowl around where she wanted.

Their liaison continued like that, soothing and benign, until one day Cyprien took to bed, unwell, suffering from earaches and boils. Then she took up post near the bed, preparing a stewpot so he didn't have to go out; she nursed him with great consideration, watched over him, indulging him, putting a bed heater at his feet, getting up to make him a drink.

He was astounded; he had long since given up hope of finding such affection, such compassion; he melted before her devotion to him, and yet perturbed by the good nature of a woman who wanted, in spite of his protests, to take charge of the mortifying and abject condition of a sick man.

When he almost lost his temper, begging her not to take on such revolting chores, she laughed, saying, "Hush now, my little man, this is women's work."

And he hugged her, weepily, and the fat woman laughed even louder, elated to be embraced innocently, contrary to what she was used to.

For the rest, she slaved away furiously because, on top of cooking and shopping, she had to sweep the apartment, cut up the old muslin curtains for poultices, fight with Cyprien, who was outraged by an invasion of medicines.

Then a whole series of purgatives followed; gassy lemon sodas that, with no good effect, filled Cyprien with gas; bitter and sweet Pullna water that he vomited up;[67] Epsom salts that that heated him cruelly; and finally, the abominable castor oil which the doctor prescribed as a last resort.

Then Cyprien squawked like a chicken. The mere smell of that drug turned his stomach. One morning, after having carefully stirred the oil in a bowl of hot coffee Mélie had to pour it wholesale down the throat of the painter, whom she scared, startling him awake, shrieking like a magpie. He cursed, swore like a sailor, shouted at her, told her to go to hell, then admitted that she had acted for the best, resignedly, smiling at Melié's puffed out cheeks and pursed lips, blowing on the bowl to cool it down, and he agreed to drink the broth with herbs, to swallow jugfuls of green water to the dregs.

For as long as he was unable to get up, she remained close to him, from morning till night, chattering, mending clothes, reading cheap, illustrated storybooks, adding a layer of gossiped tales from her own lodgings about all the scandals reported in the painter's. Her zealousness was unfailing and her stoutheartedness and good humor were a comfort to the painter who panicked at the slightest indisposition, thinking his time had come.

"When one wants something, one wants it," she said; "as for me, I could be paralyzed and still my head would make me shift my legs," and she tapped her forehead with her thimble.

Tough on herself, with saltpeter in the blood that shook off the fat, she was, however, tender with others, moved by their slightest scratch, their slightest hurt.

When Cyprien's earaches subsided and his boils burst, she continued to nurse him anyway; but toward midday she absented herself regularly for two hours every day.

The painter was alarmed; seeing her so housewifely and so placid, he hadn't dreamed of what trials the woman faced in life. Mélie happily accepted her share of the meals that she cooked, but there was also the rent, the living expenses, the laundry. Where did she get the money needed to meet these costs?

She often worked at lacemaking, with a piece of wood bristling with points that formed a pattern, on which she arranged braid that she sewed and strung with little black glass pearls gathered in her apron and stuck to the thumb of her left hand with saliva. But besides the fact that her eyes were no longer sharp enough to rapidly string these pearls, piercing them with a needle through holes at either end, this labor was too poorly paid to meet a woman's needs. Thirty-two sous were the most she could earn for slaving from morning till midnight, working at top speed; there must therefore be one or two gents who helped the poor girl out; her absences were even justified by that; and yet when he scrutinized Mélie, Cyprien was astonished. She was neither appetizing nor highly sexed.

"It must be the case," he said to himself, "that there are one or two cripples of my type, withered and weak people hanging onto a mistress for reasons different from those that have driven humanity for centuries." And he felt a certain anger, a certain jealousy about the amount of nursing she was no doubt dispensing to old lovers. His amorous petulance resembled the kind of resentment that a patient feels in a hospital when he sees the doctor scarcely bothering to examine him while spending time attending to others.

However, he couldn't reproach Mélie for not privileging him, since she hardly left his side and, besides, showed no signs of being impatient to leave. She studied the clock, wrinkling her nose, waiting till the last minute, brushing her hair unenthusiastically, murmuring while pulling on gloves through which her fingers poked, "Oh! they're not all that bad!" Then she lowered her veil and, casting a last glance around the room, scattered cinders over the fire, arranged everything so that Cyprien wouldn't need for anything during her absence.

Grown used to the to-and-fro of a skirt getting snagged on chair legs, the encouraging words thrown at the illness, the exchange of meaningless messages that are meaningful for sick people, Cyprien felt horribly unhappy when left alone. His room became doleful and he in turn looked sadly at the hands of the clock, listening to the tick-tock of the pendulum to confirm that it hadn't stopped. "How the time drags," he said, and he felt a real joy when, at the end of two hours, he heard Mélie's elephantine footsteps shaking the stairs.

The woman's measured exits remained unexplained, and without him having the courage to question her. At length, however, he was tormented by a dull anxiety; he was afraid of demands made by the persons whom she went to see, he feared a forced breakup, feared being left alone.

The idea that he might be deprived of care maddened him; he saw himself alone, during the night, restless, scourged by fever, exhausted by nightmares, sweating on his bolster, awaiting the arrival of daytime like a salvation.

He dwelt on such thoughts during those states of vague drowsiness in which the numbed spirit still pursues its course. A resurgence of his illness prostrated him once more. Then, aching all over, no longer saying anything, he dwelled at length on the terrors of a catastrophe, solitary suffering, the miserable deaths of outcasts and those ridden with scabies. The prospect of expiring miserably in a room, door left open by the carer while other tenants went up and down the stairs humming to themselves, took root, grew in his brain, fixed there by the sufferings that beset him. A terrible fear, one of those unreasoning panics, grabbed hold of him; his teeth chattered under the blankets, he was on the verge of begging Mélie not to go out that day.

Then he didn't dare to. He suddenly recognized his situation; his income was exhausted, eaten up by women, and the few scraps that had survived his losses were about to vanish, carried off on a stream of bills for medications from pharmacies. What a fool he'd been to let himself by duped by hussies who didn't give a damn about him! As always, it was the good girls who paid a price for the bad ones. Mélie had come too late . . . Suddenly the clock chimed, cutting short his train of thought.

He looked at Mélie, saying to himself, "Now's the time, she's going to cut and run." She looked at him in turn and, frightened by the distress that she read in his eyes, caressed his forehead, brought him a tisane to drink, and wiped his mouth.

"Now, what's wrong, my big boy?" she queried.

He didn't reply.

"Are you in pain? Tell me where."

He muttered, "I'm a little feverish," and sorrowfully he returned his gaze to the clock.

Then Mélie kissed him, blushing slightly, and took up her needlework again, letting the hours flow peacefully by.

At a stroke he was conquered; this simple event sealed his fate, his last struggles ceased. He began to be afraid that Mélie would refuse to live with him.

Out of decency he decided to wait until he was fully recovered before making a proposition to her. "That way I won't seem to be begging a favor," he told himself. One evening, very cheerful and in good health, he puffed on his pipe, blew out an enormous cloud and, a little embarrassed, spoke his piece in a way that was both playful and serious, finding it easier that way. "We're no longer young, old girl, and the weather's turning bad. It seems to me that now is the moment for us to play Paul and Virginie who shelter under the same petticoat in rainy weather.[68] You're fat and I'm skinny, you're brave and I'm a coward; let's combine these qualities and we'll complete each other; we'll at least have some chance of withstanding life's hailstorms. You must have had enough of trading on the black market, and besides its dangerous because the customs officers of morality, the boys in blue, are all round. As for me, the life of a bachelor does nothing for me; being on my own puts me out of sorts and leaves me on edge; when all's said and done, I'm tired and my soul's toilet bowl is full to the brim. Look now, wouldn't it make sense to come and sleep here and muddle along with me? To be like man and wife, and what's more without the chance of you getting pregnant, eh? What do you say, if you like the idea of shacking up, go on, slap my hand, it's a done deal."

She accepted straightaway; her middle-aged dream had come true; she kissed Cyprien, thanking him for his kindness, saying that he would see that she wasn't the nasty type, that she would try to make his life as easy as possible.

"I know that, Mélie," the painter replied, moved; then he calmed down again and talked about the future. He didn't try to hide from Mélie that theirs would be a tough life, that they'd have to live like laborers, but she shrugged her shoulders, declaring that she'd never been in the habit of living like a princess, that comfort and security meant little to her, that besides, by keeping things under control, she would aim to make both ends meet.

Thus commenced their union, with none of the troubles that disturb younger people. They reached an understanding, adjusting to each other's respective failings so as to avoid friction. The fat woman looked after the house, letting Cyprien idle about outside, hardly worrying about his absences, even ready to forgive some romps, as one from time to time accepts the petty tomfooleries of an urchin. "The only thing I ask," she said one day, "is that you don't 'embrace' them."

And indeed all the rest was of no consequence to her. Having retired from love, from the world, knowing from experience how small a thing carnal commerce is for people who are really worn out, she still understood the thoughtless impulse of an evening, the brutal act promptly regretted, but she rebelled against the idea that the first comer might, like her, get from her man what she considered as a sign of real affection, a forthright kiss.

Cyprien agreed to everything she wanted; he came and went as he pleased, and soon, with neither of them interesting each other sexually, a sincere friendship formed between them; Cyprien could denounce women's vices, give free rein to everything that went through his head without Mélie ever taking offense; she smiled benignly and let him talk, simply saying sometimes, the same as after Désableau's departure, "Good heavens, Cyprien, what an idiot you are, old friend."

XIV

Moved by Jeanne's departure, Mélanie wailed loud and long, then agreed to hold her tongue and didn't give the little lady another thought, save when the time came to get a bonnet at a reduced price, or have a dress run up.

Aggrieved with these expenses that were previously avoided thanks to Jeanne, the policeman at his post cursed London and the English.

Good weather had now returned, and André, installed once more on his balcony, contemplated the eternal spectacle of the same ministry employees sitting in the building opposite, in front of the same filing cabinets made of black wood, shifting the same bundles of paper, against the same background of green felt.

The look of the offices and the street remained unchanged. The mise-en-scène was that of some provincial corner, the same crippled bit player keeping an eye on the cab rank, the same waiters carrying mazagrans and platefuls of eggs, the same crowd of petitioners working up their tears, disappearing into office doors; not leaving till hours later, exhausted.

Moreover, the warmth of the sky had hatched a swarm of grooms and menials from the local hotels, even more numerous than at the late moment in the season when André had moved house last year. Clustered like flies in a corner, they were smoking their pipes and spitting, conversing with the porter of a house who was busy putting an extra shine to the door handles with an application of rottenstone; and there were other arrivals, waggling buttocks tightly encased in the kinds of pants that are pocketed at the knees and bulge out and bunch up over clogs, soon joined by stable hands in work jackets with sleeves rolled up, flannel shirts shrunk at the collar from repeated washing, their hair meticulously plastered down on their temples, caps with two ribbons squashed on their necks. And all of them were gesticulating, jawing, waving their fists. From his window André, following the movement of their shaved chins, guessed at promptly accepted invites to go for a drink, the gossip passed along from bureaus to coach houses, the greetings thrown to saddlers' dogs, sitting on their bottoms, ears cocked, sharpened by whistles, shaking their gray hair that bristled over scarlet collars with copper studs.

He rejoiced in this proliferation of dogs and hired hands in the sun.

He spent hours studying the people parading along his street, the procession of ladies and gentlemen swallowed up by the Ministry door. Suddenly his wide-ranging gaze focused on a man outlined in the distance. "That looks like Cyprien," he thought. Soon he was able to recognize the figure of the painter who was approaching at speed, jerkily maneuvering the skinny joints of his long legs.

André's face lit up; their relationship had been all but paused for months.

"Hey, you rascal, so there you are," he said when the painter had climbed the stairs, and they shook hands, both speaking at the same time, gazing at each other, laughing in delight.

"Well, my friend," Cyprien said, "you see, it's quite simple, if I haven't come to see you, it's because you were in the coils of a woman and you know as well as me that women like to make a clean sweep of everything! Just count the friends who used to visit me in my studio and those who've been kept away by mistresses and you'll soon see where the balance of power lies. You're the only one left, and I don't want to lose you too."

"I'm always by myself these days so you needn't be afraid of visiting," André replied. "Jeanne's gone." And he explained the breach, adding sadly that his prediction had proven correct, that since Jeanne had set foot in England he'd received no news of her. "And you," he asked, shaking his head as though to chase away an unwelcome memory, "what about you, what have you got to say for yourself?"

"Me," the painter said, hesitating slightly, "ah well then, you see, I've gotten . . . I'm living with a woman."

André opened his eyes wide and couldn't help but laugh.

"By God yes," Cyprien said, recognizing the irony of that laugh, "that's how it is. Well, you think it's funny because you've so often heard me make fun of people who hook up with each other. That only proves one thing, my old friend, that when it comes to women, no one is cunning, no one strong; those who rant on about them are the ones who are most afraid of them and most sure to get their fingers burnt. And that's so much the case that I can make this declaration with no fear of mistake; when you're tired of women and begin to protest in all good faith that you detest them, you might as well take the last sacrament and get ready for your shroud. Marriage and cohabitation are lying in wait, disasters are imminent.

"And yet I've now got to tell you that Mélie—that's the name of my woman—is a fine girl with really good qualities; my only option was to find a last ideal, a mature, calm, loyal woman, without carnal needs or affectations, in a word, a powerful and peaceful cow, and she meets all the requirements. Well, my good Mélie is all of that, or else, what do I know, maybe she isn't that at all, because everyone with a mistress immediately finds that she has a whole heap of good qualities that don't actually exist, and I've maybe become just as much of an idiot as they are and I'm fooling myself. So be it!" he concluded happily. "It doesn't matter, it all comes to the same thing in the end."

"So then, old friend," André cried, "we'll dine together this evening, eh? Hang it, after such a long time, the least we can do is keep each other company, so come with me. I've only just now given Mélanie time off, and I was about to eat miserably on my own in a restaurant. Your visit is a stroke of luck! Hold on, do you know why Mélanie asked for time off? No? Well, it's to go to my uncle's funeral!"

"Your uncle?" Cyprien was taken aback.

"So, you remember the day when we went in search of the housemaid at a laundress's place on rue Quatre-Vents, we saw an old man groaning on a commode?"

"If I remember him? Damned if I don't! I'm sure too there was a new girl who behaved in a way that was so extraordinary it haunted me for a long time. So, the respectable old chap has given up the ghost, just like that?"

"Yes, Mélanie told me that he leaned over on one side of the chair and was scratching the floor with his hand, while poking out his tongue at the same time. At first, they thought he was having some fun and gave him a thump to sit him up straight. But he said, 'I don't know . . . I don't know . . .' and his head fell forward on his stomach; and that was that."

"He was bled dry and he stank to high heaven!" Cyprien said. "Those words could be chiseled on the old chap's tomb as an epitaph. But, hey, on a happier note, if you don't mind, I'd much rather bring you back for a meal at my place. You'll see my woman's mug, how about it?"

"Really, you're a bit short weight when it comes to logic! You stay away from me because I've got a mistress, and now that you've got one, you want to bring me to see her; do you want us to fall out with each other, since women make a clean sweep of everything in your opinion—and you aren't altogether wrong about that!"

"Yes, yes, I know, but Mélie is absolutely the motherly type, she'll make you feel welcome; otherwise, I'd have to let her know that I'm not coming back for supper. That would be a hell of a nuisance. So, it's agreed then, you'll come. By the way, on the subject of visits, guess who visited me?"

"How do you expect me to guess that?"

"Désableau."

"Ah! . . . So, what was it he wanted?"

"I don't know, he came to have a picture refurbished; he told me that your wife wasn't in good health, that she needed a change of air . . ."

"And that I refused permission to buy a house in Viroflay, yes?"

"Yes," Cyprien said, seeming to search his memory, "I believe that Désableau talked about that. I told him that my own affairs were enough to be going on with, without getting mixed up in anyone else's."

"Do you know what Désableau is?" André suddenly said.

"An imbecile."

"Yes, for starters; and after that?"

Cyprien made a vague gesture.

"Well, he's an old rogue."

No sign of surprise showed on the painter's face.

"In a big way," André resumed. "Here's a man who proposes that we buy a house at Viroflay with the excuse that Berthe is in poor health! I'd understand if it was in Normandy, or Auvergne, Provence, or Menton, Nice, but Viroflay! He calls that fresh air! No, it's as clear as day. Désableau is eager to acquire a place in the country near Paris, near his office, so he doesn't have to carry on paying the rent on it. I'm not his dupe. So, what I said to the solicitor was, for a start, I don't see the point of buying a house when you can rent one; then, when a doctor can show me a village where Berthe's health can be restored by a stay there, in whatever locality it might be, then fine, I'll agree to as many authorizations as you want. Until then, nothing doing: I refuse."

"Désableau didn't tell me about that. You're right too. It's not at all clear how healthy Viroflay is. I hadn't thought of that." Cyprien continued, "There you go, he's more cunning than I thought, our good old Désableau! Now tell me, will you put your coat on. It's nearly six o'clock."

"So, it's decided then? We're eating at your place."

"Yes, only let's get a move on. Mélic isn't expecting you so we need at least to give her time to cook up a bigger stew; also, I want to find something extra for supper on the way; that will spare the old lady, who gets puffed easily; going up and down the stairs is an effort."

"You'd do better to tell her that we're eating out," André responded. "There'll be a hell of a fuss."

"Drop it, now. Here're some quips that'll make you change your tune: when there's enough for two, there's enough for three; you can take pot luck; feel free, make yourself at home, and so on, and so on. If you make as much as one objection, I'll rattle off stuff like this for an hour."

They both laughed and went out.

"So," Cyprien said, continuing a conversation started on the staircase, "I've taken lodgings near you, because when a man sets himself up with a woman, he should try as hard as possible to change address, and so, you'll see, the building where I'm lodging isn't luxurious, but the rooms are well situated, south-facing."

"You're not losing by making the change," André replied. "This district has got a lot to offer." And he told the painter about what he'd thought when out walking one morning. "I think I got it right," he concluded. "These streets smell of Gallican ministers and hotel porters."[69]

"Yes, absolutely," the painter exclaimed breathing in the air. "There now, thank God, you're beginning to understand modern life! Yes, this district is superb, just like all the others, too, since each of them in this adorable Paris of ours has its own individual tone; I'm pleased to see that I haven't been preaching in the wilderness, and that you're now able to credit my theories!

"Wait, look at that," he said suddenly, stopping his friend in front of a harness maker's window display, full of curb chains, bundles of stirrups, bits, rows of spurs astride a wooden hassock, displaying their upright stems so that their steel and copper rowels glittered prettily. "What a sight, eh?" he murmured, enraptured by the cold brightness that the metal threw onto the matte black of the horse blinkers, on the light brown saddle leather, on the tea-colored bridles! And he put his nose against the window, his eyes caressing the rows of riding crops resting on two rods in an overturned frame, examining, in the distance, at the back of the shop, the delightful nag, stuffed and sewn into a pelt the color of café-au-lait.

"That would be wonderful to paint," he sighed, and, while walking, he carried on speaking. "Don't you agree with me that a talented still-life artist should take shopkeeper's displays for his subject, instead of his eternal flowers and his eternal oysters, that grocer there for example, with his bottles, his bundles of macaroni, his colorful packets, his jars, or better still, the interior of these splendid coach makers full of dark-bodied coaches, with hubs shining like new-minted coins, with raised windows reflecting the surrounding colors, or else lowered and letting us see the insides upholstered in nacarat silk, lemon, dianella blue.[70]

"You see, I've often had that notion while loitering in these streets. But just you try to convey the special note of a neighborhood with a pencil or brush! That's a job for writers, not artists! It's true that you're all the same in your gang, just like in ours you make a mountain out of a molehill, so, living in this neighborhood, from father to son, you don't know the people you're so eager to portray in your books! Because there's no denying it, you and the others, you've never experienced the streets you describe. You visit them twice, take notes, and think that that's all that's needed; as if it isn't necessary to have spent time in a place and explored every nook and cranny in order to portray its life! Oh yes, by God! I know, I can hear you reply that you have mattresses and beds that you can't move every week. Okay, but a writer who describes Paris has to live in furnished lodgings, following what's demanded by his work, one day here, there the next. And after all, take the bad with the good, you can't create art when you want ease and comfort!"

André pulled a face. "While you're at it," he said, "why not make writers travel like circus folk in a horse-drawn buggy."

"That's nothing but words," exclaimed the painter, who was getting worked up. "What the hell! Six months are what's needed to fashion a work, and you can decently stay in a house for two quarters. Well, whatever. But wait, since we're in this neighborhood, do you at least know about the cité Berryer?"

"The cité Berryer?"

"Yes, the place on rue Royale where there's a market every Tuesday and Thursday? No, I see you don't know about it; well then, old chum, I've really got to ask what you've learned living in these streets for so long. I've also got to ask, what's the use of keeping a heap of dictionaries in your house, volumes of Littré, Loredan Larchey, Souviron, all of them except for Bottin, the only one who provides the particular nuance of the districts and streets, who names the trades of those who live there. In short, the only one who provides information that's useful for writers.[71]

"It's late," he suddenly said, taking out his watch, "otherwise I'd have taken you to the market."

"It'll keep for another day," André said in a disinterested voice, "after all, what's so special about your market?"

"What's so special? Ah, my friend, whatever I could tell you about it wouldn't add up to much. Go there, and you'll have something to tell me about it! Anyway, to give you the faintest of impressions, imagine a long yard shut in by four high walls. Smoke-blackened, streaked with rain, zigzagging cracks over all the buildings top to bottom; windows decked out with drapery drying on cords and hung out on every floor by women with snarled hair who empty soapy water into sinks like there's no tomorrow. On the pavement, tables with broomstick handles rigged up at each corner supporting old canvas awnings, set up in two rows, so close to each other that a couple of people together can scarcely walk abreast through the narrow path. Along with all that, an astonishing display of fish and meat, signet rings and gold-plated chains with big links for horse traders and pimps, heaps of dainty gateaux, feather dusters and dish cloths, hairnets trimmed with silk, garters dyed with crude vermilion and coarse green, clogs, draw sheets and corset stays, artificial hair and walking sticks. All that, more or less, is what makes up the table and the trimmings. In the middle of it, add an enormous swarm of people, two lines of women moving in opposite directions, shoving back whoever's in their way, shoals of breasts following in single file, masses of customers with their snot-nosed brats, slipping on vegetable peelings, bumping their noses against the coils of hair walking ahead of them, climbing on each other's shoulders, market traders calling out to them, snared by these ones here, snagged by those others there, quarreling and grumbling like harpies over rabbit carcasses and dead poultry, then moving on again, carried away by the crowd, buttonholed again by new traders whose stalls and tables are jostled in the scrum, bumped by the women's bellies. On top of all that add a furious hubbub, hoarse bellows answered by the shrill rattle of the women, then, under the gray-green canvases, on all sides, flights of blue and white smocks, the strokes of red made by long-sleeved woolen waistcoats, lilac stains left by the little stripes on the butcher boys' aprons; last but not least, the white bonnets and black caps bobbing continuously up and down in an endless stream of heads, in short an entire suburban fair, jam-packed in the yard of a destitute building, in the middle of Paris! If you see it, your ears and eyes will get a full dose, your nose too, because there are three zones to pass through, each with its own smell; in entering by way of rue Royale there's a pungent smell of burning wood chips and a stale perfume of frying fritters; in the middle of the yard, the tidal ozone takes over, salted with soft and tepid gusts escaped from cellars; at the other end, near rue Boissy-d'Anglas, all these smells disappear and you only soak up the foul breath of the waste basins.[72]

"So, there you have it. At Menilmont or Montparnasse there would be nothing bizarre or funny about this fair, but you'll have to admit that it's an odd thing to find here, in this wealthy district, on rue Royale, only two steps from the Madeleine, in the middle of these swank shops, and these restaurants and cafés with their gold trim, full of mirrors, a real court of miracles, carefully hidden behind a door.[73] This foul hole sheltering behind superior facades makes you think of a necessary sore hidden under luxurious underwear, suppurating on a well-endowed body, treated with a vesicant and a seton to expel the bile and maintain a flawless complexion!"[74]

André agreed with a nod of the head but didn't reply. He was now thinking of the supper that awaited him. The prospect of meeting Mélie hardly appealed to him. He would rather have dined in a restaurant, just him and the painter. "I can't come up with any excuses," he told himself, seeing his friend go into a rotisserie and return with a chicken wrapped in paper; and he walked on in silence, looking at the Elysée Palace which they were skirting, at the Sûreté inspectors incessantly patrolling around it and who all had the same look and the same face, frock coats buttoned up military style, black trousers reaching down to hobnailed boots, and redwood mustaches in fiery shades.

"Patience, here we are," and Cyprien preceded André up the building's stairs, grumbling, "I'm sure I paid too much for the chicken and my other half will make fun of me."

"Cyprien!" Mélie cried when they went in.

"What?" the painter exclaimed. "Here I am."

Mélie appeared, her figure filling up the whole doorframe. She curtsied politely, informed André that Cyprien had often talked about their friendship, held out her hand in a forthright gesture, and begged to return to the kitchen for the moment.

"Supper, as fast as you can make it, we're starving," the painter said and proffered the cold chicken that she subjected to a long and frowning examination.

"I'm afraid it's tough," she sighed, "well, we'll see. Now Cyprien, lay the table, supper's ready; just give me two minutes."

"Do you want to have a look round while waiting for the soup?" the painter proposed. "As you can see, this is the dining room; there's the bedroom," he said, pushing a doorknob.

André went in, trotted out the customary banalities, adding that it was splendidly polished, and he spoke true, for Cyprien's furniture, which previously had looked beggarly in a room, with crippled legs and bellies glazed with dirt, was now spruced up, gleaming and standing level on supports that had been carefully wedged with cork.

"Supper's served," Mélie bawled, holding a big soup tureen in both hands.

They sat down, Cyprien on Mélie's left, André on her right. There was a moment of silence. André unfolded his napkin and looked thoughtfully at the table. On the chalk-white tablecloth, near the cutlery's shining fillets and the bright blades of the knives, the plates deposited circles of a yellower white that were overtopped by the diaphanous gray of the glasses traversed by streams of daylight descending from the bowl to the base where they stopped, glinting in a bright spot. On the left and right of the dishes, cruet sets were spread out, opposing the salt's silvery white to the rottenstone red of the English pepper while, near carafes in whose shimmering water the guests were bizarrely elongated, a green-yellow mustard pot appeared to be indeterminately colored, hovering between violet and plum-green, drowned as it was by the shadow cast by a bottle whose curved belly reflected the latticed frame of the window in a little square of light.

"Good Lord, you don't stint on things, you two," André said, delighted by the well-laid table, having expected it to be careless or soiled.

"Tuck in, kids!" the painter said by way of reply and buried his ladle in the tureen.

"It's first rate, this cabbage broth," André volunteered, his nose lost in the aroma rising from the bowl.

"Yes, it could be a lot worse, but, as they say, better visit the baker than the chemist," Mélie replied laughing; and, pleased with these compliments, she spoke again: "So, Monsieur André, another plateful?"

"Yes please, Madame; that would be much appreciated. This soup is exquisite."

And each of them put away two helpings and devoutly wiped their mouths.

"She's ugly, but seems good-natured, the big mama," André thought after she'd brought in a platter of cabbages, turnips, potatoes, and carrots. And on another platter, grilled mutton belly, bacon, and a fat sausage tied with string at either end.

Cyprien carved the meat and then they all smiled, their noses tickled by the smell of cauliflower and the aroma from the sausage.

"Ah, but I need to catch my breath!" André exclaimed, frightened by a fresh lump of cauliflower that Mélie plopped on his plate.

"Go on, you can manage to get that down," Cyprien said.

"Now, a glass of wine, Monsieur André," Mélie continued, "and good health to us all."

"That's better," the painter muttered, his mouth full, "I was starting to feel like I could eat a horse."

"Me too, and I've had a great dinner," André sighed, furtively unbuckling his trouser belt.

"Well, so much the better," Mélie concluded. "That'll make you want to come back," and they went on to attack the cold chicken, but less voraciously.

"It isn't as tender as it should be," the fat woman said. "Men have no idea when it comes to shopping for food, but with oil and mustard sauce, it'll do."

André endorsed the use of that potent sauce; he had a feeling of great well-being just then; the fear of a frosty reception had disappeared. He was delighted by Mélie's good humor, which made her breast heave from time to time with a loud laugh. He felt completely at home. His legs stuck straight out under the table, his bottom having slipped to the edge of the chair seat, his head almost leaning on the back rest, hands in pockets, he relaxed, made drowsy by the food and wine he'd consumed.

Mélie fetched the lamp, and the dining room, with its bits of china hung on the wall, its little stove where an old Delft pot sat, its neck lit up by the flames of a peony, its tablecloth now mottled pink by the reflection of the half-empty glasses, its dishes throwing fiery flakes at certain corners under the light falling down on the table and leaping in circles on the ceiling above the glass of the lamp, seemed honest and cheerful, friendly and coquettish to André, who, looking turn and about at Mélie and Cyprien, murmured: "You were lucky to meet each other, you're both happy."

The fat girl smiled. "It isn't very complicated," she said. "You see Monsieur André, all that's needed is for good people to get together. Once that's happened, well, okay, there's your house and home for you, as they say, no? Everyone has to do their bit, and you buckle down and you push and gee up, and that's how it works!

"And then, a man on his own is all at sea; he's all thumbs, if you'll forgive me for saying so, and so lazy and hopeless. Ah, I saw Cyprien's clothes before I came here, holes big enough to put your arm through, not a button left, not a collar, not a clean cuff, it was a proper mess. Not to mention that there isn't a spendthrift to compare with this here rogue." She gave the painter an affectionate tap on the shoulder. "He'd buy a new overcoat rather than send his old one to the cleaner. I sorted all that out too, these days I save on his expenses so he can enjoy meat and wine every day to his heart's content."

"It's true," Cyprien added, "the shop is well managed these days. Now, my pet, I don't think André wants any more preserves, clear that lot away and do us the honor of coffee and liqueurs."

Mélie took away the plates and brought in the coffee cups.

"You can come in now, we've finished supper," she cried to no one in particular while opening a door, and Alexandre made his entry, skipping and greeting them with friendly meows from under his whiskers.

"Ah, here's a new guest that I didn't know about," said André, and the cat purred as he diligently scratched its red fur, drooling with delight, eyes squeezed, tail stiff.

"Mélie's son, a young scamp who wasn't exactly polite when Désableau visited," and Cyprien burst out laughing, telling André about Alexandre's bad behavior.

"You did well, old chap," cried Mélie, pouring coffee. "That gentleman doesn't like animals; he must be a nasty type." She stopped, holding the cafetière in the air, petrified, remembering that Désableau was related to André, thinking that she'd just committed a gaffe.

But André began to smile. "Oh, you mustn't worry yourself," he said, "I'm certainly not going to stick up for Désableau!"

They were sitting down, stomachs now a little away from the table, the napkin left crumpled on the tablecloth, and while Mélie splashed kirsch into her cup the men both smoked cigarettes damp from coffee that, despite their care, filtered out from their whiskers.

"Please don't mind me, Monsieur André," Mélie murmured, a little ashamed at dosing herself generously in company. "I can't help it, it's my little vice." And she poured herself another glass.

André assured her that it was a respectable vice, then, in spite of himself, he returned to the topic of Désableau. "Is that all he said?"

"Yes, I already told you. He complained that you haven't authorized the purchase of the Viroflay house."

"And," André resumed after a moment's hesitation, "he didn't say anything else about Berthe?"

"No, not a word, except that she isn't in good health. Besides, that stands to reason, the poor woman must be dying of boredom with her uncle."

"Whose fault is that? Too bad, it's only to be expected, all she had to do was behave herself. That's my revenge, to know that she's stuck with tedious philistines like the Désableaus and that she's bored rigid!"

"Don't say things like that Monsieur André," cried Mélie, "you aren't heartless, you don't like to see people suffering, do you? Good lord, I can well understand that you're angry with your wife, but if you only knew, a young woman is more naive than you think. She has her little notions in her little head, she lets herself down because some Lothario has stolen a kiss. Taking it all into account, it isn't such a big thing as it seems to you, and then, in any case, because a woman has made a mistake that's blown up in her face, that's no reason to keep beating her up, like those parents who hit their kids when they fall over and hurt themselves!"

"It's okay for you to speak," Cyprien muttered, "if you were in the same place as people who've been cheated on."

"Oh, I've been in that same place, and all my life. Times when I cried tears all over when my lover ran around with other women, but in the end, that didn't change my feelings for him, I loved him even more, and I wouldn't have wanted him to leave me for anything in the world. It's a fact that when you're young, your blood goes wild over nothing; now all that's behind me, I don't put any faith in it. As long as a man doesn't rough me up and drown me in misery, I consider myself happy. In the end, that's all that matters in life."

"There, old chap," Cyprien said to André, "pour yourself another chartreuse."

The decanter went round the table.

"I'd bet," Mélie continued, holding out her glass to toast with André, "that in the story of your marriage your wife's the one with most cause for complaint. When a woman is used to her little routines, her own set-up at home, it isn't so easy, see, to share with somebody else. No, men aren't fair, they don't want to understand what's involved. No doubt your wife has let herself down, but she loves you all the same, because, don't you see, there's nothing like going with a new person for making you immediately regret the one that's been left behind. As sure as I'm called Mélie, that's how it is."

"Ah," Cyprien interposed, striking the table with his fist, "to think that there isn't a single moment in life when a man can tell a woman to go to hell! It's really a pain in the ass because when we're old or in poor shape we need them even more than when we're young and in fine fettle; looked at this way, it's really a pity," he said to André, "that Jeanne has gone away, because you just can't carry on like this; for want of a skirt trailing about at home, you'll end up a hypochondriac."

André didn't reply; Mélie and Cyprien were openly stating what he himself was thinking. Yes, above all since the departure of the little lady, life had become intolerable. The difficulties, the betrayals, the humiliations, all that shrank to nothing as against the terrible ennui that had overwhelmed him. Basically, Mélie was right; he had messed up his life, damaged his talent, crushed during years of darkness, all on account of an unsatisfied curiosity—for he knew his wife's frigid temper—for her attempt at experiencing rapture in arms with a different shade of hair, and he thought that it would surely have been better had he, like so many others, worn his horns and kept his mouth shut.

"What do you think I should do?" he asked at last, raising a head that he had kept lowered over his plate. "In any event I can't take the initiative with Berthe. Oh, that's out of the question," he said, rescuing a remnant of strength from his loss of energy. "No, not at any price."

There was a moment of silence.

Cyprien gazed steadily at André.

"What if Berthe admitted to being in the wrong and made the first move?"

André turned crimson and stammered, "In that case, well—I really don't know . . ."

"For sure," Mélie said softly, looking at Cyprien in turn, "a man has his pride, but then again, when a woman admits that he's in the right, he must be really mean not to forgive her. If it was me in the man's place, I would kiss her with all my heart and then I would be really kind to her because at the end of the day it's up to everyone to do their bit."

André gestured vaguely.

Mélie started to laugh and delicately stuck the tip of her tongue in her little glass to lick the last drop.

"By the way, what time is it?" André asked, getting up from his chair.

"Quarter past eleven," Cyprien replied.

"Gosh, time to go home to bed."

"Well then, I'll walk you back," the painter said.

André and Mélie shook hands fondly; then, when the two young men had made their exit, she shrugged her shoulders and thought, while clearing up: "Men, they're all the same! They never want it to look as though they're backing down! Him there's one of them, but he'll end up just like the others; he'd be the first to say sorry to his wife if she came tomorrow to say sorry to him!"

XV

"Is there's anything else Monsieur needs?"

"No, Mélanie."

"Good night then, Monsieur."

André pulled out his watch, confirming that it was just six o'clock. "Mélanie's off to a concert with her husband," he thought, "so yet again I've had to eat supper twenty minutes early."

He paced up and down his little apartment, then stepped onto the balcony. "The sunset is really rather fine," he thought, and, with a touch of melancholy, contemplated red clouds in the bounded horizon, descending behind the buildings, the ridges of whose roofs were outlined in black.

He lit a cigarette and, leaning on the balustrade, looked down below his feet at the street, wet from a downpour and tinted pink by a sky that lit up entire rows of windows and walls that were reflected in swollen streams of running water.

Some passersby were splashing about here and there, casting black, almost straight shadows on the pink roadway while, on the sidewalk, some still open umbrellas were located by dark circles pearled with bright drops at the edges, hiding the hats and necks they sheltered, moving forward on bodies that walked headless.

Suddenly André laughed to himself; Mélanie, he remembered, after complaining bitterly to him that very morning that her husband no longer desired her, had, supremely foolish, boasted of her attractions.

Cheered by that recollection, he returned to his bedroom and felt a craving for pleasure, a desire to go and distract himself somewhere, at a concert, a ball, no matter where, soon followed by a sense of dissatisfaction, because, alone, without the company of a friend, he felt unable to enjoy it. "Ah, if that dog Cyprien wasn't hitched, I'd go find him, we'd both wander somewhere or other; in my present state of mind, the most ordinary things would have seemed full of charm; but that's no longer an option." And yet, as though to at least try and artificially conjure up at home the pleasure he knew could only naturally be found outside and in company, he planted himself in front of his bookshelves in quest of a volume in harmony with his thoughts. He found that nothing answered, just as in the time of his petticoat crisis when he sought from his books the alleviation of his ennui, the literature of the day being little concerned with those happy or sad sensations that often arise in a solitary man for no obvious reason.

The doorbell rang.

"Who on earth can that be?" he said, hurrying to open the door.

A gentleman asked to see a woman.

"Wrong address," André replied, shutting the door impatiently.

"It's extraordinary, there's always somebody knocking at the wrong door when I'm out of sorts and would be happy to see a friend," he murmured, and lit the lamp that Mélanie, before leaving, had placed, ready, on his desk.

He went to sit down in the armchair facing the window and looked around the room where the sparse rays of the lamp lost their orange glow as they melted into the gloom of corners, then, yawning and stretching his arms, he contemplated the still shadowy window that cut a large pale square in the dusk, and through the white flowers of the little curtains, the sky, sifted by the muslin, looked purple, motionless, beaten behind the glass by the cord from the blinds that swung in the wind, like a pendulum.

But his eyes soon stopped seeing anything. Some recent money troubles came to mind, leading him to think how much more agreeable life would be if he were to suddenly become rich. He then went off down this path, racing along in a dream. He built castles in Spain, smiling at the fancies that played out in his brain. Remembering an armchair that he had taken in for repair the previous day, he was haunted by projects of refurbishment and imagined the bibelots he would buy, the rare canvases, and he dreamed too of a splendid wine cellar and a delightful woman who would glow softly amidst of all this elegance.

Deep in these flights of the imagination, he was full of benevolent forbearance. "Of course, I'd keep Mélanie," he thought, "and employ her husband as a concierge or valet. It's annoying, though, that he couldn't also work for me as a gardener, because I'd need one, and bringing in new people always goes against the grain."

Suddenly a ring of the doorbell felt like a blow to the stomach. Startled, he got to his feet, wits not yet gathered, like people rudely awakened from a nap. "I'm an idiot with all these daydreams," he said, taking the lamp. He went through the dining room, opened the door, and stood gawping at a woman.

In spite of the veil covering her eyes and nose, he recognized Berthe.

"It's you," he gasped.

And after a minute's silence, during which they remained facing each other, both breathing hard without being able to speak, André mechanically went to put down on the dining room table the lamp that his hand could hardly hold straight.

"Come in," he murmured, closing the front door that had remained ajar.

She walked ahead of him, hesitating at the darkness of the little living room, and, in the moment that it took him to pass from room to room behind Berthe's uncertain steps, André was overwhelmed by an urgent shame at his emotions, his discomfiture, the shame of a slightly drunk man who, wanting to conceal his troubled state, tries to keep silent, to appear calm.

He showed his wife to the armchair near the fireplace, and, placing on his desk the lamp that he'd brought with him, secured the glass with trembling fingers, sighing, "Oh, it's smoking!"

Then, instinctively, he sat down on the sofa, leaning back a little to avoid the circle of light thrown out by the lampshade, not daring to stare at his wife, feeling his embarrassment and agitation increased by the nervousness of Berthe who, without lifting her eyes, fiddled with the little chain of her petite umbrella.

"After everything that's happened, I never thought I'd come here," she said, speaking low. "I've come on account of unavoidable circumstances; really, you'll see that it's a business matter. Anyhow, I've brought all the paperwork," and she groped nervously in her gown, standing up, hastily searching the same pocket several times before taking out a roll of papers tied with white thread.

She held it out to André who put it on the divan without opening it.

Berthe sat down again and, leaving her umbrella alone, she mechanically considered the tip of her gloved hand that she edged forward on her knee.

André followed this, fixing his eyes on the slight movement of the fingers.

They remained silent, their eyes fastened on that gloved hand, then André, breathing harder, grasped the scrolled paper again, turned it round and round and instinctively let it drop, having seen it becoming floppy in his hand, and that his thumb, yellow from nicotine, had left a mark on the white paper next to the thread.

"Are you unwell?" he enquired, and sought to make out her features under her hat veil. She seemed to him paler than before, with bigger eyes.

She gave a somewhat doleful smile and replied with a tremor in her voice, "I haven't been in the best of health for a while now, but I'll soon feel better. The doctor assures my uncle that there's nothing seriously wrong and that with good weather and warm sunshine I'll be as good as new."

"And how is your uncle," André asked somewhat hesitantly. "Is he well?"

She gave a little nod of the head.

Having run out of words, André took the papers again and tried to untie the knot securing them. His fingernails struggled in vain. Berthe, blushing slightly, removed her gloves and untwisted the thread.

"Ah! Here we have estimates and a plan . . ." and he plunged his nose into the documents that he was unable to read. The letters and figures danced before his eyes and the plan that he tried to view troubled his eyesight with its big squares that seemed to lift themselves and overrun the colored borders that hemmed them in.

"It's very good," he said; and after a fairly long pause, he continued, mumbling a little, "It's Désableau who's encouraged you to buy this house then? Anyway, that's understandable." And he added, with a hint of acrimony, "He's always liked to take advantage of battles fought by others."

But she defended her uncle. No, he was neither self-centered nor an interested party, as André believed, and she couldn't accuse him of lack of care or affection. He and his wife treated her like their own daughter, especially her aunt, and she carried on reciting praises of the Désableaus while André listened, tight-lipped, looking unconvinced.

Nevertheless, Berthe's resolute demeanor intimidated him. He didn't dare launch a frontal attack on her family and, slowly, he prowled round Désableau, venturing questions, baiting the ground, getting his wife to confess, make her tell him about the daily drawbacks, the regular hindrances of a life shared with insufferable people.

Blushing somewhat, she avoided blaming her uncle, but, nevertheless, between two eulogies, exaggerated so as to remove any sourness from her admissions, when pressed she acknowledged the man's little weaknesses, his shrill and bombastic character, his views about everything that steadily narrowed as he got older. "No matter, he has a good heart," she said. "When you're alone, spurned by everyone, when all your old friends turn their backs on you, it's a blessing to find relations who welcome you with open arms, and who love you."

André shook his head. "Be that as it may," he said, "for all his good heart your uncle has always despised me, and for no good reason that I can see."

"You're wrong about that," she replied forcefully. "It was your line of work that he despised, but you yourself were always excepted." And she fell silent, thinking at the same time of Désableau's hatred for what he called the bohemian literary life, remembering his rage at an employee in his office who dabbled in journalism, and whom he would have dismissed on pretense of negligence had it not been for her pleas in his defense, although she had never seen the man, vaguely believing that in this small way she was repairing the wrongs she'd done to André, taking an interest in this employee solely because, like her husband, he wielded a pen.

"Anyway," André said, "as far as the Viroflay house is concerned, it was only in your interest that I refused the purchase. I so much want to avoid distressing you or offending your uncle that if you want, I'll sign the necessary documents right away."

He was moved by the tender voice with which she thanked him. Overtaken by emotions that had loosened their hold while his resentment of the Désableaus had flared up, he walked up and down to hide his confusion. It was now almost impossible for him to talk, his mouth was parched, bone dry, and his Adam's apple bobbed feverishly in his throat. Désableau, his family, everything, all forgotten as his wife's voice touched his heart and reawakened the intimacy of those rare, charming hours of domestic life. He envisioned Berthe as she was after their marriage, letting him kiss her at the parting of her hair, saw her once more rolling a pellet of bread between her fingers at table during dessert. Once more he saw her disrobing, holding her chemise on her breasts with one hand while climbing into bed, and he was visited by a great feeling of lenience, an utter loss of firmness of purpose, of caution. He would have liked to remain unmoving, not open his mouth for fear of losing the slow somnolence seeping through him.

Then it was stronger than him. He lifted his eyes to Berthe. He was now in front of her and the glow of the lamp on her face lit the jet-black beads of her veil, fully illuminating the face under the tulle.

He felt a brief shock, stung by his wife's sad looks, her pained smile. Tears filled his eyes, he took a step toward Berthe and, choking, overcome, took her in his arms, kissing her on the forehead, the ears, the cheeks, stammering, "There, there, it's alright, it's alright," while, she, in confusion, was breathless, her head on André's shoulder, sobbing out low moans, like an infant crying, it's mouth against the pillow.

"My poor kitten," he said, now speaking to his wife fondly, as though to a mistress, suddenly forgetting the rather cool courtesies, the considered conjugal behavior he'd formerly adopted; "Look, you mustn't cry. So, now, my own sweet Berthe, give me a smile." And, putting his hands on her shoulders, he moved her back, avidly drinking her in, face pink, eyes swollen, smiling through her tears, stammering disconnected words, words of apology, asking forgiveness; and he kissed her on the mouth, begging her not to speak, swearing that he too had been at fault.

"My poor darling," he continued, rubbing his hands, circling the room, gripped by a surge of nervous gaiety. "Come now, all our stupid squabbles are over and done with. Dry your tears my love, do you want some fresh water?" And he ran to the bathroom, spilling half of the jug of water on the floor in his haste, brought back the basin, held it up while Berthe bathed her eyes, finally put it down on the parquet floor because it was stoneware and very heavy, while his wife, leaning forward, looked at herself in the mirror, ruffling the little curls on her forehead with her fingers, pressing the palms of her hands to her inflamed eyelids.

André took her by the waist and made her sit down near him on the divan. There, he held her tightly, inhaling the scent of her neck, her moist flesh, jostling her earrings with his pointed mustache. She didn't breathe a word, but she looked down at him and her heaving bust seemed to quicken.

André took hold of her fingers, turning her rings slowly round.

"Here you are at last," he said with emotion, looking her in the eyes.

She gave a little smile.

"Oh, I've waited for you so often!" he resumed, on a wave of elation, speaking to relieve himself, lying without even being aware of it.

She squeezed his hand and surprised him by speaking openly, finally acknowledging that she was unhappy, but that she would never have thought of coming if Cyprien's urging hadn't to some extent prompted her.

"Ah! you've seen Cyprien," he said.

"Yes, he came one morning while my uncle was at his office and my aunt out at the market"; and she let slip that the painter had confirmed that André would be glad to see her.

"He's a clever chap, our Cyprien," André said, moving a little away from his wife, red in the face, ashamed that the painter had revealed to Berthe how much he wanted her. "Yes," he continued in a tone of voice that he tried to keep disinterested, "Cyprien has often spoken of you, and since he understood that I would be distressed at the thought of you being unhappy or unwell, he would have concluded . . ." He stopped.

"Anyway, he did well," he exclaimed forcefully, drawing near and kissing his wife, who, in turn, had gone bright red. "If it hadn't been for him you might not have come anywhere near me. You naughty girl, the idea of coming to see me wouldn't have occurred to you without that!"

"To start with, I didn't know if I'd find you alone, and then, no, it really wasn't possible"; and she looked around, awakened, scarcely able to believe that it was indeed she herself who was sitting beside her husband, on the divan.

"I've always been on my own," André said with aplomb. "But I really don't know what's wrong with the lamp this evening," and he got up to adjust it. "Ah, men are all the same, complaining when they live alone," he sighed and, deciding it would do no harm to make himself interesting, told Berthe that Mélanie cheated him like you wouldn't believe, and, to convince his wife, looked with his finger for dust on the furniture, hardly picking any up.

“See how poorly I’m looked after,” he said, shaking his head.

“But your home seems to be well cared for,” Berthe replied, gazing round the room. “Oh! You’ve bought lots of furniture.”

He suggested a tour of the apartment and removed the lampshade.

“I’m not surprised that it smokes like that, the wick is badly trimmed, wait, I’ll see to it in a moment,” and Berthe gazed at the pictures, smiling at the ones she knew, surprised by the others. The Japanese chimera frightened her. “Oh, what a horror!” she said, and she went into the bedroom, examining the white bed, the rosewood furniture, touching the keys, whose gilt handles particularly pleased her.

“You’ve found yourself a nice apartment,” she said, going into the bathroom.

Without any motive, without any association of ideas, André suddenly pictured the bedroom of his former dwelling, the insult he’d suffered, and although his anger had long since died away he held Berthe by the waist as he had previously held Jeanne, moved by an immature grudge, by the thought of a petty revenge, born from a memory retained, for no particular reason, from his former affair, and he kissed his wife in front of the mirror above the water jug, perhaps seeing himself as strong and skeptical, definitively erasing a remnant of the offense by pairing wife and mistress, assimilating them, putting them on the same footing, in the same frame.

But Berthe freed herself and, feeling at home now, stepped with authority into the kitchen and gazed at the sparkling bottoms of the saucepans, shining like suns, the black tulle bonnet with apple green strings hanging from the ocher walls, saying, “My, but it’s really clean.”

She spoke again: “Here, give me the lamp shears, I’m going to trim the wick.”

They searched for them in vain.

In that room, no bigger than a handkerchief, which she filled with her skirts, they squeezed together in front of the sideboard, finding lamp wicks and garlic cloves, stale crusts of bread on a plate, butter in a bowl of water, white salt and flour in jam jars, lastly, near a wooden pestle and a grater that still contained grated gruyere, a little black bottle labeled "Aroma of soup, burned onion mill, Romainville."

But by dint of searching they found dirty, oil-soaked candle snuffers in the middle of an unwrapped packet of thyme and bay leaves in a drawer where their fingers mingled and where Berthe's rings glistened more brightly in the gloom.

"So," said André, delighted with the filthy snuffers, "wasn't I right to blame my housemaid, you can see for yourself whether she's dirty."

Berthe didn't reply; she nimbly trimmed the lamp; "There, it's done," she said; and she went back into the bathroom to wash her hands.

Then while she slowly soaped her fingers, André, standing behind her, followed the action of her arms whose back-and-forth movement sent ripples down the back of her dress, expiring in a slight tremor along her hips, and he felt a surge of desire.

Since Jeanne's departure, his amours had been costly and therefore devoid of the appetite that makes acceptable even the most mediocre sensual pleasures and sustenance; he was filled with a brute desire to know whether there had been any change in Berthe; furthermore, the life led following their rupture, the renewed liaison with Jeanne, had as though altered him. He had become more intrepid, less timid, less respectful. Here he was at last, chez lui, in his own bachelor quarters, and no longer in their shared domestic space, and his senses, rising in a youthful head of steam, were further inflamed by memories of the ribald fraternizing of the old days. He no longer saw very clearly, he simply went unthinkingly toward Berthe as to an attractive woman, as toward a good thing fallen by sheer luck into his lap after long abstinence.

He was also in a state of terrible nervous excitement. The shocks of the evening had left him shattered; he felt an enormous fatigue, a general ache, and it seemed to him that his brain was floating in a void. Far from bringing relief, his tears, withheld at first, then rapidly dried, had further augmented that indescribable malaise that necessarily had to culminate in a carnal détente.

He stretched his fingers, cracking them, feeling faint, having recalled a cute little fawn mark under his wife's blouse, as round as a pill between her two breasts.

On edge too, and in spite of a sensual coldness further heightened by her long-accepted habit of dieting, Berthe, tensing, felt an abrupt arousal; her cheeks on fire and her eyes humid, she dropped the cloth she was wiping her fingers with into the half-full basin. She smiled at her husband in the mirror and, bending over, her loins slightly raised, her back squirming as far as her neck, she wrung out the cloth.

Advancing on the line of her teeth, a point of light created in her mouth by the smile, or the overbite, sent André into a passion; he thrust himself against her, slowly kissed her eyes, which blinked, tickling his lips with their eyelashes.

He clutched her and led her, entwined with him, into the bedroom, willfully forgetting the light on in the bathroom. Berthe collapsed back on the bed, an arm folded over her face while the rustling of her rucked-up skirts was for a long time the only sound to be heard, along with André's panting breath.

"Oh, that's nasty!" she whispered.

And André, somewhat astonished now that his fires had subsided, wondered whether, in the interest in his future menage, he hadn't committed an irreparable error. A certain light darting in his wife's eyes disturbed him, then he noticed that Berthe's underclothes were more elegant and fragrant than before and was afraid that she had dressed up like this in order to seduce him.

Somewhat embarrassed, they went back into the little living room to sit down and found nothing to say, out of sorts, each lost in their own thoughts, she, in spite of renewed sensual disappointment, satisfied with having tasted a forbidden fruit, having undertaken, in a bachelor apartment, an escapade formerly dreamed of at home, and now honestly fulfilled, without shame and without risk, happy to shake off her uncle's yoke, to once more make an exit from a maidenly life, to regain her liberty, to return home newly empowered, feeling the joy of home-loving people at finding their own abode once more after long stays in hotels and lodging houses; he, very perplexed, rebuking himself for never learning, defenseless before a woman, foreseeing nothing good coming from the ease with which Berthe had let herself be taken, repeating, "I'm at her mercy," then consoling himself with the prospect of quitting an odious bachelor existence overrun with petticoat crises and swindling housemaids, of regaining a well-organized household, of possibly living a tranquil life.

"Shall I make us a cup of tea?" he asked for the sake of saying something.

She heard the sound of his words without realizing their meaning. She awoke from her thoughts and looked at her watch. "Ten o'clock! Good God, my uncle won't know what's happened to me. Oh, I look a sight!" she murmured, and while she did her best to repair the disorder of her hair and her dress in front of the mirror,

André, pulling on his boots to accompany her, managed to convince himself that he had acted wisely. "It's maybe the only time that I've behaved as I should have with my wife. Yes, be more impulsive, less restrained, let myself go more, be a child, a nice boy, the way I was with Jeanne, that's the way to go," he concluded, knocking the sole of the boot on the floor to ease in the sock.

Berthe was ready, he kissed her and they went down to the street, thoughtful, silent, preoccupied with the same concerns, worried and at the same time pleased, thinking of the failed life they were going to recommence, fearing that they would ruin it again, this time forever, in spite of the experience they'd acquired; and they walked on resignedly, each promising, for the sake of peace, to give way to the other, but reserving the right in certain cases when they judged it right to put their foot down, each one, while affectionately squeezing the arm with which they were linked, calculating the accommodations they would have to make, the failings that each would, inwardly, have to undertake to pass on to the other.

XVI

Once a week, on Tuesdays, André and Cyprien met together in a café toward four in the afternoon. For the first month they were strict about keeping the rendezvous, then one or other of them failed to show up.

Whichever of the two was left waiting fretted over his aperitif and, inevitably, André put the blame for his friend's breach of faith on Mélie, Cyprien on Berthe.

Each took a dislike to their friend's wife.

Moreover, a certain coolness had entered their friendship; André arrived at the agreed time but left almost immediately afterward, giving mysterious excuses, unavoidable errands, at which the painter shrugged his shoulders, more relaxed, less constrained in his illegitimate menage than André in his licensed marriage, his bourgeois lifestyle.

André resented Cyprien's advantage, was even somewhat jealous, and, in a small way, the painter pitied André's difficulties, was irritated by his constant need to rush off.

They soon ended up only seeing each other when chance brought them face-to-face in the street. André hadn't the least desire to accompany his friend home, feeling a certain discomfort, a certain embarrassment in seeing Mélie who had intervened so decisively in his affairs, and not for anything in the world would

Cyprien have set foot in André's home, remembering his frosty reception by Berthe after her marriage, thinking that, in spite of all the help he'd given, he would, as her husband's friend, yet again receive short rations at table and, as before, be shown politely to the door after the meal.

One or two months flowed by without their having crossed paths. One day however, in church at a burial mass, they caught sight of each other through people planted like pickets between two rows of chairs, and once they'd expressed their condolences, they left the hearse to jolt its way to the cemetery and walked down a side street, first discussing the good and bad points of the deceased whom they'd previously known, feeling due sympathies for those left behind; then Cyprien, switching topics, said to André, "So, since I last saw you, you must be settled in your new home."

"Yes, the arrangements are in hand, almost finished." And after a pause he added unenthusiastically, "I'm doing fine."

"Is it a big house?" Cyprien asked.

"No, five rooms, but they're well situated; used to belong to a haberdasher whose business went bust, a proper cottage with pink walls, clay-colored wooden shutters with a heart carved at the top, a door with stained glass windows looking onto the garden, and you can picture it from here, can't you?"

"Yes, not forgetting the inevitable beds of geranium around a bower near a centrifugal water pump, and, I don't doubt, baskets of roses separated by a line of box, alleyways sprinkled with river pebbles. A barrel at the bottom of the garden, with a rusted frog peering up at the sky; the obligatory garden shed in a corner hidden by a lilac bush that never flowers; finally, stacked against the aforementioned shed, a mound of fallen leaves, dead branches, and bits of broken flowerpots, the whole thing overtopped by a rope on which a kitchen apron and pair of stockings are fluttering. Can I picture that? I could draw you a spot-on resemblance without having seen it!"

"Yes, go on, laugh all you like," André replied, "all the same, you won't spoil the pleasure of being in Paris, tucked away in a little suburb, no neighbors, no concierge, a long way away from the crowds and the noise."

"It's the dream of people who are worn out by the age of thirty," Cyprien sighed. "I've dreamed it just like everyone else, except that I've found the key to the mystery of those lives lived in the outlying districts. I've seen myself opening the window in the morning, tapping worriedly on the barometer, going out in a straw hat, in a shirt, braces striping my back, to prune my plants with secateurs; lastly I've seen myself, legs dangling from the embankments, contemplating the horizon through my opera glasses, arguing for the hundredth time with my wife who's darning and yawning beside me about the name of the village that shows up as a little white patch in the sky down there, in the distance.

"That vision of my lanky person in a scrubby landscape has cured me of those raptures about the Parisian countryside that I adore when I take a walk there, but that I always detest if I have to live there for any length of time. But in any event, I'm relaxed about the whole business; when you feel sorry for your wife's boredom and you've had enough of the isolation yourself, you'll come back to live on the fourth floor, in the center of Paris, just like me!"

André scowled. He remembered Berthe's complaints, lamenting the lack of food shops, housemaids who lost no time in leaving a district devoid of dance halls and troopers. He was afraid that his break from life's troubles wasn't final, and feared that, prodded by his wife, he would gradually resume his long since interrupted pilgrimage though the salons and the ballrooms. Now that Berthe's circumstances were in the clear she wouldn't, he thought, be unhappy with a triumphant return to that world from which she'd been separated for months.

"Tell me then," Cyprien said, seeing his friend's clouded face and guessing that he'd better not persist with his theories of the countryside, "tell me, what's happened to your old housemaid?"

"Who, Mélanie?"

"Yes."

"I don't know. Ever since the day Berthe came back home and sent her packing I haven't heard news of her. I suppose that she's following her vocation and has gone to loot a new household. Ah, good for her, and you, what are you up to?"

"Me, nothing. I muddle along between Mélie and Rustbar; I also work for a wallpaper firm; among other jobs, I design Scottish tartan, you know, that paper with alternating red and green stripes and crosses, like Highland breeches or certain kinds of shawl. It isn't badly paid and there's no shortage of work."

"So, what about canvases?"

The painter rubbed his beard with his long fingers. "Canvases, pooh," he said, "When you can't sleep, it's sometimes nice to dream in bed of the ones you'll never paint!"[75]

"Yes." André replied after a pause, "When it comes to actually realizing a work we've conceived, forget it. So you see, where art is concerned we've played the part of those poor devils of lovers who, having desired a woman for God knows how long, can't get it up when they've finally got her."

"People who miss the boat," Cyprien said.[76] "Hey, apropos, what about the house you were going to buy in Viroflay?"

"It was sold while me and my wife were discussing how much to pay for it."

"Ah well, that can't have made our good Désableau's day," the painter chuckled. "Do you still see him?"

"Still."

They continued pacing up and down the street, hands behind back, unspeaking.

"So you're happy then," Cyprien said.

"Yes, and you?"

"Me too."

"Well, so much the better."

Cyprien fell silent, then after a moment, began again. "So it adds up to the same thing, and that's what knocks all known morality for six. The two roads branch off from each other, but they lead to the same roundabout. Basically, marriage and cohabiting are each as good as the other, since they've left both of us equally liberated from artistic ambitions and carnal miseries. Good health and no more talent, what a dream!"

André shook his head and blew his nose.

"Hang it!" he suddenly said, counting on his fingers the chimes that, one after another, dripped down from overhead. "That's twelve noon. I've got to run, Berthe will be getting impatient."

He shook hands with his friend, who said with a mirthless chuckle, "Being as hollowed out as we are isn't so bad, because now that all the compromises have been made, maybe humanity's eternal stupidity will make us welcome, and, just like our fellow countrymen, we'll have the right to finally live respectable and stupid lives."

"What an ideal," André sighed.

"Ah, okay, that or something else . . ." said Cyprien who, also running late, took flight like a giant grasshopper, skimming past shop windows down the length of the street.

END

TRANSLATOR'S NOTES

This translation is based on the annotated critical edition of *En ménage*, edited by Gilles Bonnet (Geneva: Librairie Droz, 2005). The notes that follow draw on Bonnet's footnotes to that edition, references to which are given as "Bonnet in Huysmans," with page number and footnote number.

1. "Whore": *fille* in French. Cf. Huysmans's early novel about a prostitute, *Marthe, histoire d'une fille.* The term is of course ambiguous; it usually means "girl" or "daughter," and translating it appropriately depends on context. *Fille* as the term for prostitute is more nuanced than any equivalent English term. The point is not merely an incidental one; Cyprien, we are told later, "only felt well-disposed toward tarts [*filles*]." Huysmans never uses the common term *putain* in *Domesticity*; it's fair to say that other contemporary French writers also refer to "fille(s)," but there's no doubt about Huysmans's tolerant, even sympathetic attitude. More commonly abusive terms in *Domesticity—cattin, grue*—come from the point of view of André's mistress, Jeanne, who is herself working class and "loose."
2. "Prior to 1975, the French Penal Code of 1810 stated at article 324 that 'in the case of adultery, provided for by article 336, murder committed upon the wife as well as upon her accomplice, at the moment when the husband shall have caught them in the fact, in the house where the husband and wife dwell, is excusable' [meaning a punishment of 1 to 5 years, according to article 326]. In practice, however, many domestic violence crimes resulted in acquittal by the juries" (https://en.wikipedia.org/wiki/Crime_of_passion#Crimes_of_passion_and_juries).
3. "Mazagran is prepared with strong, hot coffee that is poured over ice, and it is typically served in a narrow, tall glass. It has also been described as coffee taken with water instead of milk, in which coffee is served in a tall glass along with a separate container of water to mix in with the coffee" (https://

en.wikipedia.org/wiki/Mazagran). References to the beverage recur throughout the novel.

4. *Flueurs blanches* in French, technically known as "leukorrhea": "Leukorrhea also known as *fluor albus* is a thick, whitish, yellowish or greenish vaginal discharge. It has also been referred to as 'the whites'" (https://en.wikipedia.org/wiki/Leukorrhea).

5. "Mary, dip your bread [in the sauce]": a French children's song.

6. The hairdresser's fast bird/slow bird quip involves an untranslatable pun: *merle lent* (slow blackbird) is a homophone of *merlan* (hairdresser).

7. "Hippopotamus ivory [. . .] is denser than both elephant and walrus ivory. It is more hardwearing and appropriate for dental use. [. . .] Only wealthy patients such as royalty and the upper classes could afford ivory dentures" (https://collection.sciencemuseumgroup.org.uk/objects/co98260/hippopotamus-ivory-teeth-upper-denture-on-stand-england-denture).

8. *Bonnets à choux* in French. In this context, *chou* (cauliflower) is a decorative knot made of ribbons or other material. The terms *chou* and *choux* are used in Anglophone millinery vocabulary.

9. The Gros-Caillou was a district in the 7th arrondissement where the Eiffel tower was subsequently erected. The odd name—"big pebble"—derives from marker stones used to demarcate the parish boundary in the middle ages. "A neighborhood assiduously frequented by Huysmans to the point of prospectively giving its name to a novel intended to follow on from *Domesticity* and *Downstream*, but which was never realized" (Bonnet in Huysmans, 62, note 1).

10. The Odéon is a major theater adjacent to the Luxembourg Garden.

11. "Baron Haussmann changed the layout of the park due to adding new roads and streets" (https://www.eutouring.com/jardin_du_luxembourg_history.html).

12. In France at this time, Thursdays were school-free days; conversely school attendance was (and is) required on Saturdays. In 1972, the free day was switched from Thursday to Wednesday.

13. "Quicherat [is] the author of a Latin–French Dictionary, first published in 1834" (Bonnet in Huysmans, 70, note 12). Quicherat is referred to more respectfully in Huysmans's *La Cathédrale* (1898), where he is cited as an expert on medieval architecture.

14. Bonnet points out that Cyprien and Céline Vatard had already featured in Huysmans's 1879 novel, *Les Soeurs Vatard*, where, in chapter 21, Céline indeed deserts Cyprien for another man (in Huysmans, 74, note 20).

15. "Hatred of Americanization, which is a hatred of the reign of philistinism and utilitarianism, forms a leitmotif of Huysmans's oeuvre, passed on by way of the Brothers Goncourt, the Baudelaire of *New Notes on Edgar Poe*" (Bonnet in Huysmans, 88, note 8).

16. *Fra Diavolo* is an *opéra comique* by Daniel Auber.

17. *Nuait* in French, defined as covering the skin with a light cloud (*nuage*). It's the "'false coloring' specific to the woman of Paris whose 'extraordinary epidermis worked in velvet but without blusher' only [the artist] Caillebotte was, according to Huysmans, able to convey, contrasting her with the actress and whore who 'paint themselves with less restraint'" (Bonnet, citing Huysmans's *Exposition des des Indépendants, 1880*, in Huysmans, 91, note 15).

18. *Râpé*: thin, poor-quality wine.

19. *Eau de mélisse*: Melissa floral water, but translated here as Melissa oil, which seems more likely; inhaling it can calm anxiety and tension.

20. Bonnet points out that divorce was made illegal in France in 1816 and was only reinstated in 1884.

21. Waste basin—*plomb* in French—also translates as "lead." The term is a synecdoche, referring to a lead basin into which dirty water was emptied. Until the mid-twentieth century, these were fixed on the exterior of the various floors of a building. The reference occurs more than once in the novel.

22. "At that time Huysmans in fact possessed a watercolor by Degas and one by Forain, adorning his apartment on the rue de Sèvres and closely resembling these ones" (Bonnet in Huysmans, 118, note 6).

23. *Bradels* in French; this refers to a widely used and relatively inexpensive form of bookbinding pioneered by the Bradel family of bookbinders, from whom the term takes its name.

24. The reference is to *Reflections on the Mercy of God* (also known in translation as *The Penitent Lady*), written by Louise la Vallière, the former mistress of Louis XIV, after she entered a Carmelite convent.

25. Huysmans is beating his own drum here. Georges Charpentier was the publisher of the modern and naturalist schools: Zola, Flaubert, Maupassant, and also Huysmans.

26. "The hospital has played an important role in the study of dermatology since the nineteenth century and holds a wax museum of dermatological diseases" (https://en.wikipedia.org/wiki/H%C3%B4pital_Saint-Louis). The hospital is referred to again in chapter XIII, as the site where Cyprien is engaged make sketches of patients suffering from diseases of the skin.

27. The Bourse: the Paris stock exchange.

28. Both Baldick (*Life of J.-K. Huysmans* [Oxford, Clarendon Press, 1955], 60) and Bonnet (in Huysmans, 128, note 22) point out that this is a portrait of Huysmans himself.

29. A cabriolet armchair is a Louis XV style chair with open, usually wooden armrests.

30. In what Bonnet identifies as a *mise en abyme*, Huysmans here gives us a thumbnail sketch of himself, as a still relatively young civil servant, barricading himself behind official paperwork to work on *En ménage*: "Biographers very quickly informed us that among those papers precipitously hidden from the eyes of busybody superiors, the manuscript of *En ménage* drafted by Huysmans was found near the end of the 1870s" (in Huysmans, 12).

31. *Mères-nobles* in French. Bonnet explains that this is a theatrical term for the character type of the duenna.

32. Jeanne and her relationship with André derive from Huysmans's long-term relationship with the seamstress Anna Meunier.

33. *Poivrer* in French; Bonnet notes that the term is a synonym for "to deceive," and further means to infect with syphilis (in Huysmans, 154, note 14).

34. At the corner of the northern wing of the Louvre.

35. *Boum* was a word uttered by waiters in cafés when they served a drink.

36. "Jaquemin Gringonneur, fourteenth-century French painter and miniaturist, is wrongly held to be the inventor of card games, which were actually imported from Asia" (Bonnet in Huysmans, 164, note 9).

37. "Literal meaning; secondary stage of syphilitic evolution" (Bonnet in Huysmans, 168, note 14).

38. Moxibustion is a traditional Chinese medical therapy which consists of burning dried mugwort on particular points on the body.

39. Bonnet (in Huysmans, 174, note 19) points out a probable debt here to Baudelaire's prose poem, "Windows": "There is nothing more profound, more mysterious, more fertile, more gloomy or more dazzling than a window lighted by a candle" (Arthur Symons's translation).

40. *Faire de la fenêtre* in French, an idiomatic expression that designates a prostitute sitting at a window, soliciting possible clients passing in the street. The practice of what Jean Lorrain describes as "la prostitution des fenêtres" provides subject matter for the story "L'homme au bracelet" in his *Histoires de masques* (1900).

41. *Déjeuner à la fourchette*: a breakfast that includes meat and wine.

42. "Charles André Boule (1642–1732), celebrated French cabinetmaker who particularly excelled in ornamentation" (Bonnet in Huysmans, 180, note 4) (NB the correct spelling of the name is Boulle).

43. Baccarat: manufacturers of fine luxury crystal.

44. *Orléaniste* was a nineteenth-century French political label originally used by those who supported a constitutional monarchy expressed by the House of Orléans.

45. The *Second Empire* was the imperial regime of Napoleon III from 1852 to 1870.

46. "This comprises the section of the 8th arrondissement bordered by l'Élysée and Sainte-Marie Madeleine" (Bonnet in Huysmans, 182, note 7).

47. A particularly strong variety of brandy consisting of three parts of alcohol to six of a blend, hence the name, three-six.

48. "Huysmans in part realized this program, in writing texts such as 'Le Parc Monceau' published in 1881 by *La Vie moderne*, 'Le Boulevard Montparnasse' (1877), or again, 'Through the Jardin de Luxembourg.' [. . .] The neighborhood (*quartier*) seems to constitute the cardinal unit of measurement for Huysmans' imaginative topography" (Bonnet in Huysmans, 184, note 12).

49. *Mélanie poussa des cris de merluche*, literally the cries of a hake. However, Bonnet (in Huysmans, 186, note 13) points out that, in context, "*merluche* seems to be a pejorative deformation of *Merlusine*"; he refers to a later reference to *les cris de Merlusine*.

 Merlusine is a heraldic variant of Melusine, the beautiful but secretly fishtailed (or half serpent) wife of legend who disappears after her husband discovers her true form: "Thenceforward the death of a member of the House of Lusignan was heralded by the cries of the fairy serpent. *Pousser les cris de Melusine* is still a popular saying" (https://en.wikisource.org/wiki/1911_Encyclop%C3%A6dia_Britannica/M%C3%A9lusine). "Fishwife" is a very free rendering of the French "merluche."

50. Chevet: a celebrated delicatessen caterer.

51. Schapska: a flat-topped cavalry helmet; Kolbach (also colback): a busby; a furred military headpiece.

52. Laurent de l'Ardèche and Marco Saint-Hilaire both wrote historical accounts of Napoleon. J.G. Sandiford-Pellé, in a note to his translation qualifies them as "second rate historians whose work could have been buried" (in Huysmans, *En Ménage* [*Living Together*], tr. J. G. Sandiford Pellé [London: The Fortune Press, 1969], 132, note 4). Les Invalides is where the tomb of Napoleon is situated.

53. Bonnet notes that Huysmans here harks back to a passage in Balzac's *Illusions perdues* in which the Palais-Royal shops are seen as "'dives' that indiscriminately welcome bookshops and prostitutes, the two professions being really indistinguishable from each other" (in Huysmans, 200, note 16).

54. Cooked thrushes were not uncommon in nineteenth-century Europe. It seems that the cooked bird was eaten whole, and this may explain why the women find the dish inedible.

55. "A philippine is an almond with a double seed. A tradition imported from Germany proposed that an almond with two seeds be offered to someone of the opposite sex" (Bonnet in Huysmans, 206, note 33).

56. A *mendiant* is a dessert consisting of figs, raisins, almonds, and hazelnuts, also known as *quatre mendiants* (Bonnet in Huysmans).

57. The historic Hôtel de Ville served as headquarters for the Paris Commune in 1870, but the communards burned it to the ground when they retreated in defeat. Its reconstruction lasted from 1873 to 1892.

58. A "blabbermouth of a caretaker": *un pipelet* in the French; a slang term for concierge, from the name of a gossipy female concierge in Eugène Sue's *Mystères de Paris* (see Bonnet in Huysmans, 231, note 3).

59. Gambrinus: "The name of a king supposed to have invented the brewing of beer in the time of Charlemagne" (Bonnet in Huysmans, 247, note 28).

Bonnet reproduces here, by way of a footnote, a final paragraph that Huysmans canceled in the ms:

> The waiters, preparing the shutters, finally chased them away; then, on the move, they swallowed a glass of brandy by way of cleansing the palate and, heading off again with great strides, they returned home, went to bed, and, still fearful, skin burning, heads on fire, they clasped each other so hard that the wooden bedframe cracked to breaking point under the coupling of their bodies and the jerky recoil of their legs (in Huysmans, 247, note 29).

This would provide a fitting conclusion to the chapter; André and Jeanne's voracious appetite in the brasserie is followed by their sexual urgency in bed. It's conceivable that Huysmans omitted it as a cautious act of self-censorship—he was a civil servant, so a government employee, at the time of writing. But it's also possible that he wanted the chapter to end on the image of Gambrinus triumphant.

60. "Do you remember . . ." ("*Souvenez-vous en*") refers to a "chanson de M. et Mme. Denis" by Marc-Antoine Désaugiers (1742–1793) that became a popular song during the late eighteenth century. This explains Jeanne's reference to "Monsieur Denis."

61. Estimating the contemporary (2023) value of twenty francs circa 1880 isn't straightforward, but a likely figure is in the region of forty dollars.

62. "Jeanne's departure bears witness to the insecurity that struck the working classes in the years 1870–1880, badly affected by unemployment. Whence the departure [of Jeanne] for Great Britain which experienced capital development and a real industrial lift-off while the French economy still essentially relied on agricultural production" (Bonnet in Huysmans, 255, note 4).

63. "By way of comparison, the average salary of a worker in Paris between 1875 and 1880 was around one hundred francs a month" (Bonnet in Huysmans, 255, note 5).

64. Sainte-Périne is a charitable institution for geriatric patients: "An institution founded at the start of the nineteenth century. [. . .] The forerunner of our care homes" (Bonnet in Huysmans, 260, note 9).

65. The cat, Alexandre, is later also identified as Barre-de-Rouille (Rustbar), the name of Huysmans's own cat. Barre-de-Rouille reappears as Durtal's cat in *Là-Bas*, and also as the unnamed pet cat in *En rade*: "this cat [. . .] had an ashen coat streaked with rust."

66. Bonnet describes an electuary as being a mixture of medicinal powders, syrup, honey, and vegetable pulp.

67. Saline water used in cases of chronic constipation.

68. *Paul et Virginie*, a celebrated 1788 novel by Bernardin St. Pierre. Paul and Virginie are young lovers on the Île de France (Mauritius) who live in a harmonious relationship with nature.

69. Gallican: a species of Catholicism that asserts the freedom of the Church from the authority of the Pope.

70. Nacarat: bright red; dianella: blue flax lily.

71. Loredan Larchey was a prolific lexicographer who compiled dictionaries of argot and a dictionary of names, works for which Huysmans wrote to congratulate and thank him (see Bonnet in Huysmans, 293, note 15).

Souviron: "Author of a *Dictionnaire des termes techniques de la science, de l'industrie, des lettres et des arts* [1868/1871]" (Bonnet in Huysmans, 293, note 16).

Sébastien Bottin (1764–1853) was a statistician who "is known above all for the annual publication from 1819 to 1853 of the *Almanach du commerce de Paris et des principals villes du monde*, which went on to receive the generic name of *bottin*" (https://fr.wikipedia.org/wiki/S%C3%A9bastien_Bottin).

72. "Any of us who dropped into fin-de-siècle France would be struck before anything else by the smell—of crowded apartments without ventilation or water, of outhouses with no means of evacuation" (Steven Zatny, "The French Hygiene offensive of the 1950s," *Journal of Modern History* 84, no. 4 [2012]: 897).

73. A "court of miracles" (*cour des miracles*) is a slum area; the term derives from an earlier period when such areas in Paris provided refuge for beggars who faked injuries and handicaps in order to inspire generosity. On return to the slum, the injuries would "miraculously" disappear.

74. Vesicant: an agent that causes blistering; seton: a skein of cotton or other absorbent material passed below the skin and left with the ends protruding, to promote drainage of fluid or to act as a counterirritant. Bonnet is not alone in having noted Huysmans's "lexicographic erudition."

75. Bonnet quotes here a letter sent by Vincent van Gogh to Émile Bernard in 1887, in which he refers this passage: "But when will I do my starry sky—that picture which has always been on my mind? Alas! Alas! As that excellent friend Cyprien says in Huysmans's *En ménage*, 'the finest pictures are those that one dreams of while smoking a pipe in bed, but that one never does'" (in Huysmans, 322, note 1).

76. Bonnet points out here the parallel with the conclusion of Flaubert's *Éducation sentimentale* in which "Frédérique and Deslauriers acknowledge their failed lives and the stillborn projects of their youth" (in Huysmans, 322, note 2). The parallel was certainly deliberate; Huysmans held Flaubert's novel in particularly high esteem—"one of the most beautiful books I know" (see Huysmans, 322–323, note 2).

TRANSLATOR'S AFTERWORD

I. *DOMESTICITY* AGAINST THE GRAIN

Domesticity (*En ménage* in French) was published in 1881 at a time when Huysmans, as one of the Médan group, remained closely associated with Émile Zola. However, Huysmans was increasingly uneasy about pupillage in the school of Zola, and the strain shows in his novel. *Domesticity* begins with André planning to undertake some Zolaesque research in an abattoir; the plan is never realized, and there is no further talk in *Domesticity* of authorial research into lower-class urban scenes;[1] indeed, Cyprien later accuses André of inadequate research: "you don't know the people you're so eager to portray in your books!" André hardly seems a disciple of Zola's methods and Huysmans's own parting of the ways with his mentor came a few years later; *Against Nature* (*À rebours*, also translated as *Against the Grain*), published in 1884, was to prove to be his most celebrated novel, and was largely responsible for inaugurating the decadent *fin-de-siècle* in literature.

On a first glimpse, *Domesticity* and *Against Nature* stand on different sides of a cultural divide—on one side, unpicturesque realism,[2] on the other, withdrawal from everyday life into an aesthetic ivory tower. However, the streams that fed into *Against Nature* were already active in Huysmans's earlier period. Baudelaire, celebrated in *Against Nature*, was already for him (in 1879) "the poet of genius who can open up perspectives with a single epithet."[3] Indeed, Huysmans's first publication in 1874, a collection of prose poems, *Le drageoir aux épices* (*The Dish of Spices*), was written in good part under the influence of Baudelaire's recently published *Petits poèmes en prose* (1869) and included some notable exercises in proto-decadent prose.[4] In his review of the Salon of 1880 Huysmans singled out for praise the canvases of Gustave Moreau ("fantastic visions of an opium eater"),[5] to be subsequently evoked in detail in *Against Nature*.

Tension between realist and antirealist tendencies was an ongoing one in Huysmans's oeuvre and, while *Domesticity* clearly weights the scales in favor of realism, a reading of the novel in light of the later work allows us to discern some cracks in the realist foundation—allows us to read the novel against the grain.

In the feast enjoyed by André and Jeanne in the German Brasserie (chapter XI), Jeanne, with her good luck charms and dream keys, can be seen as a good witch, transporting André to a midnight bacchanalian orgy, with Gambrinus serving as a Germanic Dionysus. In the manuscript of *Domesticity* the feast culminates and concludes with an episode of riotous sex in André's bedroom. Huysmans decided to remove this ahead of publication; nevertheless it's consistent with the preceding feast and provides an instance of what Mikhail Bakhtin, in his landmark study of Rabelais, theorized in terms of the "grotesque." Bakhtin quotes a bawdy passage in Rabelais: "she'd find herself jerked up and down [*elle aura le saccadé*] as long as there was a monk within a thousand miles."[6] The Rabelais quote can be matched with André and Jeanne's sexual congress: "skin burning, heads on fire, they clasped each other so hard that the wooden bedframe cracked to breaking point under the coupling of their bodies and the jerky recoil of their legs" (*le détente saccadé de leurs jambes*). The lower body—for Bakhtin the locus of the grotesque body—is emphasized; thrashing limbs are indistinguishably intermingled and threaten to explode the containing bedframe. Bakhtin spells out the metaphysical implications of "the logic of the grotesque": "the limits between the body and the world are erased."[7] For André, the Rabelaisian feast and its orgiastic aftermath constitute a moment out of time, a brief transcendence of his crippling self-consciousness, even a sublation of self, a rare moment of enchantment (*Verzauberung*) in an otherwise disenchanted life.

Looking forward to *Against Nature*, the collection of ornaments and works of art that clutter André's living space in the rue Cambacérès apartment, including a fabulous Japanese chimera, anticipates, albeit on a smaller and lesser scale, the hyper-aestheticized interior within which des Esseintes, the aristocratic hero of *Against Nature*, takes refuge from the insufferable vulgarities of the everyday world. Later, in chapter IX, André, wandering through the shopping arcade of the Palais-Royal, gazes at turtles under a stream of water in the window of Chevet's, a high-class grocer. Huysmans remembered this passage when he came to write *Against Nature*: "[des Esseintes] had wandered at random through the streets as far as the Palais-Royal, where he glanced at Chevet's display [. . .] there in the window was a huge tortoise in a tank."[8] Des Esseintes has the shell of the tortoise gilded and mounted with precious stones, a hyperbolic version of the objets de luxe on display in the Palais-Royal shop windows ("People were transfixed in front of the jeweler's gold"). Dead under the weight of its overdecorated shell, the tortoise becomes a literal *nature morte*—a still life. As though to confirm latent links between commodification, reification, and aestheticization in Huysmans, Cyprien comments (chapter XIV): "don't you agree with me that a talented still life artist should take shopkeepers' displays for his subject, instead of his eternal flowers and his eternal oysters." We can detect here the antithetical force of the later title—*À rebours*—against the grain, against nature: "Nature has had her day; the disgusting monotony of her landscapes and skyscapes has finally proved too much for refined and sensitive temperaments."[9] For des Esseintes, nature is no better than a low-quality shop—certainly not one in the Palais-Royal—offering standard commodities: "a shopkeeper stocking one article to the exclusion of all others; what a monotonous store of meadows and trees, what a commonplace display of mountains and seas."[10]

Sensitivity of temperament offers another approach to a "perverse" reading of *Domesticity*. In his biography of Huysmans, Robert Baldick points out that while the descriptive passages of Huysmans's first two novels, *Marthe* and *Les Soeurs Vatard*, are also to be found in *Domesticity*, the latter impresses more with its characterization, underlining a "shift from pictorial to psychological interest."[11] Huysmans's portrayal of André is in good measure a psychological portrayal. He is rarely at home in himself, constitutionally incapable of peace of mind for any length of time; his prolonged petticoat crisis, which results in strained nerves, irritability, "sudden alarms and rages," provides the novel with a central theme. Huysmans also attributes his nervous temper to his artistic sensibility; we are told (chapter V) that he is "as obsessive as the majority of artists." Oversensitivity results in writer's block and tactics of delay or avoidance; rather than progressing his work, he prefers to revise what he has already written and wastes hours in a brown study. His obsessive-compulsive character is further evident in the weeks spent in mentally familiarizing himself with his new working environment in rue Cambacérès; "He couldn't even work on a table unless it was in its customary position."

A further instance of André's psychological foibles emerges in chapter VII, where he feels a need to get out of his apartment "and mingle with noisy crowds." He goes to visit Cyprien, who proposes that they go and "breathe in the delicious stink of the streets." This directly corresponds to André's wish, but, rather than promptly agreeing, he jibs:

> Instinctively, for no reason, through one of those primary impulses that decide a man, André hid the pleasure that this

> offer gave him and replied as indifferently as he was able that going to one place rather another made no difference to him. Cyprien made so much of an effort to entice him through singing the praises of these convivial locations that André, annoyed, wanted to contradict him through finding fault with the routes, one after another, over which he rhapsodized. He felt that strange need to condemn and belittle what has just been praised to the skies.

A similarly perverse mentality is at work in the following chapter, in his relationship with Blanche, a new mistress. Aware that he might not be her only lover he questions her about herself and her life. When she acknowledges visits from another gentleman, he decides, for the sake of his own peace of mind, to desist from further enquiries, "but in spite of himself broached the topic several times. . . . He questioned his own motives and felt chastened." He realizes that by obsessively "prying into her business" he is tormenting himself and damaging their relationship but is unable to stop himself. Thus the relationship that he had at first found so therapeutic starts on its downward path and soon terminates.

In these instances we can find an echo of Poe's story, "The Imp of the Perverse," where the narrator analyzes a mental state in which "we persist in acts because we should *not* persist in them. [. . .] In the case of that something which I term *perverseness*, the desire to be well is not only not aroused, but a strongly antagonistical sentiment exists." Poe's protagonist is overtaken by an irrational compulsion to publicly confess the murder he has committed.

Huysmans's admiration of Baudelaire extended to his translations of Poe. *Against Nature* was commenced early in 1882, not so long after the publication of *Domesticity*. In October of that year, he wrote a note to Mallarmé outlining the new work in progress and informing him that des

Esseintes "dotes on Baudelaire, his translations of Poe."[12] In the discussion of Poe that features in *Against Nature*, des Esseintes focuses above all on Poe as an explorer of psychology, with particular reference to "The Imp of the Perverse": "It was Poe who, in the sphere of morbid psychology, had carried out the closest scrutiny of the will. In literature he had been the first, under the emblematic title *The Imp of the Perverse*, to study those irresistible impulses which the will submits to without fully understanding them."[13] Des Esseintes's voice doubles for Huysmans's here, and it's likely that Poe's story contributed to Huysmans's portrayal of André's symptomatic impulses, albeit in a restrained realist vein rather than Poe's gothic and melodramatic one. When André and, subsequently, des Esseintes are precipitated into acute nervous crises, Huysmans modernizes Poe's romantic psychologism. Nervous disorders are appropriate to the age of Charcot, whose writings include *Diseases of the Nervous System* (1885), as well as to the era in which "neurasthenia" gained currency as a diagnostic term; indeed, the symptoms of André's petticoat crisis detailed in chapter VI correspond to a generic description of neurasthenia: "an ill-defined medical condition characterized by lassitude, fatigue, headache, and irritability, associated chiefly with emotional disturbance."[14] Max Nordau, a student of Charcot, went further in *Degeneration* (1892), his medically driven denunciation of what was, in his view, a wholesale contemporary culture of morbid neurosis. He devoted some typically moralistic pages to the character of des Esseintes, describing him as "physically an anæmic and nervous man of weak constitution, the inheritor of all the vices and all the degeneracies of an exhausted race."[15] André's psychological quirks already correspond to the characteristic ones of the decadent fin de siècle, and Nordau would certainly see his ineffective "womanishness," his "timidity of a young girl" (ch. V) as a symptom of such exhaustion.[16]

II THE DOMESTICITY OF *DOMESTICITY*

As noted above, Huysmans's French title, *En ménage*, is here translated as *Domesticity*.[17] The English title is appropriate but doesn't quite convey the full meaning of "ménage," which can signify the furnishings and spaces of a domestic household and, equally, domestic relationships—a married or unmarried couple or a larger family. "Domesticity" is a more abstract and generalized term but can serve as a convenient point of reference for some further thoughts about the novel.

Chapter IV of *Domesticity* opens with a detailed description of the Désableau residence and goes on to portray the family gathered together at home in the evening. This typifies developments in the course of the nineteenth century that saw the urban and bourgeois form of domesticity establishing itself as an accepted norm for private living.

Monsieur and Madame Désableau are paragons of conservative respectability, whereas André and Cyprien belong to the dubiously bohemian world of arts and letters. However, they too embrace bourgeois domesticity; the bachelor flat that André rents following his separation from his wife shares the same basic plan of living room, dining room, bedroom, kitchen, and bathroom.

André's new apartment is no less cluttered with decorative bric-a-brac than the Désableau dwelling, and at one point he dreams of buying more. Huysmans's novel pays close attention to shops, window displays, and shopping arcades, as though to remind us that the rise of bourgeois domesticity was accompanied by a culture of commodification and consumption. *Domesticity* ironically underlines the link between the two; after a night of intimacy in Blanche's bedroom, André concludes that "he'd found a retailer offering herself for trial, happy to grant buyers the same pleasure that she took in selling."

Toward the end of chapter II, André goes into a restaurant that functions as a convivial meeting place: it's loud with banal and meretricious conversation; he overhears a hairdresser's inane monologue, applauded by his friends, along with a dentist's cynical explanation of the class-based manufacture of false teeth and how he exploits his hapless patients.

For Jürgen Habermas, the London coffee houses of the late seventeenth and eighteenth centuries were key locations in the emergence of an enlightenment "public sphere," places where professional men—lawyers, doctors, men of science, men of letters—could meet and exchange opinions with "freedom of assembly and association."[18] In the public sphere of the late nineteenth-century Third Republic, however, "opinion" has become a debased currency; enlightenment values are no longer to be found in the bourgeois public sphere; journalism, one of its arms, is seen by André as the literary equivalent of prostitution.

Appropriately, the food served up to André in the restaurant is neither nourishing nor satisfying. This anticipates the inedible cooked thrushes ordered by Jeanne and the widow Laveau in their local eatery; in another restaurant, Cyprien asserts that the wine they ordered would taste better "if we were to sample it at home, in a deep armchair." Authenticity is now seen to reside in the intimacy of the private sphere; eating at home is generally preferable—both Mélanie and Mélie are good cooks. There is, however, a caveat: bad things can happen in homes where intimacy is absent, as in the Jayants' loveless conjugal relationship. When André invites Cyprien to dinner, Berthe treats the painter with overt hostility. Her ruthless conduct of the supper party seeks to assert a gendered control over the marital home, with Cyprien viewed by her as an unwelcome rival. Deciding that she's made a bad purchase in the marriage market, Berthe goes on to conduct "a hidden war" against André, but her experiment with adultery proves a bridge too far and, caught out by her husband, she retreats, chastened and humiliated, leaving the central terrain of domesticity in André's possession.

After an initial period of settling into his new quarters in rue Cambacérès, André is afflicted by an "undefined malaise." He desires a woman "for her skirt whisking against him. [. . .] Without her, his apartment seemed joyless." This is the *crise juponnière*—the petticoat crisis—that resonates throughout the remaining chapters. The lack of female companionship negatively confirms domesticity as a female and implicitly maternal sphere, seen in Mélie's tender care for Cyprien during his illness, and in Madame Désableau soothing her husband after his upsetting argument with Berthe. André's crisis is finally resolved in the penultimate chapter when Berthe returns to him. He now concedes the intimacy he has previously withheld and is duly rewarded in the bedroom. However, the initiative remains with Berthe; the gendered space of domesticity empowers the female: "right from the start the man and father had, of course, already been defeated by the woman and daughter."[19] André's ultimate failure as a writer corresponds to Berthe's ultimate triumph as a wife.

Prior to Berthe's return, André's petticoat crisis reaches a boiling point after his mistress Jeanne leaves him. In chapter XII, he subjects himself to a scathing self-examination: "he had been Mr. Anyone, an insignificant personality." His acute self-awareness is allied to his alienation from a materialistic social order in which, to make money, the writer has to whore himself either through journalism or popular fiction. André's artistic sensitivity goes hand in hand with his refusal of an inauthentic world of commercial culture and financial gain; these characteristics mark him out as one of the prototypical figures of modernity. Restless and estranged, he finally suffers a spiritual collapse: "Overwhelmed by an incurable distress, an unrelieved chagrin, an abdication of the self, he gave way under the collapse of a life that, scarcely rebuilt, crumbled once more, burying his last hopes under a noisy heap of ruin and destruction." What differentiates André's interior drama from later instances of psychical crisis in modernist literature[20] is that it transpires within the restricting terms of hearth and home. Rather than finding the possibility of radical new departures in the disruptive force of the crisis, André willingly accedes to a life of compromised bourgeois domesticity with Berthe. He is devoid of heroism, and Huysmans's text smiles ironically at his pretentions to combative masculine authority; going to confront the feared antagonism of his housemaid, Mélanie, he puts on his slippers "with an air of belligerence." The modern writers published by Charpentier, represented by the yellow-uniformed books in André's bookcase, are, we know, Flaubert, Zola, and Maupassant: "two rows of volumes marching tumultuously, beating the drum." But André is unfit to join the vanguard of modernity, able only to put on his slippers.

It may be significant that street life on rue Cambacérès includes a man who neuters cats; André's passivity threatens him with emasculation and effeminization. When he paces the street outside the Maison Larmange, Jeanne's garment factory, the trope of the male gaze is inverted as he becomes a spectacle for female shop assistants gazing knowingly from behind their shop windows. The disturbingly feminized space directly unmans him: he "continued walking back and forth, forfeiting his male status, acquiring that of a prostitute pounding her patch." The passage continues,

> he looked up, saw, stretching out as far as the eye could see, enormous gold letters, cyclopean inscriptions piercing the mist: "coats and gowns"; "ready-to-wear garments for ladies"; "bustles and petticoats"; "dresses and mantles." Everywhere nothing but adverts for women's clothing, running and winding the length of the facades, creeping above doors, clinging to balconies, terrace balusters, climbing up to the sixth floor, as far as the tops of roofs, and he remained there, eyeing the sky, contemplating that street that oozed wealth and bankruptcy. A street that survived from day to day, subject to the fads and fancies of a whole clientele of actresses and whores!

In "The Painter of Modern Life," Baudelaire evoked and celebrated the *mundus muliebris*, the woman-world: "[woman] is a harmonious whole, not only in her carriage and the movement of her limbs, but also in the muslins and gauzes, in the vast and iridescent clouds of draperies in which she envelops herself, and which are, so to speak, the attributes and the pedestal of her divinity."[21] But this same *mundus muliebris* almost overwhelms André, threatening to submerge his unconfident masculinity. As though in response, Huysmans's text refuses the harmonious integrity of Baudelaire's iridescent clouds of drapery, desacralizing them, reducing them to the "fallen" realms of adverts, retail goods, actresses, and prostitutes. Subsequently, however, André is able to reassert a sense of masculinity though his renewed liaison with Jeanne; unthreateningly small, she is further reduced by him to the status of pet—"my little puppy."

Sylvie Thorel-Cailleteau has commented on the disabused portrayal of adultery in the naturalist novel: "Adultery, according to the Médan group, is a false rupture that only ignites triviality."[22] Adultery certainly leaves Berthe unfulfilled and disillusioned, but, much more than that, the episode is a crisis, resulting in a nervous breakdown that, in its own way, rivals André's later breakdown. Up to this point, Berthe has been the main vehicle of Huysmans's strongly misogynistic views of the bourgeois female, but he now shows her, for the first time, in a sympathetic light. In her departure from her shallow, foppish lover she attains a significant measure of dignity; "fallen," she is no longer the spoiled and immature girl that André married. Her prolonged convalescence with the Désableaus, during which she "desires nothing," is a rite of passage which is completed by her angry confrontation with M. Désableau, refuting his contemptuous view of André's worthlessness. When, in chapter XV, she knocks on André's door, both the woman and the man, having suffered their respective crises, are ready to reaccommodate each other. Their emotional reconciliation opens the prospect of a renewed domesticity. As Berthe inspects André's residence she steps "with authority" into the small kitchen that Jeanne, for fear of Mélanie, had been too timid to enter; she has regained possession of her realm.

In his unpleasant illness, described in chapter XIII, Cyprien also suffers a crisis. Fearing a final abandonment, he suffers agonies when Mélie, a prostitute, leaves him for a few hours each day: "Grown used to the to-and-fro of a skirt getting snagged on chair legs [. . .] Cyprien felt horribly unhappy when left alone. His room became doleful." This directly echoes the earlier account of André's petticoat malaise—the absence of swirling skirts, the joyless rooms. However, Cyprien's nature is less intrinsically bourgeois than André's, and his need for a domestic female presence (for intimacy but not carnality) is more easily answered. His proposal to Mélie, that they "shelter under the same petticoat [*jupon*]," provides a constructive reply to André's demoralizing petticoat crisis. Whereas André maintains his bourgeois prejudices in refusing to cohabit with Jeanne, Cyprien, now thoroughly déclassé, becomes a cultural laborer alongside Mélie ("they'd have to live like laborers"). Like André, he fails in his higher creative aspirations, but unlike André, he keeps working.

André's lack of drive and readiness to drift, his indulgence in memories—schooldays, previous amours, first sexual experience—the details of his initial workroom obsession, his pique with the wrong kind of jam—all these can seem to affect Huysmans's narrative, making its unhurried way down alleys and side streets as well as along main avenues. These are among the factors that prompt Gilles Bonnet to define *En ménage* as "a skeptical novel that accumulates more than it progresses, privileging a structure based on enumeration at the expense of drama and its peripeteia."[23]

But readers will note that Berthe's exploration of the rue Cambacérès apartment explicitly runs in parallel with Jeanne's earlier reconnaissance. This suggests a deeper structural factor that underlies the novel's relaxed and "enumerative" procedure. A number of linked but contrasting binaries are at play in the narrative. We have already noted both similarity and difference between the respective crises of André and Cyprien; other such contrasted pairings can be discerned. Mélie is fat, low class, maternal, and unmarried; Berthe is thin (she diets), bourgeois, unmaternal (giving André cold comfort when he is unwell), and married. The miserably failed supper involving André, Cyprien, and Berthe is counterbalanced by the gratifying supper involving André, Cyprien, and Mélie; each meal comes at a pivotal point in the narrative, the former anticipating separation from Berthe, the latter setting in motion eventual reconciliation with Berthe. André and Désableau are ideological enemies, but no less importantly, they are two rivals fighting over which one has the greater claim on Berthe, each decrying the other to her. The hidden analogy between the two is glimpsed when André remembers seeing Désableau rewriting office minutes, "paused before a phrase, hesitating for hours between one word and another," thus mirroring André's own predicament as writer when, "harnessed himself ferociously to a chapter, [he] stopped, no longer so certain, sat in a brown study for hours." The two clocks that chime nearly simultaneously at the start of the novel correspond to the camaraderie of André and Cyprien while the single clock that chimes at the end marks their separation, each wanting to avoid the other's partner.

In the penultimate chapter, such contrasted binaries emerge into the open, playing a direct part in the renewed relationship between André and Berthe. André, "now speaking to his wife as though to a mistress" and addressing her as "my poor kitten," sees Berthe through the lens of Jeanne. Thus he is able to assume masculine virility, as he had with Jeanne, and to take the initiative by sexually possessing her. But he then suspects, not wrongly, that she has in fact seduced him, and that he is now "defenseless." Her "more elegant and fragrant" underwear can be read as a reminiscence of the *mundus muliebris* that André found so disturbing outside the Maison Larmange; Berthe, he begins to realize, isn't so much a kitten as a full-grown cat, well able to stalk her prey. She, for her part, remains sexually unfulfilled but has returned "home" as victor, *toute-puissante*, freed from the limiting life of the Désableau menage while at the same time fulfilling a long-cherished dream of an "escapade" in a bachelor's bedroom. The ambiguity of the relationship remains, at core, unresolved by their reunion; André will remain irresolute and beholden to his wife, while Berthe, we guess, will remain sexually unresponsive, but able to compensate as *maîtresse de ménage*.

Huysmans's writing is nowhere more sensitive than in evoking the concluding interplay between André and Berthe, involving renewed intimacy, unspoken reservations, and conditional reconciliation. *Domesticity* impresses with its exercises in virtuoso scene painting but impresses more in its portrayal of a finely balanced tension between romance and antiromance. The novel is artistically complete at this point, but this is not how things end; André must suffer a further and final defeat.

In the final short chapter we are told how the relationship between André and Cyprien gradually withers and dies, but not before they meet again. As they talk, a midday bell tolls: "I've got to run, Berthe will be getting impatient." Remembering André's situation in the first chapter as an up-and-coming young writer, able to stay out all night to undertake research, it's clear from the conclusion that the balance has tilted in favor of Berthe. André now suffers the fate of Berthe's father who had, "throughout his life, given way to his wife's slightest whim, a commanding woman [*une maîtresse femme*]." In *Domesticity*, patriarchy hardly asserts itself as a force to be reckoned with: Monsieur Désableau, patriarchy personified, is, symbolically, unable to father the son and heir he longs for; instead, he begets a daughter. André, about whose father we know nothing, has no interest in producing offspring. So, in *Domesticity*, there is a daughter in evidence, but no sons. Meanwhile, Berthe has inherited her mother's strength of character, and the conclusion suggests that she will indeed be the one who wears the trousers in her marriage. The crisis-free domesticity that André desires can only be realized according to terms set by his wife. With bourgeois matriarchy trumping bourgeois patriarchy, the line of domesticity runs from mother to daughter; in the unwritten sequel, *Domesticity II* will be Berthe's story.

NOTES

1. When André quizzes Jeanne on conditions in her all-female garment factory in chapter XI, his interest is more voyeuristic than research oriented.
2. Realism in as much as Huysmans never adhered to the pseudo-scientific theory that drove Zola's naturalism.
3. Cited by Baldick, *Life of J.-K. Huysmans*, 42. The eulogy to Baudelaire was written in 1879 in a preface to a collection of poems by Théodore Hannon.
4. See, for example, "Camaïeux rouge" (Red Cameo).
5. Cited by Baldick, *Life of J.-K. Huysmans*, 52.
6. Bakhtin, *Rabelais and his World*, tr. Helene Iswolski (Bloomington: Indiana University Press, 1984), 310–311.
7. Bakhtin, 310.
8. Huysmans, *Against Nature*, tr. Robert Baldick (Harmondsworth: Penguin, 1966, 53).
9. Cited by Baldick, *Life of J.-K. Huysmans*, 82. See also Huysmans, *Against Nature*, 36.
10. Huysmans, *Against Nature*, 36.
11. Baldick, *Life of J.-K. Huysmans*, 58.
12. Quoted in Baldick, 85.
13. Huysmans, *Against Nature*, 191.
14. This definition is from the Oxford Dictionary.
15. Max Nordau, *Degeneration* (Lincoln: University of Nebraska Press, 1993), 302.
16. "André's nervous temperament tends to ineluctably feminize him. [. . .] Huysmans invents a modality of that male hysteria that Charcot will observe the following year" (Bonnet in Huysmans, introduction, 13).

17. A previous translation by J. G. Sandiford-Pellé was published as *En Ménage* while also supplying a supplementary English title: *Living Together* (London: Fortune Press 1969). The Sandiford-Pellé translation has much to recommend it, but also suffers from a spread of local errors, some dubious readings, and a degree of stylistic awkwardness.

18. Habermas, "The Public Sphere: an encyclopedia article (1964)," trans. Sarah Lennox and Frank Lennox, *New German Critique* 1, no. 3 (1974): 49–55, 49. The term "public sphere" originates with Habermas.

19. Latter-day criticisms of Huysmans's misogyny are understandable in the light of passages such as this, but tend to overlook their specific class focus: in *Domesticity*, the misogynistic attitude is exclusively reserved for bourgeois women; lower-class women tend to be exempt, as is evident from the sympathetic portrayals of Jeanne and Mélie. The point is crystallized in a passage in chapter X where André reflects that "lower-class women help each other and almost all of them look after neighbors they don't know who are hungry or unwell, while, where the wives of the bourgeoisie are concerned, women who give them no pleasure and in whom they take no interest are, as a rule, left to die like dogs."

20. See, for example, Hofmannsthal's "Letter of Lord Chandos," Eliot's *The Waste Land*, Sartre's *Nausea*.

21. Baudelaire, "The Painter of Modern Life," in *Selected Writings on Art and Artists*, tr. P. E. Charvet (Harmondsworth: Penguin, 1972), 424.

22. Cited by Bonnet, in Huysmans, 105–106, note 30.

23. Bonnet in Huysmans (introduction), 21. To be fair, Bonnet, discussing the André–Cyprien relationship, also points out that "the rivalry between pen and paintbrush structures *En ménage*" (introduction, 13).

George MacLennan has translated works by Michel de Ghelderode, Marcel Brion, Julien Gracq, and Marcel Béalu for Wakefield Press.